6/18/14

FORBIDDEN LOVE
IN TIMBUKTU

(Woman From Another Land)

Apalena,

Thanks for the support!

Brenda

FORBIDDEN LOVE IN TIMBUKTU

(Woman From Another Land)

BRENDA SMITH

Library of Congress Control Number: 2016908351
ISBN: Hardcover   978-1-5245-0299-7
                   Softcover   978-1-5245-0298-0
                   eBook   978-1-5245-0297-3

Print information available on the last page.

Rev. date: 05/27/2016

To order additional copies of this book, contact:
Xlibris
1-888-795-4274
www.Xlibris.com
Orders@Xlibris.com
738851

CONTENTS

Titles by Brenda Smith

Insane Circumstances

Unforeseen Circumstances

Extreme Circumstances

Forbidden Love in Timbuktu (Woman from Another Land)

This book, like most of the work I have done as an adult, reflects the love, care, and concern given a small child with a wandering mind by my parents, the late Samuel E. Lane and Ona Belle Lane. They always told me I could do anything I wanted to do, even write.

A special thanks is given to my husband, Jerry V. Smith, and our sons, Brian and Justin, who tell me I can when I think I can't write another line. From being the parent, I am becoming the child and taking advice for my literary efforts from those whom I nurtured. How awesome is that!

I pray my wonderful grandchildren—Kylie, Mackenzie, Brian "BJ," Maddie, Breya, Sarah Grace, Rosalie, and Karys—will benefit from the example I continue to try to set for them. They are too young to read my musings now, but I hope they will enjoy my stories when they are of age.

My friend, Jacquie Harper, provides editorial assistance for which I am truly grateful. A retired English teacher, she works hard to keep my grammar and punctuation correct, which is no easy task. I write like I talk. I am Southern and country.

I would be remiss if I didn't acknowledge my sisters and brothers—Blondie L. Manning, Samuel E. Lane, Elvis A. Lane, David R. Lane, and Gail L. Golden—and remember with a heart full of gratitude Oleta L. Davis, our sister who went home to be with the Lord on April 5, 2015. She told everyone she met about my stories.

There are others...my Alpha Kappa Alpha Sorority, Inc. sisters, members of Mt. Pisgah Baptist Church, the 2016 South Georgia Literacy Festival committee, and the list goes on.

I also dedicate this book to the Delta Sigma Theta, Sorority, Inc., Valdosta Alumnae Chapter. Its Delta Book Club members, including Leah Baynard and Nicole Parker Gunn, read my books and review them and encourage my literary efforts. They always reserve a table for me at their annual Delta Renaissance.

Thank you for reading this book as well as ones previously written. You keep me writing and seeking new material to write about.

Forbidden Love in Timbuktu
(Woman from Another Land)

Author's Notes

This story was born out of curiosity invoked when I read an AP article about a young woman in Timbuktu who had been punished for a crime: forbidden love. She had merely answered a phone, and her life forever changed because the man on the other line had gotten the wrong number. The writer told how the duo's relationship flourished until the terrorists came and changed the rules for women in the city. The women who had obviously enjoyed many freedoms were told how to dress and how they should relate to men inside of and outside of their families.

While it was clear that both parties understood the new laws, their desire to be together trumped the law. They kept meeting. Although they exercised caution, the lovers were caught. He escaped, and she was jailed and given the ninety lashes for their crime before being returned to her family.

The reporter who pieced the story together did a good job in a short article about the two lovers. Yet I was left wanting. I wanted to know more about both of the protagonists—where they were from, what their customs were, and most importantly, where he went. Did he get caught? Why didn't he come back for her? Or did he?

I decided I could only imagine the filler that made up "the rest of the story," or I could do some research, and from this research, I could write an ending to this romance that might be feasible. To these ends, reality became this bit of fiction: Forbidden Love in Timbuktu (Woman from Another Land). As previously indicated, this reality fiction, in many places, is just what it is—a figment of my imagination. In equally as many places, it is real. It is based on research about Malians and their West African neighbors. I hope my readers enjoy the story.

PART I

In Timbuktu, West Africa

Chapter One

She smelled him before she saw the man, his scent imprinted in her mind since the first day she had seen him, and she felt him before the prints on his fingers touched her clothed skin—the man affected her that way. A soft ruffling sound reached her, and the hair on her back stood as if commanded. The girl shook her head from side to side, attempting to remove daydreams from reality, drawing her right hand over the back of her neck. Kieta Toures was exhausted, as she was studying for her final exam and preparing for the law exam. Her whole grade was based on the outcome of this one test, and she was going to have to retain a good deal of what she was learning in this clinical course and other courses for the bar exam. She had too much to do. This was no time for daydreaming or messing around. "Dang, I am so tired." She spoke more to the air than to herself.

"You got this!" A familiar voice broke her reverie. She turned in her seat at the library's table, and there he stood. Doe was there, not in her dreams this time, but he was actually standing at the back of her chair, reaching his hand out to help her to her feet so they could properly greet each other. She drew her to him.

"Doe, what happened? Where did you go? I missed you so much." She spoke into his open mouth, her words swallowed by his mouth on hers as he passionately kissed her. Lost in her mouth were the man's mumbles. "I missed you too, *cherie*. I missed you more!" He held her with one hand and stroked her hair with the other. And she held on to him for dear life. She was not letting go this time. The young woman, locked in his impassioned embrace, pinched her left arm with her right hand, wincing when her nerves verified that she was not dreaming, that the reemergence of love lost in another land was indeed taking place.

They rocked each other soothingly until the man broke the hold they had on each other. "Pack your things. Let's get out of here," he commanded. Without hesitating, Kieta Toures shoved everything into her backpack and prepared to leave the library to take the man to the comforts of her on-campus apartment. There was much to be said . . . and done. Privacy of her space was needed now. Mahmoudou "Doe" Ibrahaim had a lot of explaining to do. Too many miles and several years had passed since she had seen him. *Where had he been? What had he been doing? How had he found me?* Kieta's mind raced, its momentum accelerating like a race car, hers in the rear of the pack, trying to catch the other vehicles ahead of her. She needed more fuel.

His voice, the accelerant, propelled her. "Come on," he said as he reached out and took the bag from her, noting for the first time that her expression had changed from surprise to almost pouting. "Let's go! When we have privacy, I will explain everything," he told her as he took her hand and led her through the building, down the steep steps, and onto the open campus.

The two of them proceeded quietly and quickly through the building, down the steps, and into the open air. A barely audible "Okay!" escaped from her lips. When they were at the bottom of the steps, both turned simultaneously toward their destination.

Few words passed between them as they began their trek. Each was left to their own thoughts. His were on catching up and taking up where they had left off on the streets of Timbuktu, and hers were of how he had gotten there and how he was heading in the direction of her one-bedroom apartment on the north end of the campus. The man had not asked where she lived, and the university student had not volunteered any information, but that didn't matter. He was here with her in the United States. That was all that was important. Her beloved was here.

Kieta's worst nightmares had not been realized. Doe had not been lost in the melee in their homeland or killed. The love of her life was alive and well. The only thing that was missing was the beard he had the last time she had laid eyes on him. He was clean-shaven, his appearance healthy, and his skin clear and as smooth as a baby's butt. At least that was what she was thinking. In her dreams, Doe had been thinner, his appearance gaunt, and his skin ashen like many of the men she had seen in her last days in Timbuktu. Internal strife in one's homeland had a way of doing that to soldiering men and those who refused to participate in the struggles.

A few yards into their trek, both parties sighed collective sighs of relief. Simultaneously, their hands reached for the other's members. Their fingers intertwined, freely this time. No one was watching their every movement—at least that was what they were thinking. They took turns rubbing each other's phalanges. He relished the softness and smoothness of her skin. She appreciated the bit of roughness on the fingertips that massaged the hand he refused to let go.

No sounds came forth as they promenaded hand in hand through the campus and by the cafeteria, the president's lodging, the gymnasium, the bookstore, and on toward university housing for faculty, married couples, and finally, to the apartments where singletons without roommates resided. Quietude replaced the buzz generally heard there. Neither heard conversations of groups that milled around their sorority's plots or in their neatly manicured yards or those leaving classes talking about assignments, grades, or next classes or the cars, motorcycles, and buses that transported the university's thousands of inhabitants. They had ears for each other only.

As they approached the brick-veneered structures, Doe began to whistle a jolly refrain she had heard him emit on the streets of Timbuktu when she first met him. She smiled an inward smile. Happiness's warmth permeating throughout her being, making her mellow, the woman was inebriated by the simple unfettered act. Her thoughts took wings like an uncaged bird. They went to her homeland, Mali, and to how she had met this remarkable man and what had transpired since the last time they laid eyes on each other.

~~~~~

Kieta Toures, a house servant, was sitting home alone, staring out the window, pondering her life's journey: the trip from her home in the boondocks and her stay at the Soyinkas' compound, serving the Malian family in Timbuktu while she was attending the local university and where she would go from here. It was her first year at the university, so the beginner did not fully know what she wanted to be, perhaps a teacher. Whatever her choice, she did know she wanted to work in her homeland to aid other young girls and boys like herself who were frequently left uneducated, unemployed, and shackled by their skins' enslaving ways.

The woman let the dustrag she held in her hand fall to the floor and listlessly traipsed over to a wall mirror and looked at herself, a girly act that all young women her age did. Appearance was everything in this land. It affected lives in every way. She peered into the mirror, observing her full corps frontward; then turned, gazing over her shoulder to catch a rearview; and leaned in to get a better view of her visage. The girl brushed her cheek with her right hand and studied her features, comparing herself to the other women she knew or had known. Her brown tinge gave her solace. Despite the fact that she was not pink-skinned like some, she felt that her hue made her more acceptable than many of her relatives. For this reason, she had been offered a place in the Soyinkas' house. At least that was partially the reason for her entering into service here. She sighed a sigh of relief as she returned to the place where she was dusting furniture.

The Toures girl was indeed fortunate because the Soyinkas paid their help better wages than most in her community. Her custom allowed for these wages to be withheld if her work did not meet her master and mistress's approval. Kieta's custom also allowed her to work from day to day without pay. Not only that, but her light-skinned master could also beat her with a camel whip if he wanted to with no reprisal; that was the law in her land. Nevertheless, she was freed from such vestiges because her employer, a businessman of Tuareg and Arab Moors ancestry, was Westernized and maintained many democratic principles held in these foreign lands. His employees received full pay, and if their work was not up to par, they were warned and retrained before dismissal was considered.

Her master had been abroad, studied in France and the United States. A former military man, Monsieur Soyinka had attended training in France and in prestigious military institutions in America—that was as much as the young woman knew of the family she had found herself serving. It was apparent that his wife, Madame Ruby to all who knew her, was equally as democratized as he was, if not more. Educated, the family spoke a mix of Tuareg, French, and English, so in the last couple of years, their servant had learned a lot of words frequently used by the adults and their children. And Kieta was becoming fluent in English through her university studies.

Most people from her village were not as fortunate as she. Kieta was one of the lucky ones. The Soyinka family treated her like she was one of their children, not as their slave. As previously indicated, the wages they paid for her services were never withheld, and she was never threatened with being turned over to the Islamist, a threat used in Timbuktu after the terrorists began their takeover. Her pay was more than adequate. She could use her earnings to purchase her wardrobe and the toiletries and *parfums* that she had come to appreciate and to keep her hair done or to get a pedicure and manicure at the mall on special occasions.

Her thoughts unencumbered, Kieta thought more about her state of affairs. She was a free person. She also saved money for her future. Although she served, she was not a slave. Slavery had been abolished in the sixties when the West African nation gained independence, and all people were considered equal under the law; nevertheless, when their rights were infringed upon, few considered seeking legal actions because of the way of life that had existed throughout generations. The girl hugged herself tightly, shifting where she stood, dustrag in hand while commiserating over a future that was certain to be bright. She found herself humming a gleeful tune.

Bzzzzz. An insect flew by, interrupting her thoughts, so she waved the annoying pest away with the dustrag and returned to thoughts about where she had come from and where she found herself at the present moment. Her thoughts turned to her infancy, from her early years to her childhood, adolescence she had just come through, young adulthood, and to the present.

~~~~~

Kieta was simply born into servitude. Her parents and grandparents worked for the same extended Tuareg family in a village outside Timbuktu, so did her four brothers and four sisters. Everybody in the family worked; even the children had chores. For as long as she could remember, she would wake up before sunrise to fetch water and food for the donkeys and other small animals the family or the people who employed the Toures had. By the time she was twelve, she was tending to her family's small animals. She recalled how her chores changed when she was a teenager. The girl pounded millet for lunch, cooked, fetched wood, and cleaned their housing area.

She assumed these new chores when her mother died, just before Kieta was a teenager. Normally, loss of a member would have disrupted a family's life, but the loss for her people merely meant a shift in responsibilities. There was no time for pining and grieving. One just moved on. The Toures family continued their seminomadic existence, serving wherever their masters moved. Now the girl wondered if her destiny would have differed if her mother was still alive. Would she be here now, on mornings like the current one?

The young woman shook her head in negation and recalled how mornings would come when her father would wake them with a singular "Let's get moving!" a task that was easy because they, like other nomadic families, did not own much—a blanket or two to spread on the ground if it was cold in the desert at night, a woven mat, and a metal trunk to store their few valuables, including their prayer rug and a change of clothes per family member. They also had some goatskin water bags and a sack with a handful of kitchen utensils. Up bright and early every morning, their toileting needs were taken out behind a dune. And as time passed, the Toures family dwindled down to a handful, including her.

Kieta had pondered her destiny at length after the passing of her mother. She was certain a change was coming but did not know precisely what the change would be. Nevertheless, by the time they reached the capital city, serving one Tuareg family to the next, the child was sure she would be a servant. At the appointed time, they left their parents' house and went to work, never to return to the fold. Her brothers and sisters had inherited the family's fate as they had matured, so she was certain the same fate would be hers but was not sure of the time. She recalled asking her father about this practice and his answer.

Her papa simply responded, "At the appointed time, all must leave their father's house and make a way for themselves." A mere child, she took her father's word and did not question him further. All she knew was at the "appointed time," whenever that was, she, like her siblings, would just leave the Toures family and go to work for others. Hers would come, but she was not sure when it would arrive. Her father or someone would surely let her know.

Needless to say, years, months, and days just passed as did the seasons. True to her thoughts, her "appointed time" came. One fall morning when she was just a teenager, she was awakened early, just as the sun was breaking the day, and told to make her belongings into a bundle. "I am taking you into the city . . . You are strong enough and old enough to do work and make a life for yourself" was all that she was told. No remark was forthcoming. She obeyed her father. The girl took her meager belonging and made a bundle from a piece of tattered cloth and made it luggage.

Her father beckoned for her to follow as they left their encampment to stand beside the road to wait for a passerby to stop and give them a ride into the city. It was too far to walk, and they owned no beast capable of bearing the two of them and her belongings. As they stood there, a couple of jeeps full of uniformed men passed by, kicking up rocks and dust. The girl coughed, her lungs filling with the residue spewed from the vehicles' tailpipes. Her father waved away the fumes with an open hand. "Somebody will stop in a minute," the man assured her.

His hitchhiking thumb gesturing at a truck or two, the Toures man soon begged a ride into the city on the back of a battered, slow-poking, noisy, aging vehicle. She and her father sat together in the back of a passerby's old, beat-up truck, their backs against the sides, their rumps planted firmly on the vehicle's bed as it bumped along the rough roads full of potholes until they got to the city and passed through it until they were at their destination. Little conversation took place between father and daughter as they took what ordinarily was an hour-long trip.

When the driver came to a rolling stop, the Toures man stood first and jumped off the truck's bed. His daughter mimicked his fluid movements. After their dismount, her father reached over the side of the vehicle and retrieved her bundled belongs, beckoning with his head for her to follow him after he waved a thank you to the driver. The pair was near an open-air market, and smells from food vendors greeted them. Her stomach growled. "I am hungry," she told her father. "Can we get something to eat here? We did not break a piece of bread this morning."

"You will get something to eat where you're going," the man said as he led the way away from the food court. His thoughts were of how he wished he could afford to give her one last meal before she was on her own and serving a family thereabouts. However, he didn't have a dime to his name, not even a penny. Otherwise, he would let her journey with him a bit longer. Besides, he was hungry too.

In a minute, the man recognized the driver of another truck and called out to him, asking him for a ride into the neighborhood "just outside the city limits" where the Soyinkas resided. His acquaintance readily agreed. "Hop in. The door is unlocked." He encouraged them to get in on the passenger side.

A sigh of relief flew from her lips. She was excited about the notion of fleeing from the scorching noonday sun, which was taking no prisoners at the present moment. Kieta's quickened step was shortened by her father's hand on her shoulder.

"No, we will ride in the back," the Toures man pivoted her toward the tail of the truck. His refusal of shade of the truck's cab offered them drew her ire. It truly disturbed Kieta. Her father? His pride catapulted the man to the bed instead of the cushioned comforts of the Chevy's seat. He reached out to pull his daughter up by the hand. Noticing a shift in her attitude, he admonished her. "If you hurry up, we will be there soon!" he told the hungry child stumbling behind him, her mind on food and water. "We'll be there in a few minutes," he reiterated.

The driver turned in his seat to see if they were onboard. Hearing the thud of the bundle first and their shuffling to be seated in the truck bed, he looked at the passengers from his rearview mirror, adjusting it for accuracy. He noticed that the girl looked as if she would faint, so he took a bottle of water he had purchased from a vendor at the market from the seat, got out of the truck, and handed it to the man. "Here, take this. It is awfully hot outside today!"

Both drank sips from the bottle as the truck took off, she first then her father. Just as he told her, they were at their destination in a flash. Before they had ingested all the cool beverage that tasted like liquid gold to her and to her father, the vehicle was slowing down.

The driver stopped at the place his friend desired, and Toures asked him in their native language. "Can you wait here for me? My business here will not take long," he said before turning his attention to the huge gate. He pointed out the entrance to the Soyinkas' compound.

"Sure. I will be here when you return, *mon ami*," the driver replied as he turned the ignition off. The man headed to the gate, but his daughter waited for his command, "Come on!" before she was in motion, walking on his heels, her eyes cast down with uncertainty. Her father had not adequately prepared her for this moment. She shook in her sandals. Any child in her circumstance would be afraid. Her thoughts slowed her progress, and she found herself two yards behind the man approaching the gate. His stride was long. He didn't want to keep his ride waiting and did not want to have to walk or hitchhike back to his encampment. "Hurry along!" he spouted, his voice causing his daughter to skip a few steps to catch up. She walked hurriedly behind the man who spoke to a guard who let them pass through the gate once he made his business known.

Inside the compound, it took only a few minutes to cross the yard and go around the big house to find the door the guard pointed out to them. Kieta's mouth fell open. The gawking girl's gaze fell on and rested on the neatly pedicured yard with a few trees, some green grass, and a few budding, colorful flowers, the likes of she had not seen in the area. She noted the building was tall and looked for stairs on the outside where one could enter. Her father stopped suddenly. He emitted a sneeze that brought her back to the present. If he had not been affected by the flora, she would have walked on his heels. As it was, they were at the back door of the edifice. She walked up to his side.

Kieta's father rapped on the huge wooden door with his knuckles several times before he received a response. The woman who answered it remarked before she saw the child behind him. "You old fool. You can't remember to use the bell right beside the door. You know I work all over this house, and I don't know how you expect me to hear you." She reached around him and punched the doorbell, punctuating each word as she accosted him. "See (*ding*)? You see (*ding ding*) how simple that is (*ding, ding, ding, ding*)? What you need? Some practice on how to ring a bell before you know what to do?"

At the terse sound of the woman's voice, Toures's daughter stepped backward and grabbed hold of her father's hand. Fear was attempting to grip her in its fist. Her movements were noticed by the woman who looked first at him and the youngest daughter they had talked about a few years earlier, back when his wife was living, when he had dropped an older daughter off at the Soyinkas' compound. The man coldly shook his baby girl's hand from his with his free hand and pushed her toward the woman. And he pushed her belongings into open arms she had thrown up for rescue. Even in her culture, children turned to their parents for love, nurture, and support. All he said was "Here, Ms. Kesa. She belongs to you all now."

The old woman kept fussing. "I ain't got time for no mess. If she ain't ready to go into the service, you carry her right on back where you brought her from. I can't wean no babies off their mama's tits, their daddy's neither. If she ain't a worker, you take her with you!"

"She is a good worker," he recommended his daughter without reservations. "She took up the cooking and other duties when her mother done passed, still kept up with the watering of the animals, searching for sticks for the fire, any chores anybody around the camp asked her to do. Kieta here is a good girl." He looked downward into wanting eyes, showing in his demeanor that she would be better off in this house. "I ain't never had a minute's trouble out of her. Never even had to scold her!"

Kieta looked up at her father, noting his eyes, like the rest of him, were devoid of emotion but resolute in what was transpiring at the present moment. She let out a sigh of resignation. There was no help for her there. And then he began his departure. His leaving was mechanical like something that one would see at a theater. No visible emotion showed on his face. Kieta's visage showed a shocked resignation as he pivoted on his heels and headed across the yard toward the guarded gate. She was on her own now that they had completed their journey and were in Timbuktu on the outskirts of the city.

The remaining parties observed each other. Only a minute was spent sizing each other up. Kieta saw a round-faced, big-boned woman with wide thighs dressed in a dull colored gray outfit with a scarf covering her head. The woman was just a head taller than she. Wakesa observed a gaunt-faced, smelly, bony, malnourished waif with bright-brown eyes free of emotion, her face streaked with dust and grime and her eyes questioning. The woman tried to put the new girl at ease. "Bienvenue! Entrez-vous! Come on in! I am glad to have you here. There is so much to do in the Soyinka household." The older woman steered her into the house, shutting her past out.

The woman's voiced sentiments received little attention. Kieta was mesmerized by the house she had just entered. Her every gaze and thought was on its magnificence. She was not used to seeing the opulence her eyes beheld.

In Timbuktu, one could find a few tall buildings, but apart from those, most houses in Mali were small and modest. The typical Malian home was small and was either made of crude cement bricks or the typical building material for Mali—mud bricks. But this home was different, so Kieta could only guess that some well-to-do people lived there. Homes of wealthier people and expatriates in the Malian city were larger and usually had a garden and a swimming pool. At least, that was what she had heard from her camp's inhabitants who periodically did day labor in town—gardening, assisting in kitchens, and serving at parties in households where their relatives had permanent employment. She was anxious to see more of the beautiful house.

Chapter Two

"Come with me!" Wakesa commanded the frail girl who was dropped off by the Toures man, transporting her from reverie to reality. This was the second or third girl he had left there. The others had learned well and fast, so they went to live with other families needing their service when she had trained them. Generally, she had her charges bathe as soon as they were dropped off—they always reeked of dust and smoke from the fires fueled by camel, goat, and sheep dung—and put on new clothes before she took them around the compound, but another worker in the house needed her at the present moment. Cleansing would have to wait.

The older woman strode rapidly up a set of stairs with the girl on her heels. Without turning, she barked at her new charge, "Don't touch a thing! Your hands nasty, so don't put them on one thing in this house until we get you cleaned up! You hear me!" She understood that children Kieta's age with limited exposure explored with their fingers all their eyes saw.

The new girl jerked her fingers from the rails she'd fingered since the first step of the staircase and held them together in front of herself. She thought about how smooth the wooden rails were. Their smoothness was so different from the roughness of wood and limbs from Balanzan trees, which had sometimes left splinters in her hands. Her thoughts could do no harm. Hands in front of her, she took the

12

remainder of the steps as easily and effortlessly as the woman she followed.

Since a worker had need of Wakesa, Kieta got something few people got on their first visit to the Soyinkas' compound—a tour. The older woman went upstairs and conferred briefly with another worker in private then took the newest staff member on an abbreviated circuit of the house and environs. The Soyinkas' homestead was a walled compound with an open courtyard in the center. The house had two stories. Several bedrooms were on the top floor. A second sitting room was also there, and access to the rooftop was on this level. On the bottom floor, there was a public toilet, but each bedroom had a private one en suite.

How many rooms were there? Too many to remember! Kieta shook her head.

The Toures girl did not have time to count the rooms but thought she would do that later while they served the family. She looked up at the ceilings. They were high. They looked like they could reach the sky and meet the stars where they hang. However, this was with purpose. The novice was unaware that desert dwellers did this so heat would rise, leaving inhabitants cooler than they would be with lower ceilings. All the ceilings had rotating fans with wooden blades, and like the walls in the compound, the ceilings were white. The girl grew mesmerized with the movement of the fan and stopped dead in her tracks, moving again only after Wakesa called her a couple of times. "Girl, girl, stop gawking! Move your feet. Let's get moving. Ain't nobody got time for your foolishness. There is work to be done around here!"

The rustling of one fan drew her attention away from the older woman, who looked upward this time, pointing and still yelling, her railings leaving the girl wondering if her volume was always on "high." "Girl, you act like you ain't never seen a ceiling fan before." She fussed at Kieta for failing to attend and keep up. "I know your papa has carried you in one of those shops in the village. Just about every shop has one of them ceiling fans now! So don't be standing there looking at that fan like you ain't never seen one. And shut your mouth before a bug get in it."

The impressionable girl shook her head. "No, madame, this is the first time I have seen one of those contraptions." She admitted that while she had been in the village with her father, she stayed outside and waited until he was through with shopping for their meager belongings.

Wakesa shook her head, thinking about ignorance that would have to be overcome before this girl could move on. *Tsk, tsk!* "Keep up!" she warned her. "I don't have time to be telling you the same thing over and over." The mentor slapped her beside the head with open palm, snatched her by the shoulders of her sagging clothes, and shook her. "You can't be as stupid as you pretending. Your other sisters weren't that way. They were smart and quick on their feet. I'm glad you the last one they got! I don't know how much more I can take or how many more servants I can train before I keel over and die!" The woman's frustration as well as her age showed. She was fit for retirement, but no retirement was in sight. The workers either got sick and died or just died.

Sufficiently warned, the new girl kept up, stopped when her mentor stopped, spoke when she was spoken to, and acknowledged other compound's workers as introductions were made, most with a simple bow. She did not hold on to any names the first day. Her attention was on the lodging, its largess, and the comforts it must offer its occupants and on Wakesa. It was apparent that she didn't take any mess.

~~~~~

Kieta rested unaware, but this house was a bit different from traditional Muslim homes. Its spaces were shared by men and women. Most large compounds had specific areas for men and women, the men's areas being in the front of the house and the women's and children's in the rear of the edifices. This home, more modern than other, reflected the owners' values. The Soyinkas were more liberal than many of the other families in the area. They were well-traveled. This family was also among the small percentage of Malian families who observed Catholicism. While many people thereabouts celebrated tribal customs in addition to the religions brought by missionaries from other countries, this family had freed themselves from local traditions.

After the tour, Wakesa gave her a morsel of bread and water, she had heard the rumble coming from her insides, and showed her charge the room in the servants' quarters behind the kitchen that they would share. The older servant also made the new girl bathe, wash her hair, and dress in the attire provided for the servants—a dull gray dress and scarf. And she gave her a new pair of sandals for her feet. She also gave Kieta a sack in which to place the garments she had worn there (that and the couple of articles of clothing in the bundle her father handed her when he handed over the girl) for disposal. Cleansing done, she took her around the perimeter of the compound, telling more servants and guards who she was.

Kieta took note of the number of guards in and around the compound and wanted to know why this family needed such protection and wondered why her father would leave her in a place that was not safe, why he had not even told her he was taking her away, and why he did not respond to her question about where they were going when he told her to pack her things. It was clear that everything had been arranged through a discreet chain of contacts, but how? She wondered what could happen here that required men with guns to be at the gate, everywhere around the Soyinkas' compound. She wanted to ask, but in fear of reprisal, her thoughts did not escape her lips. She feared the woman, like her father, would box her ears or slap her face if she was too forward. After all, children, like women in her culture, were to be seen but not heard unless their opinions were solicited.

Back at the same door where her father had left her a few hours ago, the older woman opened the portal, stepping aside to let her charge enter first; shut it; and propelled the girl forward with the tips of the fingers of one hand. As they proceeded to the bowels of the kitchen, the woman asked, "Do you have questions? Comprenez-vous?" She added, "Ask what you need to know right now! We got a lot of work to do, to have dinner ready for master and his family when they ready to eat."

Not exactly sure what she should inquire, Kieta let those thoughts floating in her head be known. "Why they need so many guards here?" she asked when they were in the kitchen, and the woman was sitting in a chair just inside the doorway to take a breather.

She looked up at the girl, and her face hardened. "You know perfectly well that is not what I am talking about!" She stared in the distance in an irritated way; leaned over, rubbing her aching legs, knees down to her ankles and back up to her knees; and wiggled her feet. The woman was obviously winded. The walk around the compound had taken a toll on her aging body.

"Can I get you something?" the new girl asked, care and concern clear.

The Ayinde woman told her, "Yeah, get me that glass of water out of the refrigerator over there. It's right on the top shelf!" She pointed toward the handle of the large appliance that was almost in front of them. "Look right there on the counter beside it and hand me that medicine bottle."

Confusion showing on the novice's face, the woman pointed at all the objects she mentioned. "Yes, that one!" she voiced loudly when the girl selected the bottle of pain pills she found herself popping. Arthritis, her constant companion, was taking a toll.

Kieta waited for her to hand the water glass back to her. The woman took her pills and a sip from the glass to help her swallow it and gave it to her. "Don't put it back in the icebox. Put it in the sink."

"The icebox?"

"Don't be stupid! When I say icebox, I am talking about the refrigerator, and when I say refrigerator, I am talking about the icebox. Same thing, different name." Wakesa chastised her.

The girl did not let her face show what she was feeling. Although she wanted to cry because she had been called stupid, she was not going to give the woman the satisfaction of seeing, at last, that she had touched a nerve. Trying to act nonchalant, she gently took the glass from the woman's outstretched hand and took it to the counter, let it rest there. "You need anything else, ma'am?"

Feeling sorry that she had spewed on the girl who had just offered kindness, the woman asked again if she had questions.

Turning on her heels, the girl asked, "Why so many men with guns here? Is it not a safe place?"

"Well." The woman sighed then blinked as she considered the girl's questions. She had not anticipated this and was thrown off guard for her moment. Her question caused the Ayinde woman to reconsider the girl's level of maturity. *She ain't as stupid as most*, she thought. Most workers in the compound kept their thoughts and questions to themselves if they had any.

After a brief pause, she started anew. "Well, child, there are so many changes taking place here. Things just ain't like they used to be." She spoke more to herself than to the child. "That's why we have to have so much security! People have just lost their minds. One just can't be too careful."

The woman shook her head, looking to her charge to see if there was clarity, if the answer she provided was sufficient. She too was fearful, fear making her conscious of what she said and who she said it to. Times were indeed changing in their country, and their world was pivoting off its axis and uncertainty abounded everywhere. Their master was doing all he could to keep his family and his workers safe.

Confusion still showed on the inquisitive one's face, so she just spoken candidly. "Now see here, girl. Timbuktu is not as safe as it once was. Rumors tell of terrorists, infidels with low scruples who are taking over our lands, messing with women, taking what don't belong to them. So one can't be too careful. But you don't need to worry yourself about none of that. None of us here do! Master Soyinka is a good man, and he sees to our safety!" Discomforted by speaking of the unspeakable, she ceased rubbing her limbs, rose from her seat, and headed to their original destination with Kieta on her heels.

"Oh," the girl responded as if she comprehended what her mentor told her. However, the girl did not understand much about the infidels. She had heard her father and others in villages throughout the area use the term but had not asked. Still a child, she did not ask questions about what she overheard. He would have punished her for that. Now she had an answer to her question. Yet she remained puzzled as to why there was a guard at the gate and why there were more posted all around the compound, so no questions were forthcoming right away. She stood, her feet planted firmly, threatening to grow roots if she did not move.

The woman brought her back to the present. "Let's get busy! There is too much work that needs to be done around here to be wasting time talking about things we can't control." Moving around in the large space (Kieta thought it was ten times as big as the area she and her family called home in the tent city she and her father recently shared with others like themselves.), Wakesa pointed toward a chair and told her charge to sit. "Asseyez-vous!" The woman placed some silverware, polish, and soft rags in front or her before pulling

17

the chair she had previously propped on to the kitchen table. As soon as her hands were moving, and the girl who vicariously mimicked her movements appeared proficient in silverware's refinement, the woman quit the job and gave the novice further instructions about impending duties.

Instead of polishing, Wakesa busied her hands with the preparing of the new girl for servitude. "I am going to tell you once, *ma petite*," she began spouting rules, enumerating each aloud and counting her fingers when she pronounced her edits. "Numéro un," she commenced. *Deux, trois,* and so forth. Her talk ended with "Keep your mouth! You don't go asking the master and his mistress about nothing. You just do what they say. They will be good to you if you just keep your place, so if you got anything to ask, you ask me. Don't be worrying Monsieur or Madame Soyinka about nothing. And keep away from their children. Don't bother them children." She pointed the index finger from herself to her charge, speaking emphatically the creed the girl should adopt, "Nous nous entraidons . . . We, we are servants. We help each other. Comprendez-vous?" She looked the girl in the eye.

Her charge gave her a nod of comprehension. A bobbing of her head was not enough for Wakesa. The expectant woman held her stance until her charge emitted, "I understand, madame. Je suis d'accord."

Just for good measure, the woman asked the girl if she had a final question as she held her index finger of her right hand to the girl's face. "Just one, one question, is all I got time to entertain. Make it count! We ain't got time to stand around and talk all day."

Kieta raised her finger and spoke softly. "Just one. I have just one."

"Speak up, child. Go ahead. Spit it out. Ask your question so I can give you a response and get to work."

The girl stammered, "I forgot your name. What do they call you?"

Not remembering whether she had actually given her full moniker, the older woman sighed. After that, she told her, "My real name is Wakesa Ayinde. They call me Kesa for short, but I answer to both."

"Why your parents named you that?" Kieta asked. Her question was a common one, for every name had some sort of meaning, even her own.

The older woman explained, "Well, you see, I was born at harvest time. You know how people are. They always naming their children a name what mean something to the family. My papa and mama were showing what was going on at the time of my birth. It was time to do harvesting and gathering. The nights were growing cooler."

However, Wakesa did not leave room for more questions. "It'll be suppertime before you know it. Put that silverware over there in that drawer." She pointed toward the drawer where the forks, spoons, and knives rested when not in use. "Keep out enough for the family so we can set the table. We need a short fork, a regular fork, a butter knife, and a spoon per person."

"How many people?" the newest of the servants asked.

Remembering she had not told the girl the family members' names, Wakesa enumerated them by name, age, and position. She called out, "Monsieur Soyinka, Madame, Ms. Marissa, Little Master Taurence, and Little Petite Mistress Ife . . . Five in all, so you should have five of each kind of fork, five spoons, and five knives. I will show you how to place them in order on the table in a minute."

Kieta busied herself with her chore. The lead servant observed while the girl counted the first set of utensils. She was impressed because the novice made sets for each table setting on her own. Kieta spoke aloud, mostly to herself, as she made the sets until she had enough for all of them. "One for the master, one for the mistress . . ." The older woman smiled. "You are not as stupid as I thought. You are going to be all right." She spoke more to herself than the girl who threw herself into her task.

Kieta took a deep breath, and for a few moments, the only sound was the clack of the cutlery.

That first day at the compound, the pair toiled in the kitchen. Kieta began her training in earnest. Wakesa talked the girl through every assigned task, pausing frequently to correct her and explain how the Soyinkas wanted their food prepared. The greenhorn also had the promised lesson in table setting and using the utensils the upper class enjoyed. While she had seen others use the utensils, she was accustomed to eating with her fingers and drinking her *zrig* from a gourd. The milk from a cow, goat, sheep, or camel sweetened with a little honey was her favorite.

At the thought of the beverage, she asked her mentor, "Ms. Wakesa, I am thirsty. May I have something to drink?"

"Sure, child. Excuse my manners," the woman told her charge. "I have just been so busy with the day's duty until I didn't think to offer you a drink."

Kieta replied, "I took a drink of water from the sink when I bathed." As she spoke, she wondered if their pace would always be like today's—no time to drink or to relieve oneself of a full bladder.

The woman looked in the refrigerator and took a pitcher of goat's milk and poured a glass for the girl. She also gave Kieta a bit of gâteaux from a bread box on the counter, and she took a bite of the sweet treat for herself. The woman brushed crumbs from the counter into the palm of her hands and placed them in the sink.

In the meantime, the new girl relished the bit of pastry, feasting first on its odor, shape, and then its vanilla flavoring. Her taste buds danced with glee. The savor of the treat enacted sensations rarely enjoyed. She almost swooned. She wanted more of the sugary treat but did not ask. It was impolite. *Surely*, she thought, *this portion must be adequate*. Otherwise, the woman would have given her more.

"You like?" asked Wakesa.

She nodded in the affirmative. "Mai oui!" she told the inquirer.

The woman grinned at the obviously smitten girl. "There is more delicious food here. I will teach you not only to enjoy it but also to make it."

Kieta swooned again. She was overcome by the thought of more gâteaux and consistently nourishing foods. When she was growing up, she was lucky if she had a bit of *takoula* to go with her *zrig* or even *tadjala*. You had to have access to a mud oven to bake the pita bread-like soft, tasty bread.

The Toures family generally had *tadjala* that Kieta's ancestors made and passed down to their offspring. This traditional bread of the nomads was made of wheat semolina flour, water, and a pinch of salt. It was cooked in the sand first by building a fire to heat the sand then moving the fire to the side and scraping off the blackened sand. Next, the dough was placed on clean sand and covered by more sand. Fire was replaced on top, and generally, tea was prepared while the dough cooked. When it was done, a few hearty whacks knocked off the sand clinging to the outside of the bread. Finally, the bread was broken into bits and served with a sauce or with honey and butter if any was available. Most times, the Toures had eaten theirs "as was."

The girl's stomach rumbled. Its action was another by-product of eating the sweet treat. It did that to you if you had not eaten before ingesting the cake.

Wakesa asked if she needed to go to the toilet. Initially, the girl considered waiting until later but decided she did not know whether she would have the opportunity to go later. "Scoot. Go now." She pointed the way to the lavatory adjacent to the kitchen and the pantry.

When the novice returned to the kitchen, she received more instructions. "We will make a supper of *al kefta* and some *limonharri* for a beverage. Have you had *limonharri*?" The woman asked her about a sort of ginger ale made with ginger and lemon juice diluted and sweetened to taste before adding to the menu. "They can have some gâteaux for dessert."

Kieta admitted she had not tasted of anything on the day's menu *soif les gateaux*, but she was certain to enjoy all of it.

The woman laughed a hearty laugh. "I bet you will, you little urchin. Come on. Let's get back to work!" She set about passing items to the girl for placement on the countertop: already deboned and chopped sheep from the refrigerator, onions and garlic from a barrel, spices (jarred ones) from the cabinets, and some rice.

"We are going to put all this in that wooden bowl over there." She pointed, and the girl's eyes followed her fingers. "Get it!" was the command. "And put it here on the counter. We are going to mix it up, make some little meatballs, and fry them. Then we are going to make a sauce and put the meatballs in it. Last of all, we are going to cook some rice and put the *al kefta* over it."

"We are?" Kieta spoke, overwhelm showing in her voice. The novice had helped with making of the bread for her family but had not done much more cooking. She was totally out of her element.

"Yes, girl, I told you already—Kieta and Kesa, the two of us, nous nous entraidons. I will help you learn everything you need to know. So don't worry your little head off." The woman grinned at her inexperience and obvious sense of insecurity.

In spite of the woman's talk about being in it "together," Kieta was not certain they could make the dish. Her mother or elders and her brothers and sisters had cooked *mischoui* for the Toures family.

21

They slaughtered, dressed, and cooked their meat in the sand, much the same way they cooked bread. Nevertheless, on occasion when the family they served had a small house with an outdoor clay oven, she had seen camel, cow, and goats readied for meals and ceremonies. When this happened, her only job was to bring the sticks and clumps of dried dung or charcoal *briques* used to fuel the flames.

The girl purposed to follow the woman's lead. They made the supper, and she saw and made acquaintance of the master, mistress, and their three children at the evening meal. "Monsieur Soyinka, Madame, Marissa, Taurence, Ife"—the woman gave their names— "this is the new girl, Kieta." For lack of nothing else to do, the novice nodded at each family member. No sound would come. However, she grew more comforted when they acknowledged her with smiles and complimented the servants for the delicious meal.

Yet she was wary. The man's pink skin served as a source of consternation. And the woman, she was not sure where her master had found his bride. Her skin was like tea with cream, her hair straight and uncovered, and her teeth perfect. Their children, a blend of two cultures, multiracial, paid little attention to the brown chocolate beauty with a round face that Kieta was.

As obedient as she was wary, the girl gave their compliments a cautious, calculated smile, noticing at the same time the ease her mentor exhibited in their presence. Wakesa spoke freely to the master, mistress, and their offspring. If she was not in uniform, one would have thought she was family.

Kieta's attention was drawn to a girl her own age who asked, "Can we have a bit of brittle later?"

Her father provided the response. "Only when you have completed your studies, and if Wakesa will make some."

The older woman told them she would make some brittle. When the meal was completed, the family retired to their private quarters, leaving the servants to clear the table, clean the dishes, and make preparations for the next day.

"What is this brittle that Marissa spoke of?" Kieta asked while they washed dishes after the meal.

Wakesa stopped dead in her tracks and put her hands on her hips. She also shook her head in amazement. "Child, you ain't had brittle? I thought everybody had brittle. It ain't nothing but some sugar and

22

peanuts cooked together until it makes candy. You let it get hard, break it, and eat it."

"Oh," Kieta said. Little room was left for more conversation. They worked until the sun was set, and it was dark outside when they retired to the servants' quarters where Wakesa gave the girl additional lessons on personal hygiene, beginning with the art of brushing ones teeth. The new girl liked the brush more than the rag she had always wiped her teeth with as well as the sweetness of the paste. The girl licked paste from her lips and swallowed the sweetened spittle. "Don't use too much, just a little. It is not food, just a cleanser. Spit it out and rinse your mouth," the older woman commanded too late.

Sufficiently instructed on bathing, personal hygiene, and good grooming, Kieta passed the first night in what she later spoke of as *heavenly*. She had traded the blanket on the ground or piles of rags on shack floors she had always had for a small bed in the servants' quarters with a mattress, which was comfortable. In this cozy environment, no bugs or small creepy animals diminished the quality of one's repose, so security made itself felt. She slept soundly.

Wakesa had to shake her to awaken her the second morning in the Soyinka household. "I can't be getting you up every morning!" she told the girl. "You better get up before the sunrise. There is work to be done here, so don't be acting like you are a queen or something. Get your lazy butt out of that bed and hurry up and get dressed. We got to get some breakfast ready."

The new girl made her way in the semidarkness to the toilet and quickly dressed for the day's work. She put on the simple gray skirt, blouse, and apron she had been issued and tied a scarf around her head.

At the new place, Kieta experienced few sleepless nights. She met her fate courageously. A quick study, she paid attention to the goings on about the master's house. When she did not have duties, she longed to play with the children her age she found there but couldn't. She was the help, and the master's children treated her as such. They were respectful and paid her the same attention as they did the other servants—all except their oldest, Marissa.

Chapter Three

Soon, it was apparent to Kieta that everyone in the household worked. Monsieur Soyinka spent time at his desk in the library as well as an office on the second floor and frequently talked on the telephone and took notes. She didn't know what he was busy about, but it was clear he was a good provider for his family. Every man in the neighborhood seemed to be. One only had to stand in one place—inside the house, outside the compound, or in the midst of the courtyard—to see that.

As for Madame Soyinka, the children's mother assisted them with their lessons and periodically utilized the services of a math tutor, one who also spoke French and English. She enjoyed shopping for her family and needlepointing when she was not instructing her children or coordinating some kind of social.

Kieta, along with the older lady, cleaned the kitchen and dining area and did the cooking. The sitting room and library also were duty areas. Family members sat in these areas during the day, entertained there as well as studied and worked there.

Soon, the most recent of their servants started manipulating her schedule, so she was in the library where the master's children were taught their lessons daily. She did light dusting, brought snacks and beverages to them, and returned to take emptied dishes back to the kitchen for cleansing. Kieta always listened with one ear as she performed her chores, and the girl learned everything the children were taught.

Later, when the Soyinka family and Wakesa were asleep, she would make her way in the dark back to library, turn a lamp on its lowest setting, and peer at books the children studied from.

~~~~~

From her perch on the second floor of the Soyinkas' house waiting for the phone to ring, she now recalled that defining moment. More than a year had passed since she had come to the Soyinkas' compound, and she was feeling secure in her placement, so Kieta slipped out of bed one night when Wakesa was snoring, in her REM stage, and past awakening by the small sounds her charge made when she got out of the bed. She slipped a housecoat over her gown, tiptoed out of the bedroom, and made her way through the kitchen and dining room through the dark of the compound's hallways and into the library. When she was a few yards from the entrance, she observed a bit of light. Kieta came to a screeching halt, considering whether she should proceed or she should turn back. *What if someone is there? Stop thinking so hard. Trust your instincts*, she told herself. *So the library has a little light on. That's not unusual. If someone is there, you can say you came to get a drink of water. The light was on, so you decided to cut it off.*

Her confidence renewed by her own words, she hastened head first to her intended destination. At the library's entrance, she peered through a crack to determine that no one was in the room before widening the enclosure enough to slide her body in the room, making a pathway to avoid the desk where her master worked. Wakesa would have her head if she messed up any of the elder Soyinka's paperwork. She never even let her dust there. The girl brushed thoughts of her mentor aside and tiptoed to the area where the children studied.

In the vast room, the Toures girl took a seat in an upholstered chair beside a lamp that had not been extinguished, never thinking that someone had been there, left it burning, and might return. She took one of the books from a child's table and sat there, fingering it, moving slowly from page to page, not fully comprehending the lettering on the page but knowing by heart the story she heard her

25

mistress read to her children. She traced her finger along the page, mouthing the memorized text.

The door swung open, wide. The servant girl was so engrossed in the book that she did not hear her master when he entered the library and almost jumped out of her skin when she heard him clear his throat before saying, "Excusez moi! I didn't know you were here, else I would have left the light for you to extinguish."

She leaped to her feet, and *Le Petit Prince*, the book she held in her hands, fell to the floor while she stammered. "Oh, monsieur, I am so sorry, sir. Excusez moi!" she begged his pardon, tightening the robe around her thin corps. "I, I, I should not be here," she stuttered. It was difficult to express herself with her hands busied with concerns about her inappropriate dress. "Pleasssse don't think badly of me. I am indeed sorry and will not come here again unless Wakesa or Madame Soyinka gives me permission to enter therein. Puh-leeze!"

The man kept coming.

As Monsieur Soyinka approached her, the servant girl cowered with fear, cringing at the thought of what was going to happen to her now that she was caught. She ducked her head to one side, letting it almost meet her shoulder. Kieta thought her employer would strike her. That was what the elder Toureses and other members of their group had done when she or any of their children disobeyed the slightest of commands, disrupted them when they were speaking, or disturbed their peace.

She closed her eyes and waited for pain.

In her spirit, she felt the slap of their open palm and heard the swish of the woven lash as it touched her clothed or bared skin, whichever was the case when she was punished for transgressions committed on purpose or by accident. She recalled how if they were away from their camp, and an incident took place, she or one of the other children was sent to get a switch from a bush or tree—corporal punishment had been administered freely in her environment. Instinctively, the girl's right shoulder jerked upward, almost meeting her inclined cheek.

Noticing her recoil, the man spoke up and out. "No, no," Monsieur Soyinka told her, throwing his hands in the air, arresting her thoughts of reprisal as quickly as they had come. He read her mind and dispelled her apprehensions with "No, *ma petite*, there is no reason to fear. Or to cry?" Noticing Kieta was near tears too, he continued,

"Are you here because you want to study? There is nothing wrong with wanting to be learned. It's quite okay. I will speak to my wife. Perhaps she will permit you to come here to have lessons with the children."

Kieta's eyes flew open. Her worst fears not realized, the Toures girl wiped her eyes with her free hand. Looking directly at the man, she inquired, "You will do that for a disobedient girl like me?" Kieta diminished herself and her worth. She had done a heap more things correctly than not.

"There is nothing disobedient about wanting to be learned," the man told her as he neared the lamp, reaching for the light to put it out. "It's just that the hour is much too late to be up and reading." He shooed her from the library. "Go, go to bed. The break of day will be here before you know it," he told her, his gaze on a huge grandfather clock in a corner of the room. "It is past midnight. It will be time for you to get up and go to work soon. Hurry along and get some sleep. I will do as I said. I am a man of my word."

The girl gladly accepted his good night's bid. She fled from the room and rushed through the kitchen to the area of the house where she should have been, pausing only when she was at the door. She turned the knob and pushed the door open cautiously and tiptoed into her living quarters, exercising care to have a noiseless reentry, a feat that was indeed hard. She could hear her heartbeat and felt others could also hear it.

Needless to say, Kieta was ushered into their room in the servants' quarters by Wakesa's snores. The woman was sleeping soundly. Yet she proceeded on tiptoe with caution to her own cot where she reclined but lay daydreaming in the dark until morning came, and the older woman began stirring in the room. The girl did what was expected. She arose too and made ready for another day of service. She did not mention the night's adventure and its consequences to her mentor.

Chapter Four

The shock of a lifetime came at breakfast the following morning. "Kieta." Madame Soyinka smiled at the girl and beckoned her to come to her side of the table. She wiped her mouth for a final time with her napkin and folded the bit of cloth while the girl moved tentatively closer to her then placed it on the table beside her plate before saying more. While the woman's casual but customary morning routines were enacted, the servant girl waited, watching Wakesa who was transporting the sterling silver coffeepot to the table for refills. She let her eyes fall then raised them again.

The servants caught each other's eye. *What the heck?* the older woman silently queried her charge. Kieta almost lifted her shoulders in denial but determined that it would be best not to say or do anything except follow their employer's lead. Her mentor took the silver pot from a cart near the dining room door and sashayed over to the table, posting herself on the other side of their mistress. This place was a strategic spot where she could hear all their employer said to the girl and the latter's response.

Wakesa poured their master a refill before moving toward Madame Soyinka's cup. Both enjoyed a couple of cups of medium-roasted beverage before starting their day. But the woman raised her hand, arresting the servant's movements. "Not today. I think I am going to have to cut down on the coffee. My heart seems to flutter when I drink too much." She touched her chest.

"Sorry, ma'am," the older of the women replied. "I can get you some tea or some—"

"No, no tea."

Anxious to keep the conversation going, the woman who had been with the Soyinkas for as long as she could remember asked, "Have you spoken to the doctor about this?"

"Not yet! I just decided to cut back on my own."

The servant kept going. "Perhaps we can try decaffeinated. I can get some when I go to the market. We can see if that is better. I will put it on the list."

Sick of the small talk about beverages, Madame Soyinka held up a hand to the woman to stop her speech. "Enough talk about coffee. I will drink whatever you put in the pot. I am not choosy."

She looked at her watch, and her words rushed on. "You may be excused now, Wakesa. Just a bit of privacy, please. I want to have a word with Kieta here." The woman waved her away before she completed her offer for a glass of water with lemon, the servant's next thought. Ruby Soyinka had more pressing concerns. Her attention returned to the girl whom she had called to her side.

Kieta saw her mentor leave the room from the corner of her eye. *Whew!* She wiped her hand across her brow.

"Come closer." Ruby Soyinka beckoned the nervous girl on her left side. "I will not bite," she contended as she touched Kieta on her arm while shifting in her seat so they were facing each other.

"Oui, madame!" Kieta barely got out the couple of acknowledging words. Certain that the girl had her full attention, the lady of the house spoke up. "My husband told me you want to learn, to be educated. Is that right?" the woman inquired of her desires.

Her heart stopped. She was not expecting to hear this. She stood waiting for the woman to say something else.

No words were forthcoming. Madame Soyinka was waiting for the girl to answer her question. She didn't say a mumbling word, she couldn't, so the speaker continued, "Monsieur told me you want to learn to read and inquired about letting you take lessons with the children. Well, I don't have a problem with it. If you can manage to keep up with your chores, you may come and sit in and study alongside Marissa. She can help you catch up!"

The Toures girl's eyes lit up like a Christmas tree. She was so excited. Her master had kept his word. Gratitude showed in her eyes when they caught his.

Seeing she was not able to speak, monsieur queried jokingly, "What's the matter, girl? The cat got your tongue?"

Grateful for the windfall, she attempted to speak. Nevertheless, before she got a sound out of her mouth, Wakesa flew back into the room. She had not gone far when she was dismissed. She had stopped just outside the dining room doorway and stood there, listening and trying to peep in without being seen. Within earshot, she had heard it all, so she flew into the room to take care of the matter—the insolent girl had overstepped her bounds. The woman purposed she would teach her a lesson when they got back to the kitchen. She had told her to keep her distance from the family they served and to interact with her, her only. In her mind's eye, she recalled pointing to herself with a finger then to the girl's chest with the same finger the very first day she had entered the service at the Soyinkas. "It's just you and me. We are servants. We help each other. You and me!"

The head servant broke the exchange between the trio—mistress, master, and her mentee—who turned when they heard her voiced outcry. "Madame, monsieur! I trust this one is not being a pest. If she is, I will attend to her!" She rolled her eyes at her charge, arresting her delight and rendering Kieta uncomfortable. The woman had threatened to beat her with a broomstick on more than one occasion—a threat she had not had to carry out because she had not overstepped her bounds, at least she had not until now.

The servant girl shook where she stood, gawking. She wanted to flee from the room, but she could not even move. The sandals on her feet felt like lead restraints. She could not raise her legs. Her mouth fell open, and her heart pounded profusely. A response was provided by her bladder too. The girl thought she might piss like a camel on the linoleum-covered dining room floor, pee a river that would dampen the Persian rug the cherry wood dining table rested on. Her mistress had gotten it from the Orient, wherever that was, so Kieta knew she would be offended if anything happened to something so valuable. She twisted where she stood, impaled by tension that swept over her.

The Toures girl was so conflicted and did not know what to do. She looked from one adult to the other and back. There were three present: Monsieur, Madame, and Wakesa. She had neglected to consider what the older servant would think about her being invited to study with the Soyinka children. *Perhaps I should have told her about the conversation I had with monsieur,* she thought before recoiling again, ducking like a tortoise escaping to his shell for comfort.

Noticing her movements and sensing her trepidation, her mistress reached for the teenager, caught her by the side, and drew her even closer. Kieta acquiesced. She let her corps be limp, so pliable, in order to close the gap between her and Madame Soyinka as the head of the household continued to speak. "No need to fear, *ma petite!* You are *our* charge. My husband and I want you to come to the library each day at 10:00 a.m. to be educated alongside our children. So hurry along and get your duties taken care of," she reassured the girl, patting her on the arm gently.

No one else in the dining room moved a muscle while their exchange took place, not even the children. They were as quiet as church mice too.

Kieta nodded but did not move. She let her eyes hang low, not establishing eye contact with the woman who was her mentor. She just waited there for whatever was going to transpire as a result of the pronouncement.

When Ruby Soyinka had given the girl her instructions, the lady of the house turned to Wakesa, ordering in her peculiar way. "Ensure that she is there each day *à l'heure!* No excuses. She is to be there when we start!" Afterward, the woman nudged the girl reposing in the bend of her arm, setting her in motion again.

The youngest of the servants returned to the spot where she had been called from. She didn't know what else to do. As for the Ayinde woman, she held her spot now. She knew in her heart that she had gone too far. It was her turn to feel discomfiture previously placed on her charge. *What the heck was I thinking? I hope Madame and Monsieur Soyinka will count this to my head and not my heart. I didn't mean any harm. I was just trying to do my job, keep servants from fraternizing with family. That is inappropriate. I hope I don't get dismissed. I didn't mean no harm. I, I, I . . .* She made excuses for her misstep. Her aching joints, which were already throbbing, ached even more, and her head pounded, as her blood pressure elevated. The woman hoped she would not drop dead where she stood.

Realizing the extent to which she had overstepped her bounds, Wakesa bowed in submission, exhibiting respect. She spoke only when she realized her mistress was giving orders about the girl's schedule and itinerary. "Yes, ma'am. Oui, madame. I will ensure she is there each day at ten." The woman backed her way out of the room, away from the noises coming from a family preparing for a new day and new adventures.

The elder Soyinka smiled at his wife; the woman winked at him. They had anticipated and discussed Wakesa's likely response and actions that could follow. She was the consummate mother hen, one who took her responsibilities seriously. Once put in check, she would do their biddings. They were certain of that. The attention returned to their family. Their children had witnessed the encounter and were reacting.

Marissa let out a small, albeit quiet, snicker at the servant. Wakesa rode her back too and wouldn't let her have her way when her parents left her in charge when they were out of town, at a meeting, or socializing with other in their circle. Noticing her response, both her parents gave her a reproving eye.

Sufficiently chastised, the teenager turned to a more pressing matter. The most precocious of the Soyinkas' offspring giggled with excitement. Now she would have someone her age to study with. She had wanted to go to a public school in the city where she could be with others her age, but her parents wouldn't let her go there. Each time she brought up the subject, they inserted their parental rights, telling her that when she was of age, if her home studies showed progress, they would let her attend the university. Here, she was about to have someone her own age to study with. It mattered little that she was a servant. She was tired of studying alongside her young siblings, Taurence and Ife. Besides, they were no fun.

Noting her gleeful expression, her father asked, "Marissa, does it suit you to have Kieta study with you?" He sipped from his cup.

"That would be fine, Poppa!" Marissa used the term of endearment she employed when she was pleased or when she was getting her way. Next, she turned to Kieta, who was clearing the table of dishes and saucers pushed aside, for her appraisal of the current state of affairs, asking in her broken French, "Does that suit you, Kieta?"

Kieta stammered, "It sure does, M—" She stopped short. The girl had almost said "ma'am" to one her own age. That was not necessary.

"Can we start today?" Marissa asked her mother.

"Not today," the woman responded to her daughter, her voice as cheery as always. "We will start Monday, but it will be a while before she is studying with you. I have a battery of tests that I must administer individually before I can determine where to begin." This answer was satisfactory for both girls. They would at least be sharing space.

"More coffee, monsieur?" Wakesa brought Kieta out of her reverie. "Kieta will get a fresh pot." She gestured with her head for the girl to go to the kitchen tout de suite.

Proper decorum restored, the head servant asked, "Does anyone else have need of more food? Or drink? Kieta can get more milk if you want."

Their negative responses given, she began to remove partially emptied bowls from the table, passing them to her charge when she had given more coffee to their master. The girl put the emptied pot on a tray with bowls of leftover food on a rolling cart for transporting to the kitchen where she and her mentor would have breakfast of leftover bread, meat, dates, and goat cheese when they were in the kitchen.

In a minute, the Soyinkas left the dining room, heading to their respective places to resume their busy day. The master went to his in-home office, and the mistress accompanied their children to the library to do the day's lessons in English, French, mathematics, social studies, and science as well as reading and phonics for the littlest ones.

When they had removed the plates from the dining room table and returned to the kitchen for their breakfast, it was frosty to say the least. Wakesa was upset because her charge had done the forbidden. The girl had inserted herself into the family's life, breaking one of the rules she had given the very first day she had come into service. Needless to say, the conversation that had previously flowed freely became a question-answer session.

It was clear to Kieta that her supervisor did not think it was a good idea for her to enjoy such a relationship with the oldest of the Soyinka children. But there was nothing she could do. Obedience was better than sacrifice. Wakesa was not going to do anything to raise her employers' ire. They were good to her and had been since she had been with them, which was more years than she could count on her phalanges.

~~~~~

School time came quickly, and Kieta passed all the intelligence tests the mistress gave her with flying colors. The lessons she mentally sat in on for the last couple of years in the Soyinka household had taken effect. Content Taurence, Ife, and Marissa learned had been digested and easily regurgitated, Madame Soyinka gave her the quizzes in French. The girl had also mastered simple English phrases. So the addition of Kieta to the homeschooling process was not laborious. It was a pleasure for her as well as for her employer. The servant girl was quite gifted and had a propensity for languages. Math proved to be a bit more challenging.

Her studies never interfered with her work. She pursued her household task vigorously and was careful to exceed expectations Wakesa had for her. When her workday was done, she and Marissa frequently returned to the library on the main floor to complete their schoolwork. It was not long before they became fast friends, and the kvetching that teenage girls were involved in ensued. Much of their time was involved in talks about boys and what they thought about them, sex, hairstyles, fashions, and their dreams.

Neither girl had access to many boys. Marissa's acquaintances attended the Catholic Church the Soyinkas belonged to, and most were from working-class families like her own. Kieta listened to her talk of these young men but could only imagine them because the family did not take her to services with them. Her household duties were twenty-four hours, seven days a week every month of the year. The three hours she passed studying during the weekdays were made up for on the weekends. Wakesa ensured this.

Besides the young men from church, there were also those who belonged to other servants and those who served the family when they were of age. They drove for the Soyinkas, guarded the compound, maintained their small fleet of vehicles, gardened, or kept the herd of animals the Soyinkas raised for milk and meat. Several of these young men gained the young women's attention, but they never accosted them or tried to befriend them. They stayed in their places. However, that did not keep the girls, especially the free-spirited Marissa, from flirting with them when no adults were present.

Chapter Five

One of the most memorable occasions that Kieta was involved with took place when she had been with the family a couple of years. The Soyinkas had a dinner party. A couple of military officials, several ambassadors, and their wives were invited to the compound for dinner and drinks. When the social activity was announced, much hustling and bustling took place at the compound. A flurry of activity, including what Wakesa called deep cleaning, cooking, organizing, and preparing oneself for the party to take place on New Year's Eve, kept everyone busy.

This marked many firsts for the novice. At work, an extended table setting, which included salad and dessert forks, was learned. She received tutelage from Wakesa on how to set the table the evening of the formal dinner. While the two were engaged in this activity, boy servants s brought punch bowls, silver trays, and more rarely used utensils into the house. They also brought a couple of leaves for the dining room table as well as more chairs from somewhere—a storage area that Kieta was not familiar with. Her inquiry about where they came from brought a quick rebuff from her mentor. "Ain't no time to be talking! Just tend to your business and don't leave no spots on that silver."

Soon, the silverware and furniture were polished. And there was the washing and ironing of elongated tablecloths as well as securing matching cloth napkins from a linen closet just off the kitchen.

Her mind went back to another day when she sat with Wakesa and their mistress to develop the six-course menu for the event—lamb and all the fixings and poultry, squab for those who did not like lamb. When their mistress was satisfied with the menu, the duo scoured the many cookbooks the older woman kept on a shelf on the counter for menus, the Ayinde woman grabbing a pair of spectacles she rarely used from an apron pocket. "I didn't know you could read," her underling proffered, shock in her voice.

"Lots of things you don't know about me!" was her quick response. Kieta didn't say another word, just watched the woman peer at recipes that were already marked. The older woman traced slowly through each recipe, assuring herself that she had every spice, herb, and condiment necessary for preparing such a meal, one that she had done before.

The following week, the two kitchen workers prepared smaller versions of the larger meal, testing old and new recipes before the party. They served it to the Soyinkas for a Sunday dinner and gave remnants to others in the household for tasting and sought their mistress's approval before going into the city to secure all the ingredients they needed for the delectable fare.

While this was going on, Kieta thought her studies would suffer. She was exhausted when her head hit the bed during this busy season. Wakesa did too. Despite her aching joints, she fell out like a light as soon as her head hit the pillow. Nevertheless, her youthfulness trumped wisdom that came with age. She managed to keep up with the other children as they studied. Her energy level, sustained by adrenaline rush, brought on by the opportunity to learn, to be able to read and decipher, not labor with simple recipes like she had observed the older lady do.

A surprise took place the day following the tasting. Madame asked her if she wanted to go into town with them to assist with shopping for their attire for the party. Needless to say, Kieta was overtaken by unspeakable joy. In the servants' room that night, she told her older roommate about the offer. An "uh-huh" was her only comment. Since the day their mistress had put her in her place about

37

the girl's taking lessons with the other children, she kept her tongue when the girl mentioned something the lady of the house said, did, failed to do, etc.

The next few days, Kieta threw herself into her household duties, dusting where she had already dusted for good measure, cleaning toilets until their seats sparkled, and measuring dry goods and liquids. Wakesa used to create meals to perfection, not a grain of salt too many nor a drop of milk too much. Her studies received as much attention. The girl wanted to please both ladies. Both had something to offer. Consequently, she went into the city with madame and Marissa and got to ride in the chauffeured coal-black Suburban with tinted windows she had seen the family ride in many times and to a seamstress who kept her shop private for that day's clients.

There, the driver let them out at the entrance, and the shop owner unlocked the door from the inside, letting them whisk their way inside, Kieta the servant girl on Marissa's heels. Pointing toward a straight back chair in the waiting room, she told the last entrant, "Asseyez-vous!" Her tone terse, it drew the Soyinka woman's attention.

"She is with me." Her voice commanded the woman to let her servant girl come into the back. The corrected woman beckoned with her head for her to follow them.

Bolts of fabrics in every color imaginable greeted them. Several mannequins, some partially dressed, others with fabrics drape on them, rested by sewing machines, cutting board tables, and trash bins; everything any seamstress worth her salt possessed filled the room. There was just enough space for one or two people to maneuver easily. At the proprietor's offering, the three of them sat on one side of the table. She took a seat facing them, pulling a couple of fashion magazines from a bin and placing them on the table. "What is it that you have in mind for this occasion? Something like the last time? Something different?"

"I am not sure." Madame Soyinka admitted she was not certain about what she wanted. "I trust your judgment."

Humility showed on the seamstress's face. "Here are a few books I set aside when I got your telephone call. Why don't you ladies peruse them while I get some us some tea?" she said while pushing a book in front of each of them.

Kieta thanked her, her mannerisms like those of the family she served.

The lady returned with a silver tray replete with a platter of coconut macaroons, a teakettle full of hot water, tea bags, sugar, cream, and lemon. "My favorites!" Marissa squealed with delight.

"I remember." The woman smiled at the girl who had been coming to the shop with her mother for quite a while. "However, I forgot the silverware and napkins."

Up and out of her chair in a minute, the Toures girl offered to get the items for her if she would tell her where to find them.

"No," the woman insisted, "I am at your service today."

When she was out of the room, Marissa told her friend, they had long since become pals, "You need to forget about work and just enjoy yourself!"

Her mother poured water for all of them, including the seamstress, and passed the container of tea bags from which the girls made a selection, saying as she performed this act, "Indeed, Kieta, enjoy the moment. I apologize for having you come with us dressed in uniform. We can be so thoughtless sometimes!"

"I wasn't thinking either," Marissa retorted. "You could have put on one of my dresses. We are the same size."

Kieta swallowed, her spit threatening to choke her. She was overcome with emotion brought on by her employers' thoughtfulness. The girl made a mental note to do what she had seen the woman do on occasion, write a thank-you note, expressing gratitude for a kindness previously extended. For Marissa, she decided she was going to find a recipe for the favorite cookie in one of the books Wakesa kept in the pantry and make some for her to share with her brother and sister. She smiled to herself.

In a minute, the shop owner was back, distributing the cloth napkins and utensils to her customers. She had taken the time to fold and insert the spoon in a pocket in the cloth. Apology extended again, the women and girls fingered through the magazines, finding styles they preferred and discussing colors that would look good on them.

Several hours passed. The ladies selected dresses from pattern books, finding parts from each that they would like theirs to have. The shopkeeper made notes on a pad about the desired neckline, sleeve, length. Madame and mademoiselle were measured, and appointments were made for fittings. The servant girl watched, replying only when her opinion was asked, and daydreamed. She could see herself in vogue as she let her ears hear designers' names like Armani and Oscar de la Rente. Modern-day designers from all over the world fell on her listening ears, widened to capture all that was nouveau. She heard her employer tell the woman taking her measurements, "Your work equals theirs! Actually, I think it is better. I wouldn't wear some of those things I saw in those books to a dogfight."

Her words caused the seamstress to have a fit of laughter. "I think they are a bit overrated sometimes, but you have to ride while the tide is high!"

"We are going to put you on the map too. Isn't that right, Marissa? We are going to be looking like we are on the runway at the party."

The younger Soyinka acknowledged the woman's prowess. "Yes, ma'am. You rock!"

"Stop now! You are going to make my head swell up like a balloon until it pops!" She laughed again, shaking her head at the same time.

"Come, pick something simple for yourself! You make wages. You can buy a dress if you like."

Kieta jerked with surprise, uncertain about who the Soyinka woman was talking to until Marissa pointed out. "Mama is talking to you. We've finished getting ours."

"I didn't bring any money with me," she spoke.

"Who goes shopping without money? Only you, *ma petite*! You have much to learn!" The woman reached and drew her charge nearer, her gesture as kind and comforting as it had been the day she spoke to the girl about learning to read.

It was good she did. The girl swooned, almost lost her footing. The others, including the seamstress, laughed with her, not at her. Pointing to the seamstress, she told the girl, "Here, you pay when you are satisfied. You may bring your money when we return." Soon, she found one she wanted.

~~~~~

Kieta Toures's memory of this eventful day refreshed while she daydreamed of her adolescent days in the Soyinka household.

The girl's brain did like the computer they used for writing papers and completing their other school assignments. Periodically, the machinery would give a message to refresh, causing all functions to renew and behave properly. It took her to a place of ridicule that she had hoped to forget. The pain rested in her psyche even unto the present time.

She went into the city with her employer a couple of times for fitting of their dresses. Hers was so simple that it did not require nicks and tucks theirs required for the perfect fit. The day that she brought money with her to pay for her dress, madame found out she kept her money in a box in her room, an act she found reprehensible. Consequently, when their chores were completed, the woman took her student to the bank, helped her open an account, and gave her a lesson in economics.

After they picked up their dresses, the driver took them to the large mall on the outskirts of the city. There, the women got manicures and pedicures, Kieta too. A treat given by the Soyinkas, she enjoyed the preening. The soaking of her feet made her realize how hard she worked, how deserving she really was. Her employer also paid for the lunch they had at a fast-food place. She had a hamburger, French fries, and sweet tea.

By the time they finished, it was time to go to the hairdressers, another treat the girl did not know she would have. Madame Soyinka, the girls in tow, had swooshed breathlessly into the shop, two of them seating themselves in chairs that had previously been reserved. Kieta headed to a seat in front of the window where she would wait for the ladies to get their manes washed, dried, and styled. Her attention turned to magazines on a table beside her. She perused covers, mostly ones showing fashions as well as hairdos, cuts, and curls and made-up faces rouged with a variety of blushes and an abundance of hues of eye colors.

Lost in her own daydreams, she did not hear the woman who inconspicuously made her way from the back, securing her own place behind a third chair, which was vacant, as she called out. "Miss! Miss!" And when she had her attention, she said, "You may sit here!"

The Toures girl looked first to her right then to her left, ascertaining that there was no other lady in the shop *sauf* herself. "Moi, moi," she responded, tapping her own chest as she spoke.

"Yes, you! She's talking about you, silly!" Marissa chastised her from the chair where she sat. "You should know by now that our mother would not bring you somewhere and just let you sit!"

Still stuck in her seat, she could not let loose of it until her mistress spoke up. "Marissa, be careful how you speak. No name-calling! Kieta is no sillier than you are. She is just unaware. She had no way of knowing that I had made an appointment for her too."

"Sorry, Mama!" the girl told her mother then turned to the one with whom she shared so many experiences and said, "I didn't mean any harm, Kieta."

The Soyinka woman assured her, "Kieta, this is Ms. Rachel. I asked for her when I called for an appointment. She will fix your hair."

The waiting attendant summoned the girl to her chair, and when she was seated, she placed a shawl over her, making ready for the hairstyle she would give her that day. She removed the head rag, a part of the uniform the servant girl still wore, her wardrobe defined by her occupation, not by her wishes. Even now, as she was getting ready to have a proper hairdo, she longed to wear the styles her friend wore and told herself that she would be a fashionista one day. The woman ran her fingers through the girl's matted hair, determining for herself the texture, length, and hair strength. "You want to straighten this?" She looked around, catching the girl's eye. "I can give you a perm!"

Not sure about "a perm," the novice responded, "If you could straighten it, I would be happy."

In a flash, the girl noticed as the woman took a jar, a bottle half-filled with liquid, and a folded piece of paper with directions from a box with a girl who looked much like her on the label. The woman picked the box up, peering inside for something and not finding it, she uttered, "I don't know what they think I am going to stir this with."

"Ma'am?"

"Nothing," the woman told her as she pulled a drawer beside her open, taking a comb with a long handle from it. Her customer watched the hairdresser pour the liquid into a container about the size of a cereal bowl and stir what obviously was a substance to be used for straightening with the comb's handle. Laying this mixture aside, she took the sheet with the directions from the counter, flipped it over with one hand, and detached a pair of clear plastic gloves from it.

She handed the girl the directions. "This is what I am going to use on your hair," she said, pulling a jar of hair grease from the drawer to baste the girl's scalp. She showed the ointment to her customer. "Do you have any sore spots in your head?"

Kieta shook her head in the negative.

"Have you been scratching it with your fingers or brushing it real hard with a hairbrush?"

"No, it ain't been itching. I wash it regularly in the shower."

"A shower!" the woman exclaimed. "You are one blessed child. You got a shower? Is it in the house?"

The Toures girl acknowledged her assertion. "Yes, ma'am. I share a room with the head housekeeper, so she makes sure I keep clean and bathed."

In a minute, the woman was basting the girl's hair, parting its nappy strands with eager fingers, and dipping a finger in the grease and spreading it on the girl's scalp. She spread some of the grease on the girl's temple, around her ears, and at the edges of her hairline.

Curiosity aroused, Kieta inquired about the preparations the woman made before putting the perm in her hair.

"I baste it to keep this compound directly off you scalp. It's got lye in it! So to keep from burning the skin off you, I greased your head."

The girl cringed with uncertainty. Her mother had used lye and animal fat to make soap. She was not sure she wanted the straightening agent. *Perhaps, I should just let her wash it and give me a couple of braids.*

Rachel put the gloves on her hands and took the comb from the counter. She used the back of the toothed side to dip in the bowl, obtain some of the straightening agent, and smooth it on parcels of the girl's medium-length hair.

Feeling the coolness from the initial application, Kieta shuddered.

"You will be all right," the hairdresser comforted her. "If you feel any burning, let me know so I can hurry and wash it out!"

"Okay." Kieta shut her eyes tightly as the woman pulled her head backward to put some of the perm on her edges.

When the application was complete, and the woman was smoothing her mane with the back of the comb and her fingers, the

43

girl began to feel a warmth on her scalp and was anxious to get the perm out of her hair before her skin was cooked. "It's ready now!"

The hairdresser admonished her. "We can't take it out too early! Else it won't be straight. You want it straight, don't you?"

Kieta nodded with anxiety, glad only when the woman pumped a lever on the chair's base, letting the chair down so the girl could get out of it. "Let's go to the sink in the back so I can wash it out."

Relief swept over the servant girl when she was in a chair in the back room and at the sink where the woman rinsed her hair several times, freeing it of all the residue of the permanent. When the woman towel-dried it, she ran her fingers through one side, first, to ensure it was still there, and second, to check the degree of straightness. She smiled to herself.

"You should return when your mistress returns so I can keep it fresh," Rachel told her client when she had styled her hair and turned the chair so she could see herself in the large mirror. She spun it around, handed her a hand mirror, and showed her how beautiful and straight the back was.

Needless to say, the girls saw each other in a different light when they were both in the front. Similar height, weight, and now hairstyles, they squealed with delight. Madame Soyinka thanked Rachel and gave her a large tip and said, "I will bring her for upkeep" as they left the shop.

Anyway, when she was back at the compound, she took her dress to her room and hung it up in a cabinet that held her work clothes then went straightway to the kitchen to help finish the family's dinner, to assist with serving the meal, and to complete all the remainder of the chores before it was quitting time. Wakesa looked up when she entered, saw that her nappy hair was straight, but she didn't say a word. When the girl was beside her scooping food from pots for placement on trays as well as the serving cart, she noticed her nails were trimmed, cuticles were cleaned, and someone had polished them, a clear paint had been applied. Nevertheless, she didn't say anything. *All I know is there better not be a strand of hair in the food!* Those were her thoughts.

Her failure to say anything did not go unnoticed. Wakesa wasn't picking fights with her about anything that had to do with the mess madame and her daughter were involving her in. Kieta understood that, so she threw herself into her work. The girl tried to make up for the six hours she had spent away from the compound.

Dinner served, dishes done, everything put away in places specified by her mentor, the girl hurried to their room. She got there a few minutes ahead of the woman limping behind her, her limp more pronounced this day than some. Forced to do some of the work Kieta was supposed to do that day, the older woman was extra tired and was pissed. While she could have pulled one of the other workers from their post and let her do the chores her charge ordinarily did, she did it all herself. Anger made a fool out of her. At the present time, she was overtired. She just wanted to lie down in her bed *and just die!* Her thoughts were on little else.

Anxious to show her new dress to someone, the younger of the two servants pulled it out as soon as they were in the space they had shared since she had been there. Seeing the beautiful dress, Wakesa had laughed at her that evening, her laughter like a cackling hen. She bent over in laughter. The woman was in stitches when the Toures girl pulled the pink semiformal dress she had used her own money to purchase at the clothier's shop from the upright piece of furnishing, which had also served as her vault before she learned about banking from madame and Marissa.

When she could compose herself enough to get a few words out, the older woman told her charge, "I don't know where you think you are going to wear that! You let Ms. Marissa put foolishness in your head!" She continued, "Let me tell you what's r-e-a-l, real." The woman spelled out the word aloud. "You ain't much more than chattel. Like me, you are going to be cooking, serving, and cleaning up behind them and all their company *all* the days of your life. You must think you some kind of Cinderella or something!" She railed about the girl in the story she had heard the children read. "Where are your shoes? What are you going to wear it with, those sandals on your ashy feet?"

The reproach brought shame. The aggrieved girl balled the dress up, bent over, and pushed it as far under the bed as she could get it and fell on the bed and cried until she could cry no more, mussing the hair she had had done when she accompanied the Soyinka ladies to the hairdresser.

A first for Kieta, she had luxuriated in the comforts found at the establishment, which also offered manicures, pedicures, facials, massages, as well as waxings. This was just another piece of her formal education. Taking special care of herself, she had wanted to use some of her meager salary she had saved to get her hair done, but her mistress had taken care of it. Consequently, the beautician straightened her medium-length tresses and gave her a permanent. Her hair like the other two women, she wanted to abandon her scarf when she returned home, let it hang loose all the time.

But Wakesa insisted the morning after she berated her for buying "that little fancy dress you ain't got no use for." Before they left the confines of their quarters, she told her, "Get your head rag. Not a hair to be found in any food I prepare. You may wear it loose when you go to school but not in the kitchen. You a servant, not the slave your forefathers were but not too far removed from it. You are going to be let down after a while. All that learning you getting in your head all for naught."

When they were in the library, preparing for the day's learning, the girl confided in Marissa about the browbeating she had received from the older woman. "I started to run away!"

Her friend immediately assuaged her fears. "Don't worry about what she says! I will tell my mother, and she will put her in her place."

In a minute, Kieta realized that she should have kept her concerns to herself. "No, please don't tell madame. I don't want to get her in any trouble. I just needed to vent."

"Okay!"

"Promise?"

"I promise this time, but she better not do that again!" The oldest of the Soyinka children spoke what was in her heart.

Madame Soyinka also involved the girls in selection of music for the occasion, music which would be softly piped into the area from somewhere that the girl did not even know existed.

All too soon, the old year was gone, and the day of the dinner arrived. Wakesa got them up earlier that day to make ready for the occasions. Hors d'oeuvres had to be made, salads and vegetable dishes prepared, and the meat brought in from outside. The head cook had had the men slaughter and roast the lamb outside the old-fashioned way, so all they had to do was debone it, shred it, and place the meat on trays. Late in the afternoon, Kieta went to the dining room to set the table, which had been elongated by placement of a couple of additional leaves from storage. More chairs were in place too.

She carefully counted to ensure the correct number of place settings and placed a card with the guests' names on it at the correct seat. An odd number existed because Marissa did not have a male to accompany her. She imagined herself seated beside her friend.

The servant girl wheeled a table tray with the china and silverware on it closer to the table and began her work in earnest, talking herself through proper placement of the flatware, china, and silverware. "Salad plate atop dinner plate," Kieta voiced as she made her way around the table. On the left side, from inside to out, she laid dinner fork then salad fork. Shortly to the right of the forks' tines, she placed a butter plate with a knife on it. The girl leaned backward, observing intently the setting she was working on, considering why anyone would need that many utensils to eat any one meal. Clean fingers were good enough, at least they had been when she was with her family. She shook her head.

Her reverie was broken by Wakesa who came in to ensure her competency in completing this part of the formal dinner. *"Finis! There is much more to do. Ain't no time for daydreaming!"* The woman thrust the cart closer to the table, cutting the distance between the two of them and the table. "Now to the right," she instructed her charge. "Put the knife where I showed you. It don't matter whether it's for everyday dinner or for a formal dinner. You do the same thing with the knife. Turn the cutting edge toward the plate then put a teaspoon and a soupspoon beside the knife."

While Kieta worked on the right side of each plate, her mentor put a cake fork, tines toward the spot where the glassware would be set with a dessertspoon, its bowl facing a bread plate. Finally, Wakesa ensured placement of spotless water goblets, red wine goblets, white wine glasses, and cup and saucer for after-dinner coffee. Satisfied by the appearance of the dining table, the older woman pulled the serving cart back to the kitchen. Her charge followed her.

Almost as soon as the dinner was prepared, and the ladies had discarded their aprons soiled during the preparation stage, replacing them with clean and crisp ones, the Soyinkas' guests arrived in several identical black Cadillac SUVs with tinted windows, ushered into the compound by a police escort. The occupants' drivers let them out at the front door. A butler boy at the door let them in the house, ushering them to the sitting room where the residents greeted them. Another servant directed the chauffeurs to the garage area for parking. From there, the drivers were taken to an area of the compound where a bit of gâteaux, some meat and cheese, and *limonharri* had been left for their consumption.

When greetings had been extended, the Soyinkas accompanied their guests to the dining room. Needless to say, the servant girl was shocked by their appearances, especially by attire the men wore. All bore formal wear, the likes of which she had not known until she accompanied her mistress and Marissa to a seamstress for the selection of the patterns, fabrics, and fittings of the formal gowns they wore that night. Madame was stunning in white, and the pink Marissa had chosen was equally as gorgeous. Every lady, including her friend, was dressed to the nines and made up to perfection, their skin looking creamy and cheeks blushed, their eyelids painted in favorite colors. The men wore tuxedoes. Monsieur abandoned the traditional long shirts and pantaloons worn around the house for this formal wear.

A lot of conversation took place among and between the guests, mostly about the weather, their travels, their home countries, and their families, nothing of consequence. Kieta appreciated her comprehension of English and French. The Soyinkas' guests spoke mostly in these two languages.

After dinner, the couples parted ways. The women went to a large living room, and the men retired to the library. Madame Soyinka invited her oldest daughter's presence. Marissa was at the age where she needed practice in social graces. This was an additional learning opportunity for her.

Kieta wished she could stay in the living room with the ladies. She could not. This event served as a reminder that she was what Wakesa told her, *une domestique*, saved from the vestiges of enslavement by *grace* and employers with kind, good hearts. The girls met briefly at a table where she placed some petits fours and coffee. "I wish I was here," she told her friend, Marissa. Her reply "I would take anything to be in your shoes" was shocking to say the least. Their brief exchange was broken by a call from madame for her daughter to join her in entertaining their company.

In the library, a full bar was stocked, and bowls of nuts, peanuts, cashews, and walnuts were already in place. Everything was there except ice. Wakesa sent her charge to the icemaker in the pantry area to put some in the silver buckets for transport and placement in both areas where the guests were entertained. "Don't tarry long," the older woman warned her of both areas. "And keep your mind on your own business. If you hear anything you ain't supposed to, make like you deaf and dumb. You ain't got no business getting into any of monsieur's or madame's affairs." She wagged her finger in the girl's face as she admonished her.

Despite her best efforts to stay out of grown folks' affairs, Kieta overheard some of the men in the library talking about somebody named Usuma and the terrorists—the infidels. They wondered aloud about him, his whereabouts, and the clandestine activities media all over the globe reported whether he had actually been killed by the American President Obama or if this was just one more ruse. Her ears turned toward talk of men who she heard her father, Wakesa, and other adults talk about.

Her attention was drawn to one of the guests, an American ambassador, as he directly accosted Soyinka about the man, indicating there was talk about him ever being in their area and housed in a place on the continent of Africa. "You got some fine place here," he said, looking around. "A man like that would have been comfortable hold up in a place like this—good lodging, good food, and good drink." He lifted his sniffer of cognac in demonstration.

Monsieur Soyinka grew angered at the thought of the man or anyone suggesting his compound had served as a safe house for the terrorist. The man took a draw from his Cuban cigar and faced the questioner, denouncing his assertions that he was somehow involved with the terror cell that had set up residence in the area as a fumier and said, "That's all that is, a crock of shit. They just don't think a man like me can have what I have earned."

"Do you know where any of his followers are then?" The speaker refused to relent.

Monsieur looked around and noticed their other guests engaged in conversations of their own, appearing to give deaf ear to his talk with the irritating man. He lessened the space between the two of them. The man did not move.

"Hell, no, I don't know, and I don't give a damn where any of those bastards are!" The man let out a barrage of expletives when he was close as he could get without invading the offending man's space.

Kieta stopped dead in her tracks. She had never seen or heard her employer do or say anything unseemly. Her master noticed her as soon as she was no longer in motion and let his voice arrest. He looked squarely at her and pointed her to the library's closed door with his piercing eyes.

Remembering her mentor's admonishment, she almost took wings. The servant girl hurried from the study, pausing outside the door but a moment to hear rumblings of all the men talking about the infidels who were taking more and more control of the area. Passing through the room, she had noticed that each group's conversation had been the same although not as poignant and passionate as the one her employer was engaged in. She went to the kitchen where she belonged.

The men continued their banter, terrorism remaining at the forefront. Admitting that he had known the man called Usuma when he was in the west, the man assured his antagonist, "I have not seen him since I left *les États-Unis* . . . I went to London, and I have no knowledge of where he went or what happened after that."

"Do you swear?" The man took a sip of his whiskey.

Sincerity in his voice, Soyinka told the inquiring ambassador, "I swear on my mother's head."

One more stab was made at him. "Have you made contributions to the terrorists' cause?"

"I have not done such a thing. I want no parts of that. I want to maintain my ability to trade services with yours and other countries. In addition to that, I full well intend to send my children to the States, to Harvard or Yale or MIT, to study commerce and trade or international law when they are of age. I will do nothing to inhibit their futures." He spoke emphatically of their future.

The American ambassador followed up with. "I have known you for a long time, and I have no reason not to believe you, but I have a job to do as well. The Secretary of Defense told me I should ask, and I did. He remembered you all had come to the States and were in school at the same time, and the two of you seemed to have your heads together at one of those parties he hosted at his ranch."

Comprehension showed on Soyinka's brow, and a cooler head prevailed. He nodded then continued his assertion. "No offense is taken, my friend. Besides that, can you tell me any other reason why I have been singled out? I want to do all I can to keep from being looked at with suspicion."

"Just look around, and you will see. It is this compound that you have built, the security you have. It is almost like you have something to hide. At least it appears that way to some in our intelligence community."

"Your intelligence community is a faulty one," Soyinka replied. "All I am is a man who is using his blessings to make his family secure during these trying times. My wife does not feel safe without protection for our home and our children. She has spoken of returning to London or Paris and taking the children with her. So for peace's sake, I just give her what she wants here."

His company argued, "I am not being critical. I'm just saying why you were singled out. You know we came in peace. We came by day, at your invitation, not like thieves in the night."

"I am actually glad you shared your country's concerns with me."

Their private chat coming to a close, the men meandered over to join the group that was coming together. "If you hear anything of the man, you will let us know?" the ambassador inquired.

Soyinka gave him an affirming nod. "I will."

When the party was over, and they had seen the last of the Cadillacs' rear lights, the servants were free to clear the waiting room, library, and living room of the remainder of the foodstuffs and beverages. Kieta wanted to inquire about the terrorist from Wakesa. She wanted to know more about this Usuma, who he was, and why people thought he might be a part of the Soyinka household. However, she couldn't ask. The warning, "Child, keep out of grown folks' business," played over and over in her head like a scratched or smudged compact disc.

Nevertheless, the servant girl noticed the compound grew fortified a bit more after the party. Movement beyond its walls was limited. But one could not just hold up there forever. Soon, it was time for Marissa to go to the university.

Chapter Six

A quick study, the family sent Kieta Toures to *l'universite* when she was old enough to go, at first to accompany Marissa and later intending for her to secure a degree leading to a promising career. Her matriculation there took place when the Soyinkas, like many in the country, were concerned about their children's safety when they left the house as were others who were not supporting the terrorists, especially their daughters. Factions of the population did not want girls to be educated but to be subservient, submitting to men. Around the same time, girls were going missing, not returning from school, perhaps being enslaved and sold to others. At least, that was the talk around the city and countryside.

So the elder Soyinka and his wife equipped a chauffeur who drove the girls to school and to the mall and thereabouts with a gun. The man, one about the same age as the women he transported, who was at first armed with a small pistol, took to carrying an assault weapon later. While he initially waited with the car or went to gas the vehicle up while they attended to their business, his responsibility changed. His duties enlarged by fear, he now accompanied his charges to the classroom door, posted himself there, and waited outside for them.

One Saturday, the head of the household summoned both girls to his office upstairs, a rare undertaking. He sent Wakesa to find both of them. Soon, the two young ladies met at the bottom of the stairway leading to the side of the house where his office was. The older woman stood a foot away, her hands on her hips, watching their every move. When they were at the center of the staircase, they sheepishly took hold of each other's hands and whispered to each other about why he sent for them as they mounted the stairs together, hand in hand, like twin sisters. Kieta started the conversation. "What do you think your papa wants?"

"Je n'ai une idee," Marissa admitted her ignorance. "I don't know. You see Papa almost every time I see him," she responded.

Kieta grew more concerned, her trepidation in the voiced, "I hope it ain't got nothing to do with school. I hope he ain't going to stop me from going." She drew up and came to a full stop, and the jerk from her hand almost toppled the two of them. Marissa grabbed the guardrail, aiding them in achieving sure footing again.

"What in the world?" she asked the Toures girl. "You almost made me fall."

"Sorry," Kieta told her as they reached the top of the stairs and made the right turn into the outer area of the man's office where they seated themselves on a small couch facing the closed inner office. "Are you going to knock on the door, or do you want me to do it?"

Marissa shook her head and told her friend, "No need to do that. He will come to the door and let us in when he is ready."

As soon as the truism escaped her lips, the man was at the door speaking to and inviting the girls to come into the inner office and to seat themselves. "Asseyez-vous!" He pointed at two chairs directly in front of his desk. He returned to his chair, and when he was seated, he poured himself a glass of water from a pitcher on a tray on his desk. It held two other glasses.

A water spot on one of the beverage glasses drew Kieta's attention, reminding her of her true position in the family and transporting her to another place and time. She thought she must ensure clean, spotless glassware for her employer like Wakesa frequently told her. She had not had a "pot to piss in or a window to throw the waste out of when she arrived in Mali." And if found slacking with her work, she would be tossed out of the compound with nothing but the rags she had on her back." The girl mentally swiped at the smudge on the glass.

A conversation about being safe in uncertain times took place within her earshot, but she missed some of it, her mind overtaken with a mere smudge the man could easily have put there with unclean fingers. "Too much is going on here in the continent." Soyinka told his daughter of a school in Nigeria where a bunch of Islamic militants set fire to a locked dormitory at a school then shot and slit the throats of students who tried to escape during a predawn attack recently. "The news reported they slaughtered them like sheep with machetes and gunned down those who attempted to run away."

Marissa shiered where she sat. "What in the world?" the girl asked her father as she wrapped her arms around her rapidly chilling core.

Seeing her discomfiture, her father turned in his chair and clicked a switch, causing an electric ceiling fan recently installed to cool the small, tight workplace. "It's all about the insurgents' views on women's and men's places in society. They want women to go home, get married, and abandon the Western education they view as an anathema to Islam. These folks are killing men too who are not embracing their views. And they are acting out. There's just too much going on. We are keeping abreast of it and just want you girls to be aware of it and to be safe."

Through with his diatribe, the man paused to ensure his oldest child's comprehension. "Do you understand, daughter?" The man behind the desk pointed first to his eldest then to the other girl. "Et vous? Comprehendez-vous?"

Marissa acknowledged comprehension with a nod and spoke for both of them. "*Oui*, Papa. We understand. We will be safe." The girls were not ignorant. They had heard on their vehicle's radio and seen on the television about the scourge that appeared to be headed their way but had given it little credence because it had yet to touch their hometown and their youthful lives. The family had not discussed it until the present moment.

Kieta Toures almost swooned where she stood, his diatribe almost too much for her.

Wanting assurance that both had heard him clearly and understood, the man looked to Kieta for a response. A brief pause ensued, her affirmation forthcoming only when her friend poked her side with a finger. Their eyes meeting, Marissa indicated she had known her friend's mind had wandered elsewhere, that she should show comprehension, and she would tell her later what the man had spoken.

The girl awoke from the day's dreams and acknowledged both Soyinkas with nods of affirmation. "Uh-huh."

Momentarily, Soyinka got up from his chair, and the girls followed suit. Only ten minutes had passed since they had taken a seat, ten minutes the businessman determined were well-spent. He had made the girls aware of present dangers and told them their driver would be armed and that they should go to their classes, return to the vehicle, and make haste as soon as their schooling was done. They could no longer stop at the mall for shopping or to get hairdos, manicures, and pedicures or any other of the fun things they had enjoyed as of late, these last instructions ushering them from his workspace.

Kieta headed for the door first, Marissa on her heels. Behind them, the man placed his hand on his daughter's shoulders, turning her to face him. He drew his eldest to him and told her, "Be safe, child. It would kill your mother and me if anything happened to you." Then he planted a kiss on his daughter's forehead and rubbed her head like he did when she was a little girl like Ife before releasing her to join the servant girl who had made her way to the staircase and was on the steps.

As soon as her friend was beside her, and they began their dismount, both peered over their shoulder to see if the man still watched after them. Soyinka was not. He had already stepped into his office and shut the door behind himself.

"What was that all about?" the speaker asked a listening Marissa as they continued their dismount.

Marissa paused before opening up. "What? My dad gets like that . . . all mushy and sentimental in a moment! Especially when it comes to his girls and our brother too sometimes," she responded to Kieta's inquiry.

Kieta waved her thoughts of Marissa's fatherly gestures away. "Not that!" she exclaimed. "What in the world was the meeting about? My mind went on vacation when he started talking, so I am unsure what he was talking about."

"So I noticed," Marissa acknowledged her friend's inattentiveness. "Daddy is just concerned about all the stuff that's been going on around here and wants to ensure that we don't fall victim to one of these infidels in Mali. He said we just need to go to school and to come straight home. No shopping! No stopping! He said he was going to tell the driver the same thing."

The listener let out a relaxing breath. Her worst fears had not been realized. She had done nothing wrong and had no fear of recriminations imprinted in her psyche by the overbearing Wakesa. "We can do that." She nodded in agreement.

"Yes, we can." Marissa showed an understanding of what her father said and her willingness to obey. "We are going to do whatever we can to continue at the university."

Soon, the duo was at the bottom of the stairs, heading their separate ways. Marissa remembered what her father said about increasing security and turned to her friend to say, "Oh, don't get scared when you see a gun laid on the seat beside the driver when we go out tomorrow. Daddy is arming all the guards."

Kieta tremored at the thought of weapons. No good could come with introduction of machetes and guns. Her shudder did not go unnoticed by her friend. "That's why I told you so you wouldn't get scared," the Soyinka girl reassured her.

~~~~~

Initially, Kieta seated herself just inside the doorway at the university class where she could hear what was being taught, especially in the English class Marissa was taking.

Soon, the girls were practicing the Western language when they rode back to the house in the jeep, one of the Soyinkas' several vehicles. They bonded even more now. So the two precocious young women conspired for Kieta to gain a higher education. It didn't make sense for her to just sit there, wasting time.

Marissa pitched the idea to her father one late summer evening when the family was having supper. "Papa, I was thinking today."

Hearing excitement in his daughter's voice, the man looked up from his plate of roasted meat and potatoes. "You were thinking!" A grin broke out on his face.

"Come on, Papa. Don't tease. J'ai quelque chose de grave à dire," the girl insisted, sincerity in her voice and demeanor.

The man turned to his wife, searching her face for a hint to see whether his wife and daughter were conspirators.

"Je n'ai une idée." The woman shook her head to indicate no knowledge of their daughter's "something serious to talk about."

"She doesn't know. C'est mon idée. I have not discussed it with Mama!" Kieta readily admitted.

Seeing sincerity on his daughter's brow, he pointed his fork at her, laying his napkin and the utensil aside to give her his full attention. The man cleared his throat, and feeling what he thought might be a grain of rice lodged there, he took a swig of his beverage before speaking. "Okay, *mon petite*, have your say."

Permission gained and his full attention attained, the girl spoke rapidly, her words tripping over one another. "I was thinking since Kieta goes to school with me every day, she should enroll in the class too. It doesn't make sense for her just to be there, sitting, twittering her thumbs, and doing nothing. She is smart, and she is learning. I know she is learning. She speaks the foreign language, English, better than I. Nous parlons anglais ensemble tous les jours."

At the sound of her speech, Kieta, who was entering the dining room, stopped dead in her tracks and determining to be inconspicuous to reveal her presence in an unexpected way. She needed to stop her friend from speaking. She did not want to get in trouble and lose her employment as well as her stay in the Soyinkas' compound.

Bam! The pottery serving dish of vegetables she was bringing to the table to replenish the ones already eaten fell freely from her hands. Everyone jumped. All were unnerved by the noise made by the dish. Their eyes turned toward the commotion, and everyone witnessed the bounce of the bowl and the spew of cut carrots, beans, and roots cascading over the floor. Lucky for her that it was not the fish stew and rice that needed refilling. The porter dropped to the floor, attempting to retrieve the foodstuffs, as her friend leaped from her chair to help her friend.

Nevertheless, the older servant reached her side first. And needless to say, she began her chastisement of the girl as soon as she was standing over her. Hers, a kind of rebuke that drew their employer's ire, was arrested by an equally sharply voiced. "Stop! Wakesa, arretez-vous! Accidents happen. There is no need to fuss at her, especially with that tone of voice. If she needs correction, just do it with civility!"

Marissa who had jumped up from her seat to help held her ground and was ready to assist the workers. Her father turned to his daughter, placing his hand on her arm to keep her from going to her obviously distressed friend. "Turn around. Elles prendront soin de cela. They don't need your assistance. Asseyez y continuez!" He elicited the set of orders about the two servants who were by now clearing the floor of the vegetables together.

"Continuez, ma petite." The man restarted the family's conversation.

"I was just saying that perhaps Kieta can enroll in the university too," Marissa told her parents.

Hearing her name, the younger of the two servants turned her face toward the table. The older woman reclaimed her attention when she tugged at her sleeve. Kieta let her gaze return to her mentor. The woman's eyes told the girl, "You have broken rule number 2!" Yet she continued to listen to her friend make the case for her to attend college with her, be a student, and get a degree too. She no longer cared what Wakesa told her, what the woman's rules were. Her only thoughts were of how she was going to come from under the tyrant.

Kieta's heart raced in anticipation of the response she hoped the master would give his daughter. She got up, wiped the vegetable stains from her fingers on her apron, reached down and picked the bowl, and then prepared to return to the kitchen to get more, if any was left. She had not seen the inside of the pot. The older woman had dipped the vegetables into the bowl, and she had picked it to bring it to the table. *Oh well!* she thought.

She followed Kesa into the kitchen and was glad to see there was another couple of cupfuls in the bottom of the pot. The girl scrapped the dish and hurried back to the dining room. Wakesa remained there, resolve intact not to offend her employer further. Besides, her knees were aching. They had kissed the floor when she fell down to help the "ungrateful brat." Resigned, the woman took the chair in the corner the girl used when not busy and let her arthritic body sit.

Back in the dining room, the Soyinka family continued. "Umm." The man put his hand on his chin then spoke. "That might not be such a bad idea, *ma petite*," he told his daughter who was bouncing in her seat by now. She squealed a delighted squeal, leaped from her seat at the dining table, and ran over to the spot where Kieta was working.

In a moment, the girls were leaping leaps of joy together, dancing a circle in the middle of the room.

Momentarily, Kieta remembered correct etiquette. She tore herself from Marissa's embrace and turned toward her benefactors. "Merci, monsieur"—she curtsied—"and you too, madame. I am most appreciative." She spoke with humility showing in her voice and her mannerisms. She cast her glance toward the floor.

"Come back to the table," the man told his daughter. "Finish your supper. Let them complete their work. Your mother and I will contact the university to see what will be required of Kieta."

Rewarded for her diligence, Kieta was loyal to the family and had not entertained the idea of leaving them when her education was completed. Consequently, there had been no thoughts of further education and a career choice.

The young woman had found solace in the fact that unlike many she had known before coming to Mali from her homeland closer to the Nile River, she had a roof over her head and rested unaffected when the winds came and stirred the Sahara, dusting her everywhere—in her eyes, nasal cavity, ears, and mouth—if she did not have a shawl to cover them. She also had use of a toilet with a bidet that could be admired by many and access to soaps, oils, lotions, and *parfum* when she bathed—daily, not periodically. And her diet consisted of more than the grain and vegetables her family enjoyed when she lived and migrated with them from place to place as her father sought work.

Kieta Toures was indeed very happy!

True to their word, the Soyinkas enrolled her into the university the next session, and she took a seat alongside Marissa in the core classes. Consequently, their studies together continued, and both girls made excellent grades. Neither declared a major because they didn't have to do so until their junior year.

And they played together, the shopping mall in Timbuktu their playground. They ceased to have their garb customized by the tailor in the city Madame Soyinka used. The girls bought matching outfits off the rack. They also distanced their mores from those of the woman by getting their hair done, manicures, pedicures, etc., at the one-stop shopping place. Sometimes they had a late lunch in the food court with other students as their circle enlarged.

Chapter Seven

One could say that Kieta was feeling especially blessed on this fall day before the school was supposed to open back up for the second term, her sophomore year, Marissa's third year. She was looking forward to the return to the university and to being immersed in the goings on at the school. It was vibrant there, lively. Music abounded everywhere on the campus, and stories were shared in the theater there, ones that bore her history and ancestry. And she would renew the acquaintances she made the first year. She and Marissa would also make some new friends too.

The woman's thoughts were arrested by a chime from the residence's telephone. *Ring, ring, ring, ring.* It kept making itself heard. She waited for a moment to see if her mistress would pick it up. She was home, in the house's upstairs area. The girl was certain of that. *Perhaps she was in the necessary,* she thought. *Ring, ring, ring.* When the woman did not respond, Kieta fled from her perch in front of the window to answer it.

"Bonjour, good morning!" she called out, her voice unpretentious, fresh, and full of cheer. She did not have time to add the customary salutation, "Soyinka Residence," before the person on the other end of the line was talking.

"Fatouma, Fatouma Sanago?" the caller replied, his accent thick with French. The man thought he was calling a relative. When he heard Kieta's voice, he apologized. His voice was polite but firm with the authoritative cadence of a man in his prime.

"Are you sure? This is the number I have for Fatouma Sanago."

"No, no Fatouma here," she said. "I am sure there is no such person here," she told the caller and hung up.

The man on the other end of the line looked at the instrument in his hand, removed the piece of paper with a handwritten number from his pocket, and dialed the number, repeating the digits (223-803-2039) aloud as he punched the telephone's keypad again.

This time Kieta did not wait for her mistress to answer. She picked it up on the first ring, instantly recognizing the voice on the other end of the line. She shook her head. "Do you always call the number again when someone suggests you are in error?" she responded to his greeting, her voice flirtatious.

Caught off guard, the man paused.

She giggled, and her laughter betrayed her youth and inexperience.

"No! No, I do not," he insisted, "only when I like the sound of the voice on the other end of the line."

She blushed and giggled, almost swooning at the sound of his enchanting tone of voice.

The caller smiled inwardly, shook his head, and then he asked her, "What is your name?"

"Kieta," she said tentatively.

"Kieta, do you always answer for Fatouma? Is she your mistress?" The man refocused, his mind now on why he initially dialed the number.

The girl confessed, "No, I generally do not answer this phone. My mistress, Madame Soyinka, did not pick it up, so I did."

He responded, "I am glad Madame Soyinka did not answer. Otherwise, I would not have made your acquaintance." His response surprised her as much as his next comment. "I will call you the same time tomorrow, mademoiselle." The nameless figure spoke anew. Then he hung up, leaving her to look at the handset she held in her right hand when she had removed it from her ear. She placed it on her heart before returning it to its cradle.

"Was that for me?" The voiced question from her mistress who was entering the room brought her back to reality.

"No, ma'am. The call was made in error. It was a wrong number." The declaration made, the servant girl turned back to her work, and her employer proceeded on her way. Kieta sighed a sigh of relief and took up her dusting where she left off, her movements jerky as her thoughts vacillated between him and the assigned tasks. Thoughts of the caller thwarted her productivity. But her reverie did not last long because soon, her supervisor was calling her name aloud to assign more chores, one after another, keeping her busy with duties that came with her servitude for the remainder of that fateful day.

The Toures girl did not have a moment more to reflect on the call until dinner was served, dishes done, preparations made for the next day's cooking, and some clothes laundered and put away, and she was on her small cot in the servant's quarters that night. In her bed, Kieta replayed the Wednesday morning telephone call until sleep overtook her, putting it out of her mind until the following day when she consciously posted herself near a telephone in the study when it neared 10:00 a.m.

Right on time, the mechanism gave off its almost alarming blare. The young woman picked it up almost before its chime made a full blast. "Hello!" She spoke almost breathlessly, peering to see if her mistress was nearby. She was unnerved by the prospect of getting caught doing something that she was not supposed to be doing. Consequently, her legs threatened to fail her, and her bladder seized. She thought she might pee on herself and make a puddle on the room's hardwood floor.

A smooth, charming, confident voice emitted. "Good morning, *ma cherie!*" She swooned and fanned herself to keep from falling over the armchair beside the end table. Her voice betrayed her. She couldn't speak.

"Hello, hello. Are you there?" he asked a couple of times. In the confines of the office of the petroleum company his family owned, the man removed the receiver from his ear, looked at it, returned it to its proper place, and inquired anew, "Are you there?"

In her weakened state, she expressed a short, breathless "Morning."

The caller asked, concern in his voice, "What's the matter? Did I startle you? Are you busy?"

"No, no," she responded to the trio of questions simultaneously, "I am not busy."

He teased her, "So I caught you doing nothing. You were waiting on my call?"

"No, no," Kieta managed to get out before he asked about her morning and what she hoped to accomplish that day. A brief conversation ensued, and after they had talked about her day for but a few minutes, he was gone again, leaving her with the promise of a call the following day.

"I love hearing your voice," he assured her. "It is so full of cheer. It makes my days much more meaningful to feel your care and to hear your warm voice. It's like a smooth cream and warms my heart." And then he was gone, leaving her as weak-kneed as he had the first day.

The obviously smitten young woman removed the receiver from her ear, placed the instrument over her heart, pressed it to the point of making a lasting imprint, and then covered her right hand with her left and pressed even harder. She closed her eyes, willing her brain to repeat his voice over and over, her longing to hear from him again increasing. After a second or two, she placed the handset back on its cradle and took up the dusting she had pretended to be doing so she would be in this room at the present moment.

A whole week passed before Kieta found the courage to ask his name. He simply told her, "Doe, my friends call me Doe."

"Why do they call you that?" she queried the man, her need to know more about him steadily increasing.

"Actually, I am Mahmoudou." He gave her his first name only, which was sufficient at the time. They were mere telephone acquaintances. The likelihood of their relationship being extended beyond that were nil. Kieta did not enjoy much freedom. When she was not at the house working or at school with Marissa, there was no time for other social activities or other people for that matter. Of course, this did not stop either of them from wanting to lay eyes on each other.

By the time two weeks had passed, he had gained full knowledge of who she was, where she lived, who her employers were—Soyinka was one of his customers—and about her attendance at the university. "Kieta, I need to see you! I think I am falling in love with you," he whispered these words and other sweet nothings in her ear when they managed to converse on the phone. There were days when the lady of the house or someone else beat her to the telephone, and when this happened, he gave the salutation "Sorry, wrong number!"

Soon, Doe ended their daily phone conversations with the phrase "Je t'aime," "I love you" in French, his preferred language, the one still spoken widely in the former French colony in which they resided. And instead of Kieta, he called her *cherie*, sweetheart in the language of romance, then spoke more of the language of love yet to be requited. "I need to touch you, to know your caresses and your kisses," he implored, his tone quite throaty, his need for her making itself clear.

She resisted his relentless pining. "There is no where we can meet," she argued, almost tearing up at the thought of never being able to see the man. Her desire to see him matched his own, to lay eyes on her.

However, Doe would not take her reluctance for a final answer. "I will come there, *cherie*!" he told her on more than one occasion. "I will come to Soyinkas' door and ask for you by name."

Hearing sincerity in his voice, she implored, "Doe, please, Doe. No, you can't do that. The guards will not let you in the compound. You cannot come here!"

He raised his voice, asserting his manhood. "Then you come out!" he hollered in the phone while he paced the warehouse's floor. "I will come outside and wait for you!"

"No, please, Doe. You know I can't come out unaccompanied," she pleaded for understanding.

"I am coming there, and I will see you! I know where the Soyinkas' place is!" The man spoke emphatically, leaving Kieta with no doubts that he would make his words come true. She didn't know how he would make his way to the Soyinkas' residence, but she was sure that he would come, so she pondered how and where they could meet discreetly.

An idea popped into her head as she lay on her bunk, waiting for the morning to come. *I don't know why I didn't think of that yesterday.* Her thought, one she unknowingly gave volume, made Wakesa raise her head and ask, "What?"

"What?"

The older inquired again about what her charge should have thought about yesterday.

"Nothing. I must have been talking in my sleep." She let the tale float to the other side of the room on a yawn.

Her roommate gave her yawn a reply. Soon, both workers were snoring. Mornings in Timbuktu had a way of coming awfully soon, and labor came with their advent.

~~~~~~

Needless to say, Doe was on it as soon as he had her on the phone. "I couldn't sleep last night. The only way I will get some rest is when I see you."

His pleas led her to say, "No! Please don't come here. I can meet you on the campus. We can meet at the student union in the cafeteria." Kieta gave a feasible solution off the cuff. While she had the idea the previous night, she had not considered sharing this option at the present moment. She needed to think it through and talk with Marissa about it. The two friends talked about everything. *Everything except these phone calls*, she thought.

Nevertheless, his persistence made her thoughts come forth. And once spoken, she could not take the words back. She knew she would see him there; if not there, somewhere. As soon as she said it, she knew she would have to tell Marissa about him before any meeting could take place. Her friend would handle the driver for her. She would do that for her. They were like sisters, two peas in a pod.

"No, not there!" Doe did not want to meet her there, and he told her so. He wanted to meet her in a place where he could not only feast on her apparition but where he could also hug her, kiss her, and make her his. He was sure that she was beautiful. Her voice was like an angel's. Surely, the vessel that bore it had to be equally as stunning. It made mush of him every time she emitted a sound, when she breathed and when she spoke.

She pleaded with him for the public meeting. Safety and enlisting the aid of her friend in their affair were on her mind. "Just think about it, please, Doe, and give me a little time. I need to get Marissa on my side."

Lust for her brought agreement, "Okay, I will wait, but I won't wait long, *cherie*. Use the number I gave you and call me later when

65

you have spoken to your friend about me," he told her. "I want to know what she says tout de suite!"

She promised she would talk with Marissa that very evening, wiping the nervous sweat raised by his insistence with her dustrag. "Dang!" The expletive flew from her lips. "Now I have to go wash my face!"

~~~~~

Privately, the man explored other options for meeting and spending time with the university student. Doe remembered his friend Kunto Boro had a place near the university, so he got on his motorcycle and sped out of the town to the village where he resided to find him and to see if he would allow him to rent space for a rendezvous with the girl who had gained his full attention.

The motorcyclist had to pass the compound where the desired woman lived and worked, so he had to contain himself fully to keep the vehicle on the poor desert road and not to veer off the main road, just go into the compound where he knew the woman was hold up and haul her out. He let up on the throttle, cutting his speed in half. He had a mind to just fight his way in there and get the woman.

Wisdom spoke to him, reminding him that he had not seen her. He would look like a fool running through the place yelling, "Kieta, Kieta Toures, *cherie*, where are you?" He might frighten her away with his folly or catch a bullet from one of the weapons the guards at the gate held. He sped up, and in a minute, a jeep coming from the place intersected him, but he gave the vehicle little attention. The driver yelled, "Imbecile!" and blew the vehicle's horn at him and threw a warning finger at him to no avail. Doe hurried on to his destination. He broke the speed limit, ignoring traffic signs while simultaneously watching for the police.

Kieta saw the man on the scooter kicking up dust and a few rocks as they passed. She and Marissa were headed into the city to the university. Her heart rate soared at the sight. Doe rode a bike like that. She wondered if that could have been him. He had told her that he passed the place she lived and worked every day. That was about all the man had divulged about himself in their telephone conversations. She was anticipating questions she would ask when they finally managed to meet in the cafeteria, but first things first.

She cleared her throat, drawing her friend's attention. "Marissa, there's something I want to talk with you about," she told the young woman she shared the backseat of the vehicle with.

Her friend turned in her seat toward her. Their knees almost touched. The jeep they shared was small. "What is it, *ma petite*?" Her friend used the term of endearment to make Kieta feel at ease. She had sensed the tension in the girl's voice. "You know you can talk to me about anything."

Kieta immediately responded, "I met someone, and we were talking about getting together and having lunch somewhere."

"Oh!" her friend exclaimed, her brow raising. She had not anticipated this. The pals talked about family and schoolwork, but the duo had never broached this topic—dating. And they generally accompanied each other wherever they went. If they were not together, her friend was working alongside the head servant or carrying out duties specified by the older woman. Consequently, Marissa was confused. "Where did you meet him? In the marketplace when you and Wakesa went shopping?" Her mind turned toward the classes they shared. "Is it somebody in one of our classes?"

The girl, seated directly behind the driver, stopped her friend with a touch on her knee. "No, no, not when we were shopping. Or at school."

Anxious to hear more, the other girl said, "Where then?"

Kieta took a breath then began her full reveal. "Actually, I met him on the telephone." The obviously smitten waif divulged her and Doe's story to her best friend. She exercised caution and spoke in undertones so the driver would not hear all that she revealed. Periodically, she let her gaze wander to the rearview mirror to see if the man had his eyes on the road and was not trying to attend to her affairs. He rested attentive to his task, driving safely.

Marissa clasped her hands with glee, expressing her delight about what the woman revealed. "That is exciting! Girl, I wish I could meet somebody! When are you all having lunch? I can go to the cafeteria with you . . . and just sit at another table! You don't even have to let on I am there!" she squealed. Her friend shushed her to lower her volume.

The driver cleared his throat; the terrain was dry and dusty. He coughed and took a rag covering his mouth, spitting phlegm into it. His unnerved passenger watched as he laid it on the seat beside him. He toggled the radio's knob, changing the channel to news of the insurgents' encroachment in nearby villages. She observed intensity on his brow in the rearview mirror as he turned the volume up so he could hear better, above the crackling noise the instrument was making. Reception was not always the best in Mali.

Kieta breathed a sigh of relief. It was clear the man was not attending to her affairs. Her attention returned to the disclosure of her and Doe's affair of sorts. She could trust Marissa to keep her secret and to cooperate so she and Doe could meet face-to-face and render a relationship that was yet to be made, complete, and whole.

The love-struck girl bubbled over, excitement in her voice, "We have been talking on the telephone every day for several weeks, and we are anxious to meet each other."

Marissa gave the typical young woman's response. "Girl, I can't believe you've been keeping this to yourself! I would have told you!"

~~~~~

By the time the girls were at the university, Doe had arrived in Bouri and found his friend working some leather to make bags to sell at the market. After a while, when exchanges about their wives and families were exhausted, Doe asked Kunto about his place near the university.

"Do you still maintain that cottage near the university we used to hang out at when we were taking classes?"

"The one on Baker Street?"

"*Oui!* That one."

"*Certainement!* I sure do. It is without an occupant at this time," the man volunteered. And before his friend could probe further, he told him, "Renters are not easy on property that does not belong to them. The last college students I rented it to left holes in the wall and broken furniture. I need to do a little work on it so I will have it ready for some students to rent during the next term."

Then after pausing for a cleansing breath, the man threw up his hands and said, "I probably just need to go ahead and sell it!"

Doe was ecstatic. He realized he had hit pay dirt and was glad he had followed his mind. "Uh, ugh! Don't do that, man! You ain't got to sell it. I am looking for a little place in town and will rent it from you and make the repairs," he told the owner, putting extra emphasis on the "and." "What will you take for it?"

The man turned his head sideways and cocked an eye at his buddy, the offer one almost too good to believe—rent and repair. *Who does that?* the Boro man queried himself silently. *And why, especially when you got property of your own? Hmmm.* Shrugging, the man posed a couple of questions. "Why? Do you need a place for one of your wives?" And he commented, "You know, you are my friend. Whatever you need, I will do. How about I just charge you a little bit of rent and use the money you pay for the repairs?"

Shaking his head in negation, Kunto's bestie confided, "No, *mon ami*. It is not for any one in my family but for a friend."

A girlfriend? He wanted to ask. Instead, he told him, "That's fine." The man, unlike others in the rental business, had no concerns about subletting his property or letting someone stay over, so he reiterated, "You just give me a little rent, and I will do the repairs at my leisure just as I have always done."

The two men bantered back and forth for a bit before Doe finalized the deal. "No, you let me have it, and I will pay you *fair* rent in francs *and* make the necessary repairs. That's the only way I can use it."

They talked a bit more about the place and its needs. Some walls had holes, a couple of windows had cracks, indoor plumbing was present, but work was needed to be done in the kitchen and bathroom. "It's got a couple of pieces of furniture still in it, an old couch and a chair."

"That's all right. I can dispose of it or get it repaired. You just tell me what you want to do with it," Doe contended.

"Once I give you the key, you do what you want with it," the property owner responded.

I just want it to be fit and nice when she comes were Doe's unspoken words. The opportunity was present, but Mahmoudou Ibrahaim did not tell Kunto about Kieta, his reluctance supported by their beliefs.

Both of these men were men of faith though not as devout as their forefathers. Periodically, each of them did not offer up the prayers like they should, ignoring the toll of the bell calling for prayer when their occupations required their attention. Their religion piecemealed, they had more than one wife and family, which was acceptable. Doe had more than his friend though. Kunto had only two, so he was still "eligible," but his old friend had four wives already, the maximum number their faith allowed, one reason he didn't mention the girl.

Anyway, Kunto knew a deal when he was offered one. He acquiesced, accepting his friend's offer. There was no need of a contract. He knew Doe was a man of his word and would honor their verbal agreement. "Let me get the key," he said before going into his work hut to retrieve it.

"Don't do nothing I wouldn't do!" Kunto teased his friend when he returned with the key.

Both men laughed. Doe winked a wink of acknowledgment at his boyhood friend and reached for the leather chain holding the key. His grinning buddy shook his head as he gave it to him.

Key in hand, Doe grabbed him, and the men shared a Western custom. They slapped each other on the back and gave brief hugs before Doe was on his way to the cottage on Baker Street to make it ready for his rendezvous with the girl with the angelic voice.

The following day, Kieta eagerly anticipated the call from Doe. The hours between five o'clock in the morning and the ten o'clock call passed slowly. The minutes seemed like hours, and the clock's coordinated collective bits boomed instead of clicked like they normally did. Her heartbeats aligned with them. A minute until a quarter to ten, she took matters into her own hands. She called the telephone number he had given her and was surprised to hear a woman's voice. "Bonjour."

The caller stammered, "Hello." The word out of her mouth because she had been poised to utter it but could not arrest the imploding sound, she hung up. Kieta was stunned to the corps and was glad she had used a one-word greeting, that she had not called Doe's name. *What the heck?* she thought as she returned the handset to its cradle.

Time elongated, the remaining fifteen minutes passed by at a snail's pace. Her breathing grew labored, and the young woman thought she would expire. Her death would come if the man did not hurry and telephone her. Her bladder and colon joined her heart and lungs, making spur-of-the-moment physiological changes. She rushed to the bathroom, used the potty—her bowels would have betrayed her in a minute if she had gingerly walked into the room—then flew out of the necessary to stand beside the phone and wait on the telephone call.

An unnerved Kieta held her hand over the handset, and feeling it vibrate before blaring, she grabbed it and answered it. "Allo! Soyinka Residence. May I assist you?"

"Hey, I found us a place!" the caller said, excitement in his voice quite clear.

"A place!" She raised her voice then threw her free hand over her mouth to muffle her own voice. She didn't know what she would do if Wakesa, the master, or his mistress walked in and caught her on the telephone talking to a stranger. She tipped over to the door and peered out the opening around the corner. The long telephone cord trailed behind her. Ascertaining that no one was near, she backed into the room and pulled the door shut before sliding down on the floor, pressing her back to it. Simultaneously, she pushed the receiver as close to her ear as it would go, listening harder, attempting to make her breathing quiet. It had grown louder, almost asthmatic, as she became more excited. Her full intent was on finding out if he had said what she thought he said.

"A place. You said you found us a place." She took a cleansing breath and let her body relax. The Toures girl didn't know how to feel about what she was hearing, whether she should be happy or what?

"Yes," Doe hastily told her about the rental he had made the previous day. "C'est au milieu de Baker Street. It is within walking distance of the school. You can come there afoot to meet me, or I can pick you up on my bike and take you there," he said of the cottage halfway down an alleyway two streets over from the university.

The listener grew hesitant, ceased breathing for a moment and could offer no response. Feeling her reluctance, the man quickly assured her she would be safe. "There is no need for you to be afraid, cherie. I will be watching every step that you take. No one will harm you. I promise you that!"

Despite the man's assuring words, fear took a grip on her. The hair on her body stood, but she decided to throw caution to the wind. She had to see him! Kieta wanted to see Doe as much as he wanted to lay eyes and hands on her.

"Come there tomorrow," he told her. "I will be waiting."

She hesitated, "I need to talk with Marissa about it."

"Talk to her while you do your homework!" the man commanded. By now, he had full knowledge of their schedule.

She hesitated again, but his insistent tone clarified his intent to wait no longer to see her. "Tomorrow, I will see you tomorrow, *cherie*. At the cottage or at the compound, I will see you tomorrow." Doe made a vow, not a threat.

"How will I know it's you?" she relented, knowing any excuse would fall on a deaf ear.

"You will know it is me. I will be inside the house and will let you hear my voice," he responded. "The question is 'How will I know you?'" The man pondered more to himself than to her.

"I will be dressed in blue," she told him. The woman described one of the dresses a seamstress in town had made for her when she started to college. "I will be wearing a royal-blue, two-piece outfit with a flame-like flourish of gold brocade on the bodice."

"Beautiful colors for a beautiful lady," he complimented her. "Did you make it?" He learned more of her each time they talked.

"Actually, my mistress had some outfits made for me when they put me in the university. She had Wakesa to accompany me to the market to pick out the fabrics though."

"Is blue your favorite color?" He asked of the *bazin* fabric, the hand-dyed, polished cotton, which was the mainstay of Malian fashion.

"Yes, it is," she admitted, thinking to herself how she would look when he set eyes on her the following day.

Chapter Eight

Kieta, like most Malian women, was a round-faced, big-boned girl with the wide thighs still fashionable in the desert. Her hue was deep brown, not chocolaty though, toasty brown. The twenty-year-old woman weighed about 120 pounds, and her body bore no stripes of childbirth or disease. She had never been sick, nor did she have a child. The woman was a virgin. Her pearly white teeth were straight and even, and she still had a full set. By all standards, Kieta Toures was as beautiful if not more attractive than her pink-skinned friend, Marissa. She turned many a head when she was at the university.

Later in the evening on the same day she and Doe had determined they would lay eyes on each other, she and Marissa went to the library at the compound to finish their homework. As soon as her friend was in the room, and the door was closed behind her, the two co-conspirators engaged in a conversation about the upcoming rendezvous. "We will see each other tomorrow," Kieta said of the day's phone call.

Marissa posed the question about the location, and the Toures girl told her all she knew about the cottage, ending this portion of their talk with "It's there or here!" She hunched her shoulders in resignation.

Her friend asked Kieta what any concerned friend would ask, "Are you sure you can go alone? I don't know whether I could go meet someone I have never seen in a place I have never been. Are you sure you want to do that?" The questions came faster than Kieta could formulate an answer.

She stood and flung her head back, shoulder raised to show bravery and assurance that all was well. "I am certain. Doe will be watching out for me." Kieta spoke confidently of the man she had never seen.

"Okay. What do I do if you do not return?" Marissa asked, fright on her countenance. She wished she had not gone along with the ruse the girl was pulling on her parents or that she had not even confided in her. She went over to where her friend was standing, looking out the library window into the courtyard.

When she was beside her friend, she tried to assure her that she was not being a spoiler, but her intentions were noble. She was a true friend. "I am not trying to mess up your fun. It's just that he might not be who you think he is . . . He might be a kidnapper. Or a rapist. Or one of those infidels I keep hearing Daddy talk about." While she said all the right things, she was not convincing. No apprehensions showed in her voice or on her face. It could not because while she was not certain that her friend was making the right decision, she knew in her heart of hearts that given a chance at love, she would jump on it herself.

Kieta waved off her friend's apprehensions. "Don't be silly. I will be back by the time history class starts. Let's get this paper completed so we can get some sleep." She yawned. Her brain needed fresh air. The servant was forced to think about more than she wanted to entertain at the present time. *What if Doe was not who he said he was? Supposed he was going to take me and sell me into slavery or to one of the new groups, human traffickers, who took girls from their families and made prostitutes of them. I had heard of such when a girl from my village had gone missing the year before Papa had left me at the Soyinkas' kitchen door. What if? Am I being foolish to compromise my safety by going off on my own? Was Wakesa right about times being so perilous?*

She led the way to the desk where the girls put their heads together studying until it was time to go their separate ways—Marissa upstairs to her bedroom to shower and read until it was time to go to sleep and Kieta to the servants' quarters to bathe and make ready for work and the following day's activities.

Needless to say, the servant was glad when their study hour was over, and each of them could return to the privacy of their own rooms. All she wanted to do was bury her head and her thoughts in the pillow and go to sleep.

The Toures girl got up from the desk first, something she rarely did. It was she who was driven to study and learn as much as she could, a privilege she did not take for granted.

"You've had enough!" Marissa remarked as she looked first at the watch on her wrist then to the grandfather clock against the wall. "I don't have to be upstairs for another hour."

"I'm just a bit exhausted." Kieta was honest with the girl.

Clearing the desk together, both grew pensive. When the chore was completed, Marissa bade her friend a good night. "Sleep tight! Don't let the boogeyman get you," she said as she left the library, leaving the lights for her friend to extinguish when she was at the top of the stairs.

Her friend's "Good night. Sleep tight! Don't let nightmares chase away sweet dreams" held special meaning when she returned to the servants' quarters that night. Wakesa, the woman she shared space with, was already asleep, and Kieta was glad about that. She needed to be alone with her thoughts. She got her sleepwear and headed to the washroom to take a warm bath, wash her hair, and make ready for her impending date. The girl administered special care to her body. She trimmed her hair with shears she found there, cut her fingernails and toenails, and cleaned the dusty wax from her ears. Kieta scented the bath water with jasmine.

Doe, at his own home, made ready for their date too. He feigned tiredness and did not give either his wives or children much attention. The man took a bath, freeing his own members of dust and grime as well as the scent of fuel. And he took extra care to trim his mustache and beard. He had business to attend to the following day, business apart from petroleum he sold for a living.

The night short and the morning as long as the drive to school proved to be, the two girls did not talk a lot. Both were engaged in their private thoughts about Kieta's new venture. She was overly excited, and Marissa was wishing it was she. The latter spoke first.

"Kieta Toures, you better tell me everything when you get back. Everything!" She emitted under her breath "Everything!"

"Everything?" She raised a brow at her smiling friend. Kieta shook her head as she smirked. Momentarily, the girls' visages cracked, and they smiled at each other then giggled like teens and twenty-somethings do.

"Oui! Tout le monde!" In French, her dearest friend told Kieta she wanted to hear everything. "Every little detail!"

When their morning class was over, the duo split up at the classroom door. Marissa told the driver who also served as their bodyguard, "Come with me to the cafeteria. Kieta will be along soon." The man followed her lead. He did not question his mistress. It was her safety he was charged to ensure. The other woman enjoyed the same status as he. They served the Soyinka family. If Marissa dispatched Kieta to another location, she had to go there too or risk her young mistress's ire and the subsequent reprisal that could follow the action or inaction, whichever was the case.

Kieta left the duo and slipped quietly out of the building, stood a moment, and then tried to get her bearing before setting off to meet Doe at the cottage. Her stomach rumbled. It was lunchtime. She could have brought some snacks from the kitchen but figured if she did, it would prove to be futile. Her nerves would probably cause her stomach to seize and make her throw up the nuts, raisins, and cookies she had thought about bringing or even some brittle. And her feet, flighty as they usually were, made tentative steps. They too felt unsure.

In a moment, a man brushed past her. "Follow me!" the familiar voice ordered. He never missed a step, and instinct propelled her into action. She marched after him with lowered head, keeping her eyes from others on the street, following the man as close as she dared, who before long slid in a darkened alley. The sun did not shine there. Kieta stumbled on the edge of a brick that raised itself from the street, pausing briefly to get her groove back. When she looked up, she had lost sight of him, but she kept walking. There was little else she could do at this point. The young woman hastened along, anxious to find her suitor again. Fear tried to climb her backbone, so she almost broke into a run but didn't. Moving at a frantic pace, she did not stop until a hand grasped her right arm, pulling her into a doorway.

Kieta gasped in the darkness but had no time for real fear. "It's me. It is me, Doe," the man voiced as he brushed her mouth with his before kissing her, taking her in his arms, and suckling her tongue, instantly taking all her apprehensions away. He maintained ahold on her with one hand as he flicked the light switch on with the free member. They caught sight of each other for the first time. The man smiled, and the woman he had spent hours in conversation with returned a smile. Her teeth glistened; every tooth was perfectly in place. The man had an urge to lick them. Instead, Doe ran his fingers around the rim of her pretty mouth before letting his hand rub her temple, her cheek, and her jaw. She leaned her head to one side, enjoying the warmth from his hand. The woman groaned inwardly, the sound making itself felt by the caressing fingers.

He couldn't take his eyes off her face. His gaze moved from the parted lips upward. The man brushed her hair back with one hand. That was all he could use, as the other would not leave the small of her back, the base of her spine. Both marveled at the fit of his hand there, and both felt it burn there. She leaned into it, willing it to caress her too. Doe kept peering at her wanting eyes. At close quarters, her eyes were mesmerizing, and he couldn't stop staring, especially at the ridiculously long lashes she had. Little did he know the girl wore mascara she and her friend learned to apply by practicing first on each other then independently until they perfected a makeup artist's craft. "Beautiful!" he spoke to her, his voice throaty and soft. She blinked, her eyes twitching, as she was amazed at how his voice matched his visage.

The expression in her eyes widening, then narrowing eyes jerked the man out of his reverie. "You are every bit as beautiful as I thought. Your looks match your voice," he told her, mentally snapping a picture of her to keep in his head and hide in his heart. He wished he had brought a camera with him. He did have one.

Now that they were in full view, neither could stop staring nor complimenting each other.

"And you are equally as handsome," she told him. Kieta noticed that he was a bit older than she. She did not know by how much, and at this point, she did not care. She was certain, however, that he was no college boy. Like her master, he was a mature man and must be self-sufficient. Her master! She shook away thoughts of monsieur. Feeling the change in her demeanor, he made the next move.

Now that they had their bearings, he switched the light off, took her hand, and led her in the semidarkness to a rickety couch where he seated himself first, bringing her to his lap. The woman followed his lead. It was as if they were preparing to dance. She let her body behave naturally and was soon seated on his lap where she curled herself up into the sling he made for her with his lean, tight, muscled body. He smacked her on the lips, and she reciprocated. They exchanged a few more kisses before he said, "You like that?"

"Uh-huh," she answered, given Kieta voluntarily launched more on his kisses, and they spent some time fondling each other. They knew each other's upper bodies by the time their hour and a half had passed. They had explored with their hands and tongues what words had suggested. All too soon, it was time for her to get back to the campus and the next class. Both knew without a doubt that their first encounter would not be their last.

They left the cottage and reversed the route they had taken to Baker Street. Their same posture taken, he in the lead and she following, they made their way back to the university.

"Call me later," he told her at the dropping-off point.

"At the same number you gave me earlier?" she asked.

"What was the number?" he asked of the phone number she had committed to memory. The woman responded with the digits he had previously told her.

"No!" he spoke brusquely before giving her yet another telephone number. Doe had given Kieta the number to his compound, which housed his four wives and their children. *I have got to be more careful*, he said to himself. There was no shame in what he was doing. Most men he knew had more than one wife. He just wanted to tell her everything himself in his time, in his own way. However, he knew instantly that he needed to tell her sooner rather than later. The man knew what lies and misinformation could do to relationships. If she found out anything about him from another person, she would not trust him. He also knew from experience that once trust was established, it could be lost with just one bit of indiscretion. He wanted her to trust him and to love him! So he purposed to tell her everything about himself soon.

When several meetings had passed, Doe decided they should have a more comfortable place to repose and pass their limited time. He had the holes in the cottage's walls patched and painted as he had promised Kunto, the friend who let him have it. The man also bought a bed and had it delivered to the cottage. He took sheets from his linen trunk at his house and brought them to the rented space. He stopped in at a nearby shop and bought a broom, swept the floors, and made the place feel like one's home.

Instead of meeting and leading Kieta to their lair, one day the following month, he took the day off from his regular employ to make the place even more livable. He made the bed, exercising care to smooth the sheets and square the corners. A second thought took him back to the same store to get some perfumed soap for bathing and refreshing oneself before leaving their love nest. Needless to say, when she got there that particular day, he kissed her, grasped her hand, and took her straightway to the bedroom. "Shut your eyes!" he ordered her as she followed his lead. The woman smiled as she awaited the surprise and giggled.

"You can laugh all you want to, but you better keep those eyes shut tight!" the man commanded.

Kieta submitted to his will. She followed him, stopping only when he told her, "*Arretez!* You can open them now!" The woman's eyes and mouth flew open simultaneously. She threw her hand over the gaping member. He pushed her closer, causing her knees to touch the side of the bed. The woman leaned over and touched the bedroom's furniture. The bed was large, its mattress and pillows as plush as those she covered and laundered at the Soyinkas' compound. The sight rendered her speechless. She couldn't imagine lying there!

"What's the matter? Did my angel lose her voice?" Doe teased the woman beside him.

"Is this for me?" she asked when she could make her voice noise itself.

"Only if you will share it with me, *ma cherie!*" he exclaimed with glee.

Kieta Toures turned to Mahmoudou Ibrahaim and flung her arms around his neck, and their lips locked in passion not yet consummated.

The "Yes, yes!" she said when they came up for air was the confirmation the aroused man needed. He picked her up and placed her ever so gently on the bed.

She swooned at the feel of the Egyptian cotton sheets on the back of her arms and her legs and the side of her face. Kieta knew the roughness of the cotton on the thin mattress in the servants' quarters and had enjoyed that when she had come to the Soyinkas four years ago. It felt better and slept better than the desert grounds her nomadic family had reclined on for years. And while she had been tempted to lie on Marissa's, she had never known the sumptuousness she felt now.

Doe removed her sandals, rubbed her feet, and kissed them and her legs. He pushed her hem up and caressed her thighs. His hands were almost too hot to bear. The man lifted his head, searched her eyes, and saw full approval. His experience showed. In the wink of an eye, the woman was fully disrobed, and he was feasting on her with his eyes . . . and his hands.

She was thrashing restlessly on the bed, his warm touches making her move involuntarily. Her body ached. She wanted him to take her. He waited for her to ask.

Her "Please, please" caused the man to disrobe and let his shirt and pantaloons drop and to join her anew on the comforts of the bed. Before long, they were engaged in full intercourse. Experience met inexperience. Inexperience joined the former. Their two bodies meshed. They found lovemaking's rhythm, and their voices were no longer words but sounds of pleasure, ending only when both lovers felt total release. Both grew still when their thirst for each other was quenched, and they were satisfied.

The man who inclined on top of his beloved Kieta spoke first. "Are you all right?" He swiped his hand across her brow and kissed her forehead.

"Uh-huh" was as much as she could emit. The woman's tongue was tied.

He got off her and pulled her with him to the small washroom to refresh themselves before she returned to school and he to his office. A successful gasoline merchant, he provided fuel for smaller businesses to sell in cans alongside the roads, so the Ibrahaim man was free to come and go as he pleased. She, however, did not have the freedoms he enjoyed. "Come on. Pick your feet up," he teased her as he twirled her onward to the basin. The man pushed her to the mirror where they saw their visages. He was a head taller than she. Her hair was a mess, but her face glowed. He kissed the back of her neck. She turned to the right, and he nibbled her ear before sucking on the skin of her neck. While he kissed her, she felt his manhood stir anew.

"Uh-uh."

"Uh-uh what?"

"No more, not now."

He ground his manhood against her rear, pulling her to him and told her, "Don't uh-uh me. You are my woman, and I am your man!"

Kieta told her lover, "You know I have to go back!"

"This time . . ." He went along with her. "Let's wash." The man slapped his forehead. He had not gotten bath cloths for them. "Wait right here," he told her. The resourceful man went to the bedroom and grabbed a pillowcase off the pillow, and they cleared the remnants of their lovemaking with it.

The two lovers dressed quickly and went back to their daily occupations.

Kieta was flushed and still sweating when she headed back to school to reconnect with her friend. Her hair was napping too. The desert heat was dry, so this was different. You never saw moisture on the desert people unless some sort of sickness was making itself known. "Darn," she spoke to herself. *I wish I had worn a scarf! I will wear one or at least put one in my bag next time. Next time! Yes, there will be a next time.* The Toures woman's thoughts propelled her forward briskly.

When she was back at the university, she slid uneasily past the driver who had posted himself more closely to the door than on previous days. Their eyes caught briefly as the student entered the classroom and took her seat beside her friend. Her books and notebook were ready. Her companion saw to that. "Are you all right?" Marissa questioned her almost before her bottom hit the seat.

"I am okay," Kieta whispered, a bit unnerved, her eyes falling on the school supplies.

"Hey!" Her friend beckoned to her to lean over, so she did. "You let him do it to you, didn't you?" Marissa said. "You had sex with him?"

Kieta's hand flew over her mouth, and she grew even more flushed. She had anticipated her friend's query but thought she would wait until they were in the car or at the compound in the library.

Marissa laughed and let her head fall on her desk so the professor could not see her face and peered sideways at Kieta. Her friend gave her a look that would kill, and she felt it. The professor called the class to order, and both girls threw themselves into the day's lesson.

Admittedly, the hour seemed long, as both girls were anxious to get out and head for home.

When class was over, and they were back in the jeep and headed back to the Soyinkas' compound, the two girls bantered back and forth. Needless to say, Marissa wanted to know what her friend's deflowering had been like, but Kieta refused to "kiss and tell." "Can we talk about something else?" She tried to get her friend off her back.

Marissa threw her hands in the air. "What else is there to talk about? If it had been me, I would have told you everything!"

"Sure!"

The friend gave up and decided to wait another opportunity to get Kieta to tell everything. Both girls slid to the corners of the vehicle and let their attention turned to the music flowing from the radio. The driver, noting it had their listening ears, turned the volume up. Soon, the trio was humming along with the songs, or he whistled, his whistling and the engine's whirring replacing the chatter and laughter, which usually took place when he took them to school or the market or the mall . . . wherever he was assigned to take them.

As soon as they returned to the house and were in their respective rooms undressing and redressing, Kieta enjoyed a few private moments while changing from the street clothes worn to school to her work uniform. She relived the time she spent with Doe. All she wanted to do now was take to her cot where she could bask privately in the day's lovemaking. The sex had exceeded her expectations. It was almost overwhelming. The girl went to the bathroom, looked in the mirror to ensure there were no telltale signs of her and her lover's tryst, and rubbed her stomach, hoping he had not planted a seedling there. *That would be a big mistake*, she thought.

Her daydreaming was interrupted by the call from Wakesa. "Hey! You in there? Come on, girl. It's time to get supper ready!"

Kieta threw herself into the assigned tasks and kept as far away from the woman as she could. She did not want the woman to smell the afternoon's romp on her. She had bathed, but Doe rested in her nostrils, on her skin, and inside her. At the thought of the latter, she squeezed muscles she did not know she had until their lovemaking. "Dang!" she muttered more to the air than to herself. Minutes passed like hours the day of Kieta Toures's deflowering, hours seemed like days. Night in Mali, Timbuktu, just wouldn't come that particular day.

When she and the older woman completed their chores, she decided to go to bed early. "You must be sick!" Wakesa told her when she made her aware of her decision. The older woman shook her head before adding, "You make sure Ms. Marissa know you ain't going to be studying with her tonight so she won't be coming to the room, knocking on the door, and keeping me from my rest. Morning come round here before you can get to sleep."

"Okay," the young servant responded. She went to the library to render an excuse for skipping the customary study time with Marissa, feigning a stomachache of all maladies.

"I hope he didn't impregnate you!" Marissa wouldn't let it rest, so Kieta fled from her to the side of the house where the Soyinkas rarely, if ever, wandered.

Needless to say, Kieta passed another sleepless night before their ten o'clock call the following morning. "I am missing you already," Doe told her.

"Me too," she admitted before they confirmed their next of many couplings. When she was off the phone, she went to the bathroom and put soap and a couple of washcloths in her book bag, assuring proper hygiene when they met, and, from a drawer, a multicolored scarf.

On the way out, she reconsidered her holdings and returned to the cabinet for toothbrushes and toothpaste. Admittedly, she had not used the brushes until she came to work for the Soyinkas, but this was one of the many guilty pleasures she acquired. She brushed at least three times daily. The woman let her tongue pass over her teeth, feeling their smoothness.

Chapter Nine

The longer the two Malians enjoyed the affair, the more enjoyable the time they spent together became. And he gave her a full reveal, one that was of little importance. By then, Kieta was so in love with him. She didn't care if he had ten wives.

The petroleum merchant shared his every thought with the young woman. She became his friend and confidante. She got him! Unlike his wives, Kieta's communication was advanced, so the man who had been schooled at the university too appreciated her learning and scholarly pursuits. She also had a sense of what was going on around them and the world. The young woman had an affinity for history and geography as he as a businessman did, so they had a lot of things to talk about.

She read newspapers in the university library and turned her ear to the radio in the vehicle as they traversed the desert and came into the city for school and shopping. And whenever a television or radio was on, her eye, ear, or both receptors would turn to the commentators' voices. Consequently, her lover grew to value her opinions, and everything political, economic, and social was inserted into their daily lives. Smitten to the core, Doe wished he could marry her, but the law allowed for four wives, not five.

Around the time of their uniting, things were changing faster than anyone could imagine. They, like many inhabitants of Timbuktu, discussed the chaos in their country and on their continent almost every time they talked—on the telephone or when face-to-face. Of great concern were talks of governments everywhere in their environs being overthrown daily. Right in their backyard, the rebels and later the terrorists and radical jihadists had come and were imposing a harsh interpretation of Islamic law, creating unimaginable events. They were turning the once-moderate Muslim country into a place where women were whipped for going out in public without veils.

As tensions heightened, the duo listened even more closely, the private Malian station, Africable, his source more than hers. It, the media that reported the changes taking place around them, would later share their fate with the world. Neither knew or anticipated this fact.

They kept commiserating over the current state of affairs in their homeland, the acknowledging that Timbuktu had historically enjoyed a place in the world, a crossroad of sorts between Africa and other continents, and had been a center of intellectual and artistic life for centuries but noted that years of warring among the competing factions had rendered it unstable and on the brink of uncertainty.

"I wish we lived somewhere else," she told Doe on more than one occasion. "I don't like living around here anymore. I just wish we could just go somewhere where we could be free to do as we please!"

Hearing anxiety in her voice or seeing it on her brow, he would frequently change the subject. However, the chaos in the land rested the elephant in the room. It would pop up later in the conversation or the next time they talked.

Sometimes the torn woman added to her rant, "I am tired of slipping around and not being able to tell everybody about us too!" And when she had the monthly blues, her conversations were accompanied by tears, ones he could barely stand.

One particular day, he leaned up on his arm and looked over at the woman who rested in a reclined position in their love nest. "All right! I get it!" he said when they were eye to eye. "Where would you like to live? If you could go and live anywhere in the world, where would it be?"

She paused, humming as she did a bit of pondering a bit about destinations she had previously let herself fantasize about. "France, England . . . maybe even America." She regurgitated faraway places she had put on her bucket list as she grew more learned. "Europe, North America, I will visit countries in both continents one day," she vowed before asking if he had been anywhere besides Mali.

"Of course, I have been to other places on the continent. My work in the petroleum industry has gotten me as far as England," he responded before adding. "I wouldn't mind going to the United States one day, to New York City, but only if you would go with me."

"What do you know about New York City?" she inquired.

He told her, "Not much, but I've just heard talk of it from other merchants."

She raised from the comfortable spot where she lay, anxiety abated by forgetting their present situation, looking toward a brighter future. "Hmmmm, New York City. New York City, New York." She let the city's full moniker roll thoughtfully out her mouth. "I will look it up in the library sometimes to see what we could do there," she told him on this one of the few times they allowed themselves to converse and to dream of a life somewhere else together. Their passion took a backseat. Years later, they would consider their time well spent.

Chapter Ten

After almost a year and a half of meeting at their secret location, Doe came to the cottage alone, earlier than usual, and waited for her. The man sat around a while but soon found himself pacing the floor while he waited. His mind was busy! Things were going awry all around them. Everybody everywhere seemed to be going berserk! The terrorists were there, in the city, all around Mali.

New groups were forming, and people were taking sides. Family members were experiencing different allegiances—brothers were being pit against brothers. Friends were alienated from each other, a civil war on the horizon. Sufficiently divided, their strength reduced, alien groups showed their heads. One such organization, named DOOR by its leader, had set up in their environs, and men were being drawn to it.

A few men like him (Mahmoudou Ibrahaim) were trying to just stay out of the fray. *All I want to do is just take care of my business! Ain't got time for no shit! Damn! Damn!* Yet here he was being drawn into it. He stopped his pacing for a moment, looked at the piece of paper in his hands again, and seeing its content, renewed the fuming, fussing, and cursing he was already doing.

The new group had made some new laws and rules that were disconcerting to say the least, ones impacting women in the city, how women needed to dress and behave, rules that would set the city back a hundred years, ones that would adversely affect women like his beloved Kieta. She dressed fashionably, new vogue, modern like her mistress and other women in the Soyinkas' compound. A servant, she did her job but was not subservient. She was a free woman. Wakesa could attest to that.

He didn't know how she was going to take it. The man himself wasn't handling it well. Doe threw the paper on the floor, kicked it, and fell on the sofa. His head was throbbing, his blood pressure the culprit. The man rubbed his temple and leaned back on the furniture to get himself together before the woman arrived.

Too restless to actually relax, he looked at his watch, finding the minute hand in the same position that it was when he checked it earlier. He removed the gold timepiece from his wrist and shook it. An audible tick accompanied by the hour hand's movement showed the instrument was indeed keeping time. He returned his watch to his left wrist, nervously running a finger from his right hand under the watch's band while pondering. *She should be here soon. I just hate like hell to tell her this.*

The Ibrahaim man groaned aloud, the mournful sound alien to him.

What had happened to bring about such discomfiture was while eschewing any contact with women, DOOR members in and around Timbuktu handed leaflets with the new rules out to every man they saw—at their employ, in the marketplace, before and after prayer time, wherever they gathered, and whenever opportunity presented itself. Men, regardless of what they thought, were charged with sharing these regulations with all the women in their households and about and ensuring that they were not only enacted but also obeyed. Like all societal rules, these also had consequences, consequences placed alongside infractions.

However, Mahmoudou had not been in a public place where the rules were distributed. He had actually gotten the rules from his friend Kunto, who tracked him down to share them with him and to warn him to be careful. Handing the leaflet to his friend, the man told him, "I brought you these because I don't want any trouble with the insurgents. If they find you and your girl in my house, I could lose my house . . . or even my life!"

The encounter caught Doe off guard. Eyebrow raised and voice slightly elevated, he asked the landlord, "Who sent this to me? Somebody trying to send a bone by you?" His query raised his friend's ire. He was not a dog and was not carrying messages for anyone. It was what it was.

"Nobody, man!" He gave the man the side-eye and a stern answer. "Like I said, I just don't want no mess! You running around here acting like you don't know what's going on. I just don't want you to get caught with your drawers down around your ankles."

Document in hand, Doe surrendered. He was not ready to be evicted from the Baker Street location or to lose a friend. The man backed off, his desire to be with the girl overwhelming. He would do nothing to keep them from being together. "Excusez moi!" he acknowledged his insolence. "I beg your pardon. I know you don't mean me any harm. You are just looking out for a brother. I will talk to her. I promise I will. We will be careful."

The shift in attitude apparent, Kunto slapped his friend on the back, accepting his apology. "Je suis d'accord!" The two men hugged each other, loosed each other, and then grappled playfully, wrestling like a couple of high school athletes as they had done since childhood and broke out into laughter; things were right again.

Sufficiently assured, the Boro man got in his truck and left Mahmoudou to his own thoughts and devices.

~~~~~

Once accosted by his bestie, Doe literally kicked himself in the rear because he had not frequented the meetings in the city or kept abreast of the changes that were happening in his backyard. Instead, he had listened to the news and chewed the fat with Kieta about the happenings.

His participation had actually been sought by relatives and acquaintances. He was well respected in Mali, but he had resisted active participation and the leadership role the group had tried to thrust on him. Occasionally, he opined when asked. That was the extent to which he was willing to participate in what he labeled "government."

He stirred on the sofa, his thoughts now, *Perhaps I should have gone to a few meetings. I could have dissuaded them from setting these absurd rules.* This was the same thing he had said to Kunto a couple of times since the manifesto was made public.

"That way, I could have looked out for her!" *Her.* It had taken him a while, but he had eventually confided in Kunto about his love for the beautiful, alluring, and intelligent university student. He never questioned Kunto's loyalty. He knew the man would not tell even if his life depended on it. Besides, it wasn't anybody's business but his, hers, and theirs.

Even so, when full disclosure was given, his friend made him comfortable. Loyalty made Doe say what he said about the noisome pestilence the rules were. "Don't sweat it! I will be careful to take care of this important business," he assured his oldest, dearest, and most trusted friend. He meant what he said.

The two men had grown up together and were thicker than thieves. They were more like twin brothers. They had played together, learned together, hunted game together, and had even fished together and became relatives when they were a bit older. One of Mahmoudou's wives, wife number 1, had been introduced to him by her cousin Kunto. The others had been arranged as custom allowed.

Needless to say, the very day Kunto gave the rules to him, the Ibrahaim man read and reread the communications' content, sharing it with his wives before taking it to his and Kieta's love nest. It took little thought for him to read the rules to his relatives. He just did it, pointing out, "You know the rules, so act accordingly! If you get caught, you can't say you weren't sufficiently warned." Every member of his household gave nods of comprehension and talked among themselves about how to be safe when he returned to his daily occupation.

In bed that very night, he tossed and turned, his mind replete with thoughts about how he would share the insurgents' rules with the Toures woman and what this would mean for them. The more he thought about his current state of affair, the more pissed he grew. Angered at the idea that they would have to proceed with caution not previously required, the man got up and dressed.

Exercising care not to disturb his family, he did not turn on a lamp. He sat up on the side of the bed to reach for clothes he had thrown on a chair the night before. His companion rolled over, touching him in the back with searching fingers. The man reached backward, pushing the woman's hand away as he spoke quietly in the dark. "Go back to sleep. It's not time to get up. I just need a glass of water."

He sat still for a moment, his feet flat on the floor. The moment was enough time for wife number 1 to yawn, expire a relaxed breath, and snore ever so gently. That was all the time he needed. "All right, you gone back to sleep. I can get up now," he told himself. Searching for and finding his outer garments, he slept in a T-shirt and drawers, the man put on his pants and went to the kitchen for a drink of water. Doe's throat was really dry and scratchy; he had not lied about that.

The man switched a light on, the single bulb enough to light the small space, and reached in his pants' pocket to see if the paper he had folded and put in it was still there. It was. He withdrew it, looked at it, and threw it on the kitchen table and got a drink. He drank from the glass as if it was his last drink and did not come up for air until he had emptied it. *Ahhhh!*

His thirst quenched, he put the pitcher back in its place and the glass on the table. In the privacy of their small kitchen, he revisited the rules, this time applying them to his lover. Anguish accompanied sleeplessness. The tired man, angered by circumstances beyond his control, did the only thing he could do at the present time. Mahmoudou balled the piece of paper up and threw it against the wall, cursing it as it met its mark and slid down the wall. *No, nothing, nothing, not even these damn rules will keep me away from my cherie!*

He sat on a chair at the table for quite a while, his head in his hands. Then he got up, went over and collected the wad of paper, and smoothed the wrinkles out as best as he could, refolding it as he headed to stretch out on the bed to wait for morning when he could and would get on his bike and head to their hideout. *Hideout*—the word took on new meaning.

~~~~~

Now he thought he heard something or someone, so he got up from the sofa and commenced looking around the small cottage. The creak somewhere outside or, he thought, *Maybe it is inside*, raised the hairs on the back of his neck. His nerves were shot, and he willed her to hurry from the campus and to exercise caution. He thought he would die if anything happened to her! Women had been stolen off the streets in the last few weeks for sex; innocents were being made sex slaves. At least, that's what was reported on the news. *Who knew what in the hell was happening?* Mahmoudou shook in his sandals at the thought of something like this happening to his beloved.

He was more than glad when the woman got to Baker Street. When Kieta entered the cottage, the living room was well lit. Doe had turned the lights on when he entered and left them on. And he had searched the house, more than once, before she came to determine that it was indeed empty, that no one was there to accost them. He took her in his arms almost before the door was shut and kissed her, his passion checked by the need to protect her. The man waltzed with her where they stood. It was she who broke the embrace. "What's wrong?" she asked, her sixth sense kicking in. "Something is wrong. You can't fool me!" Fear showed on her face.

The man shook away her apprehensions. "No, no, it's not like that!" he told her as he took her hand and led her to the couch. He had previously shored it up by placing some stones under its wobbly legs and sagging belly. "Sit here. I need to share something with you," he told her.

He patted the spot where he wanted her to sit. She sat first, and he followed suit, leaving enough space where he could turn and face her.

Noting exasperation on his brow, she looked him in the eye when they were seated and asked, "What is it, Doe?" Fear that he was going to tell her that they would no longer be able to see each other raised the hair on her body. Her trembling voice elicited, "What's wrong, baby?"

He paused, searching her soul through her eyes. The man pulled her to him, erasing the gap between their corps. He resisted anything that could come between them, even space. He loved her more than life itself, and he would die for her. Mahmoudou Ibrahaim rubbed her arms, erasing the goose bumps from which the raised hair peeked. He was clearly thinking how he would broach the contents of the communication DOOR required him to share.

Kieta's lover took the wrinkled paper Kunto had given him and handed it to her. He was uncertain about whether he could read it to

92

her without his voice cracking or without tearing up. But he was going to give it a try. He cleared his throat and pursed his lips but could produce no sound. The man thrust the document at her, recounting then that the college student could read. She was proficient in more than one language.

She took it and perused it fairly quickly. The Arabic words and their French translations immediately jumped off the crumpled paper, leaving her stunned. When a few seconds had passed, she looked up from the sheet at the man and spoke up, concern showing in her voice. "What does this mean, Doe? Should we stop meeting here?"

The man threw up his hands, arresting any further thoughts about not seeing her. Mahmoudou had to see her. He had to have her. Doe needed this woman as much as he needed air in his lungs. She was his soul mate. Kieta satisfied him carnally, emotionally, and intellectually. That was more than he could say of the other relationships he was in. He spoke loudly, more forcefully than she had ever heard him. "No! Nothing will separate us! Nothing! Give me some time to think about what we should do."

Her attention returned to the rules, which she read aloud this time, not for his hearing but for her own. She remembered that the militants had long been trying to institute their strict moral code known as *Sharish* in this region, which had people who generally embraced a moderate version of the Islamic religion, but up until this point, they had not been successful.

"This has been a long time coming," she told him. "My papa used to speak of such. You know how old-fashioned he was. Women, even my mother, were little more than chattel in his sight!" Her mind vacillated and turned to the day he had dropped her off at the Soyinkas' kitchen door. He had never even mentioned he was bringing her there . . . to leave her and never return. He would be proud of these men for what he called putting women back in their places.

"I am not for this!" he argued. "And I am not about to follow this 'shit.'" He let one of those expletives loose. Mahmoudou Ibrahaim showed resolve but decided they should proceed with caution. Blood was already being shed in their homeland, and while it had not reached them, he could smell it coming. He was sickened by the thought of what was approaching.

The most even keeled of the two at the present moment, his lover suggested they look at the rules one at a time and discuss them.

"No," he resisted spending the little time they had together talking about rules. "Come on," he said as he got up from the seat. "Let's go have a little fun!" He pointed to the bedroom with his head.

She rejected the notion. "Uh-uh. Not today. This is much too important for us to lay aside." The woman picked the paper and patted the seat for his return. Her lover slunk back to the couch and let himself fall back onto the uncomfortable cushions.

"I got to get us a better chair if we are going to be sitting going over rules," the man said, sarcasm showing in his voice and with a pout that replaced the usual smile on his face.

With an "Okay" given to his remarks, she started reading aloud that which he had already read for what seemed like a hundred times. "Numéro un. Women should *not* speak openly with men in public." Kieta paused right away, looking to Doe for his take on the rule. Since their first tryst at the cottage, they had occasionally met on the street and just chatted for a few minutes. And there were the men on the university campus, her and Marissa's driver, Nouhoum, and her master, Monsieur Soyinka, shopkeepers. She found this rule ludicrous, snorting her disapproval as she proceeded. "This is so old-fashioned!" she commented more to herself than to the man.

The Toures woman got up from her perch on the couch and marched from one side of the room to the next as she read more from the pamphlet in her lover's hearing. "Women should wear veils in public, *black long ones . . .*" The university student resisted this idea. She enjoyed dressing and being fashionable. Her resistance to the plain, colorless veil prescribed to cover the whole body was made known. And while she occasionally covered her head, she loved the permed coiffure her mistress and Marissa wore loosely so much that she let her own loose some days. "Doe," she asked, "did you see this?" She thumped the page with a finger.

"No, I don't see nothing! You got the paper!" He raised his voice. He was so disgusted. Tired and sleepy too.

Kieta droned on, "I don't like black." Her preference for the vibrant colors were the same ones most of the sub-Saharan African women like the yellow she wore now. This was true indeed, as much of the money she received from her employers was spent on shopping and getting hair done while on excursions in the city with Marissa.

On occasion, the girls also got manicures and pedicures and had spoken of going into the back of the shop to get waxings done; Marissa's mother did that. While her daughter's companion had not seen it for herself, she had told Kieta that her mother not only got her eyebrows, chin, and top of her lip waxed, but she also got the bikini wax and had the hair removed from her legs anywhere.

The paper fell from her fingers, an act that brought her out of reverie and back to the present. She bent and picked it.

"What do you think about that one?"

"Which one?" he replied. He had not been listening. The man had barely heard her as she droned on, alternating between the reading, fuming, and fussing about each rule as she read it while she paced the cottage's bare floors. His thoughts were elsewhere. He had recently seen an older man and his wife punished in the town square for some act unknown to him, so he did not want to face such punishment himself, nor did he want Kieta to be punished . . . His gaze turned to her, and his heart ached, and his manhood stirred with longing. Here they were, she was reading rules, and he was experiencing all the physiological changes love brought.

The man's wandering mind brought back to the present by her sweet voice, he shook away any thoughts of never seeing her, having her, and making her his. Doe hit the palm of his left hand with a fisted right one. "Uh-uh!" Refusal escaped his lips. His desire for Kieta Toures so much greater than any threat, he had already determined they would proceed with their affair but would do so with caution.

At the sound of his voice and the smack he gave himself, she paused and stood in front of him, waiting for a comment. He looked up, and their eyes held each other's gaze for a moment. Doe did not make any more comments. When none was forthcoming, she took up where she left off.

She read more, and the more she read, the greater her consternation. Kieta did not know what she would do if she could not see Doe. He was more important to her than anyone in her life. She loved and desired him as much as he did her. He was wind beneath her wings. The document signed by an organization that called itself Defenders of Our Religion (the DOOR) fell from her limp fingers. She started to cry, and her lover got up from the couch to comfort her. He wrapped her in his strong arms, her face fell on his shoulders, and they rocked and swayed a mournful dance.

His spirits sank even more than they had before she had come that day. He felt dumb to having been blinded by his own vanity, to have imagined that he could keep her secreted away and free from the things that were happening all around them in Timbuktu and surrounding towns and villages.

Time flew; it took wings that day, and when it was time for Kieta to leave, Doe told her they had to be careful. "We will continue to see each other, *cherie*! But we must be careful," he insisted throatily. "These men are serious!"

In months past, they had walked out of the mud cottage together and parted ways at the corner. This particular day, he peeped from a crack in the door to see what he could see before letting her go first and following her from a safe distance to the corner of the street.

They walked back down the street with their figures a yard apart and did not speak again until they reached the corner where he slowed, his stride shorter than it had been a few minutes ago, and she, like a vehicle that was behind him on an open highway, sped up, increasing her stride and bypassing him as she rushed to get back to the place where she would meet Marissa and the driver. "Be careful, *ma cherie*," the man spoke softly to her as she slid by him.

"You be safe too," the Toures girl told the love of her life as she glimpsed him from her roving, searching right eye.

The two lovers breathed a collective sigh of relief when no one on the street approached or tried to stop either of them.

With her head down, she mournfully made her way back to the university for the remainder of the day's classes. Today's pronouncement made lead of her usually supple feet and flexible legs. She plodded on, her sandals making themselves heard each time her feet struck cobblestone, until she was at the university's entrance.

Back on campus, she did not tell Marissa about the rules. She barely said a word. Her quietude did not go unnoticed. Her friend questioned her about her mood because worry that was not there when they separated for lunch had etched itself on her brows, and her friend was jumpy. "Are you all right, Kieta? Did something happen with you and Doe?" the Soyinka girl probed further when they were seated in the back of the car and headed back to the compound. Her voice was a bit too loud for her friend.

Kieta put her finger to her lips to silence her friend who was speaking her lover's name aloud. One didn't know who to trust anymore, who was friend, and who was foe. Her friend sensed her apprehension.

"We can trust him." Marissa spoke of their driver as they zipped past a group of bearded men in khaki uniforms on the bed of a beat-up, battered, greenish pickup truck. Kieta turned her head, peering in the cloud of dust and rocks stirred by the wheels on both vehicles, to see if they would turn around and pursue them. Her heart was pounding in her chest; fear had a grip on her. Her eyes widened by their apparition, she looked at Marissa who appeared quite normal.

She shook her head in negation. This day, Kieta rested, reluctant to talk in front of the man she had recently let her guard down with. He participated in the ruses she and the Soyinka girl participated in, such as her leaving them alone at lunch while she met a friend, their occasional skipping of class to shop, or their failing to reveal holidays to her parents and going into the city for a day's folly. After the conversation she had just had with Doe, Kieta did not know who was who anymore, so she said little until they were at the compound.

By the time they were at the Soyinkas' gate, a convoy of trucks was approaching. No one in their jeep made an observation. However, Kieta knew in her heart that they, the bad men, the infidels as Mahmoudou called them, were making their presence fully known in their area. She wondered silently if they would wage war like they had in other places.

Her mind turned toward the Toureses. She was longing for her father or one of her relatives: a brother, a sister, an aunt, or an uncle. Kieta had lost track of all her family members, which was not peculiar. Times were changing, and her family was affected the same way as everyone else was affected. Nearly a quarter of a million Malians had been forced from their homelands, and some were in refugee camps in neighboring Niger.

Many people were trying to get out of the country before they were run out of town. She had recently heard the fate of a group that had taken to the river by boat because it was easier for them to travel by river even though their journeys took several days and nights, and it was easier than traversing the region's poor desert roads.

An Associated Press article she read in a local newspaper at the university library also indicated that one boat headed from the central port of Mopti to the northern desert town of her native Timbuktu packed full of people traveling ahead of the Muslim holiday of Eid al-Adha had capsized, killing hundreds, ones who could not be properly identified because the ship's owner did not keep full lists of passengers. Many were from the village of Bouri where her father's people and sister and brothers inhabited sometimes. *Some of my family members could have been on that*, she thought, *but I would never know.*

That boat disaster came, as Mali had been gripped by more than a year of crisis, starting with a rebellion early in 2012 and a subsequent coup, followed by seizure of the country's north by Tuareg separatists and Islamic extremists. The French army intervened early that year, pushing the militants out of the cities, but violent attacks still took place.

And here she was, facing an uncertain future with Doe because of the rules and consequences they had shared and were considering disobeying. She longed for her family: her deceased mother, her father, and the many sisters and brothers she had been separated from by circumstances. However dysfunctional her family had been, they were still family. They shared a bloodline and memories, good ones as well as bad ones.

Ironically, the Soyinka man met with his family in the library the same night Doe shared the militants' rules with her. He also invited Wakesa and Kieta to attend the family's meeting. The servant girl noted the pamphlet in his hand as soon as she entered the room. It was the same one her lover had shown her hours ago, but she did not say anything. "Asseyez-vous!" the man commanded his charges to take seats. He continued speaking while they made themselves comfortable. "I have news about some new rules being instituted by the DOOR," he told them. "I am going to read them, then we will make some decisions about how our family will respond. I have had some time to think about what I think we should do, but I want to hear from all of you."

"Moi, aussi?" Wakesa asked, fully aware of her position and rank in the pecking order. She was in charge of the house and servants when the master or mistress allowed her that duty. And she watched over their children in their absence. Nevertheless, she felt her opinion was not valued as much as that of Marissa, who was becoming an adult. However, she felt honored that her opinion was being given added value. The older woman straightened in her seat, her chest up and outward.

Kieta shook her head and glanced over at Marissa, who rolled her eyes. The girls were sick of the older servant woman and her posturing. The teenagers, who were almost twenty and twenty-one, frequently complained to each other about her "trying to act like she was better than anyone else" and her being "so opinionated all the time." One of the younger two scooted over to where she sat and pushed her over so he could sit beside her. It had not been so long ago that Marissa was doing the same thing. The trusted servant served as surrogate whenever her mother traveled with their father, or they went on a date night. Naturally, she would be included.

Their employer and Marissa, Ife, and Taurence's father told the servant, "Yes, you too, Wakesa. I want to hear from all of you."

The older woman looked at Kieta, and the younger servant returned her gaze, noticing a new confidence in her mentor's demeanor. Wakesa had not been the same since the Soyinkas had allowed her charge to first study with their children while the other servants labored then to let her attend the university alongside Marissa.

Monsieur Soyinka propped himself on the large desk in the library and waited for all the ladies to take their seats. He took his reading glasses from his desk and put them on. He commenced reading aloud from the list all the demands the terrorists, the Taliban, imposed on the women in their environs. Shock showed on all their faces, but none spoke until he had finished reading, laid the pamphlet on the desk's top, and taken off his glasses, laying them beside the paper.

"Well!" Madame Soyinka exclaimed, her voice elevating as she vented. "These mongrels will not make me practice hijab! I'll have no parts of it. And I will speak to whoever I want to wherever!" She ran her fingers through her long tresses, raking her bangs to the side.

"My girls either." She pointed at the college students. "We will not give up freedoms we enjoy to please anyone!"

Her husband cast a warning glance at her but did not respond because his daughter's whine drew his attention from his wife's tirade.

"Papa, do we have to do all that?" Marissa queried her father as Wakesa emitted a strangled "Lord, have mercy on us." The older woman held her hand over her heart. She had practiced the Islamic faith when she was a mere child, but once in servitude, she let go of her family's customs and embraced the mores and values of her employer.

Kieta dropped her head, her thoughts on pulling the scarf that was a part of her uniform off her head, throwing it to the floor, and stomping the piece of clothing on the floor with her sandaled feet in protest.

"This is as vocal as I thought my opinionated lot would be," the man said. "I would have been shocked if you were leaving it up to me to do all the talking and the thinking." He shook his head and took a seat in a nearby armchair just as his spouse relinquished her own seat and got ready to leave the room. She was disgusted, fed up with it all.

"I won't stay! Taurence. And neither will my children!" his wife yelled at the businessman as she left the library. "I have never liked it here and only came because this is where your work is. The children and I are leaving! You should procure our tickets on a commercial flight so we can leave as soon as possible."

"My dear, I thought that would be your immediate response," Monsieur Soyinka called after his wife as she headed to their living quarters.

The man's attention turned toward his speaking daughter. "No, we can't leave now. We have classes at the university! I love it there, and Kieta loves it too. Isn't that right?" his oldest daughter looked to her friend for support for the notion that they should stay. "We can get some black cloth and get those veils made. If that's what it takes, we can change our style and wear our other clothes when we are in the compound."

Her father acknowledged Marissa's response. "That's exactly what I expected you to say, my precious daughter." And he told his child, "I will speak to your mother about this later." He looked to the other ladies. Nothing was forthcoming, so he dismissed them, frustration showing through. "Let's just get back to our work!" His thoughts, *When madame is rational, we will let everyone know what we will do.*

Feeling hopeful, Marissa ran to her father and hugged him. "Thank you, Daddy. If you will let me stay here, I will do as you ask. Everything!"

The man looked into his daughter's eyes, seeing excitement at the possibility of not having her life disrupted. "Okay, baby," he said as he returned his daughter's hug and left to go to his wife to make things right with her.

~~~~~

Kieta kept her thoughts to herself. Her mind was on Doe and the possibility that her employer might prohibit the girls from going to school anymore after this day. This, a notion she could not bear to think about, she attempted to suppress.

Nevertheless, when she and Marissa were left to their own devices in the library, she had to speak on the unspeakable. Her friend immediately accosted her going to the cottage and fraternizing with the man. "You know you are going to have to stop seeing him!"

Her ire raised, the Toures girl spoke up, her tone quite threatening. "Says who? Certainly not you!" She wagged a finger at the other girl.

Shaking her head from side to side, the accoster attempted to assuage the beast that was arousing in her friend. "Uh-uh. There is no need to bow up at me!" She pointed a finger to her chest, arguing, "Not me! I am on your side. You know that! All I was thinking about was your well-being. I was just thinking about your safety, that's all."

The truth be told, Marissa was engaged in her own secret relations with a couple of fellows on the campus, ones that Nouhoum, their driver, and Kieta were aware of. So for her to suggest to her constant companion that she should stop seeing her man was reprehensible. That's why the girl had behaved like she did at her friend's suggestion that she stop seeing Doe.

Consequently, she paid particular attention to, not only her voiced concern but also her mannerisms, what she did not say of major importance to Kieta about the man she loved more than life itself.

Sensing care and concern in the Soyinka girl's voice, she quickly apologized. "I am sorry. I know, I know you are concerned about me. It's just that I can't imagine life without Doe." She teared up as she spoke.

Marissa reached for her friend to comfort her. Both of the girls started to cry.

In a few minutes, they were reduced to whimpers. Marissa grew nostalgic because she was certain her mother would make her father get them out of the country and into England fairly soon. Kieta mourned prematurely for friendship found, requited, and soon to be lost. They reached for the box of tissues on the desk, each taking one sheet from the box, and instead of using it on herself, she passed it to her friend.

Chapter Eleven

As more incidents in and around Timbuktu happened, the family stayed close to the compound, venturing out only when necessary. Monsieur Soyinka, like most of the affluent members of their community, beefed up security in and around his property. The driver who took the girls to the university was more heavily armed than he had been when they first started to matriculate there. Nouhoum kept his weapon on the seat beside him when he drove them and threw it over his shoulder as he walked with them on the campus, to their classes, to the library, as well as to the dining hall where they took two of their meals, breakfast and lunch.

Like all the other security providers, the man got trained on how to ensure safety of the family members he served; the Soyinkas' head of security spoke with the girls' driver on the following Sunday evening. His instructions clear, Nouhoum spoke to Marissa in private, when they were at the university the next day, about Kieta leaving the campus to meet her "friend." "Maybe now is the time for her to stay with you to eat her lunch in the cafeteria," he told her.

She cut him short, reminding the man that he was to take orders from her. "Perhaps you should keep to your driving and keep your nose out of other people's business."

The man let his head drop. He wished he had not let the teenagers drag him into this ruse. He contemplated speaking to the head of security or to the master himself, but he did neither. The driver was certain he would lose his much-needed job.

Both girls kept doing what they were doing: Marissa hung out with her university friends between classes, after classes, at the mall, and on other occasions when just the two were in the city.

The Toures girl and her beau kept meeting at Kunto's cottage yet exercised caution as they passed along the streets into the alley and along the route. But they were in each other's arms as soon as the door closed behind them. Neither felt as free as they did before the man brought the rules.

Now they made love with one ear for each other and the other on the door, and their couplings were always at a frantic pace. Admittedly, neither was enjoying. Both initially kept their thoughts to themselves. It was she who broke silence brought on by their current situation; her conscience needed clearing.

"Doe, I am so afraid that I am going to lose you, and I just can't imagine life without you," she confessed.

He attempted to assuage her fears as much as his own. Taking her into his arms and holding on to her as if he were holding on for dear life, he said, on the first occasion in which she aired her consternations as well as on subsequent days, "No, my *cherie!* You won't lose me. Nothing will separate us!" That first day and on the others, he tried to kiss away her apprehensions. He would hold her face in his hands and kiss her lips, right cheek, chin, and left cheek, creating a pattern that ended with his lips on her forehead and a breathed, affirming, assuring "Nothing!"

However, the man's efforts to reassure her were met with bits of information she gleaned from conversations in the Soyinka household. As soon as they were on Baker Street, behind those closed doors, she would talk with him about things she could never share with Marissa.

The man listened but never commented. Doe knew more about DOOR's underground activities than he could or would share with the woman. Early on, before he met her, he had attended a few meetings with friends and some family members. His interest waned, so he quit going. However, others kept him abreast of what was going on. Every time he stopped by to pay rent, the Boro man filled his head with information, preaching the group's half-truths and suggesting that they should perhaps fully participate in the group's activities.

"That way, we can keep our families safe," he would tell the Ibrahaim man, his argument always thrown at his friend's back when he was on his bike or in his work truck and departing. Kunto could not maintain his lifelong friend's attention long enough for a serious heart-to-heart conversation like the ones they had had before Doe met Kieta. This disturbed the man so much. Consequently, he went to the petroleum company to have a one-on-one with him.

"*Fumier!* I won't have any part of that crap." Doe initially waved him off. However, he attended a few more meetings. He thought it would be better if he had inside information, a necessary precaution, as Timbuktu was becoming more and more restless. Soon, his name was being tossed around for leadership training in the organization.

In the meantime, more covert operations were taking place daily in their part of the country—kidnappings, beatings, murders. So about three months after the family gathering to talk about new rules enacted by the DOOR, the Soyinkas had a meeting of minds and decided to send Madame and the children to England.

This time as soon as the family and a few of the servants who were "like family" met in the library, the father's pronouncement was immediately met by resistance from Marissa. "No, Papa, no, please don't make me go. At least until the end of the current semester. Don't make me drop out of school now!" The girl fell to her knees, begging her parents to leave her behind.

Having anticipated and fully discussed their daughter's protests, the Soyinkas had already decided that Marissa would remain with her father in Mali to continue her studies and join the family in Europe at the end of the year. So he decided to wave away her concerns and Kieta's too. If he didn't do that right away, he would not get his business complete. Pointing toward his child, he ordered, "Get up from there!"

The simpering girl obeyed and took tissue being pushed toward her by Wakesa. "Wipe your face, child." She propelled the girl to a seat beside the window. Kieta made her way to her friend's side and rubbed her back to comfort her.

Her father continued, "You can just cut the tears out! What I have to say does not affect you older girls." He pointed toward the servant girl and the oldest of their brood.

Hearing that, his daughter blew her nose and gave the tissue back to the woman who took it from her and dropped it in the trash before finding herself a seat.

Order restored, the head of the household pointed toward the two friends. "You girls will continue with your studies, for the moment. However, if conditions deteriorate, you will be withdrawn for your safety and sent to your mother. I have already made plans if they are needed," he told the girls who looked from one to another. Surprise and delight showed on their countenances.

He pointed to both of them, this time for comprehension. "Do you understand? If conditions deteriorate, we'll have to change this. I hope you two hear me!" Marissa left from her seat and ran to her father who was still leaning on his desk rather than sitting where he usually sat, jumping around his neck, her glee at her parents' decision being manifested.

A thankful Kieta showed both the master and mistress her appreciation. "Thank you, monsieur! Thank you, madame!" she said as she gave a brief curtsy.

Most of the time, Madame Soyinka left the family business be taken care of by her husband, but this time she spoke out, charging Wakesa to assume her maternal duties. She turned to the oldest woman in the room. "Kesa, I am leaving her in your charge. Take care of my daughter. Make sure she eats her proper meals, completes her studies, and dresses appropriately. She is not grown yet."

The woman cast her eyes and warning finger toward her offspring who was turning away from them. She was anxious to get to her friend so they could celebrate this moment.

Hearing her mother gave the servant instructions about her care, a pivoting Marissa rolled her eyes, shrugged, and twisted her lips. She didn't want any part of this. Wakesa was quite the taskmaster. She had noticed how she kept Kieta in check and wanted no part of the servant's telling her what to do. She actually thought it would be better for her to leave now with her mother, Taurence, and Ife. The girl did not stand a chance with the stern Wakesa.

Noting her daughter's posturing from her seat, her mother also told the woman, "Marissa thinks she is grown, but she still needs discipline, so make her father aware when she is less than ladylike. He will quickly withdraw her from the university and have her transported to me!"

Sensing her parents' sincerity, Marissa let go of her young adult posturing and became more demure in her apparition, respect for their choice swiftly intact and evidenced.

"Mother," she said, causing Madame Soyinka to turn her gaze from Wakesa to her. "Mother, dearest, I will honor all your requests. I will make you proud! You will see!"

The girl flew from her father's side and threw her arms around her mother. They stroked each other's back as they embraced. "I will miss you so much, Mommy!" All the wonderful times they had flashed through the girl's mind—shopping together, preening, and celebrating special times. Her mother was the best at birthday party planning and giving. She always used themes and involved her impressionable daughter in preparations. Her thoughts were that she might be better off with her mother than in Mali.

"I will miss you, child," her mother told her, "but it would be better for you to finish your schooling at the university. That way, you won't lose credits, which usually takes place when you transfer." She looked her daughter in the eye. "We, your father and I, need for you to step up and be the mature young lady that we raised. Do you understand?"

"I will, Mother. I will." Marissa kissed her mother's cheeks.

"And I need for you to take care of your father too." She held both of her daughter's hands in hers. "Can you do that?"

Marissa assured her mother that she could and would see to her father's well-being, while she took care of the little ones.

The woman turned her attention back to Wakesa. With her hand raised in a swearing position, the older of the house servants spoke to the Soyinka woman earnestly. "I will. I will do everything to take care of the family in your absence, ma'am," Wakesa promised. The childless woman continued, "I will take care of Ms. Marissa like she is my own! Ain't nothing unseemly going to take place with Mademoiselle Soyinka while she in my charge. You can trust me to see to her like she is my very own."

107

And to herself, she vowed she would separate Marissa from Kieta because she was convinced the latter of the two influenced the girl she now had charge of in a negative way.

The compound's owner looked at his watch. Time was flying, so he encouraged everyone to get moving. "Okay, now that we have all that taken care of, you should finish your packing," Soyinka told his wife. "The plane is leaving this evening, and the driver will be here soon."

"So soon?" Marissa piped up. She had yet to realize the urgency under which her parents' decision had been made.

"Yes, it is imperative that we get everyone out now. Go help your mother and brother and sister make ready," her father replied, his voiced insistence, raising the hair on Kieta's back.

Everyone in the library went up the stairs to make ready for their leaving. Marissa and her father accompanied their loved ones into Bamako to catch a private plane waiting at the airport to take them to safety. Their good-byes quick, they hurried home, their eyes peeled to seek out insurgents they had heard about but not seen.

During a telephone conversation the following day, Kieta told the Ibrahaim man that the Soyinka woman left Mali in the night and took the younger children, Taurence and Ife, with her. He breathed a sigh of relief when he learned that Marissa was left behind and that the young women would continue at the university and spoke to her about what was on his mind.

The man cleared his throat. "You know I was thinking we probably should cut down on our meeting days," he spoke to her, his demeanor more like that of the businessman he was than her lover.

Her heartbeat raised as she anticipated first a reduction in the time that she could see the love of her life to never seeing him again. "No!" she exclaimed, a sob escaping her mouth. "No, please. I can't bear that!"

Doe shushed her. "Ecoutez bien! Listen! I am not talking about us not seeing each other at all. It's just that we must exercise caution. These men are serious, Kieta." He spoke her name, something done infrequently. "I would die if anything happened to you. I could not stand to breathe the air in Mali if I could not see you or hear your voice."

Feeling the passion in his tenor voice, she became consoled. After a bit more conversation, she admitted that she understood where he was coming from. She agreed to cut down on their rendezvous on Baker Street, to meet the man every other week, twice a month, "until times are better!"

"I will call when I can, but if I don't call, don't fret!" he told her near the end of the telephone call.

She replied, "I will try not to worry."

Her lover offered more encouragement. "I will be fine, and I will not fret either. Soyinka is a wise man. He will ensure your safety. Just remember, *ma petite*, this is just until times are better."

She repeated, "Until times are better," and let the phone fall on its cradle. The instrument had grown as heavy in her hand as her heart had grown when she felt she would lose the love of her life.

~~~~~

Almost a year passed before the daring duo, Kieta and Doe, met their fate. They had exercised caution but became of interest when some DOOR members who patrolled the street noticed their movements. The insurgents reported the activity of the university student and the gasoline merchant to their superiors, first to ascertain if he was one of them, as DOOR members were made up of all classes of people in the area, then to determine when they should detain the two lovers. With the group being so fragmented, no one was sure who was who, especially in the upper echelons of the organization, and they could ill afford to accost a superior; they could lose their own heads. Consequently, these others watched and waited.

They watched the lovers meet, spend time alone together in the cottage, and part ways in the same place on the streets of Mali. Who was this girl who had Mahmoudou Ibrahaim on a leash? The insurgents learned where she lived, who her employer was, what daily schedule she followed, who the pink-skinned girl was that she hung out with, and whether the driver was loyal.

Doe's infrequent attendance at DOOR meetings gained additional scrutiny. Leadership questioned his loyalty. Was he one of them, or was he there to protect the girl? Was the need for his petroleum so great that they could turn their eyes and ears the other way? How would having a possible traitor in their camp impact the organization? What about Kunto Boro, who kept his name in their mouths, was he loyal to the cause, or did he just have his buddy's back? There were more questions than answers.

Soon, some foot soldiers were ordered to catch them in the act, to capture her, but to let the fuel merchant go free. The insurgents decided they had need of his services and thought they could persuade him to take a greater part in their organization once they got the girl out of the picture.

Accordingly, when the two lovers got caught in the cottage, the man was verbally chastised, and an attempt was made to let him go. "Allez-vous! Leave here! Go, you imbecile! Go home! Take care of your business and your family! See after your four wives and their children" was the order rendered by the insurgent leader who was with the group of six involved in their discovery and subsequent capture. His beloved, Kieta, was grabbed by two of the men.

Seeing his loved one being physically restrained by the men, the Ibrahaim man refused; he went ballistic. The man leaped at his adversaries, and they met him with four times the force he exerted alone. Fists flew, and curses did too. "Lose her! Take your hands off her, you slimy bastards!" he yelled as three of the men were holding him back. "Arretez-vous! *Stop!* Take your hands off her less I will kill you!" Threat after threat was spewed at the perpetrators. Mahmoudou Ibrahaim tried to fight the men off with his bare hands but was unsuccessful.

In spite of his best efforts, her lover witnessed Kieta being led away in tears, reaching and begging the insurgents to let them go. "We won't do it again. We won't! We promise we won't meet again. Please! S'il vous plait! *Please!*" were the last words he heard.

A screeching "No!" emitted, Mahmoudou kept wrestling with his captors, pulling away from them before plunging headfirst toward them like an angered bull. They leaped out of his way, trying to arrest him with words. "Come on, man. Get ahold of yourself!"

He was not hearing them. The insurgents took the grappling, wrestling man down, and held him on the floor until they felt resignation in his corps. One would have thought the man had seizures. While the men could have left him maim or dead, they followed orders. Their leader had told them to let him go. "There is

FORBIDDEN LOVE IN TIMBUKTU (WOMAN FROM ANOTHER LAND)

need of his service in the DOOR. He might put up a fight! But don't hurt him!"

The leader of the pack fighting with him on Baker Street was certain that when his countryman came to his senses, he would man up, fully support the movement, and advance their causes. So he ordered, "Get up! Let him go!" which they did.

However, it became apparent that all the fight was not out of him. The wounded man sprung catlike off the cottage's walls, so they engaged him further until he could resist no further. Fists flew, his and theirs; skin separated from flesh; and bones cracked.

The third time was the charm. After another ten minutes or so of the battling, Mahmoudou and they were exhausted. The men who held him captive booted him callously aside.

"See you at the next meeting, Ibrahaim!" The leader spoke his last name as he prepared to leave the cottage, the other men on his heels licking their wounds and wiping perspiration and blood from their faces with their garments' sleeves. The broken man looked up from his perch on the floor, resolve in his face to kill the murderous bastards who had taken his woman. The cottage door slammed as he lost consciousness for a while.

His wits regained, Doe wept profusely, his thoughts on the fix he had found himself in. *What was I to do? Fight the insurgents or join them? How could I get Kieta back?* He knew they would kill her for certain if he did not do what they wanted him to do. The aggrieved man crawled along the wall, weeping until there were no more tears.

In a little while, he gathered himself, lugging legs unwilling to hold him up, and got up to leave but not before a pause to clean himself up. He went into the bathroom, grabbed a towel out of the sink, and wiped his face with it. The scent of the soap and his beloved almost overtook him. He sobbed again, wiping away fresh tears before looking in the mirror.

Mahmoudou Ibrahaim saw grief in the place where a happy visage used to show itself. The Toures woman had painted a smile on his face since the day he heard her voice on the Soyinka's telephone, one that DOOR wiped away when they took his *cherie*. He hit the mirror he had placed on the wall while making the cottage habitable with an already bruised fist; the glass cracked. He winced; his hand, like his heart, hurt like hell.

After going to the bathroom to wipe his face and gather himself, he hobbled out of the Baker Street cottage and fled on foot to his motorcycle. *If the bastards didn't take that too*, he thought. He moved sure-footedly on the cobblestoned street, his resolve intact that he would gather some friends, relatives, and coworkers then go to the jail he was sure she would be placed in to enact a rescue. The man gave little attention to a passerby who noticed his condition and moved aside to let him pass without questioning his appearance.

When he rounded the corner, he did run into one person who accosted him. "Watch where you going, idiot!" Mahmoudou paused to give him a side-eye then proceeded. His thoughts turned to who would lend him a hand. As usual, Kunto was the first person who came to mind. He purposed to go to his best friend's abode first. He nodded in the air, assuredly, knowing that Kunto would help him if no one else would.

Doe was relieved when he got to the place where he had parked his bike. He was not sure that the men had not taken it too. He grimaced as he threw his left leg over the vehicle. Once he was successfully seated, the cyclist headed off Baker Street and to one of the main throughways but did not make it to his destination.

Blinded by rage, he gave traffic little regard. The biker did not yield to a stop sign, and when he saw the big supply truck approaching, he swerved to avoid it but hit the side of the vehicle, sliding along its girt until he was at the back of the truck. He fell, and the back wheels of the vehicle rolled over him and his bike, crushing them both.

Chapter Twelve

Kunto arrived at the hospital early the next morning, finding his friend in dire straits, not expected to survive. Word had come to him from Doe's family, who like many in the village were gathering their meager belongings and heading away from the countryside. The infidels were out of control. "Go there, into the city, to the hospital, the one where the foreigners go, and see after him," one of the elders in the Ibrahaim clan told Mahmoudou's friend. "We are not certain we will be here when you return."

"Where are you going?" the Boro man questioned the relative, considering whether his own fleeing family could join this group. *It would probably be easier to find them when this conflict was over. Doe and I could seek our family members together*, he thought.

The bearded, white-haired elder hunched his shoulders. "We are not certain, but we are getting out of Timbuktu. It is no longer safe for us. It has come to our attention that a group of refugees is taking to the river at Bamako and going to safety. If we can catch up with them, we will join them."

"Is everybody going?" Kunto asked, his brow lifting simultaneously as he questioned the elder about his friend's wives and other family members.

The elder affirmed, "Everybody! Our entire family! Wives, children, in-laws, all the Ibrahaims and anyone attached to them!" He also told him, "Mahmoudou's belongings are boxed and in a corner of his lodging if you would like to retrieve them and take them to him. Otherwise, he can secure them for himself once he is cured, if he survives." The man threw up his hands in resignation.

Finally, the two men looked at each other, consternation on their faces, doubts that they would ever see each other again in this life evident. For a moment, neither of them knew what to say next. They reached for each other simultaneously and hugged and bid each other a simple "Adieu." Both wiped their noses on their garments' sleeves.

Knowing his friend would collect his meager belongings if the need existed, Kunto turned on his heels and went into the cottage to salvage the boxes that held Doe's clothing and personal effects. The man took the three containers and placed them on the passenger seat and floorboard in his truck. He squeezed his friend's belongings into the truck cab with the elder's help, leaving a corner for him to sit while steering. He wanted to be able to lock it up when he got to his destination and did not want someone to see it on the back of the truck and steal it. Trust had been thrown out the window in his land.

When the two finished, the aggrieved man bade the elder Godspeed before he raced to the hospital to see for himself if his friend had indeed been injured by the insurgents and to determine the extent thereof.

Kunto Boro drove like a bat out of hell, jumping out the truck cab almost before the vehicle rolled to a complete stop. Taking just a minute to get his bearings, he headed to what he perceived to be the front entrance of the building he had passed many times. The medical facility was a four-square building with yurt-style roofs strategically vented to let hot air escape, connected by covered hallways, but coated with brown dust. No similar buildings were in the area.

The visitor had never been inside of any kind of health facility. The elders in his family doctored his family using traditional medicines, herbs, or whatever had been passed from generation to generation.

And nowadays, caretakers could always be found on Avenue du Fleuve in the central market in Mali where young men sold dried dogs' heads and pick from piles of them or heads of house cats by the dozens or stacks of monkeys cut into parts, all their assorted parts with sun-dried faces shrieking silently and hairy dead hands clutching empty air. They could also shop for dried bats, rats, and warthogs; desiccated bird carcasses of all varieties; live vultures, falcons, and chameleons; the skin of an eighteen-foot python; bottles of lion urine; cruets of python fat; and jars of lizard blood to mention some. Practically everything needed to treat whatever bothers you could be found there.

Trouble in your love life? A bad cough? Business is lousy? Don't like your neighbor? Your baby has a fever? It didn't matter what the sickness was. If you didn't have a family member to treat your ailments, you could always find someone in the village to help you. Traditional medicine, faith healing, juju, black magic, witchcraft, sorcery, gris-gris, whatever one preferred to call it flourished throughout Africa, particularly West Africa, and nowhere with more vigor than in Mali.

Despite this, his friend was here in this hospital. At least, that was the message that had been passed to Kunto. He was going to find him and get him out of here too. His thoughts running wild, he proceeded to an open door and stuck his head in, peeking both ways before putting his foot in the entrance. Surprisingly, the halls were free and his way clear. The same dust that was outside was in the building, and windows were wide open. And the stifling heat from outside was a constant companion. The air reeked of rotting flesh, and his attention was turned toward moans coming from further down the hall.

The visitor stopped to get his bearing. A few horseflies swarmed, one of the pests buzzing him. The man stopped and flailed at the busy fly with his hand, turning around, fighting off others in attack mode. "Git! Git out of here!" he emitted. The air reeked of rotting flesh; he held his breath. Doe's confidant saw a desk at the end of the hall, so he headed there.

"Huh, huh." He cleared his throat before speaking to the woman who raised her head from the paperwork in front of her.

"May I help you?"

"Mahmoudou Ibrahaim? I am looking for Mahmoudou Ibrahaim." His inquiry fell from his mouth anxiously.

The receptionist at the emergency facility verified his friend was there, and his condition was grave. "We are surprised that Mr. Ibrahaim made it through the night."

The Boro man asked the woman, "Can I see him?"

"Are you family?"

"I am not family! We are friends, have been since we were boys," the man responded.

"Only family. Our policy will allow for visitation by his wife or parents only," the woman voiced, her speech stern and full of warning. It was apparent the man facing her was quite impatient. Unruliness showed in his eyes, so she implored him, "Leave now, monsieur! Don't make me have to call security, please."

"What if he has no family? I am his *ami*. We have been friends since childhood." The woman hunched her shoulders and turned back to her paperwork. Other patients and their families were waiting to be called to the desk for their medical needs.

Doe's friend threw up his hand in surrender and fled from the reception area. Not willing to create a scene, Kunto hasted away and secretly made his way to another wing, following signs that pointed him to the unit where the most critical of patients received care.

Arriving in the critical care area, he stopped at a nurses' station and inquired of his friend, insisting that he be taken to see him, but met resistance much like that he had at the receptionist's desk.

"Sorry, monsieur. Only family can see him and only for a few moments at a time. Doctor's orders." The nurse dismissed him.

"Just—" His voiced plea to just see his friend for but a moment was met with woman's open palm. She halted him. "I have rounds to make, monsieur! The exit is there." She pointed in the direction that he had come from with a chart she picked from the desk while she spoke. "Go now, please!"

Her attempts to wave him off were not met with resistance. The man knew she was serious and would call for security if he did not leave right away. The receptionist had told him the same thing, so Kunto turned on his heel to leave; however, his resolve to steal his way into the intensive care unit where critical care patients were hospitalized rested intact.

Disappointment showing on his face to appease the nurse, he turned and slunk down the corridor toward the exit slowly. When she noticed him leaving, the nurse went about her way, her gait swift and with purpose.

Momentarily, the Boro man looked over his shoulder, and as soon as he was sure she no longer watched, the visitor pivoted on his heels and rushed through the unfamiliar area, checking doors for patients' names or charts that identified the room's occupants. "I'm coming, buddy!" He spoke to the air, as no one else was in the hallway. "I'm coming. I got your back! I'm coming!"

Just a minute passed before fate delivered him to the door with his friend's name on it. Letting out a sigh of relief, the man quietly turned the knob, peered in the room through a tiny crack he made in door, and seeing no one else except a bedded patient, he slid snakelike into the small space holding several beds separated by hanging curtains. Inside, he held his breath anew and pressed his back against the wall beside the door then let the air out of him slowly, careful not to wheeze, else he might get caught in the forbidden area.

The space was dimly lit, so he took a little time to become acclimated. He noticed for the first time that a nurses' station was right in front of the bed, a mere couple of yards away from the foot of the patient's bed. *Whew!* No one was there, and he was glad about that. He could have gotten caught right away if someone had been attending the desk.

Swoosh! Swoosh! Noise from a machine breathing for his friend brought his attention to the mass that was in the bed in full body cast with IVs, catheters, and other devices attached. He shivered where he stood frozen. For the first time, he noticed the area was cool. The area was powered by a few generators the American missionaries who helped build the unit brought from their homeland, consequently some modern-day medical devices. *Swoosh! Swoosh!* His attention returned to his raison d'être. Kunto stepped forward and turned toward the noise, uncertainty on his brow. He squinted in the dimness, peering directly into the patient's face.

Bruises and abrasions peeking from a mass of bandages left him almost uncertain about the true identity of the man who lay there in a medically induced coma; he was unconscious. The truck had run over Doe's corps, missing a face already bloodied and beaten to a pulp by the men who separated him from Kieta. *This has to be him though. The receptionist said he was here!* the Boro man thought.

"Damn, boy! What did you get yourself into? They beat the crap out of you!" He spoke more to the room than the man on the bed, his thoughts interrupted by voices on the unit. Kunto slid back toward the door, hiding behind the upraised hospital bed's back.

"Let's check on Mr. Ibrahaim next." He heard a masculine voice from the other side of the curtain, one that set him in motion again. He backed cautiously and carefully out of the same door he entered, peering through a crack to see that the two speakers, doctor and nurse, were indeed in the space he had just relinquished. Sweat beaded on his brow. "Whew! That was close!" he exclaimed as he drew a rag from his pantaloons' pocket to wipe the moisture from his face. Kunto pressed his ear to the door, desiring to hear the medical professionals' observations.

"Monsieur Ibrahaim is lucky to be alive," the doctor spoke first. "Every bone in his body from the neck down is either fractured or broken. It's a good thing his spinal cord was not severed. Paralysis would have been certain. Whoever brought him in is to be complimented for the way his back was stabilized on the scene. As it is, he will have to wear a back brace for a while, but that is a much better option."

The accompanying nurse nodded as she voiced, "Je suis d'accord! He is one lucky man!"

Kunto removed his ear, opting to peer to the crack to see and hear the nurse's reaction. The woman gave a nod of assent as she spoke of Doe's luck. The man nodded in agreement. His friend, like a cat, had nine lives. He remembered other near-fatal experiences one or the other had alone or together.

His eyes followed the medical professionals taking care of his buddy. At the head of the bed, the physician fingered the patient's face, looking at bruises, separating his eyelids with his left hand to view the ball. He used a light to look therein then cut the miniature flashlight he held in his right hand off and put the object in the pocket of his white coat. "Another inch and his cranium would have been smashed!"

Then he looked again at the patient's chart and repeated his accomplice's assessment, "Mr. Ibrahaim is one lucky man!"

"He is, indeed," the woman replied. "And strong too. He is a strong one! I was looking at his face while you examined him. Even in his current state, as sick as he is, he appears resolute! He must have been going somewhere important. Witnesses to the accident reported that he didn't pause or yield the right-of-way to that big truck. They say it seemed like he tried to lay his bike on the side and slide under the bed of the truck to get to the other side. He was in that big of a hurry."

The doctor shook his head. "Such a young man! And as I said, a lucky one too. The gods must be on his side . . . all of them. It's a small wonder that his lungs were not punctured or deflated. We'll keep him sedated for a couple more days and then bring him out slowly, check for his response. Let me know if there are any changes."

The doctor pivoted on one foot, the nurse doing the same, the two prepared to leave the patient and continue their rounds.

"I will," the woman spoke assuredly as they made their way from Mahmoudou Ibrahaim's bedside. The man on the other side of the door let the doorknob loose and pulled it until he felt its closing click, his original intention laid aside. There was no way he could pilfer his friend away from the facility and take him to the village so the elders could care for him. He would surely die and die young. As it was, most people in Mali did not live to be fifty years old. Only one of nine made this milestone.

Kunto left the hospital, his intent on finding out more about what happened on Baker Street before the accident. Word was that the insurgents had caught Doe with his mistress and that the woman had been taken away. He recalled one man's account. "Three men dragged that woman what Mahmoudou Ibrahaim was seeing out of the cottage. She wasn't no bigger than a moment, but it took every one of them to handle her. She fought like a lioness, and as small as she was, it took all three of them to put her on the back of the truck. One had her head, and it took two of them to hold the rest of her. They had to knock her out before they could drive away with her!"

He shook his head, invoking his mind to return to the present. While things were looking bad for "the home team," Kunto had heard what the medical professionals said, but they didn't know Mahmoudou like he did. That cat had nine lives. He knew his friend would survive. The man had the strongest intestinal fortitude of anyone he knew. And as soon as he was able, he would demand to know where Kieta Toures was and would find her.

What would he expect from Kunto? He would expect his friend to have that information, so he left the hospital, his intent to find a woman he had heard much about but never seen. She could pass him on the street and tap him on the shoulder, and he would not know

119

who she was. *I wish I had at least stopped by Baker Street when they were there. Surely, he would have introduced us!* Thoughts assailed his senses, propelling him onward, toward discovery of his friend's woman.

A couple of weeks passed before Doe was removed from the critical care unit and placed on the ward. Nevertheless, he still rested infirm and was hospitalized for months in a body cast. While he was at the facility, infections cropped up and, as small as they were, had to be treated with antibiotics. Fevers too, which came and went, had to be cooled. So people were in and out of the patient's room. There was no peace to be had.

During this critical period, the infirmed man did not acknowledge anyone. He seemed to have just turned inward, his spirit man his only companion. There was no medical reason for his failure to communicate. He just didn't. Not even a groan was given the pain he obviously experienced. He refused to whimper or cry.

His friend kept coming to see him, sitting by his bedside, speaking encouraging words. "Come on, *mon ami*! We got this. Together we are going to make things straight." Kunto spoke about the tragic event and loss of Doe's beloved in the best way he knew how. Since one did not know who was who and who could be trusted, it was better not to say anything directly about things that concerned both of them. *Come on, mon homme! You got to get up out of that bed. I got everything you need!*

Despite Doe's failure to acknowledge him, Kunto kept vigilant during the ordeal. His presence no longer discouraged, he made daily treks to his friend's bedside, his thoughts always on what he would say to his friend when he was lucid. "It won't be long now," he told himself as he observed the wounds on his buddy's exterior heal, and the abrasions left on his face by the insurgents' knuckles erased themselves.

When the man's countenance was clear as were his eyes and his face clean-shaven, the Boro man grew more hopeful. Doe was going to come out of the funk he was in soon. He was sure of that. So he kept speaking to him those things he believed. He mouthed softly on these uninterrupted visits. The staff no longer paid him attention and let him sit as long as he wanted to stay. "Come on, Mahmoudou. You are better than this, brother! You are the man! You can't let no knuckles, fists, or collision take you out of the game. Come on, man. Talk to me!"

Some days he just prayed; others when patient was not his best virtue, the man was tempted to reach over, grab his friend by the shoulders, and shake him until he spoke. Regardless of his attitude, he always told him, "I know you are going to talk soon. The doctor says ain't no reason for you not to talk. Anyway, I'll be here. You can talk to me. About anything! Man, you know we are like brothers. You can tell me anything that's in your heart!"

True to his thoughts, a month to the day of the accident, Doe spoke to him when he came to his bedside. Kunto's butt had barely hit the seat when he heard sound. *Doe was talking!* A strained voice made raspy by insertion and removal of tubes and reinsertion when a bout of a staph infection occurred as well as ones that kept him breathing until he could aspire on his own emitted. "Where is she, Kunto? Did you find out where Winston's men took her? I know he took her! I know that bastard took her!" His voice raised as he spoke, calling attention to him by others in the room.

The visiting man jumped up from his seat and leaned over the patient. He shushed him. "Shhhh. We will talk about that later!" Kunto rolled his eyes toward the door, indicating there may be listening ears. "Hush, man!"

"Hush, hell! Your ass been standing over me for days begging for some conversation, and now you don't want me to talk!" Doe shook his head, an action that caused him to wince a little. His feelings were returning, all of them. He closed his eyes before he piped up. "Now look what you have done. You have made my friggin' head hurt." He rubbed his temple with his right hand.

Hearing his friend speak and observing his personality attempting to make itself known anew, Kunto laughed aloud with glee. He was so happy until he could not contain the joy he felt at the present moment. The boom in his voice drew the attention of a passing nurse who stuck her head in the door. "Is everything all right here?" she asked as she stepped into the patient's room.

"Yep!" The laughing man spoke excitedly. "Everything is all right here. He just started talking, and he said something funny," he told the inquiring woman as he pointed to his friend.

The nurse did not stop until she was at the head of the bed. At the bedside, she touched Doe's face, asking how he felt. "Oh, so somebody is communicating. How are you feeling, Mr. Ibrahaim?"

"Like new money," he told her as she continued to minister to his beaten and battered corps, checking his pulse and heart rate and rearranging the bed covers and pillow as she continued their first conversation.

"I am glad you are feeling so much better," the man's nurse told him. Then added, "And that you are speaking. We have been worried about you. You were one sick man when you were brought into the hospital after your accident. Do you recall the accident?"

"How can I forget? I hope I didn't hurt that truck too bad!" He attempted a joke, causing Kunto to shake his head. His friend was back.

The woman continued her probing, poking here and there, causing her patient to do a bit more wincing, nothing of consequence, however. Any pain he felt was replaced with the aroma of her perfume. His mind briefly flashed back to Kieta standing over him as he lay on their bed in the cottage on Baker Street. He shook his head and groaned.

"Sorry," the nurse told him as she ceased her ministrations to him and turned to address the friend she had been talking to since the Ibrahaim man had been admitted. The woman spoke assuredly as she was preparing to leave Doe's room, "The doctor says we will remove more of the casts this week, okay?"

"I'll be glad. I am itching like hell all over!" the patient insisted, drawing her attention away from his friend and back to him.

The nurse acknowledged, "That's a good sign. You are healing and will be as good as new before you know it."

Chapter Thirteen

When Kieta did not reappear on the university campus at the designated time, Marissa grew concerned. She mentally whipped herself for participating in the ruse they were involved in. Regrets about keeping her friend and Doe's affair to herself and away from her parents assailed her. The coed frantically paced the length of the passenger side of the jeep, inquiring of the driver what they should do when more than an hour had passed.

"We should head home now, mademoiselle!" His anxious reply brought greater consternation. "There is nothing more we can do here. It is past time for our departure." He looked at his watch and said, "Let's go, mademoiselle! Monsieur and madame will worry if we are not at home right away." He reached for her elbow to assist her with her mount.

"I don't know why I asked you what to do!" she replied before jerking her arm away from him. Experiencing her recoil, he leaped aside, tossing his hands in surrender while speaking more frantically. "S'il vous plait, mademoiselle. We must leave now, else it will be dark when we get back to the compound. Your father will not be pleased. I will lose my employ."

His charge did not budge. He begged more, his mannerisms showing his sincerity. "Please, Mademoiselle Soyinka" came as he stomped the ground with his right foot. "Please."

"No," she insisted, "we can't leave her! Allons! We must search for her. Kieta is not far. I believe she may be near Baker Street. Let's go there tout de suite!" She turned and started her trek away from the vehicle. When she noticed that he was not following, she stopped. Bravery was not one of her strong suits.

The man held his posture. He refused to budge, and the passenger door's handle in hand, he encouraged her silently to mount the step so he could begin the drive to the Soyinkas' compound. Angered by his defiance, Marissa sashayed back to the vehicle and stood by it. Soon, it became apparent that the two co-conspirators were at an impasse, a stalemate of sorts. Marissa folded her arms under her breasts and planted her own feet firmly on the dusty terrain, and she let her bottom lip drop.

"Come on, Mademoiselle Marissa. Don't be so stubborn!" Nouhoum continued to beg the pouting girl. "Master is going to have my ass when we get back to the house. Please, come on. Let's go!" he repeated incessantly for lack of anything else to say.

Over an hour passed before an overactive bladder brought the impasse to a screeching halt. *Why didn't I go to the restroom before I left the building?* she thought. The truth of the matter was that if she did not get in the car and go home, she would wet herself. Consequently, Marissa, unassisted, took her seat and slammed the door.

The relieved driver scurried to his seat under the wheel, ignited the engine, and sped off toward the compound.

Momentarily, his passenger began to cry, out loud. He adjusted the rearview mirror so that he could observe her without her knowledge. The man drove on, weighed down by a misstep that could have been easy avoided by telling the girls "No!" when they involved him in their folly.

In spite of persistent cries, the man now attended to the task he had been hired to with fear on his countenance, his heart heavy. He wished he had told the captain in charge of security. The man would perhaps have made it known to their master, but it would have been worth it. He would not be in the car with the weeping, simpering, bereft young woman he was transporting to the compound tout de suite.

They got to the compound in record time. Kieta's friend jumped from the vehicle before the driver braked and parked it and ran into the house. She flung the front door open and ran in, shouting, "Papa! Papa! Where is Papa?" All the occupants' attention was drawn to the girl as she took the stairs in twos, heading to the man's office.

Wakesa fled after her, calling, "Qu'est-ce qu'il y a? What's the matter? Are you all right, child? What's causing you so much trouble? Why you coming running in the house like that?"

The driver made his way to the house and stood in the doorway, waiting his fate. The man threw his hands in the air and banged his head on the wood frame. *Fumier!* he cursed himself and the day he had agreed to participate in the girls' folly.

Soyinka, his attention drawn from the computer, papers, folders, memos, notes, and bills, including the fuel invoice he was getting ready to review in front of him by the frantic cries of his daughter, let go of his chair and ran from the room. He met his daughter at the top of the stairs then grasped her gently by the shoulders and pulled her to himself. "What's the matter, child?" he asked the same questions Wakesa had already spouted but with a tone gentler than that of the servant. "Speak up! Tell me what is wrong!" He pulled his daughter's chin upward so he could catch her eye. "What's going on, Marissa?"

"Kieta is gone! She didn't come back to the university. We don't know where she is! Kieta is gone!" the girl wailed, sobs distorting her normally clear, crisp voice. Her declaration made, she clung to her daddy, crying loud enough for all to hear. The whole compound grew silent, every ear attuned to the girl's conversation with her father. "We have got to find her, Papa. We have got to find her!"

"Hold on, ma petite!" Her father assuaged her fears. "It's all right. We will find her. Stop crying and talk to me. Tell me what happened."

Wakesa was in their circle by now. The two adults heard an abbreviated account of Kieta and Doe's love affair. Neither commented until she stopped talking. "Sit," the man commanded as he steered his daughter into his office and to a seat in front of his desk. The maid sat beside her and reached for a box of Kleenex on the desk. "Here, blow your nose. Wipe your face!" she said, her usually gruff voice tinged with what appeared to be sympathy.

"Can I go to the bathroom? I've got to pee! I didn't get to go before we left school," she said.

Her father pointed the way to the restroom across the hall. "Sure," her father told her, his action causing Wakesa to take the girl's arm, to help her lift herself from the chair. The woman took the used tissues from her as she moved aside to facilitate an easy exit from the small office.

"Where's the driver?" the man asked before his daughter was out of earshot.

"He's down there by the door! I'll go get him!"

"No, you sit in that chair over there!" The man pointed to a second chair in the office, reserving the one nearest the door for his daughter's return from the necessary.

The man stepped to the entry way and stuck his head out. In a minute, the driver was called from his perch. A simple "Driver!" from the Soyinka man set his employee's feet in motion. Fear for his job accompanied the man who squired the young women around Mali daily as he mounted the stairs.

"Sir, I am so sorry, sir! I know that I should have come to you. Or I should have told the captain. He would surely have come to you. Je le regret!" Nouhoum immediately started apologizing when he was at the office door.

His master held up his hand, arresting his thoughts and fears. "No, no! No need to fear! I know it is not your fault." The man did not blame the servant. He knew his daughter had asserted authority she had not been granted. "All I need to know is who has her. Keep your ears open and let me know if you hear anything," he told the man in his employ, more for Marissa's sake than for anything else. He had little thought about the Toures girl.

I am just glad that Marissa is home safe. There is so much to fear in Mali at the present time. Madame is going to shit a brick when she finds out about this! She has been bending my ear every time she hears news of the goings on from her friends when she is in the city. Those were the man's thoughts.

Marissa's father wiped his brow with a handkerchief and looked at the driver. "You may go now!" He waved the man away, an action Wakesa found reprehensible. She purposed to make the head of security at the compound aware of the driver's failure to take care of his assignments.

"I'll take care of this! You take care of the house and my womenfolk!" He dismissed the woman. "See about that girl in the bathroom. Make sure she is all right."

Wakesa gave his admonishment a nod and the brief curtsy the man despised. "Stop stooping and bowing!" He rejected her training. "I am not your master, and you are not a slave!"

"Oui, monsieur!" emitted the woman, backing out of the office and heading to see after her charge.

Whew! Relief swept over the man trusted to get the girls to the university and back. He hastened from the doorway and hurried down the staircase. Nouhoum took the steps in twos. It was not until he was at the foot of the stairs that he paused to wipe sweat from his brow. While he had heard what their employer told Wakesa, he still worried. *I must go to him and tell him myself. If that old busybody tell it, she won't tell it right!* The driver left to park the vehicle and to seek out the captain of security who managed transportation for the Soyinkas.

Back in the office, Soyinka revisited the last hour's happenings and rested comforted. His conscience was clear. He had given the Toures girl a home and a place of employ and even allowed her, at the insistence of his wife and daughter, the opportunity to receive a degree and better herself. There was little else he could do for her. He had a family to take care of. His thoughts turned to Marissa. He would send her to her mother. He was certain that the best place for her was in England with her and their other children.

The man heard someone clearing her throat. "Monsieur, Mademoiselle Marissa wants to speak to you again."

He nodded, and the two women, the older steering the younger by her shoulder, returned to the seats they occupied a short time ago.

Contrition showed in her voice and mannerisms as Marissa begged her father's pardon. "I am sorry, Papa! I will not disobey again. Please don't punish Nouhoum! He just did what I told him to do."

"I was certain of that!" he spoke, annoyance his companion. "I knew without a shadow of a doubt that the two of you persuaded him to participate in your ruses. Girls have done that since the beginning of time."

A hiccup escaped her lips, so Wakesa took a glass from the tray on the man's desk, poured water from a pitcher, and gave it to the girl to sip.

"Just a little bit at a time! Them hiccups will be gone in a minute." The woman ministered to her charge. She had encouraged the girl to apologize to her father before retiring to her quarters. Her mind was on her mistress's confidence that she would take care of her daughter while she was away.

"I know you will obey! It is imperative that we do what is necessary to keep you safe," he told his daughter. "You will not leave the compound until we have sorted this out. Do you understand, my child?" he asked his simpering daughter.

She nodded a nod of comprehension, her mind on whether she should ask what he was going to do about Kieta.

The man let his gaze leave his daughter and turn to the servant as he stood. "Wakesa," he said, "go downstairs with her, give her something to drink, comfort her, and watch over her until she is better!"

Marissa let go of her seat, rushed out of the office, and flew down the stairs. The woman, her mother charged with her care before she fled Timbuktu with her younger children, closed the distance between the two of them.

"I will do that, sir," the housekeeper responded.

~~~~~

True to his word, Nouhoum kept an ear out and did hear of the Toures girl's fate. He told his boss his findings, and the man, in turn, told their employer what had happened on Baker Street.

Once Marissa's father found out where Kieta was, he did not attempt to intervene. He had given the waif an opportunity of a lifetime, but she had chosen her own way. That in itself was more than most men in his position did for their workers. Besides that, he did not want to antagonize any of these clandestine groups. He and his household were safe, so he would not put them in jeopardy to save a servant.

With little deliberation, he told Marissa her best friend was dead, and grief overtook her. The day he called her into his office to tell her of the woman's demise at the hands of the insurgents, she wailed and moaned like a banshee when her father gave the grave news. Soyinka almost wished he had not ended Kieta's life story with such a final blow.

Hearing the fate of her friend, Marissa whipped herself relentlessly, her grief making her ill. She couldn't sleep, and she lost her appetite. The girl thinned rapidly. Her appearance became gaunt like one who was anorexic. Her clothing began to drop off her shoulders. Nothing her father or Wakesa could say or do gave her solace. She no longer wanted to be in Mali, without her friend, so she acquiesced to her parents' wishes. Taurence Soyinka's oldest child implored her father to let her take the next flight to England to join her mother and siblings.

He did. "I will join you all as soon as my business is completed here," the Soyinka man told his daughter when they were being transported to put her on the plane at the airport in Bamako. "Help your mother out until I get there," he told her, and for lack of anything else to say about Kieta, the father spoke sympathetically to his daughter as he rubbed his hands through her hair. "I am sorry about your friend, *ma petite!*" Then he loosed her.

~~~~~

The men who separated Kieta from the love of her life threw her on the back of a truck with a couple of bearded beady-eyed men seated on their rumps. All bore AK-47s. She fell in the vehicle's bed knees first, tumbled forth, and banged her head on some object. Her skirt lifted, exposing her behind for all to see. No sound came from her. She refused to give way to the pain. The Toures girl lay where her body settled, pushing her skirt down with her right hand.

Her captors were entertained by her fall. Her awkwardness drew laughter from everyone except the leader who ordered brusquely, "Shoot her if she tries to get out of the truck's bed," before he retook his seat on the passenger side of the truck's cab.

Momentarily, the driver ignited the engine and sped over the cobblestones away from Baker Street. Tears that had been suppressed involuntarily cascaded down her cheeks, making her weep. She shifted where she lay. The simpering waif sunk as low in the bed of the bouncing truck as she could. The girl wanted to die. Kieta wished her captors would shoot her right then and right there. Soon, the vehicle came to a stop in front of what used to be the city jail.

At their destination, her captors dragged her from the truck and steered her along the way with the butt of their weapons until she was inside a dirty and dank building. Shortly, she found herself in a cell with a horde of other women who were seated everywhere on the floor, their eyes cast down and voices silent. The guard opened the door and poked her in the base of her spine with his weapon, prodding until she was just inside, and enough room was left to lock the enclosure.

An older woman rushed to the cell door and tried to push her way out as the novice was forced inside. The man elbowed her brusquely, causing the inmate to fall backward. Hands from somewhere flew up and caught her, and another set pulled her backward. She cried aloud and was shushed by yet another imprisoned one.

The Toures woman nearly gagged. The smells of body odor, vomit, and spoiled food were almost too strong to bear, making this experience more disgusting. The young woman held her breath but refused to cover her nose. She tried breathing through her mouth instead of her nostrils but could taste the stench when she did this. What a fix she was in! She did not want to draw unnecessary attention to herself. Her condition was the same as all the other women on the unit. They were imprisoned for what? Perhaps they, like she, were ignorant of charges that landed them in jail.

Kieta Toures let her body cascade downward into the empty spot where she stood. She knew she would be there just for a little while. Doe would come and get her. She was certain of that.

Seated in a space the size of a box, she raised her eyes to scan the room full of women as soon as the guard was gone. She couldn't even catch an eye. Each and every soul dressed in *habib*, dark greens, was into herself and her own situation, so their eyes were cast to the dirty, unkempt floor they all shared. Kieta heard a moan nearby, and her eyes followed the sound her ears picked up on.

A woman sat hovering in a corner, holding her face, rocking. *Maybe she is sick*, Kieta thought as she considered making her way to her side. She raised up a bit but was pulled back to her seat by the woman on her left side. "Asseyez-vous! Sit! They beat you if you don't stay in your place!" she evoked.

Kieta took the stranger's advice and let her mind and body relax. She had already been physically maligned earlier in the day. She didn't want any more punishment. She only had to tolerate the environment until morning. Her mind turned toward her upbringing out in the desert with her family. Conditions had not always been the best but seemed to improve when the morning light showed itself. Sure her lover would get everything cleared up and would get her released tomorrow, she sighed a sigh of relief.

Soon, her stomach growled. She had not had a bite since breakfast. *Surely*, she thought, *they will feed us before long.* Someone farted, and Kieta briefly held her breath, now dismissing thoughts of food. She shook her head. With this stench, she was not sure whether she could get it down, but she had grown accustomed to the three meals and an occasional snack available to all who served the Soyinkas. A rumbling from within her bowels caused Kieta to put her hand on her middle to quiet her innards.

The minutes passed and felt like hours. *What time is it? What time was it?* She marked time with hums. Tunes from songs played on the radio as she and Marissa rode to and from school chorused in her psyche. She knew the melodies lasted no more than two or three minutes each, so she counted on her phalanges the songs she now played in her head. That was one way to mark time.

There was no way to tell what time it was. No clock was on the wall, and no one had a watch. Needless to say, no food came on her first evening at the jail. Soon, it was apparent that it was later than she had imagined. The sun going down, darkness turned the cell into grayness then to the black of night, so it became apparent that she had to wait until morning. Pools of saliva swelled in her mouth, and she swallowed over and over as she tried to fill her empty paunch.

The night dragged. Silence was broken frequently by the women's dreams, nightmares, and thoughts, even by screams or shrieks that came from across the way or down the hall or, maybe, from outside. She was not sure where the sounds came from. Nevertheless, they unnerved her. Kieta had not slept for a couple of days. She bit down on her lip and began to sob in silence. Never in a million years had she imagined herself in jail. She hugged herself tightly, self-soothing until sleep came and took her away from this awful place.

Wakesa came to her in a vision. "Told you so!" The apparition mocked her for trying to be like Marissa. The old woman wagged her finger in the dreamer's face. "You ain't one of them. You are no better than me. You ain't nothing but a servant. You see if anybody come see about you! You think that little bit of college they give you make you better than me. You like me, nothing but a servant!"

Kieta cried out, waking herself. It was early morning. It was lighter in the cell, and the caged women were shifting in their places, trying to make stiffened muscles supple. She wiped saliva from the side of her face that had escaped her lips while she napped fitfully, stretched her arms upward, and emitted a yawn, echoing those of others around her.

The waif heard scrapping and raised her head up, noting for the first time that the man from last night was back. The keys clanked loudly as he opened the cell door. The girl vaulted to her feet. Surely, he was there to get her. Doe must be outside. Her heart fell when she realized that she and the remainder of the women in encasement were being herded out for a potty break and a bit of bread and water for breakfast. As bad as she desired food and a toilet, the latter first, she wanted freedom more. She leaned back, waiting her turn as she considered who and how many cellmates she had.

One, two, three . . . twenty-five. She counted the souls as they came out of the cell. *There are twenty-five of us in this space, one smaller than the room I shared with Wakesa ever since Papa dropped me off at the Soyinkas' compound almost ten years ago.* Tears streamed down her face as she experienced a series of flashbacks while they went first to the toilet then to a room where the prisoners shared a meal. Everyone took a seat at the table that already had the foods on it.

"You better eat! Keep your strength up!" A woman seated beside her on a bench at the creaky wooden plank table they all shared. A bowl of gruel and some bread drew her attention. Her stomach growled. So she pulled the bowl close to her, took her spoon, and started to taste. The odor of slop assailed her senses, and her mind returned to her place of employment. Back at the Soyinka household, the cook maintained a slop jar for placement of leftover food. One of her duties had been to take the bones and put them in an earthen vat then scrap the leftover from plates, pots, and dishes into the jar. The jar was taken out to the livestock pen to feed the animals and returned to the kitchen.

She thought now about how grossed out she was initially by the task. She gagged when she took the top off the jar to place new scraps in it. Before long, though, she mastered the task by holding her breath until the top was on, and she had turned around and headed away from the animal's feed. That was what this gruel was, a combination of whatever the jailers brought. The jail's cook threw the scraps in a pot and put it on the fire, cooking it until it was mush. Kieta pushed the bowl away, pulled the crust from the bread, ate that, and drank from her cup. Others cleaned their bowls and cups.

After the morning meal, the women were taken out to the yard. They separated, this space appreciated by all of them. Some fell to the ground and prayed, their faces to the east. Others stretched, exercising their limbs, or took to the yard and walked it like it was a track. A few talked among themselves. Most of the women simply kept to themselves, trying to avoid eye contact and conversation.

The guard ignored all of them. He pulled a rolled cigarette from a pocket, lit it, and smoked. The new girl's mind wandered. She paused for a moment and contemplated going over to him and decided to act. Kieta drifted over to the man to ask about charges against her and a release. He took her in for a moment then laughed before shooing her way from him. The other women shook their heads, commenting to one another, "That one right there, she must be touched in the head!"

All too soon, the women were returned to their cell. That day passed, and others did too. Doe's lover grew more troubled as the minutes, hours, and days passed. *What happened to Doe the day I was taken? Why hasn't he come or sent someone to get me? Did Marissa tell her father what happened? Will my employer consider my fate and enlist the aid of some of those high-powered people he knows to broker my rescue? What is going to happen to me?* The longer her imprisonment, the more questions.

~~~~~

While her lover did not come soon, someone did. Kieta did not recognize the camouflage-wearing, rifle-toting, bronze, tall foreigner, but he seemed to know who she was. He stood outside the enclosure for a little while, observing her. She stood, and their eyes caught each other's, an act that did not go unnoticed by the other women who were hunching one another as they witnessed the encounter. "Take that one out of there"—he pointed at her with his finger—"and put her in a cell by herself. Don't let nothing happen to her!" he told the men who accompanied him. And then he was gone, leaving her planted there in the spot she had claimed the evening of her arrest.

One of the Timbutuktuian men who was with the stranger returned shortly and took her to a washroom to bathe and change before she was placed in a cell by herself. He gave her a towel and a bar of soap. She smiled a smile of thanks, a gesture he gave little attention. Inside the room, the guard pointed out some clothing on a stool before telling her, "I will wait outside."

Kieta started to remove bright-yellow garments she wore then stopped, her gaze turning to the entrance. She tiptoed to the door to see if it was locked. Her hand on the knob, she tried to open the door just to peer out to see if anyone was there. Its creak drew the guard's attention. He looked up from a stool he sat on. "Finis?" he questioned her. "Have you finished your bath?"

Her reply "I have not started yet" drew his ire.

"You better wash before the water run cold," the man insisted. "I will rest here. No one will enter!"

Hearing and believing that she could bathe uninterrupted, she shut the door, undressed, and stepped into the tiny enclosure, noting that it could not hold a candle to the shower stalls at the Soyinkas' compound. However, it was a shower with warm water. The common one used by the prisoners did not have this amenity. She forgot where she was and set about cleansing herself. She scrubbed herself until she felt raw. Kieta Toures did not know when she would be afforded this comfort again, so she took full advantage of the situation, her attitude the same as it had been the day she entered into service at Marissa's house. That of a survivor!

Warm water spewing from the showerhead washed away some of her apprehensions but not all of them. She was still a prisoner, a wandering one at that. *Is Doe all right? Does he know who took me?*

Or where I am? Her mind also returned to her friend Marissa. *What happened to her when she got back to the house without me? Was her father so angry at her/them that he sent her to be with Madame Soyinka, Ife, and Little Taurence? Why did I let myself get into this?* She shook the last thought away, for she had no regrets about meeting and loving Mahmoudou Ibrahaim. *I would do it all over again just for one day of love!* she spoke to the open room before she turned the water off, toweling first her wet hair then the remainder of her corps.

Head high, Kieta traipsed across the room; retrieved the same drab, dark-green vestments the other prisoners wore; and put them on. She placed the scarf that was also provided on her head. Dressed in the clean garments, she opened the door so she could be led to the cell the stranger told the guards to put her in.

Months passed. The days seemed like years, hours like months, and minutes like days. The first few days, the woman rested hopeful. She knew in her heart of hearts that Doe was coming for her. She saw his face every night in her dreams. Every time she closed her eyes, he would be standing there, staring at her, so she awoke each day confident that her lover would come, and he would get her out of this mess.

After a while, she was no longer sure of a rescue. So time dragged as Kieta remained in the jail in the city with other women awaiting sentences for a variety of infractions ranging from prostitution to theft to disobeying her husband. She had learned their fates when she began to communicate freely with them as they dined on the meager subsistence in the common area or on the few occurrences where they were allowed outside the facilities' walls to walk around in the sunlight.

Like the other imprisoned women, Kieta survived on the odious gruel of sorts and water, eating and drinking every drop as if it were her last meal. Kieta continuously missed the comforts of the Soyinka household, especially the toiletries she had had access to and her toothbrush. She rubbed her tongue across her teeth each time she thought about brushing. She could not complain, though, because at least she could clean her mouth in the weekly shower she got, one most women in the jail were denied. She washed her teeth with soap and water, rubbing her teeth and gums with her fingers briskly.

A few at a time, the prisoners were allowed in the commons area outside every day or two, and Kieta looked forward to these times, often longing to be enclosed in the cell with the rest of the imprisoned instead of suffering isolation ordered by the unknown man. They were allowed to bathe twice a month and their garments tossed in a pile. They selected another clean one from a pile on floor that was washed. Several women did the laundry for all the captives. Kieta preferred the socialization these encounters allowed. It was not healthy to be alone with her thoughts. There were days when she thought she might lose her mind.

~~~~~

Finally, her trial came. She had no idea what month it was. No calendar was made available. Initially, she tried to keep count of the days but soon gave up. There was nothing to make marks on or nothing to write with, and when she had tried to keep up with the days, she would often forget what the last number had been. Newly captured women, however, gave her and the others as much information as they could.

One fall day, a couple of guards appeared at the cell door. One of them called her name, "Kieta Toures." She hesitated a moment and had to be called again before she was in motion and walking toward the speaker who was unlocking her cell door.

When she was at the portal's opening, the man pushed the door open, allowing her to step into the hallway. "Follow me!" the other man ordered, while his accomplice shut the cell up, locking it. He only walked a couple of yards before she was on his heel, making her way to wherever he was leading her. The other man followed closely behind the two of them.

Her heart started pounding an unsteady beat, one she could not only feel but hear. "Where are you taking me?" she asked, fear taking its grip on her. Too many women had been removed from their cells and had not returned. Each occupant was replaced with another. At least, it seemed that way to her. Was she coming back to her cell? Would she be tried? What form of punishment would she receive? Where could she go if she was freed? She didn't know where her family was, nor did she know if the Soyinkas would have her back. Or *if* Doe would be able to find her when and if she was released.

The young woman shook her head, attempting to shake the *ifs* away. And her feet involuntarily stopped moving. Her own unanswerable questions brought her to a screeching halt. The man behind her bumped into her, prodding her onward and forward. "Keep moving. Follow him!" were commands emitted as he prodded her with an open-palmed hand.

They rounded a corner in the dirty, dank, and musky building, and she found herself in a simulated courtroom. A man sat on one side of a large table, and an empty chair rested on the other side. The guard grunted for her to sit, and he stood on one side of her while the other armed man guarded the exit.

"Your name?" the man who sat in judgment of her asked when he looked up from the paperwork he pulled from a manila folder.

"Kieta, Kieta Toures." She spoke evenly with respect. It was apparent that she was sitting in judgment's seat, so she did not want to antagonize the man and heightened her sentence. *Perhaps he will let me go. I have not done anything. If he lets me go, I will follow all the rules to the letter. I will not be impudent. I will obey. On my honor, I will do what my master wants me to do, that is, if Monsieur Soyinka will let me return to his employ,* she thought.

The bespectacled man looked her over, catching her eye. "It says here that you were caught in a cottage on Baker Street engaged in an illicit affair with a man who already has a family. You and he were seen in public together. You refused to cover your head and hide your knees, and you conversed openly and freely with him as if he were your equal," he droned on and on, recalling for her hearing the same rules that her master and Doe himself had shared with her.

When he completed his tirade, he paused but a moment before determining her guilt and her fate. Disdain for her disobedience clear, he barked at the guard, "Ninety lashes!" He pointed a wagging finger in her face. "You are guilty! For your punishment, you will be administered ninety lashes in the public square." Her mouth fell opened, not a sound escaped her lips. They were frozen, and her voice box was too. All she wanted to know was when. *Maybe Doe will arrive before the beating takes place.*

Then she heard the man telling the guards that her punishment was to be carried out *immediately without delay.* His "Teach her to mind, do what she is told!" set the guards in motion, the one beside the door coming to the other side of the judgment seat. Her spirits sank; they fell to the floor.

Hearing the judge's final pronouncement allowed for relaxed members and released wails and sobs to escape her lips. "Oh my god, my god," she cried out for mercy as she fell to the floor, pleading her case. Hands clasped in front of her, her posture that of a submissive, Kieta begged, "Please, no, please. I will obey! I will do what I am told. I will follow the DOOR's orders."

Her pleas fell on deaf ears. The judge let go of his seat and headed out of the room. The guards grabbed her arms and pulled her upward, a task that was difficult. Her knees were gripping the floor, suction created by perspiration, fear, and filth on the floor. They grappled with her until she felt herself being uprooted. The suction removed by their strength, the guards dragged her, toes first, out to the streets where the crowd was already gathered. It was sentencing day.

In Mali, trials and sentencing took place simultaneously, so hordes of men, women, and children were already there and had taken up their perches in the square near the jail. They had not needed to be notified. When they were out of the building, Kieta could see their apparitions in spite of the bristling heat ushered by the blazing sunshine. She lifted her head, trying to catch sight of someone in the crowd she knew or who knew her. "Doe! Doe!" she emitted, her longing for her lover swallowed by the din from the waiting crowd, her expectation of being rescued by him diminishing.

~~~~~

It was noon on August 1, the beginning of a new month, when Kieta Toures was taken to the same place where she bought the beef for the brochettes she made at the Soyinkas' compound and the flour used to make Wakesa's flatbread where madame had taken her to buy the fabric for the beautiful dresses she had worn before her capture.

Through eyes reddened by salty tears of regret, she recognized some of the merchants, and they recognized her. She was a "privileged" one. Often, she was with Marissa and her mother when she shopped.

Unlike most servants, the family that had taken her in when she was "of age" had spoiled her, allowing her to attend the university and to get an education alongside their daughter. Most who recognized her felt little sympathy for her and were thinking she deserved the whipping she was on the verge of receiving. One of them used his phone to record what happened next, deciding he would share the video with her employer.

The guards prodded her along with the butt of their weapons and their commanding voices, and when at the appointed spot, they made her kneel in a traffic circle in the marketplace. They covered her in a gauzelike shroud. They made her remove her dress, leaving only the thin fabric to protect her skin from the whip.

Men looked on, their pride showing because this one had disobeyed, and if she was allowed a pass, their own women might revolt. Some women in the audience pitied her, and others placed blame on her for being disobedient. Their curious children jostled and jockeyed for positions for a better view of the woman's punishment.

The executor announced the Toures woman's crime and her punishment. Then he began flogging her with a switch made from the branch of a tree. Her high-pitched cries were contorted with pain. Observers heard the slap of the whip. And they heard her labored breathing. Kieta was hit repeatedly, rapidly, and for so long that at one point, she wasn't sure if the veil had fallen off. She experienced pain but not what she expected. Yet the woman could feel the mixture of blood, sweat, and urine seeping through.

When it was over, the flogger told her that if they ever saw her with a man again, they would kill her. She sighed a sigh of relief as she prepared herself for the release that was sure to come now that she had been publicly shamed. Some of the other women in the jail had told her she would be allowed to return to her family when her punishment was over. However, she did not move a muscle. A lesson in the consequences of disobedience just received, she waited further instructions. Needless to say, fate took an unexpected turn, one that confounded even her.

Her punishment completed, the crowd moved away, the woman was dragged back toward the jail by the ones who brought her to the marketplace. All were silent. She did not mutter a word, her mind on how the whipping had been bad, yet it was still not unto death. *What now?* she thought. *Will they return me to the jail to clean myself and put on some clothes before I go home?* Her spirits began to soar. She could taste freedom.

~~~~~

The young woman was unaware that the flogger was a relative of Mahmoudou's, an extension gained through marriage to his first wife. He turned the girl to make her behind more accessible, and when he did, she thought she heard him say under his breath, "Holler loud!" Kieta rotated her head to avail him of her ear, an attempt met with a push on the side of her head. "Don't move!" voiced for the onlooker. The man, experienced in inflicting of punishment, flailed quickly, striking the cloth more than he did the young woman.

She thrashed in the dirt, making new utterances, ones she never emitted before even in the throes of passionate encounters with Doe. Her grunts and groans made the theatrical more real. Yet she was no less hurt. She was embarrassed in front of her community. One of the final thrashes drew blood. Kieta swooned first then fainted. The odor of her own mix of blood, sweat, tears, and dust too much for even her.

Sufficiently punished, the girl was dragged back to the cell and rolled with a jailer's foot onto the hard floor. Winston, leader of the local group, DOOR, had told the jailors to return her there instead of letting her return to her master or her family, which was frequently done once the punishment was given. He had need of her. A DOOR leader, he thought Ibrahaim would be more cooperative once he found out how she had been spared.

Out of the corner of his eye, the man who administered the punishment spotted the man who recorded the flogging on his phone. When he was finished, he let the switches fall where they lay and quickly followed the man to his business. He marched up to him and put his hand out, saying, "Give it to me! You did not have my permission to record my work, else—" He did not have time to complete his threat. The offending man hastily gave the telephone to him. He placed it in his pantaloons' pockets and left as quickly and quietly as he had come. The man destroyed the telephone later the same day. No good could come from having such a video viewed by his ailing cousin.

Chapter Fourteen

Under the watchful eye of his best friend, Doe recuperated, spending more than five months in the hospital as back and ribs cracked in the fight and femur, tibia, and phalanges crushed in the collision healed. When the cast on his lower body was removed, he found that he was no longer able to walk and had to utilize services of orderlies at the hospital to get him back on his feet and mobile again. He was constantly in pain but fought through the torment, fueled by desire to get out of the facility and reclaim his life . . . find Kieta and rescue her.

Most days, the orderlies and nurses had to cease with the sessions, their apprehensions intact because the obviously angered man was in jeopardy of reinjuring breakages on the brink of healing. Their consternations were frequently met with crutches and/or curses catapulted at them. They were no match for a man crazed by events of which they had no knowledge. If he was not fighting, he was down and almost out.

Needless to say, depression's thwarts to overtake him were abated when Kunto also made him aware of the fate of his four wives and their families, news he received with meager concern. The man's truest thoughts were of his beloved Kieta. Bathed in guilt over her capture and full of consternations about what had happened to her, what those dogs had done to her, he railed about finding out who had taken her and getting revenge. There was little his friend could do but pray and watch over him. The man was out of his mind; Doe was loco. His friend was as crazed as anyone Kunto had ever seen.

"I will kill Winston, cut his heart out, and make lunch of it!" he yelled at Kunto about the previously unnamed leader of the DOOR one day when he came to the hospital. "Then I am going to kick his bloodied corps all the way back to America."

His fingers to his lips, his childhood friend tried to shush him. "Please, Doe, calm down. Don't speak his name aloud! You do not want to get us killed before we can rescue Kieta and get her out of here." He spoke nervously as he hastened to the door to check the hallway, ensuring for himself that no one was in there, and no one heard Mahmoudou rail against the man who had originally come to Mali with no intent to establish and nourish a group to fight against the insurgents but to serve as an independent contractor.

When he returned to his companion's bedside, he pulled up a chair, and a sincere conversation ensued about their involvement with DOOR and the rescue of Kieta.

"Are you sure she is still there, at the jail in Mali?" Doe accosted his friend.

"Yes, I am certain."

"Do you know who took her? Has anyone spoken her name at a meeting? Which one? Which one laid his filthy hand on my woman? All I want to know is which one."

Kunto confirmed for his friend that while he did indeed know that Winston had the lovers separated and her jailed, he did not know who had carried out their kidnapping and whipping, her incarceration, and her punishment. He assured his friend that no mention had been made of her "by name" at any meeting he attended, yet the situation was railed about by the leader himself.

He threw his hands up in the air. "Man, they weren't supposed to touch a hair on your head, but you put up too much of a fight. You brought this on yourself! All Winston ever wanted was your full participation in the group. I heard him say as much with my own ears," he confessed, making his conscious clear. Mahmoudou raised himself on his arm, let his eyes lock with those of his companion, ensuring that there was no misunderstanding about what he had to say. "Fuck him!" Doe cursed the day the man had come to their village, the day he had let Kunto convince him to come to a meeting, as well as his refusal to let Kieta go when she encouraged more caution than he was willing to give their affair. He railed until he tired of his own angry outbursts, and his friend prayed he would not take leave of his senses. Doe concluded his rant with the same phrase he had starting the swearing, "Fuck him!" He took in a cleansing breath when he was through.

Hearing his breathing regulated, Kunto lifted his downcast eyes, asking for clarity. "You through? You all right?"

The listener nodded a nod of assent. "Yeah, I'm through! I just had to get that out!"

"I know," his friend assured him. "I can relate." That was as much as he could give Doe's anguish. His empathy was based on the relatability of the situation his friend was in, not his experience. Consequently, he could not tell him "I know how you feel."

The patient breathed a cleansing breath and fell back on the bed. His verbal tirade completed, he said, "Bring your chair closer, buddy. Let's think this through together."

His friend scooted the chair until his own head almost rested beside Doe's on the edge of the bed. The men spoke almost in whispers, plotting for Kieta Toures's release from jail and removal from the country.

Their conversation complete, Mahmoudou inquired of his friend, "You got that?"

Kunto gave his friend's question a thumbs-up then said, "I've got this!" He left the room, his full intent to make preparations to enact the plan the two friends had just devised.

~~~~~

A fortnight after the conversation about the leader of the group who originally organized to protect their city and countryside, Doe dreamed Winston came to his room and stood over his bed with the doctor by his side, telling him that the man was physically capacitated and would be able to take care of himself.

"His return to DOOR may be fraught with challenges. Mentally, Mahmoudou Ibrahaim is not the man he was before the accident." He thought he heard the doctor say to the man who had just asked, "Will he be all right?"

The patient squirmed in his bed, moaning aloud, his moans putting the two men in motion; both of them were startled. "I thought you said he was asleep," the bald-headed, bearded visitor dressed in camouflage jacket and pants said to the physician. "Let's get the hell out of here!" Another grunt from the bed set his feet swiftly in motion.

Following after the man, the medical professional offered assurances. "There is no need to hurry. He is harmless. We administer sleep medication nightly," the doctor told the visitor who had come at night well after visitors' hours were over as they left the patient's room.

"Take special care of him," Winston spoke forcefully when they were in the dusty hallway. "You are aware that we have need of him. He can secure petroleum for us at a better price than we could ordinarily get it, and we are running low at the moment. In addition to that, he will make a good lieutenant. He has the respect of most men in the community. The defenders has need of his service, so whatever it takes to make him well, do that."

"That he does! Consequently, I will." The doctor slapped the American on the back when they were at the hospital's exit. He offered up more reassurances. "Monsieur Ibrahaim is getting the best care we have to offer. We will do as you command, sir." A salute given, and one following the first one, the men bade each other "Adieu!"

When Kunto came to visit the following day, Doe spoke to him about the dream. "I had a nightmare last night. I dreamed that bastard was right here in my room, standing right there where you are standing."

The man let go of the spot where he stood, moving a bit more to the right as his friend spoke.

Scooting to a seated position, the patient continued, "He had on that same jacket he wears all the time. You know the one I'm talking about!"

"I doubt that. He is too big to visit the likes of me and you," his friend responded as he pulled a chair up to the man's bedside.

Kunto's response given, the Ibrahaim's man turned to his business. "I don't know what I am going to do when I get out of this joint. I don't even know whether I got a business left or any work to do." Worry showed on his brow for the first time in a while, and he tried to wipe it away with the back of his hand.

The visitor attempted comfort. "Your men have been working right along just like they did before the accident. We just got to get you well and out of here. Many of your customers are still around here. And there are some new ones, ones who came with the insurgents. It's just folks like my family and yours who had to flee and find refuge." He let his head drop, an action that did not go unnoticed.

For the first time in the half year that he was in the hospital, Mahmoudou thought about someone else besides himself and his personal problems. He raised his upper body, and seeing that his friend had let his head fall, he asked a series of questions, "How is your family? Is everyone all right? Or did they have to leave too?"

Kunto shook his head then looked Doe squarely in the eye before telling him, "Everybody's gone . . . To where, I don't know, but they are all gone. It's just me and you, *mon ami*, just the two of us. The elders tried to get me to leave too, but I couldn't leave you behind."

By the time the man had finished telling him of his own family's fate, Doe was seated on the bedside, facing him and patting his companion on the back. "Bring me some clothes when you come tomorrow," he told the obviously aggrieved man. "I don't have a damn thing here."

"Are you being released then?" Kunto spoke up, excitement replacing melancholy.

"You just bring me something to put on. Don't make me promenade out of here with my ass showing! This gown don't close all the way in the back, and I don't even have a pair of drawers to cover my crack. Comprenez-vous? Understand?" He lightened the mood in the hospital room.

"I didn't know you wore any," Kunto told him while giving a nod of assent. He exhilarated; his heart was happy. Doe was back in the fight. He smiled all the way out the building that day.

He would bring some clothing tomorrow. Glad that he was not the doctor who would have to deal with the man, he jumped in his truck and hastened away to make ready for his buddy to come home and resume life such that it was in Timbuktu.

~~~~~

Out of hospital, Doe did not return home. No one was there, not even the huts and houses, and tents. They had been ravaged, trashed, and burned. Consequently, Kunto took him back to the cottage on Baker Street where he had left the belongings secured from his fleeing family. He had had the place cleaned and old linens replaced with new ones. He also purchased a new couch in the living room to make it more comfortable for his tenant.

"So you tried to get rid of anything that would remind me of *ma cherie*!" Doe told him the day he brought him from the hospital.

"No, just trying to make your ungrateful ass more comfortable," his friend told him.

Doe bantered back, "I bet your ass is going to raise the rent!"

"You bet!" the Boro man chided him before he left the Ibrahaim man to his own devices.

He looked around the eight hundred square feet building with new appreciation for it. At least, he still had a roof over his head. In the kitchen, some food was in the cabinet. The bedroom had new bedding and pillows. The man took one of the pillows and held it to his face, sniffing for traces of Kieta's scent. It was gone from there, but it rested boldly in his sinus cavities, brain, and psyche.

When he got to the bathroom, he had an ever-greater surprise. "Damn. He even replaced the cracked commode top! And the mirror I beat up before I left!" He thought about how much his friend had done for him. He would have done the same.

In a minute, Mahmoudou took to the couch to rest. His body healed, he still needed to rest and fully recuperate. *Start life after Kieta!* The man shook away such thoughts and began to consider his livelihood. Time would take care of some things. Besides that, he and Kunto had done a bit of strategic planning for the future.

His physical injuries healing, he was able to go back to his daily occupation. Nevertheless, his back worried him, so he frequently wore the back brace the doctor gave him on the day of his dismissal and took pain medicine as well as drunk teas from herbs he bought at the market to make himself more comfortable.

However, his mind rested on his beloved Kieta, so he tucked his tail between his legs and did what they had discussed at the hospital—*that* he thought he would never do. A couple of weeks after he was home, he telephoned the Soyinka Residence, this time to speak openly with the man of the house, not to chat with his servant. The connection made, he asked if he could come to the Soyinkas' compound to confer with monsieur. "I have some business I would like to talk to you about."

One of Ibrahaim's customers, the man's mind went directly to petroleum. "We don't require as much fuel as we used to," Soyinka replied. "I have reduced the number of vehicles we use. My folks also stay close to the compound now that those infidels have made their presence so fully known and felt," he told the businessman.

"No, sir," the Ibrahaim man told Monsieur Soyinka, "it is not that business that I need to talk with you about. I have a personal favor to ask, and you being a fair and just man, I felt that I could come to you."

On the other end of the line, Soyinka mulled over the caller's request. He knew who he was and anticipated the business he wanted to discuss. "All right. Come by anytime. Just give me a call." And then he hung up.

Hearing the click, Mahmoudou looked at the receiver he held in his hand for but a moment. He redialed the number he had dialed so many times before with reckless abandon.

The telephone on the man's desk chimed anew, threatening to jump off its cradle. Soyinka picked it right back up. "Allo, Soyinka here!"

"I know. Can I come now?" The urgency in his voice reached the listener's ear.

He looked at the clock on his desk. It was just after one. There was a lot of daylight left, and as previously said, his calendar was open. "Sure. Come on out to my compound. I don't have any evening appointments."

"Okay!" proceeded the click that the head of the household heard.

Doe drove his truck to the property he had passed thousands of times, contemplating how he would broach the conversation about Kieta. Time dragged, and ten miles outside of town seemed like a voyage across the entire continent of Africa, as vast as it was. He let out a sigh of relief and leaped from the cab like he used to before the accident. Pain hit him. "Damn!" he emitted as he hobbled toward the door and destiny.

He rang the bell then knocked. Anxiety would not allow for patience. Mahmoudou rang the bell a second time.

Wakesa quickened her pace to get to the portal. She opened the door for the limping stranger. She looked him over, from head to toe and back, snorting disapproval because he was not dressed and did not look like the company her employer usually kept. "What can I do for you?" she asked, her disapproving eye raised as she spoke.

The man removed his cap before telling the woman, "I am here for a meeting with Monsieur Soyinka."

"Is he expecting you?" the woman inquired of the man whose apparition was hardened by pain he still felt when he overexerted himself.

"Yes, ma'am," he responded to her inquiry, one he perceived as intrusive. He sensed her desire to know what his business was but refused to engage her further. Using a contrite tone with the woman, he implored, "Please let him know that Mahmoudou Ibrahaim is here to see him."

"One minute." She reached for the wall phone to ring her master in his office to ask if her employer was expecting anyone.

"Okay, okay," she replied to the man on the other end of the line. "Yes, sir, I will."

His appointment verified by her master, Wakesa led the visitor to the library and gave him a seat before she used the phone perched on the desk to let her master know the man was in the room before asking if he would like something to drink. "Some coffee, tea, *limonharri*, water?" Wakesa named the beverages that were in the refrigerator.

"Some water, please," he acquiesced. His mouth was dry, felt like cotton balls, so he knew he would need something to help him get out of his mouth the thoughts that were in his head.

"Okay," she agreed, acknowledging the "glass of iced tea for me" given by her master as he entered the room.

Doe stood when the homeowner approached him. The two shook hands and made small talk, talk about the weather, how things were going downhill in the city, and the prices of fuel until the lady returned with their drinks.

She carefully placed each beverage on a coaster on the end table beside the chair in which they sat, noticing that Monsieur Soyinka was not seated at his desk, the stance he usually maintained when he conducted business. The men turned their attention to their drinks, each sipping from his glass, while she made her way to the door that she'd left ajar. Noticing this, the master laid his beverage aside, got up, and ensured its full closure.

Turning on his heels, the homeowner crossed the room, speaking as his bottom hit the cushioned seat. He looked at his watch too, a gesture noticed by the visitor. "Okay, what business is this we need to talk about if it is not petrol?" Soyinka cut to the chase, his thoughts of what was going on all around them.

Doe's mind flew there too. *The militants, whose struggle for an Islamic state had killed thousands and made them the biggest threat to security in Africa's top oil producer, were increasingly preying on civilians: Muslims and Christian.* Since he was in the petroleum business, they would do whatever they could to ensure his cooperation. This was certainly the case in the kidnapping and jailing of the love of his life. At least, those were his thoughts.

His attention drawn to the matter he came to discuss by the clearing of Soyinka's throat, Doe unconsciously mimicked the gesture. He cleared his own throat before emitting, "Kieta . . . Kieta Toures."

At the mention of the girl, her master's full attention was gained. He sat up in his chair. "Kieta Toures? What about her? She no longer works here."

"I know, sir," the Ibrahaim man admitted. "She is in the jail. The insurgents, they took her . . . from me." Tears welled up in his eyes, and his bottom lip quivered. He took a pause and wiped his eyes on his garment's sleeve. His head dropped, his chin almost hitting his chest; his pain was apparent.

Soyinka took another sip, giving the man time to get his emotions in check so he could finish his story.

The Ibrahaim man raised his head and spoke up. "You see, Kieta and I were lovers." He shook his head and ceased talking a moment before starting anew. "No, we were *in love*. We were not engaged in some petty affair. I still love her, and she loves me!" he spoke as he got up from his chair. It hurt to sit for any length of time. His spine could not take the pressure, so he paced as he told Soyinka their full story. He concluded with "You see, my refusal to fully participate in DOOR's clandestine activities caused our capture! Me, I got a brutal beating that almost cost me my life, and she, they jailed her! Those bastard caged her up like an animal!"

He choked up, and a sob escaped from him. "And whipped her. The judged ordered ninety lashes in the public square, and she took them! All of them. Then they locked her back up!" He retook his seat after his ten-minute disclosure and wept unabashedly.

Kieta's former boss looked on, watching the man fall apart before his eyes, and didn't move a muscle or say a thing until the other man stopped crying.

~~~~~

Both men just sat for a while. "What is it you want from me?" the listener asked when he had sufficiently mulled over the story the man had told him.

His spirits sinking fast, Doe cleared his throat and answered, "I am not totally sure of how you can help me or if you will, but I feel certain I can get her out of that holding pen, but I don't have the resources to get her out of the country. That is why I came to you. Once she is out of the stockade, she will need somewhere to go . . . somewhere, somewhere far away from Timbuktu. She will not be safe here!"

The Soyinka man retorted, his voice elevating as he spoke, "What resources do you think I have that you don't have access to? I am not a wealthy man. Like you, I work and provide for my family and my household, but as a working man, I have not amassed wealth that many of my constituents have."

Doe slid to the edge of his seat, closing the distance between him and the man. He told him about the party that Kieta had worked at the residence during the holidays. "She told me every one of import was here. Even an American ambassador and his family were in attendance. And I was thinking that you could use your influence to get her out of here, to America, New York, someplace like that."

This time Soyinka took to pacing the room, lecturing the Ibrahaim man, throwing his hands in the air as he spoke. "I did as much for that girl as I did for my own daughter. She was homeschooled alongside my children, and when she was of age, I allowed her to attend the university with my daughter at my expense. I paid her more than adequate wages, never withheld a dime when she was on duty, treated her like my own Marissa. What do I get in return? She was skipping out of school, whoring around with you on Baker Street, forsaking the rules imposed by those insurgents, talking about whom I entertained in *my* damn house, and then getting back in the car with my daughter, endangering her life because of your folly! And you want me to do what?" The man's voice rose higher in volume as he spoke.

The Ibrahaim man wrung his hands in regret, standing to meet the man eye to eye. He clasped his hands in a praying posture. "Please, monsieur, please don't blame Kieta. If you find fault in someone, find it in me! It was me who insisted that we continue to meet! I beg your forgiveness, monsieur, and plead with you for her life, not mine. She will die if she is left there . . . I am certain of that!"

At the mention of "death," the Soyinka man was startled. He had not thought about her losing her life. He paused a minute before agreeing to help get Kieta out of jail and the country. "Give me a couple of days to speak with some of my contacts, and I will see what I can do. You think about how you will get her out of that putrid stockade, all right? You do that, and I will do my part."

"Merci, monsieur! Merci beaucoup! Thank you, sir!" Kieta's beau appreciated her boss's willingness to assist with her release and getaway from Mali.

Doe floated out of the Soyinka's house, out of the compound, and headed to Kunto's place to nail down plans for getting Kieta out of jail and the hell that Timbuktu had become almost overnight.

~~~~~

When Doe and Kunto met later in the evening, they chatted a while about the interaction that took place at the Soyinkas.

"I went in there feeling so secure but was reduced to tears when I got ready to tell our story."

"What's that all about?"

"I don't know why I was so presumptuous and thought he would be jumping to help get my girl back. I guess I was thinking everybody loved her like I do." He welled up again, his thoughts of Kieta still so fresh.

Kunto decided this was a good time to change the subject and help his friend refocus. Now wasn't the time for him to go all soft on him. They had more pressing matters that would require their full attention. He arrested Doe's wandering emotions with "Winston has called a meeting tonight. Are you coming?"

Retrieving a rag from his pantaloons' pocket, he blew his nose. "You bet your ass. I am going. I wouldn't miss it!" he told his friend, facetiousness the tone. They had discussed this in detail when the man was out of the hospital and in the cottage on Baker Street. The Ibrahaim man had promised Kunto he would come to the meetings from now on, fake cooperation until the time was right before avenging his beating, and together, taking care of Kieta's misfortune.

His flippant response made his friend chide him anew. "Come on, Doe. Act right now! Don't forget what we talked about. It's better to be on the inside than watching from afar sometimes. So suck it up! Let's show up and do what we got to do! All right?"

Doe gave his friend's advice some thought. He would go along to get along, right now, but there would be hell to pay as soon as Kieta was a safe distance away. *Winston's white ass was going to be his. He was going to make him wish he had stayed in America instead of coming to the continent of Africa to wage war where no war was desired.*

Chapter Fifteen

After the Soyinka-Ibrahaim meeting took place, a conspiracy began to get the imprisoned girl out of the country. Soyinka called on his ambassador friend and some of their associates who had attended the New Year's Eve party. All agreed to help but acknowledged it would take time. Documents had to be made, a visa and passport; transportation to the United States secured; and a family to take her in once she was in the receiving country was found . . . in New York City. Needless to say, some doubted the efficacy of such a plan, but the man kept his resolve. His consistent reply to any bit of naysaying was "We don't have time. We must act now! It is a matter of life and death!"

Just a couple of weeks passed when the ambassador called to inform the girl's employer that the CIA had an operative on the ground in Mali who would handle everything. "Dubuya will see to it. He will take care of the transportation out of the country, secure documents for the girl, and find a host family."

"Who?" Soyinka asked about the man he had not previously heard known. "Dubuya!"

"Yep, Dubuya!" The man chuckled. "That's what he calls himself. He is one of those George Bush's loyalists, so he enjoys using that moniker. Don't you know him? I was thinking you did."

The man shook his head, more to himself than the caller. "I can't say that I have met anyone called Dubuya since I have been here. Are

153

you sure he can handle this business?" he asked about the man whose name was pronounced like the letter *W*.

"We will have to trust him to handle it," the caller told him. "There are some questions in the field about whether he is as reliable as he once was though. Some say he has gone rogue and is hanging out with a clandestine organization, DOOR. Anyway, they say he is the best we got on the ground in Timbuktu right now. So we are going to have to go with what we got."

"Okay."

The men talked a bit more before the caller remembered the one thing the man couldn't do. "Oh, before I forget! It may not be New York. She may have to go to Florida, which seems like the best entry point right now. And there's a host family there who will help her."

"That will work! Once she is out of here, I don't care where she goes. That girl has been more trouble than she is worth."

~~~~~

It was soon apparent that Winston was indeed the man. No more than two weeks passed before the Ibrahaim man was summoned back to the Soyinkas' compound. His appointment was free from distractions, and Wakesa made him welcome and brought his tea immediately. This time when her master came into the library, the two men met each other in the center of the room, taking each other's hands, hugging each other like brothers. Their encounter was fueled by adrenaline that came with both having full knowledge that plans had been made to get Kieta out of Mali and into America. Mahmoudou reached for his tea to take a sip. Soyinka took the glass from him, inviting him to get a drink of cognac from the bar. "I feel like celebrating!"

His host poured as he watched, and Doe took a glass of the beverage pushed toward him. He held his drink and waited for Soyinka to pour a finger for himself. The two men lifted their glasses, toasting their impending success silently, then tapped the containers before taking a sip. Doe threw the liquid in his mouth and let it slide down his throat. It scorched the man's inside as he infrequently partook of any alcoholic beverage. He shook in his sandals and shook his head side to side before laying the emptied shot glass on the table.

The Soyinka man sniffed the cognac, enjoying its fragrance before drinking, then swished his beverage in his glass before taking first one swig then another.

The Ibrahaim man was extremely anxious to hear of the plan put together by his nemesis, Winston, so he cut to the chase as soon as Soyinka let his emptied glass rest and took a seat. "Now what is this plan that that bastard has put together?" he asked, disgust for the agent apparent.

His host spoke with ease. "I am not privy to all the plans. I am just a go-between. The less I know, the better," he told Doe before offering him a seat at the desk in the large room.

Once his guest was seated, the man took a key and opened a drawer on one side of the desk. He retrieved a nine-by-eleven envelope with a clasp from it and pushed it across the desk. Doe took the communication in his hand and attempted to open the dossier, but his action caused an immediate, unexpected reaction.

"Nope, no, sir, take that with you!" Soyinka told him as he threw up his hands in surrender, coming up out of his seat while talking. "Take it to your own house! And open it when you are not in my presence. If I am ever faced with an international court case or anything pertaining to this ploy, I want to be able to say with a clear conscience 'I know nothing! I saw nothing! I heard nothing!' Is that clear? I can ill afford to get into anything that may cause me to lose my job or my life. I have a wife and family that needs me and my support. So leave here with that."

An equally anxious Doe was out of his seat in a minute and heading to the door with the folder and its contents in hand before you could blink an eye. He did not wait for any of the household servants to let him out; he let himself out, a rare occurrence indeed. Prior to his visit, the head of his household, Soyinka, had told Wakesa, the one who he knew kept vigilant and watched every move made at his residence, that her service was not needed when it was time for his guest's departure.

When the man was out of his house, and the door shut behind him, Soyinka sighed a sigh of relief. The couple of hours that he had had the folder in his possession had made his graying hair even grayer.

As soon as Mahmoudou was in his vehicle, he took his new toy, a cell phone, from the glove compartment and called Kunto. "Meet me at my place" was all he said, and then he disconnected.

However, before he could ignite the engine, the chime from the phone drew his attention. It was his friend calling him right back.

"Hey, what you need? You didn't give me time to say a word," he said. "I got a little job I need to finish. I will swing by your place later."

Doe barked, "I don't give a shit about what you doing! You can finish that later! Bring your puny ass over to my place right now!" He turned the phone off this time, wanting any message to go to his voicemail. He looked at the envelope and spoke to it. "I've got to get you to the house."

When Mahmoudou arrived at the residence on Baker Street, Kunto was already there inside. He still maintained a key to the house, and it was a good thing he did. He had used it on more than one occasion to assist his friend with something, a repair; to secure clothing for him when hospitalized; to bring medications after he was let out of the hospital prematurely; and to bring him subsistence until he could provide for his on needs.

The man jumped up from the sofa. "Okay, what's so urgent that I had to drop everything I was doing to get here?"

Pointing the dossier toward him, he responded, "This, this is what's so important. And if you will give me time to take a piss, we will take a look-see and see what's in it." He kept walking, pulling down the front of his pantaloons with his free hand as he headed for the commode, Kunto on his heels.

After he relieved himself, he turned around, knowing his best friend was in the doorway. "Back up. Get out the way so we can see what gift I got today," he said, glee in his voice.

"What's up? Your birthday come early?" Kunto asking, knowing full well that his friend's special day had already passed. Then he said, "You must have gotten some good news from Soyinka today."

"I got more than news. Let's go have a little look-see!" By then, the two friends were on the sofa, and Mahmoudou was preparing to open the envelope. It had been sealed with glue, and the clasp was also fastened, tape over it. He took a small knife from his pantaloons' pocket and was poised to open it when Kunto stopped him. "Wait, you don't know what's in there!"

"I know. That's why I am trying to open it. As a matter of fact, I am going to rip it open with this little blade as soon as you release my arm." He snatched his member from his friend's tightening phalanges.

"Suppose it's got some of that ricin shit in it! Your ass will be dead in a minute. And mine too!"

"Your little paranoid ass is about to make me regret I called you. I should have just looked in here myself and told you what it was later."

Kunto grabbed the package and ran around the room, shaking it. "It's got more than one thing in it," he told Doe.

"If you don't give me that envelope, I am going to rip your little butt to pieces with this blade."

"For real?"

"For real! Now let's see what we got there."

Seriousness overtook them, and his friend handed the package back to Doe. "Be careful. Don't cut nothing you ain't supposed to," Kunto contended.

Doe opened the envelope and peered inside, seeing what looked like a passport and visa as well as some typed instructions. He poured its contents on the coffee table. Kunto saw the navy-blue cover with gold embossed block letter "PASSPORT" on it, reached for the brochure, and opened the passport, seeing for himself a picture of Kieta. "Damn, man. This is a real passport," he acknowledged Winston's work.

"I know. It says it on the outside cover! Now hush! Be quiet so I can read what this paper says," Doe spoke, impatience, distrust, and a serious of emotions making themselves known. "I hope everything is like it's supposed to be. I don't trust that dude to do the right thing."

Kunto quietly admitted he didn't either. "I don't trust Winston and Soyinka neither!" And he waited for Doe to read and to share with him the full contents of the envelope.

The Ibrahaim man read the instructions slowly, word for word, before passing them to the Boro man for his scrutiny. He made a small noise as he came to the last line, an action noticed by the onlooker. After this, he handed the information to his friend.

The last to read, Kunto took as much time as he needed to read and ensure full comprehension. His friend kept as quiet as he had while he was reading and did not move a muscle or make a comment. When he read the last line, he understood why Mahmoudou had emitted a small, also whimpering sound. He leaned over, pointing to the line he just read, and the duo looked at the words simultaneously.

Both men hummed hums of acknowledgment when they reread the postscript, which, unlike the rest of the manuscript, was typed in bold, italicized, and reddened. The threatening words "Burn this document as soon as you have read its contents. Follow it to the letter, else the captive remains captive, and her freedom rests elusive!" jumped out at them, setting them in motion.

"Get some matches! Let's burn this shit!" the Ibrahaim man told his friend. "There is no step here that I will forget. Kieta's life depends on it!"

~~~~~

On the night that the woman was removed from the jail in Mali, three men went to the facility where they were allowed entry without question. The driver remained in the car, while the two friends went inside. They met no resistance. Everything had been previously arranged, and they followed the script they were given, no questions asked. A man who appeared to be in charge of the facility handed the key to Mahmoudou and pointed the men to her cell.

In the cell, they found her seated on her haunches in a corner, whimpering like a bruised dog, her head on her knees. Kieta's rescuers prepared to enter.

Hearing noise, she lifted her head, seeing them.

Although it was a bit dim, Doe knew instantly that it was she. Kunto had never met her, so he had to depend on him to identify her. He touched his friend's arm, and the man nodded a nod of affirmation. They were not speaking because they didn't know who was listening.

While she had lost a few pounds, her lover had recognized the woman instantly, but he was taken aback by the setting. She was in one corner of the small space, a piss pot was in the other, flies swarming over it, stooping on the rim. The only other furnishing in the room was a table constructed from two sawhorses covered with a board.

Doe, the key holder, shook his head in disgust at the sight of his beloved entrapped, her setting not fit for a dog, so he hastened to open the door and get her out of there. Becoming increasingly infuriated, he grew nervous, finding it difficult to keep his emotions in check. The sight left him unable to put the key in the keyhole and turn it. Growing increasingly unnerved by the sight, he almost dropped the key.

Seeing his inability to perform such a simple task, his friend took the key from him and unlocked the door. Doe pushed past him as soon as the door swung on its hinges and hurried to the spot where his beloved Kieta sat, cowering and shaking at their approach, motions causing him great concern.

The woman, unaccustomed to such forward movements, drew up, cowering in fear, and opened her mouth to scream. Her voice was arrested by the putting of a clothed hand over her mouth while a familiar voice whispered briskly for her to be quiet and to play dead. She paused, holding her breath against a noxious odor emanating from the rag the man held to her face, thinking for a moment that she recognized the voice and the scent of him. *Doe! Doe has come for me. I knew he would come.* Thoughts of her beloved assailed her senses, replaced by odors, fumes from gasoline . . . or something.

Her hand flew up, touching a bearded face. *No,* she told herself, *Doe never wore a beard, was always clean-shaven. This man could not be him.* She began to struggle.

Her attempt to shake him away was met with a stern but gentle "Uh-uh. No fighting. Don't pull away from me! Close your eyes and relax. Just breathe. I got you, *cherie!*"

Cherie! No one calls me that except Doe! Through the haze evoked by the chloroform, the woman determined her beloved had come for her. This was no dream. Reality made itself evident.

Certain now that the man in her cell was Doe and that no harm would come to her, she relented and acquiesced to his will. Her actions, easy feats, for she had dreamed this rescue over and over in months past. Kieta let her eyelids fall, drew the odor in with a series of short breaths, and let go, her confidence in the man who loved her and in whom she put her heart and her trust intact. Momentarily, she fell on the man kneeled beside her.

"Damn. That chloroform is the thing!" the man told his companion. "You are going to have to help me get her up off this damn floor and out of here. You know I ain't worth a damn since that accident."

"Yes, I know. You can hardly tote a gallon can of gas!" He shook his head and went to his friend's side, removed her weight from his still-recuperating friend, and swooped the woman from the floor, leaving the man to get himself afoot again. "She doesn't weigh much!" he told him when he had taken the petite woman into his arms. He tossed her around so she was facing him.

The woman's arms instinctively fell around the neck of the man who bore her deadweight. "Doe," she spoke her lover's name to the shadowy figure removing her from the jail, and then she swooned for a second time. The man who bore her corps made no reply. He was anxious to get out of the building and finish their assignment.

Mahmoudou grunted aloud as he pulled his frame from the floor, using the wall as a crutch. His knees popped, making themselves felt and heard. Upward, he hobbled over to the table and leaned on it.

"Give me that sheet so I can wrap her up," the Boro man spoke up. "It's kind of cool out there." He nodded toward the sheet he had laid on the table when they had entered the jail and cell unchallenged.

Doe's best friend bundled the love of his life in a sheet that he handed him and tossed her over his shoulders like he would a sack of potatoes. And they headed to out the facility, each hoping that the car was still there, and everything would proceed without a hitch.

Needless to say, the driver, Nouhoum, was antsy too. He was equally as glad to see them step out of the building and coming to the parking lot where he sat, engine running. The man with the girl slid into his seat, keeping her on his lap, and his unencumbered companion took up the remainder of the jeep's backseat.

The co-conspirators fled the scene, taking her to the airport to board the plane that would spirit her out of Timbuktu and to freedom, to another country where she would not be oppressed. Their journey was made in silence. Every man's attention was on their surroundings, as danger was prevalent in Mali, in Timbuktu, on the continent. Even the night had eyes!

It only took about thirty minutes to make the road trip from Mali to the airport in Bamako. There, they were accompanied to the runway by a couple of men in a jeep similar to the one that bore them.

A small Learjet waited for them on the tarmac. Short greetings given, the wrapped woman was passed from one set of hands to another. Kieta Toures's countrymen and friends watched as she was ported up the steps of the small jet and into the cabin. The door shut, and the plane headed toward the runway.

Kunto put his arms around his friend's shoulders, and they walked back to their vehicle, the former's gait swift and smooth, and the Ibrahaim man limping with pain evoked by the sending of his beloved to parts unknown. Since the beating and the accident that took place after the first event, any stressor made him miserable. Even the supportive hand on his shoulder brought pain that he bore quietly. Neither man said a word. They just moved in concert, step by step, until they were at the right passenger door. Kunto helped his friend with his mount before going to the other side to seat himself.

Their silence was broken by the Boro man. "You will see her again." He attempted to comfort Doe. "Winston will let you know where she is when he is made aware of her whereabouts. You will see her again!"

"Fuck Winston!" Doe retorted. There was nothing good that anyone could tell him about the man. "There is nothing good you can tell me about that jackass!"

~~~~~

As soon as they had gotten the girl taken care of, Kunto and Doe dumped the driver that had been provided to help spirit her away. They took to the streets and headed to the DOOR meeting where they heard the group's leader rail about hardheadedness of the villagers. "No matter how we punish them, they don't do any better!" Both men experienced collective epiphanies. They could not be a part of this. They were better than that. They were their brothers' keepers.

In private, they decided to report the insurgents' activities and plans to ones targeted for reprisal. So they kept attending meetings.

"Like I told you before, if we are going to change things, we have to be on the inside," the Boro man reminded his friend of his insistence that he come with him to the meetings early on, an invitation that man had rejected.

Now Mahmoudou agreed with Kunto, so he threw himself fully into DOOR's activities. The man became a part of the group. He participated in the clandestine group's military-style training, an activity that gave the physical therapy he needed for his physical well-being and was successful. The man's mental ability improved as his body strengthened. His competitive spirit made him lead in most activities. No one could jump higher or run faster than he or do more pull-ups and push-ups. At the firing range, no other's aim was truer than his. The man never missed his mark. He became a beastly warrior.

Chapter Sixteen

Needless to say, all Mahmoudou Ibrahaim's activities were reported to Winston. Hearing of his physical prowess, mental acuity—he was sharp as a tack, and his judgment was sound unlike it had been when the broken man initially attended their meetings . . . and how accurate his shot was—it was not long before Winston invited him to come to his tent for a private meeting.

At what he determined to be "the appointed time," the DOOR leader summoned the soldier to come to his camp for a meeting. His sentry's message shared with Kunto, the man went to the camp outside of Bamako for the appointment. "If I don't come back by nightfall, come get me!" he joked with his friend.

"Don't play with me like that," his friend told him. "This is serious!"

Playfully sparring at his friend, Doe countered his friend's admonishment with "Don't worry your head off about me. If I go in there, I am coming out alive. As for Winston, ain't no telling how he gon' be looking when I finish with him." The man, feigning a shot straight to the head, blew smoke from his pistol like he had seen done on one of those American/Western shows when he had gone to England with his father when he was a teen. Standing wide-legged, he placed his imaginary gun in a holster on his side.

His friend shook his head and told him, "Man, you know you a fool if you think you are going to get that close to him. He is going to have bodyguards all around him."

"We will see what's what, and I'll let you know when I get back," he said as he got behind the wheel and made ready to meet Winston.

Accompanied by his thoughts because he did not let his friend accompany him, Doe spent the driving time reflecting on the last couple of years he had spent with Kieta. His primary focus on the last time he had seen her.

~~~~~

When she had been passed from Kunto's arms to the man who took her aboard the plane, his heart had fallen to his knees and basically rested there. There was too little room left in his chest for the member. Love for the woman had taken up all the space not occupied by blood and molecules of oxygen. Mahmoudou had thought he would die, right there.

Nevertheless, the man, heart breaking right then and there, had feigned bravery when he was at the airport and in the company of his friends. When the aggrieved man was back on Baker Street, he had taken to his bed, cried all night, regretting he had not been physiologically capable of bearing her corps and passing her off himself. He mourned because he had not had time to hold her to himself, caress her, kiss her brow, explain what was going on, address her concerns, and make her understand before whispering an "Au revoir, ma cherie . . . See you later."

~~~~~

Shaking away regrets, the man raced along, the speed so high that he almost passed the narrow road that led to the camp. All too soon, he was at the appointed destination but was ahead of appointment time. He had to wait for more than half an hour before he was allowed in the tent for his one-on-one with Winston. For want of nothing else to do, he got out of his truck. Pacing the ground and moving along the length of the truck under the watchful eye of Winston's guards, he calmed himself. *Down, boy. It's not time. Patience, patience is the virtue that will help you achieve your ultimate goal. Patience . . ."*

This was a meeting that he had looked forward to, and it wasn't the kind of opportunity one blew by losing his temper. He looked at his wristwatch, noting that it was a few minutes past the appointed time. His gaze left the guards posted at the tent's corner to the flapping doorway. He imagined the man sitting inside, looking at his own time piece while considering how much longer he could toy with him. *That's all right! Time is all I got!* He continued with the self-talk, a calming mechanism. *He is just testing me to see what I am going to do, how I am going to act. Uh-huh, that's what he's doing. That's all right. I get it.* Doe was certain that the impetus for making him wait for the meeting was to intimidate him, make him feel he was not as important as the DOOR leader, that he deserved his invitee's respect, so it was best to try to be cool, calm, and collected and pretend he didn't give a damn. He leaned against the vehicle's door, his nerves knocking on it so loudly its sound echoed in his psyche.

A horsefly buzzed him, and he hit at the insect with his hand and caught it, his aim that true. He dropped the insect on the ground, wiped its blood on his pantaloons, and looked up to see if it was time for him to go in. He shook his head. *Nope, not yet. That bastard is just sitting on his ass in there, making me wait!* he thought. He was certain the man was in his tent. Men were traipsing in and out at will. He hit his left palm with his right fist, causing himself to stop and to wince. The man attempted to shake the pain away. His hand hurt like hell. His injuries much better, he sometimes struck a nerve somewhere, causing a bit of pain. He looked at the member. His gaze lowered. He, therefore, did not see a man almost in front of him.

"Monsieur, monsieur!" The guard who was sending him into the tent for the meeting spoke a couple of times before he gained Mahmoudou's attention. Called to attention, he jumped, startled because he had been so lost in thought and had missed his cue. "Got to be more careful, got to stay focused," he told himself as his escort led him to the tent, pulling the door open for his entrance before he could do it himself.

When he was in the tent, his mouth fell open. He could not believe what his eyes saw. There in front of him on a couch, not a box covered with cushion and rags but a sofa in much better condition than the one in his cottage on Baker Street sat Winston. Doe almost shook his head in disbelief. The self-important grandeur leaders liked to surround themselves with what would have been scary if it wasn't so ridiculous. A table was in between a coffee table, and a couple of chairs with padded seats for visitors were there too. A cursory view of the tent also showed a couple of potted, almost fully grown palm trees and a cot for its occupant to rest on when tired. Artwork, that is, paintings were on the walls. Coming to see the DOOR leader was like having an audience with a world leader or being at the Vatican with the pope. At least, that was his initial impression. At least, those were his thoughts.

He stopped where he stood and waited for further instructions. Initially, he kept his eyes on the other man in the room then gave the furnishings in between them a few more cursory, inconspicuous glances. A gun on the coffee table caught his eye. Mahmoudou observed it, willing the weapon to keep its place. He did not want the Royals man to use him for target practice. He focused outward, catching Winston's eye.

His host engaged in some theatrics of his own. Winston was thumbing through some papers and doing his best to look relaxed and in charge. He looked the man in his tent over. Mahmoudou Ibrahaim was looking much better than the last time he had seen him up close when he was in the hospital bed recuperating from the accident. Manly posturing completed, they exchanged mere glances before he made the first move. Remembering another weapon on the couch beside him, one Doe had not seen, he took a minute to unthreateningly move it from the seat to the floor and slide it under the sofa. His actions were noticed and welcomed by the invited guest.

The Ibrahaim man sighed a sigh of relief and cleared his throat. His nemesis looked up, acknowledging his presence as he shoved more papers on the coffee table aside, choosing instead to stack only the ones he needed neatly on the right side of the furniture. He leaned his supple frame to the side of the sofa, let his fingers search there for something, and then he stretched more to see what he was looking for. Doe watched his every movement. The visitor's eye fell on a Styrofoam box on the floor between the sofa and several boxes. "Oh, there you are," he said as he brought it into sight. The two men's eyes met.

166

"Drink?" Winston inquired as he opened the cooler and pulled one of those imported beers he enjoyed from the container. He held it out to his guest who rested where he had since his entry into the tent. He gestured with the bottle for him to come over, his thrusting of the drink toward Doe setting the visitor in motion.

Doe closed the distance between the two of them with a few long steps but stopped at the back of the chair. He held his stance, careful not to sit in the chair he stood next to without being asked. One hand was on the back of the furniture, his other lay freely at his side. He waited for further instructions. His mother had told her children on more than one occasion not to make assumptions. "It is better to be invited up than to be asked down." He had not understood many of the adages she had spoken when he was a child, but their meanings became clear as he aged and matured.

Their game of chess, fueled by each man's perception of his masculinity, continued. Each man waited patiently until it was his move. Both men, knowing their game, had too many solutions to chance, making the wrong move. Each man's desired outcome rested elusive to the other, so neither took a chance of making a mistake. It was Winston's move.

"Take it. Sit," Winston told him as he got up and pushed the beverage toward him. Mahmoudou was as close to this man who seemed like a giant when he was on the field, noting for the first time that he was his size, and he was merely a mortal man. He was about five feet ten inches tall and probably weighed about a hundred and eighty. They were evenly matched. *I can snatch his arm, yank him across the table, wrestle him to the floor, and break his fucking neck.* Those were Kieta's lover's precise thoughts. *I can take him out now!* Check! No, he wanted more! He wanted a "checkmate!"

His opponent felt his apprehension but didn't give it extra attention. If the Ibrahaim man started some shit, his men would be all over him before he could utter a sound. He'd never get to see his wench again. Never. No one could tell him her whereabouts. He had kept that bit of information close to his chest, so he was better to him alive. *Check!* "Here, man! Take the drink," he urged Doe on, "and relax. We'll get down to business shortly."

Doe reluctantly took the bottle, sat, and read the Samuel Adams label before twisting its cap. He was not much for beers, ales, or any alcoholic beverage but deemed it better to share in a cold one with the man. He took a sip. Its coolness proved to be refreshing. It was hot as hell outside the tent and almost as warm inside the enclosure. *He must have ice in that chest*, he thought. *Where he get ice from?*

The man finished the refreshing beverage in record time, resisting the urge to belch loudly when the bottle was empty. Doe swallowed the inclination. However, bubbles escaped his nostrils as he placed the emptied bottle in a trash bucket that was in arm's reach.

Winston took another beer from the cooler and placed it on the table so Doe could have another one if he wanted. This action completed, he retrieved the papers from the table. He also retrieved a pair of eyeglasses nearby and perched them precariously on his nose then read aloud from the documents all that he knew about Mahmoudou Ibrahaim: his family history, his schooling, his work history, everything. The dossier review completed, he chucked the papers back on the table before telling the man sitting across him, "Monsieur Ibrahaim, your people have need of you and your skills to help wage this war to maintain their basic freedoms. They respect you, and you have their confidence. On behalf of *your* people, I offer you a leadership position in the DOOR." His punctuation of the word "your" was accompanied by a pointed index finger. A recruitment tool, the member kept wagging as he appealed to the man's conscience.

Doe stirred in his chair, bringing his torso upright, locking eyes with the offering man. "Tell me more of this opportunity," he spoke assuredly. *My people, not for my people*, his thoughts. He recounted why he was fooling with the man. His interest was fueled by his desire to exact revenge on the organization's leader for what had been done to him and to Kieta.

Check! Winston thought he had made his mark. He offered the man a higher position in the organization, from a foot soldier to upper management, a lieutenant. He would report directly to him and be one of his advisors. That way, he could keep a closer watch on him.

"That's something I might be able to do successfully! Can I have a few days to think about it?" *Check!* Mahmoudou was on the inside. He would take his mark down, tear the DOOR down inside out. After that, he would kill the bastard.

"Take a week!" Winston continued, "Get your affairs in order. Get somebody to handle your fuel business. You will be with me!" His fait accompli, he picked his bottle and pointed it toward Doe who followed suit. His in the air too, the men pushed the bottles together to hail and celebrate their individual and collective successes.

Their business taken care of, both men jumped to their feet. The man who had just received a promotion headed out of the leader's tent. However, Winston was by his side in a flash, accompanying him to the doorway. When his visitor was leaving, he slapped him on the back with an open palm, put his arm around his shoulders, and pulled him closer to his side, an act that Doe found reprehensible. He grew nauseous. His current state was not brought on by the couple of beers he drank but by Winston's actions.

Chapter Seventeen

When Doe parked his truck on Baker Street, Kunto was already at the cottage, standing in the doorway, people watching. The renter hurried afoot to his home. Seeing the Boro man standing there, he thought he noticed an odd, almost nervous look on his friend's face. So he looked around too as he moved along but did not see anything out of the ordinary. *What the heck?* were his thoughts before he realized his friend was freaking out because he had stayed longer than either imagined.

Anxiety was now abated. Mahmoudou was there. Kunto was glad he had made it out of what they had previously labeled "a den of iniquity." He stepped aside to let the man in, widening the archway as he moved. The door swung freely on its hinges. It grew wide open in a matter of seconds, creating a gulf. In his haste, the Ibrahaim man almost fell in. He grabbed the doorframe and wrongly twisted a wrist still sore on the inside. He had pins in it. "What the fuck?" he emitted as he recovered from a stumble, a near fall.

The man who had waited there for him lit into him. "Man, I was worried shitless about you!" His comrade paced the floor while he told his friend how unnerved he had been. "I just about walked the bottom off my sandals while you were gone. What happened? Did you see him? What did y'all talk about?" These rolled out his mouth.

Seating himself, Mahmoudou leaned back. His head in his clasped fingers, he recounted his visit with Winston for his friend.

The tale fully told, Kunto cut to the chase. "So he offered you a position in the DOOR?"

"Uh-huh! That's what you said he was going to do." The speaker affirmed his friend's earlier assertion.

Hearing his friend speak and not liking the tone of his voice while he spoke, Kunto encouraged Doe. "Give him a break. He has proven to be a man of his word, on every count. What happened with Kieta is just as much your fault as anybody's. I kept telling you to come to the meetings, to get involved. If you had done that in the beginning, he would not have had to force your hand."

The listener raised his right eyebrow, a sign of suspicion. His hair rose on his back. *What the fuck is Kunto thinking?*

Doe sensed his friend's differing attitude. He wondered, *Has he bought into Winston's shit? Whose side is he on? Is he just scared shitless? Or just a coward?* He could have asked him, but he decided not to confront him.

Instead, he determined that he was on his own. So he turned his friend's conversation a deaf ear. He heard the Boro man's voice, but his words grew indecipherable. Doe decided right then and there to infiltrate the organization and take the man down without Kunto. It would be Ibrahaim versus Royals. He would be the fighter, his manager, his supporter, and the "winner." No ring, no audience, and no bettors, the ring at the place of his choosing, the day, the hour, the time, already appointed by destiny. He would not be encumbered by a friend with a wavering allegiance.

When the speaker had finished, he directed his attention to the only other person privy to their conversation. The Boro man saw too that his friend was no longer listening. He was speaking to the air. So he sat on the opposite end of the sofa, and seeing a bug of some sort creeping, he moved his foot, stomping softly so as to not disturb Mahmoudou who rested full of *his* private thoughts.

A quiet fell over the room, lingering in the still air.

For a moment, neither of them spoke. The silence that made itself felt soon filled with the lilt of noises that came from outside on Baker Street and the tented marketplace nearby.

Kunto got up from his seat, reached in his pocket, took the key to the cottage off a ring he kept, and gave it to Doe. He too sensed a difference. The newly found distrust making itself evident, the man grew sad. All he had done was try to protect his friend, but he knew Mahmoudou wasn't buying what he was selling.

The other man stood too. They walked to the door together, their footsteps matching each other's. At the door, Doe dropped the key he held in his right hand in his pocket. "See you later," he told the Boro, his customary, cheery adieu reduced to a flat colloquialism.

His friend nodded in agreement. "Yeah, pick me up when you head down by the way." He attempted to speak in a way that was familiar. After all, they were the best of friends and had been since before either of them could remember.

~~~~~

After that time, whenever the DOOR met, the Ibrahaim and Boro men were there, frequently front and center seated on their haunches with their ears attuned to the rhetoric spewed by the organization's leader or periodically from one of the lieutenants or even a guest speaker. And when military-style training sessions occurred, their presence was assured. Both became marksman extraordinaire. They could and did hit the homemade bull's-eye the insurgents used more frequently than not.

Simultaneously, Mahmoudou endeared himself to Winston and became a trusted servant who turned traitor. He breached the man's confidence by giving away secrets whenever he could. He warned shopkeepers and merchants when they were mentioned at meetings. Sometimes he ran interference and prevented punishments for those men and women who were breaking the group's canons. The aggrieved lover sabotaged the DOOR's efforts day in and day out, sometimes with Kunto's knowledge; at other times, he did these deeds on his own.

Since the day his friend showed what he perceived as "true support" for Winston, he consistently weighed the contents of their conversations and the degree to which an act benefitted Kunto before he involved him in any ploy. Mahmoudou worked hard to ensure that Kunto would not report his misdeeds to Winston.

Needless to say, after a while, they were discovered. Word came to them by another sympathizer that the leader was on to them, so they had to flee, abandoning their employ. Neither man could go to his workplace any longer or to his home. Doe nor Kunto wanted to be jailed or killed.

Both men had already paid a price for failure to participate in the DOOR's activities and their lack of faithfulness. They had already lost their families . . . Now their employ was gone. For a while, they managed to maintain their own lives by mimicking other resisters' lifestyles. Doe and Kunto spent days asleep in homes of other sympathizers or wherever the enlarging group of homeless Malians gathered to rest, their hobo-style existence tiring and distressing.

Soon, the duo came to the attention of another group that opposed the insurgents, so they hooked up with them. They were tired of being hungry and not fed, sleeping any and everywhere with one eye open, and constantly looking over their shoulders. So they signed up readily with this newly formed yet unnamed group. Within a matter of months, the two lifelong friends received more training in guerilla warfare and use of weapons, the popular AK-47s, and in bomb-making. Side by side, they exercised true grit, fighting against DOOR members, one on one or in groups. It was like old times, the thing that had come between them lost in the melee.

Doe stole a handgun, a small thirty-eight-caliber pistol, during one of these marksmanship training sessions. He did it free from worry because no one actually kept up with the small arsenal, so he was not in any type of jeopardy for this act. The weapon actually could have been his for the asking. He simply pilfered it and a box of bullets when an opportunity presented itself.

When he showed the gun to Kunto several days after he had swiped it, his friend wanted to know his intentions, so he asked, "What heck?"

Glee showing all over his face, he spoke up. "Meet Winston!" the Ibrahaim man told his friend of the weapon he had secured with an express purpose. "This piece has a name on it. I took it because it's small enough for me to hide yet powerful enough to make its mark sure." He held the weapon eye level with outstretched arm as he envisioned discharging it in the eye of the man who had taken his Kieta from him. "Pow!" exploded from his pursed lips.

"Man, you are loco!" Kunto told his friend. "Winston Royals ain't gon' to let nobody get *that* close to him!" He chuckled aloud. "No damn body! After what we did, you think you gonna to get *that* close to him, close enough to use that little piece?" The man hunched his shoulders then continued his verbal tirade. "You would have been better off taking one of those AK-47s!"

Hearing no response, he looked directly at the man. Kunto noticed that his friend was giving him little attention, the weapon his object of affection. Doe continued to speak, talking more to himself than anyone else. "Nobody but me and my Winston! We'll figure out something," Doe spoke assuredly with endearment of the weapon before he kissed the chamber that held the bullets.

Kunto yelled, "Man, you crazy as hell! You are going to get both of us killed!"

His argument fell on deaf ear. His friend countered, "You are going to get your own self killed! All I know is you better get you a weapon and stop waiting on these infidels to give you one. War is everywhere. You don't know who to trust anymore, so you better be ready!"

The Boro man shook his head again.

"Come on, come on!" Doe cajoled him, thrusting the weapon toward the crazed man. "You know you want to try it out!" A brief pause took place before his friend let out a sigh, reached for the weapon, and spoke, resignation in his voice. "Why not? Let me try her out."

"Wait a minute. Let me load it," Doe said as he took some bullets from his pocket and reloaded the revolver. Clicking the cylinder back into position and checking the safety first, he offered the gun, grip first, to his bestie.

The awaiting man took it from his hand. He looked around, trying to find a target.

Seeing a clump in the desert, the gun's owner pointed toward some debris several yards away. "Hit that!" he told his friend.

Pow! Pow! Pow! Kunto missed with the first shot but hit the debris five times in a row after the miss, making shreds of it.

Amused by the surety of the gun's shot, the weapon's owner asked, "What you think about that?"

"It's the bomb!" Kunto used an expression that was not part of his customary vocabulary. The words simply tripped out of his mouth, one after another.

~~~~~

Shortly thereafter, they came across one of Doe's business associates, a member of Winston's security team, at a relative's funeral.

"Man, we miss you!" the DOOR member told Mahmoudou. He kept talking, not giving the hearer a chance to reply. His sentences tripping over one another, his wanting to make Doe aware of Winston Royal's desire to have him back in the organization clear. The speaker said a couple of times, "He talks about you all the time. He says he know you was mad about what happened with your girl, and it wasn't about the movement. I know he will take you all back. I will talk to him for you if you want me to."

The messenger's speech did not go unnoticed, the Ibrahaim man's ears opened, wider. His interest obviously peaked, Doe and the man made arrangements to continue their conversation later. "See what he say," he told the man. "And meet me over near the marketplace in a weeks' time." He spoke easily, willing the excitement he was feeling at the prospect of meeting with Winston to be patient. His mother had told her anxious son on more than one occasion, "*L'enfant*, you got to be patient. La patience, c'est une vertu." The thought of her brought a smile to his face. "I'm going to wait 'til the time is right," he responded aloud to a past encounter. "I am going to be patient all right."

Mahmoudou Ibrahaim had created a wealth of scenarios of how he was going to meet the DOOR leader, but none had seemed feasible even to him. The few he had proposed to Kunto had also fallen on deaf ear or disbelieving psyche. Although they still hung out together, there was little that they shared in common anymore, just space. The Boro man, war-wearied and sick of the whole thing, preferred to talk about the past, not the matter he found so pressing. So he decided to share this information with his friend solely when he was certain that a meeting could take place and there was a real, not contrived possibility of rejoining Winston's group.

~~~~~

Winston's security team member kept the conversation between his distant relative and himself alive. "What tent? Where do you want me to meet you?" He wanted to be certain of their meeting place before they left the funeral. He had no way of contacting the Ibrahaim man after their departure.

Doe cocked an eye at him then spoke. "You just be in the marketplace! I will find you!"

The man hunched his shoulders. "Okay, that works for me," he said before the two shook hands and separated.

The week passed rapidly as Doe awaited the meeting. He was actually surprised to find Winston's man there in the marketplace. He was near a hut checking out a bunch of medicinal herbs the following Thursday, the very spot where he was supposed to be. No one of consequence appeared to be around him. A bunch of women and some children—mothers, wives, and single women—often congregated there to get herbs for teas. The only man, the shopkeeper, was behind the counter. Nothing suspicious there, but the Ibrahaim man still proceeded with caution.

Close to the stand, he stopped. The man he was meeting looked up, catching his eye. Mahmoudou paused as their eyes met. Kunto was with him, so he touched his friend's arm, causing him to stop. "Wait for me here," he said. "I am going over there to talk to him," he pointed toward the DOOR member.

"Shit! You know who that is!" Kunto exclaimed as he came to a full stop. His sandaled feet dug into the packed dirt street. He wanted to flee but was planted there by fear.

"Yeah, that's Winston's man. Me and him got a little something to talk about. I'll tell you about it when I get back." Doe spoke with more confidence than Kunto currently showed. "Go over there!" He pointed out a spot where he would catch up to his friend then sauntered off, his air of confidence intact, whistling as he made his way over to the back of the medicine shack.

"Excusez moi," he said to the women and children as he crossed their path. And he spoke to the medicine man. He knew the man, and the man knew him. He had been a regular customer. He had purchased from him an herb that made his sperm less fertile. The man had not wanted to impregnate Kieta, so he drank tea made from the herbs the elder prescribed before their couplings. At the thought of her, his manhood stirred. He adjusted his pantaloons and followed the man to a more private spot.

"Hey!" The medicine man tried to flag him down, but Doe kept moving.

Kunto threw his hands up to his head. Shocked beyond measure at his friend's revelation, he did as Doe bade. He moved inconspicuously to another shanty replete with foodstuffs and pretended to shop, his mind on what in the world the two men were talking about.

He had seen them talking at the funeral but had not accosted his friend about their conversation. Since the day they had had a falling out of sorts, he waited for Doe to speak, never asking questions, for his desire was for things to be like they used to be. They had been the best friends and had been since childhood, could talk about anything. He wouldn't trade their friendship for all the tea in China, so he did as the man asked.

Once the two men from differing camps met, they greeted each other, and without either suggesting it, they moved away from the crowd. They talked, still keeping their voices low and even. No emotion showed on either's visage. This was strictly business. Winston's man made the Ibrahaim man cognizant of the leader's willingness to "let bygones be bygones" and arranged a meeting in a tent outside Timbuktu near a small clump of trees.

"Okay, I will be there Tuesday." Mahmoudou gave the emissary his word. His thoughts were *And I don't want no mess!* But he didn't say what was on his mind.

Knowing full well that trust was indeed an issue, the other cut to the chase. "I will be there to ensure your safety as well as his," the man told Doe before departing. Their business had lasted about five minutes; nothing more was forthcoming from either man.

Kunto watched as his friend turned his back to their foe and walked away, his gait sure and his head high. He never bothered to look over his shoulder. He knew his pal was watching his back. In a few minutes, in less time than his meeting took, he stopped near a path leading out of the buzzing marketplace. A tossing of his head sideways set the Boro man in motion, and he headed to the spot where Mahmoudou stood in wait.

"Come on. Let's get out of here," Doe said as soon they were beside each other. Kunto fell in step, his footprints paralleling those of his friend. Silence joined them as they headed away from the marketplace so they could speak in private about the arrangements Doe had just made.

When the friends were sure of their privacy, Doe told the Boro man about the impending meeting between him and his adversary.

"You sure you want to do that, bro?" Kunto asked him.

"As sure as I am standing here speaking to you," Mahmoudou spoke, certainty in his voice.

The listener grew nervous, and a slight chill overtook him. His own voice quivering slightly, Kunto asked the question he thought his friend expected. Clearing his throat to release words that threatened to stay where they were, he managed to emit, "You want me to go with you?"

Doe stopped, the cease in step not anticipated, and the two almost collided, Kunto rear-ending him. He turned to face the quizzer. Coming to a screeching halt, his companion found himself eye to eye, nose to nose with the man who told him without reservations, "That's on you, man. If I have to go by myself, I will do just that."

Chapter Eighteen

Tuesday came fast, and after submitting an inquiry to the gods, Kunto did what he had always done. He followed his *ami*. When the Ibrahaim man borrowed a jeep from one of their acquaintances to make his way out to the spot where the meeting was to take place, his friend leaped into the passenger seat of the vehicle almost before the driver was in his seat. This time he strapped the harness. He did not like to wear a seatbelt but did this time. His psyche was preparing him for the flight that this ride would be. When he finished, he looked over at his friend. Seeing an unusual creasing of his forehead, he noted to himself that the man who was always so cool, calm, and collected may be stressing beyond measure.

The driver turned the vehicle's ignition and received an immediate response from its engine. He set the rearview mirror to suit his needs then gave the ones on the outside scrutiny.

Momentarily, they sped out of the city toward the appointed place. The wheels on the truck spun, knocking dust, rocks, and debris as they rolled on toward their destination. The two men rode in silence for a while before Kunto cleared his throat, the sound causing an immediate reaction.

"What? You don't want to go. You can get your scary ass out right here." The driver hit the brakes as he spoke, causing the tail end of the jeep to swerve a bit.

179

The passenger, thrust forward by the vehicle's movements, threw his right hand forward, touching the dashboard to brace himself. He used his other hand to keep the seatbelt from choking him.

A spew of expletives flew from the driver's lips as he took off again, accelerating as he maneuvered the vehicle more carefully, thankful he had avoided a rollover that could have come with overcorrecting his steering.

As soon as they were aright, an adequate response was given the "darns and damns" Doe had given the simple clearing of a throat.

"Ain't nobody said a damn thing, man. A person can't clear the dust out of his throat without you acting crazy. I tell you what! You just drive. That's what you do! And keep your eyes on the f—ing road!" Kunto shifted in his seat, ensuring comfort anew, and pointed ahead to their destination.

Doe broke into a crazed laughter. He hit the seat beside his friend and apologized. "I am sorry, man. I know I am being a little melodramatic! I promise I will do better."

"Okay." Kunto accepted his apology as they continued their trek. They skipped and hopped over bumps made on roads by explosives that had been expelled by one faction or another in squirmishes and battles taking place as Mali had grown more divisive.

The driver hummed along with the engine, no particular tune in mind. His tune soothed the savage beast inside him. He knew Kunto was on to something. He needed to keep himself calm, in check, else he might make a terrible mistake.

Soon, Winston's camp that was bathed in orange appeared on the horizon. The hum from the environs met their ears, causing the friends to attend more to their surroundings than anything else, even each other. Just outside the camp, they were waved to a stop by armed guards. "You got business here?" one asked them when he was at the driver's door.

"Got an appointment with him." The driver pointed toward a tent that was obviously that of the leader of the group.

Before more interaction took place, the man who had made the arrangement was beside the other guards. "They are all right. Let them pass," he said.

Doe didn't wait for more. He drove quickly but cautiously as close to the tent as guards would allow and got out to go in. He reached in the cab and got his weapon, the trusted AK-47. Kunto mimicked his movements.

The guards reached for their guns, and both men gave up their weapons before they were allowed entrance into the doorway of the tent.

Upon entry, with no words exchanged between the two, Winston passed his own gun to his guard, a sign of his sincerity, his desire to befriend a man who could advance his personal agenda—to make DOOR legitimate, a force to be reckoned with. The guard waited for his dismissal, which came momentarily.

"I'll call you if I need you!"

One of the guards peered suspiciously at the two men who were inside with them. "You sure, boss?" he questioned the man.

Winston gave his apprehension a wave of his hand. He confidently told the concerned comrade, "It'll be all right. I got a couple of things to do when they leave, so we will get down to business now. I will be sure to call out if I have need of you."

The men quickly left the tent so their boss could do his bidding.

"*Bienvenue!*" the DOOR leader greeted the men in French, a language he was fluent in. He knew that Mahmoudou Ibrahaim was a student of languages as well. The Ibrahaim man had attended the university in Mali. The language had been part of his curriculum when he studied international trade and marketing. While he had not graduated, opting instead to work in his family's petroleum business, he was indeed a learned man.

We must make peace with him, whatever it takes. He will certainly get better when we reveal the whereabouts of the girl. I hate we had to resort to kidnapping and spiriting her away . . . but we couldn't let him disrespect us like he was. Others would have thought us weak were Winston's thoughts as he offered Doe and his friend seating in his tent. "Us." The crazed leader had come to think of himself as a trinity of sorts. He never spoke singularly, never owned up to what the "I" did.

While Doe was taking his seat, Kunto's attention was drawn to the ornate, the well-furnished and decorated fissure plunked out in the desert, almost in the middle of nowhere. His friend's description of Winston's tent had left him wanting. He never could have imagined the likes of this here, in Mali, especially since they were not at some billionaire's home. It was even cool in the tent. A ceiling fan and another on a stand in a corner were whirring, an indication that the man had use of a generator. A whistle of awe escaped his lips.

Both of the other men looked at him, their eyes off each other for but a moment. Trust had not yet been established.

"Come over here, Boro, and sit," the Ibrahaim man spoke before Winston could call his guards and have his accomplice dismissed. His mind on those things he had not shared with Kunto, he felt secure with him at his side for today's meeting.

Their host made them welcome to beers from his cooler. Both joined him in downing a couple of bottles, each sipping and seeing as they sized each other up. Each man's thoughts were on achieving their personal goals, the purpose for their meeting. Winston's mind was on making Mahmoudou a member of the organization's leadership team and Doe's on beating the crap out of him until he told him where Kieta was.

Soon, the men were making small talk about the weather, dry as it was. It was 86 degrees Fahrenheit outside with passing clouds, but it felt more like 83 because the humidity was about 30 percent. Their city, how it had grown, then suffered loss; the future, how if they cornered the petroleum market, they could advance their own agendas. All things masculine but nothing about what they were there to discuss, nothing about forgiveness because Doe had failed to respond to DOOR's call to action, and nothing about anything of import to Kunto's friend.

Their comfort level fueled by alcohol, Winston made yet another warm gesture. He reached for his hookah to share a smoke with the men. He salivated, the thought of the good stuff he possessed, almost overwhelming.

The Royals man had abandoned the use of tobacco in the water pipe he had secured in Egypt on one of his many visits there. He had replaced the tobacco with another substance for which he had an affinity—ganja. His intent on making peace and bringing the men over to his side, for good, this time he set the apparatus on the coffee table separating him from his guests.

His visitors watched while their host filled the base with a bottle of water that was already on the table. Winston leaned to his right and retrieved a bottle of liqueur from the floor, uncorked it, and splashed a shot of it in the water before ensuring that the shaft was submerged about an inch. Next, he inserted the neck of the pipe into the base semi-filled with the substance and screwed it in to ensure a snug fit. He was trying to get a reasonably good seal. He didn't want any of the smoke to escape.

"Now!" he emitted when he was sure the apparatus was ready for filling.

Doe and Kunto watched in silence while he reached under the coffee table and put a box from the floor on the table. The box held a variety of tobaccos and shisha as well as the coveted marijuana. The man fingered a couple of containers, and seeing his favorite one labeled Lebanese Bombshell, he put it up to his nose, taking a whiff of the cedar flavor it held. His apparition changed, the transformation noticed by the two friends who were seated side by side. Kunto touched his friend with his knee; Doe kept his eyes on the man who couldn't seem to make up his mind about what he was going to put in that ceramic bowl that laid waiting to be filled.

~~~~~

Winston Royals's whiff of shisha, his favorite Lebanese Bombshell, transported him from the tent in the desert on the continent of the African country to a cedar forest in his own homeland in the Pacific Northwest, USA, in a small community between Seattle, Washington, and Vancouver, Canada. His mind took wings, traveling 6647.7 miles or 10698.4 kilometers from Timbuktu, Mali, to his hometown, the 13-hour, 48-minute trip taking a nanosecond in "brain time."

He faded out for a short time. Soon, he was standing on his family's property, gazing at the nursery, seeing the saplings that grew to mature trees that not only bordered their property but also that of others in his neck of the woods. A breeze stirred, sending the fragrance of cedar to where he now sat in Mali, outside Timbuktu. Mahmoudou Ibrahaim saw his mind take leave and peered to see if he could see where the man had gone. He could only imagine.

At the cedar trees bordering his family's property, the DOOR leader's life flashed before him: skipping around the tree farm, helping his father water the saplings, running down the treelined dirt lane, his older brother and younger sister and he racing to catch the school bus to elementary school, not having to seek employment elsewhere when in high school, cutting and trimming cedars for Christmas trees, and then banking the money that he made to take care of his needs during the remainder of the school year and first date and subsequent trysts with Janet. He had been a pretty good basketball player, and the cheerleader had sought his attention.

The man's countenance changed when he thought about the girl who had broken his heart. "Dang," Doe said more to himself than to his friend when he saw the sadness that took Winston over.

"Huh?" Kunto asked.

Doe shook his head and put his finger to his lips to shush the man. He had eyes and ears for Winston only.

The thinker and Janet dated all the way through high school and attended college at the local school. An athlete, his thoughts like most young men his age had been on going to the pros, but his dreams were thwarted by injury and inconsistency. His parents hoped he would return to the cedar tree farm when he completed the bachelor's degree in marketing and management. However, by that time he and the love of his life were married, and with her encouragement, he left home, she did not want to live there, and "grow Christmas trees." The woman wanted to see the world, so soon, Winston found himself serving in the military. A seriously decorated Gulf War veteran, the man who did three tours was jilted by his wife while he was gone. She fell in love with his best friend.

Almost twenty years after giving up a lucrative business to satisfy that woman, here he was in Timbuktu in Mali. An independent contractor because he did not want to live in the United States, be on the same continent with her, he did construction work. Any odd job he could pick up, and periodically, he served his country when there was need for an American to do some intelligence or counterintelligence activity. He was also a CIA operative of sorts . . . one full of secrets. He had gotten those papers to get Doe's girl out of the country, arranged her transport, and secured a host family. His thoughts at the present time. *Nobody knows where she is except me!* He was almost exhilarated but kept control of his face, would not let the smile threatening to show itself appear.

The man looked across the table at the Malians, catching their eyes briefly. Afterward, he shook thoughts about Mahmoudou's woman

184

out of his mind. His psyche was conjuring up the cute, nondescript yet enticing redhead he had fallen in love with when she asked him to come to her church.

In spite of the fact that Seattle had almost a hundred churches— Baptist churches, Methodist churches, Roman Catholic, Pentecostal, nondenominational and all types of Christian churches, and even synagogues—Winston's family did not go to church much. The only times he could recall going was when there was a funeral or wedding. His father was driven, spent most of their waking hours at the nursery or in the fields tending trees. Winston had to work in the cedars on weekends, including Sunday morning worship hours. If one were to ask if he was "atheist," he would decline that label because he did believe in a higher power, especially when he was in a jam.

And he had been in quite a few when he was in "the war" in the Middle East. He had seen action on more than one occasion. His mind took him to Bagdad. *Boom!* All of a sudden, he could hear bombs. *Boom! Boom!* And screams.

He was in a Humvee, riding in the middle seat between the driver and his best buddy, riding along, joking, and talking about "taking leave." *Boom! Bam! Bang!* They were just cruising along. Their smooth ride took a turn when the vehicle they were in was struck and its side blown off.

Winston thought about how he and a couple more men in his unit scrambled out of the damaged transport, hauling a hundred pounds of gear, including his body armor. The man had wanted to sprint like he did when on his high school's track team but couldn't. For a moment, he stood, frozen, dirt, and debris making things dim.

The man patted himself down, feeling for all his limbs, and determined he was safe and still whole. He parted the mist with his fingers and coughed loudly to clear his lungs, the same thing other survivors were doing. Soon, a cursory view showed that the Humvee's driver was dead; both his legs were blown off, one arm too.

He forgot himself, noticing that a couple of others were barely alive; his best friend was one of them . . . eerie quietness after everything was over. With little thought of the enemy that was among them, he dropped his pack and searched for other survivors. He followed the groans of the wounded and started plucking fellow soldiers from wreckage. He attended to them until medics who had not been far behind were there.

~~~~~

The man shook his head where he sat, attempting to shake away the past and return to the future. Here he was in another war zone, a different one, however. He had been so lucky while in this African nation. While the insurgents had fire power, they rarely seemed to be able to aim mortars with a lot of accuracy; however, a few of the near misses had caused "Lord, have mercy!" to have flown from his lips on more than one occasion.

The Royals man had gone to the Baptist church back home, some after he was "with Janet," but he had no affinity for organized religions. He had never believed in fate or destiny or whatever people liked to think or blame for what befell them. His philosophy was that life was whatever it was. Survival was merely a matter of "if it was your time, it just was." It didn't have nothing to do with luck. You got what was yours, and the next man got his.

He smirked, his mind on being affiliated with DOOR, an organization with goals to defend citizens of Mali and its environs against insurgents who wanted everyone to embrace their beliefs, especially women who seemed to have gotten out of control in recent times. That was the only thing he could relate to, *women out of line*. Janet, *out of line*, divorced him and married one of his friends.

She ought to be over here! he mused. *I would cover her ass up all over! Keep her in the house, barefoot, pregnant. She wouldn't even be able to drive!*

The tick and tock of an alarm clock he owned garnered his guests' attention. Mahmoudou and Kunto's lids raised simultaneously as if they had been orchestrated. Both men let their eyeballs' glance fall on each other before returning to the object of their collective ire. They breathed sighs of discontent, their breaths in sync too. Both men were ready to get the hell out of there. Their business was taking too long.

Some thirty minutes! The Boro man's mind was on the amount of time his friend told him they would be there when they were on the way to Winston's camp. Thirty minutes had come and gone. *How much more time is this going to take?*

Doe, on the other hand, was not concerned about the time. He was wondering *if* he could carry out his plan. *If I don't, I don't know when I will get another chance.* His mind turned to *his own Winston.* That *thirty-eight* was weighing him down. He cleared his throat, bringing the DOOR leader back to the present.

Attending anew, their host asked casually, "Want another beer?" Both men turned him down, so he finally laid the package of cedar-tasting and smelling shisha aside, opting for the ganja, the intoxicating substance he perceived would be a treat for his guests. The dope he had was not easy to come by. When the water pipe was ready, he took a drag, giving it to first Doe then to Kunto. Doe was careful to stay lucid enough to take care of his personal business. He let his friend smoke as much as he wanted to smoke.

When Winston took a long, albeit final drag, his mind returned to reverie, and he relentlessly whipped himself for his current state of affairs. *How in the hell did I get here? I am not one of them. I am me. My face is not black like those dudes sitting on the other side of the table. What the fuck? I could have been anything I wanted to be! A tree farmer, a politician, even president. If that college cheerleader, George, the one who was president when I found my way over here could do it, I could have done that too. Instead of trying to help these jackasses over here get their women in check, I could have been home, leading my own country.*

The DOOR leader's mind went futuristic. A dying man was supposed to have flashbacks, his life up until the present moment visit him, not be flashing forward like his was doing or blinking like a lightbulb before it blows. Maybe, just maybe, he would live another day. Doe considered this as he watched Winston and read his mind. The hunter shook his head at his prey. *Your number is up today!* was his adversary's only thought.

Winston shifted in his seat. His thoughts turned to being invited to a service by one of the guys who worked with him, listening to an Imam and considering conversion. He liked their views on the man being the head of everything as well as subservient women.

If he had kept a tighter rope on "his woman," he would be back in the Seattle area, enjoying the comforts of home. He loved to go out to Pike's market after work on Fridays, get some fresh salmon, and take it home to be blackened like his mother taught him.

The Royals family always had fish on the last day of the workweek with green salad, potatoes, and hot bread. Someone would make a raspberry vinaigrette for salad while spuds baked in the oven (sometimes paring them for frying) and stir some honey into butter to be heaped on hot buns as soon as they were pulled from the oven. The man who loved real butter, he was not a fan of margarines.

The man almost drooled, catching his spittle before it could drop from lips, relaxed by the mere act of smoking. He was getting hungrier by the minute. That shit always made him ravenous as a wolf, so he anticipated grabbing a bite of meat being roasted in a pit not far from his tent. One could always find food in his camp.

Doe's mind rested on his target. He was considering when he would make the destined move. His adversary continued with entertainment, attempting hospitality where there was no need. *What? What's he doing now!* He peered at the man, his patience being tested. His thoughts were on how sick of the charade he was.

As for the other man, his attention turned to "the good stuff." Laying the canister of Lebanese Bombshell aside, Winston "Dubuya" Royals instead opted to enjoy a bit of cannabis. It was, after all, a special occasion. He smiled briefly at the men across from him as he did his business. The man loosely filled the apparatus's bowl to the required height. With experience, he had learned how much a person needed to put in the small vat. It depended on how long a person wished to smoke.

Next, he took a small amount of foil, just bigger than the top of the ceramic bowl, and covered it with a piece of foil he kept in his "smoke box" for this express purpose like he was trying to make a lid for it. Then he got a large safety pin and poked some small holes into the foil.

His guests watched as he worked his nimble fingers quick and sure. Neither owned such apparatus, and neither smoked frequently, only on occasions when they were in the company of someone who used tobacco and who, like Winston, wanted to share.

Their nemesis picked a coal from the pack and simply lit it with a lighter, heating what he labeled a "quick coal" until it was red hot. He spoke aloud as he proceeded. "You see," he told them, "you have to wait 'til the coal stops 'fizzing' and is no longer giving off any smoke. This is what makes a difference in the flavor!" He drooled at the thought of tasting the dope.

It was Kunto's turn to question why they were still there. He told himself, "This fool is going to get us high and kill us!" He shivered where he sat, his movement drawing his friend's attention. Doe gave him an assuring eye. So he let anxiety loose and watched how carefully their host placed the hot coal on top of the foil around the center.

After what seemed like forever, Dubuya spoke, excitement in his voice. "Ready!" he announced then demonstrated inhaling. He was not sure whether these boys had had any smoke and had not asked. Winston rested hospitable. He hunched his shoulders and began his smoking ritual.

The man bent his head and inhaled through the hose until smoke was bubbling down through the water and out of the pipe. He inhaled with his lungs while "hitting" the pipe, exercising care not to further inhale like one does a cigarette after he takes a hit. Winston gestured to his guests to take a hit from the water pipe; they did. Doe first as one would expect. Kunto mimicked his friend's actions. Their host hit it again after them.

As they smoked, Winston relaxed. He almost swooned. The smoke's taste perfect, it brought euphoria that was almost orgasmic. *Damn. This shit sure is good* became his thought.

Not Mahmoudou Ibrahaim; he did not let himself melt away with the smoke. Instead, Doe's resolve grew as he watched the DOOR leader enjoying the drug he had already heard was his "delight." He shook his left leg as if to straighten the leg on his pantaloons and leaned over, his movement quick and fluid, then came up, firing a single bullet from the weapon he had concealed there.

Kunto, on the other hand, grew content and just wanted to lie down on Winston's brocade-covered couch. He was almost as messed up as their host; nevertheless, his mellow was interrupted by a singular "Pow!" His eyes flew from his friend to their foe, and he did not believe what he saw.

Doe's friend jumped up from his seat, his buzz fleeing as well. "What the fuck? What did you do, man?"

~~~~~

Comfort established, Mahmoudou had put a bullet in his adversary's head. Utilizing the weapon he had named after the man, he made a clean shot in the middle of the eyes, a shot that left the deceased with a visage frozen in surprise.

Winston barely had time to react before the trajectory made its mark. When he realized he was headed for assassination, his heart ceased. Consequently, blood coagulated where it was. Not a drop was wasted. No movement was made by the corps that had just a moment ago been warm, vibrant, self-assured, and headed for making its murderer his right-hand man.

If one considered the lack of running blood, not a trickle cascaded down the forehead toward the deceased man's brow, an autopsy report could possibly indicate he suffered cardiac arrest and was already deceased when the bullet went through his cranium.

Silence permeated the air and was broken when his companion hurriedly relinquished his perch. "What the fuck? What have you done? Doe, you are crazy man! Look what you did! How are we going to get out of here?" Questions and comments tripped over one another as they fell from Kunto's lips.

"Just like we came in, through that door. Ain't nobody coming in here until he calls for them." Doe pointed to the opening where they had made their entrance. He returned his weapon to the secret place and went over to the couch. The man laid the dead man's corps on its side and checked for his wallet. Finding it, he took the wad of American currency out of it and placed it in a pocket on his dusty pantaloons.

Without being prompted, Kunto rushed over to the doorway. He wanted out of there, and Doe was not moving fast enough for him. He peered out, and noticing Winston's men still in their places, he proffered, "They still over there, by the canteen. Come on, man! Let's get the hell out of here."

"Why are you acting like a pussy?" Doe spoke harshly to his friend as he sauntered over to the opening. Pointing at the men in the camp, he continued, "Those buttholes out there can't hear a damn thing that is going on in here. Can you hear them over here?"

Kunto shook his head in negation.

"See." The Ibrahaim man turned his attention to others. "Look at that bunch over there. They are over there filling their bellies. They don't give a shit what is going on in here!"

His friend craned his neck as his friend assured him they were going to be all right. Doe stepped in front of him and beckoned for him to come on.

"Follow me!" he ordered his companion as he stepped outside in the open air, pausing just a moment before making his way inconspicuously across the length of the yard over to where the other men sat, munching on bits of bread and meat.

Kunto followed on his heels, his breath hitting his friend on the back of his neck.

"Damn, man. Get off my back!" the Ibrahaim man uttered, causing the distance between them to enlarge.

Doe reached the group first, seated himself, and took some meat from a fork held by one of Winston's men, pulling a bit of the *mischoui* for himself before putting it on a bit of bread and partaking it. He exercised care to be as normal as he had been when they come in the camp. Mouth full, he asked one of the other men to pass him a beer, which he did.

"Y'all finished in there?" another asked as he gestured with his head toward the huge tent they had just left.

"Yeah," Mahmoudou told the speaker, adding, "your boss say he'll call you when he finish."

Winston's security detail lead nodded in agreement. It was not odd for their boss to take a nap after he had visitors, especially when they took to the pipe and made peace. While "smoke" left most folks munchy and having to snack right away, the American would often fall asleep when he was high. He would call out for a feast when he came back down to earth. The listener rested certain that his boss would have already called out if he had had need of them.

The guard turned to Kunto who stood waiting for the man with whom he had entered the camp to make a move. "Go there. Retrieve your weapons." He pointed toward the ones they brought with them.

The Boro man did not move quickly. His feet were planted in their places. His legs felt like they had lead in them. He had no idea what was going to happen next. Doe had gone off script. His friend had not revealed his attentions to him, and admittedly, he was peeved. He had a right to be. The man had placed his life in danger without his permission. He was thinking about how he was going to give him a piece of his mind when he heard the guard say again, "Your guns are over there. Your man here can get them while you finish your beer."

"You hear that?" Doe asked, elevating his voice to get his friend's full attention. "Get our weapons." He gestured with his head toward the place where his friend needed to go.

Despite the weight he currently bore, Kunto willed his legs to transport him to the spot where the man pointed and gladly secured the guns they brought with them. Their weapons in tow, he hastened back to where his friend squatted on his haunches, joking with the DOOR members.

As soon as he was by his side, Doe stood, and his accomplice pushed his weapon in his hands, pressing it firmly. The retriever felt the urgency in the man's body. His friend's anxiety set them in motion to the borrowed vehicle and away from the camp.

Arriving at their transport first, the shooter got in the passenger seat. He needed to watch the road and their backs. He thought it would be better if Kunto drove this time.

The unnerved driver backed the truck up a piece, rotated, and headed out of the camp, his speed the same as it had been when they had come, slow and with caution. However, he put the pedal to the medal when they were outside the camp and on the main road. Silence accompanied them these first couple of miles toward freedom.

Both men sighed a sigh of relief when no one pursued them. "Whew!" Doe exclaimed, his verbal expiration more for himself than for his friend. He had to let go of some of what had been bottled up in him for months.

It was at this point that the Boro man let go too. He was indeed sick of Doe and his mess, so he raked his friend over the coals, emotion showing in his voice. "What were you thinking? You could have gotten us killed!" he yelled at the man while pummeling and pounding the steering wheel with a fisted right hand, he steering with his left one. "What are we going to do now? Shit is going to hit the fan when they figure out that bastard ain't napping. And they know we were in there last! What the hell are we going to do?"

The vehicle rolled along, bumping, jumping, and rattling as they made their way. His passenger, equally as thoughtful about what he had done and what the consequences for his actions would be, gave his friend's questions much consideration.

When Doe heard enough of the driver's rants, he proposed what previously was "unthinkable." He summed it all up with "It's time for us to part ways! We'll stand a better chance if we split up and go our separate ways."

"Fine! That works for me," Kunto agreed with him.

Doe's "Just drop me off on Baker Street!" was met with a sigh of relief.

~~~~~

Silence accompanied them to town. Each man's thoughts diverging then converging as he reviewed their childhood, youth, young adulthood, and life now that they were in their early thirties, both anticipating their demise. Mahmoudou Ibrahaim and Kunto Boro were certain that DOOR members would certainly seek them out, kill them, and make an example of them before throwing their bones to the wild animals.

When the truck came to a screeching halt, Doe reached over and gave his friend a hug. "Love you like a brother!"

His accomplice hugged him back. Both men patted each other's backs before turning each other loose.

"Love you more." The last words Doe would ever hear from his friend escaped from Kunto's lips before he jumped out of the vehicle.

"You know where to take it," the latter said to the driver who gave him a wave before he sped away. A nod of affirmation given, the Boro man was gone. He would dispose of the truck and go his way.

Doe watched the vehicle until it was at the end of the street and turning left. He rushed into the cottage he had rented from his friend a while back and quickly gathered a few personal items. Just one change of clothing, for he could not carry everything. The man also secured his passport and some money. He had a bit of Timbuktuian currency, some West African CFAs he had horded and hidden at this location while preparing for his "hit-and-run."

He ran his hand in his pocket and retrieved the money he had taken off Winston Royals's corps. There were a few folded euros and some American dollars. He hit his head with the palm of his hand, his thoughts now on his failure to share the bounty with the Boro man. "Damn!" He cursed himself for the straits he had put his friend in. "I should have told him everything so he could have made ready!"

He threw the contraband to the floor but picked it. His future uncertain, he might need it. Mahmoudou Ibrahaim renewed his effort to escape from Mali and find the object of his affections, his *cherie* Kieta Toures. After all, this was what caused him to do all the things he had done lately, all of them, including involving his friend in a murder.

A picture of the bullet floating on the air, hitting Winston Royals squarely between the eyes, and making a hole from which no blood escaped assailed his senses. Nausea swept off the man. He rushed to the toilet where he heaved and vomited until he felt emptied.

He rinsed his mouth at the sink, looked in the mirror, and saw the crazed individual he had become staring back at him. Sorrow and grief showed on his face. He wished he had not involved Kunto in his mess.

Despite his regrets about stiffing his partner, he shook all thoughts of him aside. He had to get out of there and go somewhere. Where? He was uncertain, but he knew he must leave right away. Winston's men would be on his trail soon.

The Ibrahaim man grabbed a pillowcase off a pillow from the bed, stuffed the few belongings he would take with him into it, and prepared to leave the house. At the doorway, he turned to look at the place where he and his love had enjoyed countless hours, knowing full well that the likelihood of either of them returning here was nil. The man left after the pause and went to a nearby building that had a public telephone booth to make a call for assistance with his current dilemma.

Chapter Nineteen

Doe turned again to Soyinka to help him escape. He dialed the number he had subconsciously committed to memory.

"You again!" Soyinka responded to the man on the other end of the line when he answered his business phone and recognized the caller's voice.

Drawn to babbling by the man's obvious disgust, Mahmoudou was reduced to apologetic begging. "I know. I promised, but this time I will keep my word. You will not hear from me again! Please hear me out. I just need a little help. I have to get out of Timbuktu! I must go now!"

His persistent pleas fell on deaf ears. "No, I won't do it!" Soyinka denied his requests. Kieta's former boss put the phone back on its cradle to turn his attention to his own affairs. He felt he had done enough.

Hearing the disconnection, Doe let the phone fall from his hands. He grabbed the small bundle of goods he took with him when he left home and stepped into the street. The man walked listlessly through the town, considering his fate as hours passed, and evening and night were on the horizon.

Facing westward and noting the orange sky, exhaustion caused him to scoot in an alley, sit in the street, and let his wound-up body relax. The last forty-eight hours had been a whirlwind. The Ibrahaim man, his freedom relinquished when he took out the DOOR leader and causing him to become a fugitive, let his belongings fall in place beside him. Sleep overtook him.

The man spent a night unfettered and free of distractions. No one came into the alley to disturb him. It was only when the sun came up in the east, and he heard the calls to prayer in the city did he stir. He yawned, stretched, and looked over, and noting his belongings were still there, he grabbed the bundle and pulled himself up from the street's hard-packed dirt floor.

An urge to relieve himself overtook him. He looked toward the street fleetingly then turned his back to the opening and urinated.

His stomach growled with hunger. Scents and sounds from the nearby open-air marketplace assailed all his senses, so he proceeded to go there.

When he was almost at a tent where he could get a morsel of bread and a bit of beverage, he came to a stop and looked around. More people, armed ones, were there than he had ever seen. They swarmed the place like bees. A couple were at each vendor's spot. There were more of them than merchants or patrons. DOOR members were out in droves, large numbers.

Doe recognized a few of them, and he knew they were acquainted with him, were probably looking for him. A day had passed and a full night too since he had snuffed the life out of Winston Royals and left him resting on the sofa in his tent.

The fugitive stumbled backward, hid himself in a store's doorway to consider his options, and then turned and hurried away to begin his exodus. He knew he could never go home again. If he did, his capture was certain, and he would certainly suffer persecution.

For the next couple of weeks, the man wandered aimlessly, foraging food at the back doors of restaurants and in trash containers near the marketplace. He slept in abandoned buildings on bare floors, wherever he could find a spot. The man was always careful not to entertain anyone and was comforted by the fact that he was not the only homeless person there.

Each person he saw had his own story, and no one bothered him, so he bothered no one. Mutual respect of these night owls made him secure. Periodically, a mongrel dog barked, but they too were homeless. He learned to keep an offering of food to toss to them so he would not become their next meal.

His thoughts clouded by his current situation, Mahmoudou was not sure who would come for him, whether it would be DOOR or the U.S. government or who, but he was certain someone would come. Or when they would come, it was spring now. No matter when they came for him, he would not go easy.

While the May days were quite warm, the man grew cold at night. Sometimes it was the weather observing nature's mores, and other times his physiology was the culprit. Whatever the case, nights in Timbuktu were quite lonely for a man who truly enjoyed socializing and being with loved ones, especially his *cherie* Kieta Toures.

He fell into a depressive state, was listless many times, and would have, on occasion, preferred death to his present conditions. The man was obviously rest broken. Whenever he had the opportunity to enjoy a restful repose, rodents and bugs scampered about, crawling, creeping, snipping, and gnawing on his exposed skin and members, preventing the much-needed sleep. He had to get away.

~~~~~

Early one morning, the Ibrahaim man fell asleep on the floor of a vacant warehouse. It was a peaceful sleep. Out of the elements and unfettered by canines, rodents, and insects, he dreamed of his beloved Kieta, their meetings, their couplings, and their love for each other and their separating at the hands of the insurgents, her rescue, and her being spirited away to parts of the world unknown to him.

He woke with a start. His heart pounding in his chest, he thought how he had killed the man who had made arrangements for her to be sent away from Timbuktu, a killing he now perceived as immature, too hasty. He'd snuffed the life out of him before he told him where she had been taken.

Doe smacked his forehead and cursed himself for not finding her whereabouts before he shot the man. Perhaps he should have played along with him a while longer. Maybe he would have told him where she was. Or he could have tortured the Royals man until he told him where the Toures woman had been taken. He could have muzzled him and cut off his fingers, one at a time, until he gave the information he needed. "Damn!" His word of choice accompanied his would haves, could haves, and should haves. The deed had been done. The man let go of thoughts about that eventful day.

He leaned up on his elbow and prepared to get up. He reached over to get his bundled belongings, feeling first before looking to where he had laid it before he had fallen into a deep sleep. Everywhere his probing fingers touched was empty, his fingers flailed in the air.

The man jumped up and looked around. His eyes fell on the space where he had had put the dirty pillowcase with his change of clothing and bits of food pilfered from garbage cans. It was not there. He looked around, his hopes dashed in a moment.

All that he owned in the world except the bit of money in his pantaloons' pockets was gone. He had been victimized while in one of the abandoned warehouses the homeless frequented.

The man cursed aloud as he continued to scan the area around himself. Shaking off the remnants of sleep, he pissed in a corner before beginning his descent from this place to a yet unknown and undetermined place. His thoughts accompanied him out of the building and onto the streets.

His mind returned to the airport at Bamako, the one where Kieta had been secreted out of the country by night. Doe recalled how isolated it appeared that night. Most of the employees worked during the day when flights were few and far in between. They generally took care of commercial flights. The commercial ones didn't fly at all after the sun set, yet private planes such as the one that had removed the woman often came and went. Consequently, a skeleton crew worked to assist with comings and goings of these small jets and were always available for government officials' needs.

Mahmoudou Ibrahaim listlessly made his way there. He caught a ride on the back of a truck that transported and taxied a number of people to work at the airport and back home. There, he hid for a couple of days, observing the place, its employees, and noted there was not much security. While there, he also ate better than he had in the last couple of weeks.

Remnants from vendors who set up in the small airport as well as foodstuff the passengers dumped were in abundance; much of the food was packaged too. It was so plentiful until he did not have to hoard anything. Yet he put a couple of pieces of fruit in his pocket.

Needless to say, he was strengthened physically when he had a bit more food. The first night at the airport, he prowled around the facility until he found an open locker in the break room. Its content put a smile on the man's face. A worker kept a spare set of clothing there and some deodorant too. The man removed the items from the locker, went into the restroom, and washed at the sink with paper towels using the hand soap to cleanse his skin. He almost swooned at the notion of having warm water with which to bath.

He washed his hair and his bearded face with the soap too and kept splashing until he thought he heard someone walking in the hallway. He froze where he stood, holding his breath and hoping he would not be discovered.

In a minute, whoever was outside left, so Doe let out a sigh of relief and quickened his pace. The man put his spoils in the trash can, tossing paper towels on top of them to conceal them. He made himself comfortable at the airport, and when morning came, he exercised caution. The man could and did roam freely as the number and volume of workers and passengers arriving and departing from Bamako increased.

In the evening when chances of discovery decreased, he found places of refuge in the corridors, behind the desks where attendants checked passengers in and off flights, anywhere he wanted to take a load off his feet. He exhilarated, his thoughts on how he could stay there forever and not be discovered, but he chased away such thoughts by refocusing on what his real intent was—to get out of Timbuktu, to find his *cherie*.

The third day at his new respite, he abandoned the inside comforts of the airport and went outside to observe its functions from another angle. Soon, his attention was drawn to the sky by the engines from a particular plane. As the plane came closer, it grew so loud that it almost hurt his ears. Doe ducked behind some barrels outside the airport's main building. The man stuck his fingers in his ears, removing them only when the huge cargo plane came to a rolling stop.

He noted it was nothing like the mid-sized plane that had taken Kieta out of Timbuktu. It was huge. The man whistled with amazement at the size of it. He had seen the big bird in the sky but never been this close to it. Workers flew past where he kneeled. He ducked.

As soon as the C141 landed, there was a scurry of activity. Maintenance person set about fueling the aircraft. The cargo hold at its rear opened, and baggage handlers rushed in and carried but a few pieces from it. However, some crates were taken in there. Lastly, the crew disembarked and headed into the airport.

The hiding man snapped to attention. Doe knew in his heart of heart that this was his plane. He had to get on it. If he did not get on this one, he was certain to die in the West African nation.

The Ibrahaim man kept his eye trained on the workers, trying to determine when he should make his move. "On the mark, get set, ready, go!" The man told himself to make a run for it. *All I have to do is get into that hold before the door shuts. If I don't do it now, that big bird is going to leave me right here in Timbuktu.* He leaped upward from his perch, his form that of a basketball player going for the three-pointer, but fell down when voices a few yards from him made themselves heard.

His heart raced; he almost had a heart attack. There were six American soldiers porting a box with a flag for placement in the hold. "Poor dude." He heard one of the passersby say about the boxed corpse they were taking to the plane. "He wasn't worth a shit, but he didn't deserve to die like he did," the man continued. In a minute, Doe heard a response.

Another acknowledged, "I know. You are right. I don't have much compassion though. You just can't fool around with these infidels like he was doing and expect to come out alive."

As they passed by the man in hiding, the first speaker spit, his spittle almost hitting Mahmoudou. They were that close. Doe thought it good that the wind was still, else he would have been bathed in the man's harked phlegm.

"Hurry up. Let's put his ass on that bird. I got something else to do!" a third voice said.

"Like what? Play with one of these local girls?" Another man spoke, levity in his voice.

Acknowledged and responded to, another one argued, "Don't forget to cover your shit up. You don't want to catch any disease to take back home to your old lady." The men laughed, their laughter dying only when they were in the plane's belly. Doe shook his head.

The detail was out of there in a few minutes, and as soon as the building's metal door hit the last entrant's back, Mahmoudou jumped up and started running. It was if someone were behind him, and he was running for his life. His feet flew, and the beat of his heart matched that of his pounding footprints. The man ran so fast he almost lost his sandals. At the back end of the huge plane, he leaped into the cargo hold and pushed his way in between some boxes. He willed his heart rate to decrease and his breath to become regular again as well as the pain from overexertion to ease.

About five minutes later, a couple of Timbuktuian airport employees came to the hold and peered in, their glances more out of curiosity about the transporter than anything else. "This is one big bird!" one of them exclaimed.

"And it ain't even half full? How much you reckon will fill it?" his companion asked as he hopped inside the hold and walked toward the area where the stowaway had hidden himself.

Doe responded silently, facetiously, "Why you need to know? You ain't got a pot to piss in and nowhere to send it! Why don't you get off this fucking plane?" The man was freaking out. He needed for them to get away from the plane, let whoever was supposed to shut the door do just that, and let the plane leave.

The stowaway started to perspire, his glands making a sour rain. The intruding man sniffed air, and catching scent of the fugitive, he walked over and kneeled, and he saw him. Doe pulled his pistol out of his waistband. It was the same one he had used to execute the Royals man. He waited for the man in front of him to react. He knew he was going to have to kill him. Sweat beads swelled and merged, making his face slick. He looked the man in the eye, daring him to speak, to call attention to him.

He didn't. Instead, the man held his stance, exercising care not to incite the armed man. He shook his head gently, side to side, showing there was no need to fire. Compassion also showed in the man's eyes. The airport employee waved the gun down with a downward fanned hand.

Both men put fingers to their lips, shushing each other for fear of being discovered.

The worker backed away, his failure to even make his companion aware that there was someone else on the plane fully appreciated.

Mahmoudou Ibrahaim let out a huge sigh as his body relaxed, fitting himself neatly between boxes already strapped down and secured so there would be no movement in the hold.

The encounter between the two had only taken a minute or two, ones that seemed like hours. When the men were off the plane, he sank further into the abyss to await the unknown.

Momentarily, the two at the tail of the plane left. It took another half hour for the plane to be fully serviced and loaded. Doe could hear and see everything from where he sat. He started to relax. He was so sleepy. The man shut his eyes.

His reclined state was interrupted before he could allow his tired frame to rest fully. The man thought he heard something or someone. So he leaned forward and craned his neck so his eyes could check his surroundings.

From his perch, Doe caught the glint of metal from an approaching vehicle and heard it come to a stop, and the car doors opened and shut as well as approaching footsteps. Then he jerked his neck back into the locks of his shoulders. His instincts his guide, his mind froze in disbelief.

~~~~~~

There were two men who got out the backseat of a black limousine. Their driver got out of his seat too but did not join them. He stretched where he stood and leaned against the vehicle. He removed his cap, fanned with it before returning it to his head. The man on the side closest to the plane waited for the other to join him on the passenger side of the car before he joined him in their trek toward the plane's wide open tail.

When they turned around to come to the plane, Doe exclaimed audibly with disbelief. The man threw his right hand over his mouth to quiet himself. He could not believe what his eyes saw. The duo briskly walked over to the plane's tail and, without much ado, got in the hold.

Taurence Soyinka, Kieta's boss, the man who had helped him get his *cherie* out of the country, was there, almost in front of him.

He could reach out and touch him, his proximity almost too much for Mahmoudou's racing heart. He did not know the man who was with him, but he was certain he was someone who knew about him. *What have I done? Lord, please don't let me be found here. Keep me covered! Please!* he thought, begging the elements to keep him concealed from the men's roving eyes.

Swoosh! They passed by his hiding spot. He let out the breath he had started holding when the men were coming up the steps. He focused on the men, his interest peaked as they went in the same direction the men who ported the casket had gone.

The Ibrahaim man observed that Soyinka was dressed quite casually—in khakis and a short-sleeve shirt. The man with him was fully suited, his black suit the same color as the vehicle they rode. He had a white dress shirt and tie. Their movements seemed orchestrated. Both men came to a halt and removed their shades so they could see better in the dimly lit cargo hold. They pocketed their glasses before continuing to their destination. Side by side, their gaits matching, they walked right past the observer and over to the casket the soldiers had brought in earlier.

He heard one clear his voice then speak. "Too bad we got to take Winston back to Seattle in a box! At one point, he was one of our best agents," the man in black suit told Kieta's former boss.

Hearing the deceased's name, the stowaway nearly lost his bowels. Mahmoudou barely heard parts of their conversation. Their voices lowered a bit, the two spoke of other things—how long they had lived in Mali, how times were changing, and the probability that they two would have to leave West Africa and return to the States—before returning to talk about the departed and how Soyinka knew the departed.

Kieta's boss acknowledged he wished he had not assisted with getting the girl out of the country. "If I had followed my right mind," he told the man beside him, "if I had not let that servant girl's boyfriend convince me to help get the girl out of Mali, I would never had heard about Dubuya and how he could help!"

Doe shook away the man's apprehensions. He was glad Soyinka had helped spirit the girl out of Mali. Regret at having to kill a man attempted to make itself felt, but the man shook that away too. *I know I did the right thing!*

"You want to have a look-see?" He heard the man ask Soyinka as he reached for the center of the box.

"Hell, no!" Soyinka exclaimed, his voice elevating. "I don't need to see nobody with a hole in his head!" He backed away from the box as he spoke.

The other man removed his hand from near the coffin's latch, chuckled, and exhorted his accomplice. "Don't be such a pussy, man! They already patched that hole up, and he looks quite well. I don't know Ibrahaim, the one accused of shooting him, but I can tell you one thing. He is quite a marksman. The wound was clean as a whistle." The man whistled.

Hearing his name, Mahmoudou attended more to their conversation. He turned his head so his best ear could filter their talk's contents better.

"So you already saw him?"

The agent answered, "Sure. I saw him at the morgue. I just brought you here because I thought you might want to see for yourself that he was dead. Get some closure."

Soyinka commented, "I didn't need to see him! I was just pondering what happens with guys like Dubuya and the outcome of their illicit and illegal activities."

"Well, this is it!" The man paused, let his head drop for a moment, and hit the top on the draped coffin.

"Yep, this is what happens when they go rogue, when they let this power shit get in their heads! We have to box them up and send them back to their families. I wish it wasn't like this, but it is!" The man who appeared to be acting in some official capacity hit the coffin with an open hand as he spoke.

"I think it was more than that. That dope didn't help!" Soyinka added his two cents to the conversation. "They get to smoking that stuff, and it messes up their heads!"

"You are right! That doesn't help." The man looked at his watch and added, "Let's get the hell out of here before we find ourselves shut up in this thing and on the way to Seattle too! This plane is supposed to leave in a few."

He took the lead, and Soyinka followed him. Almost as quickly as they had come, the men were gone. Doe let his breath come freely when they had passed by him when they were leaving the hold. "Damn!" he spoke in disbelief to himself.

~~~~~

As soon as these last two men were out of the plane, the loadmaster peered in, and the door to the cargo hold shut. Doe breathed a big sigh of relief. He was safe, on his way out of Timbuktu and to Seattle, Washington, a place he had never been but one he had heard about. Perhaps he would find the love of his life there.

Maybe that's where Winston "Dubuya" Royals sent Kieta for safekeeping! After all, that is where he is from! Doe exhilarated at the thought of finding his *cherie*. "Makes sense!" He cleared his throat and spoke aloud this time. No one could hear him.

The plane taxied down the runway and was soon in the sky soaring above the clouds. From where he sat, Doe could see out of a window and became euphoric as the plane climbed to thirty-five thousand feet, was above the billows, and cruising toward a new life in a new land.

He laughed aloud with reckless abandon, drumming a happy tune with his hands as he enjoyed the sounds that came from inside him. The last few weeks had almost been more than he could bear. Life as a fugitive had not allowed the joy and freedom of speech one could enjoy when not hiding, or running, or keeping discreet.

They were not long into the flight when he began to get cold. The flimsy shirt and pants he had pilfered from a worker's locker at the airport were not adequate. He wasn't wearing any undergarments. "Brrrr!" He let his lips release what his body felt. To no avail, the Ibrahaim man pulled his arms around his corps.

Hearing a fan start up, he realized that it was probably cooler in the hold than up front where the pilots were seated. It had to be. All sorts of cargo was being transported, including a corpse.

He shuddered, not from fear or trepidation but because it was growing increasingly cold as they flew. Doe longed for a jacket to cover his arms and boots and socks to put on his freezing feet.

After a while, his attention turned toward the deceased man with whom he was sharing the cargo hold. He wondered about the man in the box, what he was wearing, and asked aloud, "What you got on, asshole? I ought to get up and take the clothes off you. You can't use no clothes where you going! No need for clothes in hell! They are going to burn in the fire just like you are!"

The plane lurched and dropped. It hit an air pocket. Doe, though he was tossed around a bit, remained in the area where he was squeezed between two boxes. He looked down, noting for the first time that he was seated on metal. "No wonder my ass is so cold. I got to get off this piece of metal."

Again, the man attempted to pull himself up from his perch but found himself plopped back down into his place.

Bump! Bump! Bump! He fell back into his spot to wait for the plane ride to get better.

After three more drops and a few jerks, the plane evened out. Like a ship on the ocean, its occupants enjoyed smooth sailing.

A couple of hours into the flight, the stowaway pulled himself up and from in between the huge wooden boxes; they came to his shoulders.

His bones cracked, and aching joints made him feel insecure. Twisting his neck and head, he looked around, seeing not only boxes but also bundles, some seemingly covered with burlap or some material.

Doe considered making his way about the hold and checking to see if he could utilize some of this material to cover himself.

He shivered, the cold almost too much for him to bear. And he coughed, feeling pain in his chest. "I hope I don't get sick," he told his companion, the corpse. His nose itched, and he sneezed, spraying moisture in the air. "Nope!" He attempted to make the impending pneumonia go away.

The man put one foot forward. The plane shook and shuttered. He determined he must proceed with caution. He could ill afford to step out of his perch and into the open cargo hold then become unable to fit himself tightly and snuggly in place as he was at the present time. In addition to that, he also thought he might be thrown around and suffer injury if he was too far away from his nest and unable to grasp something to hold.

Another thought caused him to snap his fingers. "I don't know why I didn't think about that a while back," he spoke in the abyss. His full attention turned to the flag on Winston Royals's coffin. It was within reach, and its cover might be useful. Consequently, he held his place with one hand and reached with the other to secure the covering.

He forcefully snatched the flag draped on the casket and wrapped himself up in it. "You can't use it! I might as well," he said to Winston with whom he made monologue all the way to the latter's final destination.

Their sixteen-hour trip was replete with "What's next?" What was Doe going to do once he got there? Would he be able to get off the plane as inconspicuously as he had gotten on it? Where would he go when he left the airport if he left on his own? Where would he stay? The questions too many and with no correct answers were forgotten after a while. Mahmoudou Ibrahaim finally dozed, gave way to his body's systems, and fell asleep. He let Winston rest in peace too.

~~~~~

The stowaway did not awake until he heard voices. "Hey! Come over here and see what we got!" One perfect stranger spoke to another in his native tongue.

Another told him, "Come on out of there, brother! We will help you to safety. Just be quiet and stay put wherever we tell you!"

Doe could find no words, so he just stayed where he was. Not only that, but he also felt so bad. He knew sickness surely would follow. His throat was scratchy; his eyes running and ears hearing a humming, buzzing sound; and his chest hurt like the dickens. He touched his head to see if he was feverish. He was quite warm. The man suffered from more than exhaustion. He was certain of that.

"Gimme that dead man's flag," the man who had seen him first ordered while taking the red, white, and blue drape from him. He spread it back over the casket before the worker picked it to carry Winston's remains to a hearse waiting his return home.

"Sit still! We'll be back in a minute!" another said.

Doe nodded at the speaker. There was little else he could do. Exhausted and sick, he was safe, albeit he had almost used all the nine lives his friend Kunto Boro had referenced during one of their conversations on his lucky estate.

While waiting on his rescuers to return, he thought about the man who had been his friend since childhood. He didn't have any idea about where he was, whether he had made it to safety the last day they had been together, whether he were still alive. He tried to shake away such thoughts.

Whatever the case, Kunto was probably better off than he would have been with him. He had spent most nights in the elements on the streets of Timbuktu; gotten in a few fights with other homeless people over space, food, and dregs of beverages; and then hid in the hold of a plane, trusting that wherever its destination was safer for him than Timbuktu was at the present moment. Mahmoudou Ibrahaim was a wanted man. He was wanted not only by his government but also by the DOOR,and by the Americans.

PART II

On Foreign Soil

Chapter Twenty

Kieta's trip across the Atlantic Ocean led to a stay in Florida, South Florida. She was taken to a family, man and his wife, the Smarts, an elderly white couple. How she got there, she could never tell, for she did not know. It was as if she woke up from a dream and found herself in a beautiful home, in a bed similar to the one Marissa Soyinka slept in. The room had a private bathroom. It was three times as large as the one she and Wakesa had shared off the kitchen back at the compound in Mali. She rolled over, leaned up on her elbows, and saw the commode directly in front of her. It was apparent someone had left the door open so she could access the necessary.

When she sat up, her gaze fell on the gown she wore. Confusion showed on her brow, and she was afraid to move. Thoughts cascaded from her mind while sitting there. *Where am I? How did I get here? Who put this gown on me?*

However, an overactive bladder set her in motion. "I can just sit here and pee on this nice bed!" She turned where she sat on the bedside, let her legs hang over the side, and slid off the queen-sized mattress until her feet touched the bare floor. She shivered; the tile was cool. When she looked down, a pair of slippers were right beside the nightstand. The young woman slid her feet in them and hurried to the bathroom where she relieved herself.

When she was at the vanity, she checked her countenance. Her face was clean, except for crust in their corners, and her hair too. It was clear she was no longer in the stockade in Mali.

Mali! Her thoughts returned to the night some men had taken her from the jail and what had happened afterward. *Did Doe get me out of there? Did he really come? Am I in a place he arranged?* Question after question tripped over itself as she stood looking in the mirror.

She rubbed her neck, her hand automatically went where her nerves led it. "Humph? What in the world . . ." fell from her lips as she looked more closely at her upper body, craning her neck to see what her phalanges touched.

A scar on her left shoulder drew her attention. Seeing its pointed tip, she pushed the gown's strap aside. "Where did you come from?" she asked aloud about the wound. She rubbed the fingers from her right hand lightly over the raised abrasion. Feeling no pain, she expressed, "At least, you don't hurt." Then Kieta pinched the welt between her fingers, feeling firmness that came with healing.

The Toures girl had been a bit feverish when she arrived in the States. So she was taken to a military base where a doctor examined her. During her entire journey, she was unconscious. Her rescuers injected more anesthesia while she traveled. Her unconscious state was maintained for a few days after she was dropped off at the hospital, secreted in a room not near other patients. And while under, she was bathed and given all the required immunizations recommended by the CDC. The amount of medicine given her was enough to kill a horse, and she lapsed, unexpectedly, into a semicomatose state. Her condition was so dire that even her doctor questioned whether she would survive.

The young woman also had bruises and abrasions on various parts of her body. However, a gynecological examination showed no evidence of violation. She was not pregnant. But few scars from her punishment had not fully healed. One in particular concerned the physician, one where the tip of the whip broke skin.

Something had to been done to save her flesh and her. That singular wound on her shoulder had festered while she had been in the jail. It was exacerbated by the change in climate as well as squalor-like conditions. It was humid where they brought her, the air wet, not dry like it was in her native land, Mali in Timbuktu, West Africa. The medical staff at the facility paid the sore extra special care. So the welt on her shoulder that had gotten worse while she was in captivity soon started to heal after several rounds of antibodies had been used. However, it left a scar.

Another scar, the one on her psyche, required attention too. The girl moaned, cried, and simpered even when sedated as they cleaned it and ministered to the spot and hollered loudly and mournfully even when left undisturbed, frequently calling for Doe. So her physician added some anxiety medication to the regiment of medications that dripped intravenously from a pole at her bedside.

It took a couple of weeks of medicating, feeding, and nurturing her until she was better and ready to be taken to a safe house the Intelligence Agency had secured for her when she was spirited out of her homeland.

When they were sure she was going to survive, she was transported to a "safe house" on the East Coast. Her tracks sufficiently covered, she was dropped off in the dead of night at the house where she found herself, standing looking in the mirror, studying her countenance.

~~~~~

A light rap on the bathroom door brought the Toures girl from reverie to reality. "Miss, miss, are you all right in there?" She heard a woman's voice.

Her heartbeat rushing, she sputtered, "Yes, yes, ma'am! I am all right!"

"Good!" came from the other side of the door. "When you have freshened up, check the closet. There are some clothes there for you. When you have dressed, come out and come to your left. We will wait for you in the dining room."

For lack of anything else to do except follow after the voice she just heard, the Toures girl set about making herself ready for the day. Perhaps, just perhaps, she would get some answers to her many questions.

She began with her teeth. She brushed with reckless abandon. A treat she enjoyed at the Soyinkas' was returned to her. Finished, she licked her teeth, relishing the smoothness, and rinsed with the scope from the glass decanter on the marble counter.

Considering whether she could skip a bath, the girl sniffed her own armpits, marveling at the fresh, clean smell. She wondered who had bathed her and dressed her in the soft pink gown she saw in the mirror. The Toures girl had not taken leave of her senses and knew she had not done these things herself.

Despite her state of near clean, she stepped out the gown and locked the bathroom door. She took a brisk shower and hopped out to dry herself with one of the plush towels draped on a chair in front of the vanity. The young woman dried the mist from her face and put the large towel to her nose, enjoying its scent. She almost swooned, her thoughts on how she managed to be enjoying this spa-like facility. Neither Madame Soyinka's nor Marissa's bathroom could match this one, decked out in lavender to match colors in the bedroom on the other side of the door.

When she had dried her body, she took other liberties—used the Ban roll-on antiperspirant fresh scent from a tray on the counter as well as a grapefruit scent body spray. She combed and brushed her hair, noting that someone had trimmed it. The girl pulled a few strands toward her eyes to see it, and she also smelled it.

It was clear someone had taken better care of her than she had been able to take care of herself lately. Kieta, body wrapped in the towel, unlocked the bathroom door and peered out of it. Finding no one in the room, she hurriedly tiptoed to the entrance and locked the door. The girl turned the knob once for good measure.

She headed to the closet. When she opened the door, her mouth fell open. Her hand flew to it in amazement, and the towel she was wrapped in fell. The walk-in closet, one unlike anything Madame Soyinka or Marissa had, yielded clothes in abundance. A "Wow!" escaped her lips. After another pause, the Toures girl kicked the towel aside as she ventured inside what she labeled "a pure fantasy land."

Inside, she found herself touching everything that her eyes saw. The closet was filled with every item of clothing one could imagine, shoes to match, as well as accessories, all in a rainbow of colors, ones that brought tears to the young waif's eyes. Drawers and shelves had been labeled for her convenience.

Her cries were put into check by a solitary rap on the bedroom's door and a voice from the other side. "Miss, Ms. Marie! Are you dressed for breakfast yet? Miss?"

Kieta ran over to the door, responding as soon as she was there. "Yes, I am fine. I will be out in a minute. As soon as I put on my clothes, I will come out."

"Okay," the soprano in the hallway told her. "Please hurry, Ms. Marie! You won't enjoy the breakfast cold."

"Marie, who is Marie?" Kieta asked herself who she had been mistaken for as she dressed. "Oh well," she told herself, "at least she and I wear the same size!"

The girl put on a sundress. The variegated fabric in her favorite color purple drew her attention. Her eyes fell on a pair of white sandals, so she slid her feet into them.

~~~~~

Kieta hurried from the bedroom and paused to peer through the open doors into the dining room. Just one man, his face to her, and a woman on one side were seated at a dining room table that could easily seat twelve people. If asked to describe them, the only thing she could tell from where she stood was that he was taller than she, and both had long hair. Hers in a ponytail like his but penned up, causing the tail of her mane appearing shorter. His, with a band on it at the nape of his neck, cascaded down the back of the blue polo he was wearing. Both were sipping coffee.

For lack of anything to do except do as she was told, the girl slid into the room. Her entrance noticed by the man first then the woman.

"Good morning! Good morning!" man said as he saw her enter the dining room and approach the table. He laid his cup aside, got up from his seat at the head of the table, and pulled a chair for her to sit in on his left side, waving with his hand for her to take the seat. His wife was already seated in the one on his right side.

The woman wiped her mouth with a cloth napkin and returned it to her lap before uttering, "Good morning, dear! Mr. Smart and I are so glad you are feeling well and able to join us for breakfast this morning. We were worried about you for a minute there." Kieta looked in her face, noting her beauty and her state of fitness as well as the tank top from which peaked arms toned to a *T. This had to be the voice that came through the bathroom door.*

"It was me who knocked on the bathroom door." *There, she said it! It was her.* The woman's voice droned on, "It was not Jan. Did you see her? I told her to have you come to breakfast before it got cold." Kieta was still standing, waiting for further instructions.

Confusion showed on her brow. The man pulled the chair a bit further from the table, an action that caused her to sit. He returned to his place and patted the table gently next to the hand she laid on the table. "No need to fret, little one! Mrs. Smart and I will help you catch up after breakfast."

"I am Louel, and this is my husband, Harold," she introduced themselves to their houseguest.

"Thank you" were the only words she was able to get out before a woman who could have been her sister pushed a serving cart into the room and started placing food in front of each of them, their guest first then the couple.

His wife joined him in assuring her that she was in a good place, one with good food too. "Look at the breakfast Jan made for us! We don't eat like this all the time! Both Harold and I would be as big as house if we ate like this every day!"

The man added, "I know. You are right. I would be good for nothing if I ate everything Jan prepared for us. Not to say it is not good, but I have to watch my cholesterol."

"I know! I know!" The woman sympathized with her employers. "Just enjoy it this morning. I will bring your usual oatmeal, juice, and coffee in the morning!"

Kieta watched as the woman worked. She toyed playfully with the couple and ensured their every need was met. "Or I won't bother about making you nothing and just fix whatever miss want."

The man winked at his wife. "I guess we better stop complaining and clean our plates, else Jan ain't going to give us nothing but bread and water."

"Both of you all could stand a little more meat on your bones!" The girl watched as they bantered back and forth about eating.

Louel told her, "I am going to eat every bite of this, but I am going straight to the gym when I finish. Ain't no way I am going to eat like this every day!" She pointed to the platter in the woman's hand, noting, "My metabolism isn't what it used to be! You don't realize the amount of work I have to put in to get rid of all those calories."

"Stop fussing, Ms. Louel. Your guest will eat if you eat. Ain't that right, honey?" She looked to Kieta who rested silent. Her mind was on where she was and how she got there and who these people were.

When the woman who reminded her of Wakesa placed a plateful of potatoes, scrambled eggs, and equal portions of bacon and sausage in front of her, she asked, "Would you like toast or pastry?"

The Smarts' houseguest waved both of the items away. She was not certain that she could eat everything on the breakfast platter in front of her.

"What would you like to drink? Coffee, hot tea, juice, some water?"

Their guest asked for water, which Jan poured from a pitcher on the cart. Kieta drank all of it before the woman left her side and pushed the emptied glass toward the woman.

"Awwwww!" She unconsciously emitted a long expression of relief. She had not realized how thirsty she was. Little did she know her dehydration was created by the wealth of medications she had had the last few weeks. "Can I have another glass, please?"

The woman smiled at her. "Sure, you can have as much as you want to eat and drink. Mr. and Mrs. Smart, they are generous, good-hearted people. They always tell me to make sure company has plenty, not to scrimp on anything." Pivoting to return the pitcher to the cart, she told the woman, "Just call out, and I will pour more if you need more."

"No!" Kieta refused to be served. "If you leave it here on the table, I will pour it myself. Or if it goes on that serving cart over there, I can go there to get it for myself."

The two women's eyes locked, and both acknowledged their equanimity. They were both invited here and received quite well. It would serve them well to always be kind to each other. Neither wanted to make a faux pas, so neither moved.

The woman who served the Smarts was glad when her mistress gave the final word. "Just leave it there, Jan! Marie can get it for herself."

Kieta looked at the woman across from her. There, she heard it again. *Marie, who is Marie?* She fixed her mouth to ask about this Marie person and what made them think her name was Marie but was interrupted.

Her thoughts were broken by the head of the household who told her, "Now eat! We will talk when breakfast is finished."

She acquiesced. The girl dove into the platter, first quite tentatively then with reckless abandon. The food was good. She had not had any as good since her last meal at the Soyinkas' compound. Kieta Toures's face softened as her palate was teased and satisfied.

When madame and the younger Soyinkas went to Europe, she left the Ayinde woman in charge. As soon as she was on the plane, the older servant sat about, rearranging their lives. She made the girls get up earlier and eat a hearty breakfast before Nouhoum drove them to the university. Initially, they had rebuffed her efforts, opting to put some fruit and nuts in their bags to snack on later. The woman, however, won the battle. She reported their insolence to Monsieur Soyinka who told Marissa he would send her away if she did not obey. So the last meal at their table had been breakfast—cooked cereal with nuts and dried fruit; tea, a green one; and buttered bread with fig preserves.

The Smarts watched her eat, her mood shifting throughout the meal. She ate every bit on her plate and cleaned its remnants with a bit of toast then rinsed her mouth with juice and another glass of water. She pushed her chair back from the table to wait for her hosts to clean their own plates. Neither did.

As soon as breakfast was over, the Smarts and Kieta took to the library in the mansion to talk.

Inside the huge room—it was bigger than the Soyinkas' library— the occupants took turns going to the bathroom just outside the door, their bladders begging to be emptied.

Jan, like Wakesa (the woman the Toures girl served alongside in Timbuktu), busied herself bringing water, juices, and coffee into the room. Next, she placed the pastries on a small table beside the beverages, her hands busy and her ears wide open. *Must be a head servant thing!* That's what Kieta thought while Mr. Smart dismissed the household's only helper when they were ready to talk.

"No need to check on us, Jan! If we have need of anything, we will buzz you!" the man exhorted the help. The woman backed out of the room Wakesa style, shutting the door behind her.

"Okay, let's get at it!" The man started talking. He told the girl their services had been sought out. "I am a criminal justice professor. Before my current employ, I was in the military and saw action in the Middle East. As a matter of fact, both of us, Louel and I, were military police. That's how we met! Anyway, we married shortly after our tours of duty were over, retired here, and I took position at the university. Shortly after we arrived here, we were contacted by the Feds and asked to serve our country in yet another way, the one that brings us to where we are today." He paused to get a drink.

She did not move a muscle. The girl kept her eye on him, willing the man to hurry up and tell her what she wanted and needed to hear.

He took up where he left off. "As I was saying, we acquired a new opportunity when we relocated. Louel and I maintain what they call a safe house. We keep people who need to get away from their past for one reason or another and make a new life for themselves."

"A safe house?" the girl questioned him. "Like a haven!"

"Yes," he replied, "a haven if you want to think of it that way. We help people in trouble be safe! Louel and I had kept political figures, stars, and people who needed their identities concealed for one reason or another for short periods. Not only have we kept individual, but also periodically, witnesses from high-profile cases have stayed here with us until their identities could be changed, and they could be relocated."

He looked over at his wife and added, "Generally, individuals in need of respite and care until their situations are worked out are not left alone. That's where Louel comes in! While I work outside the home, she attends to our clients and ensures their safety. She is a certified bodyguard, and a good one at that."

Kieta looked from one to the other, becoming increasingly aware of where she was, why she was there. She had to be removed from her country; she was not safe there. *But how did I get here?*

Winding down, the man ended with "When our clients' identities have been changed and documents secured, they go on their way.

We never hear from them again, and they don't hear from us!" He hunched his shoulders.

The girl gave his story her full attention but was left wanting. Not only did she still want to know how she got there, but also other questions had arisen. "Why do you do this?" the girl asked. "Do you just do it because you get paid to take these people in your home?"

The man shook his head, telling her, "No, it's not just for the money. My wife and I have big hearts. We have no children, and it's a pleasure to help people we meet while we provide this service. There are, however, perks, if you will, that come with this work. Right, honey?"

His wife acknowledged the efficacy of the work they did with the federal government. "We get to live in this big house, one we could never afford otherwise, in a neighborhood like the one we are in! Drive nice cars. Dine at the country club. Have our yard work done free! Things we could never have enjoyed on a professor's salary!" she told the girl, the exuberance in the woman's voice matched only by the glee on her face.

"In addition to that, we would never have met some of the characters we have met or gone to some of the places we have gone if we did not do this work."

"Like who?" The Toures girl was caught up in the moment.

Louel calmed down. "Sorry, I cannot tell you. We can't disclose anything about anyone who has passed through here. A slip of the tongue, and someone could be exposed and their covers blown. Their lives in jeopardy, they would be back where they started."

She grew serious again. "We are sworn to secrecy. If our employer loses confidence in us, we lose our livelihood! However, they basically ensure our success! Most times, we don't have people's real names or know where they came from or, for that matter, how they got from their homes to ours. They show up at our door anytime! Sometimes they are mobile, just walk up to the door, envelope in hand! Others have come on stretchers, the porters presenting their envelopes to us!"

There, she said it! That's how I got here. They, whoever they were, brought me from Mali to Miami and dropped me off here at the Smarts' house. Kieta got the answer to one of her questions. She knew full well she had not walked up to the door, rung the bell, and been made welcome. She was certain she would have remembered that.

Hearing Louel's voice drone on, she turned her attention back to the woman. "Several of our clients have labeled me Harriet Tubman and said we were running the Underground Railroad out of our house." The Smart woman chuckled as she spoke. "Do you know that story?"

"Yes, I know who you are talking about!" Kieta Toures, a U.S. history buff, was indeed familiar with the Harriet Tubman, the Black Moses, who led slaves to freedom using "safe houses" where they were available so her passengers could rest up, be revived, and make their journey from bondage to freedom in one piece from the county's southern states to Canada.

The Smart man gave support to his wife's explanation of the work they did. "I also view it as *my mission.* People sometimes find themselves in dire straits, and it sometimes takes some extraordinary measures to help them get out of their misery." The man showed his Christian roots, adding, "I just try to do what the savior would do!"

Hearing what they said, the girl was still not satisfied. She had more questions than they could or would answer.

Her impatience showed. "Can you just tell me how *I* got here?" She was not interested in what happened with all the other people they mentioned. It was indeed all about her need to fill in the blanks, to connect the dots, and to put the puzzle her life had become together.

Sensing the girl's frustration, Mr. Smart tried to help her comprehend, his actions mimicking those he used in his criminal justice classes when trying to help his students understand.

"Actually, young lady, we can't tell you where you came from or how you got here! We are not privy to that information." He pointed a wagging finger at her. "You alone know where you came from!"

Then he pointed the member at his mate and himself as he interjected, "Neither one of us is privy to that bit of information."

Finally, he made a circle in the air to encapsulate their collective knowledge. "The three of us know for certain that you are here. Neither of us knows what your future holds!" The man's voice elevated as he spoke.

Her tone and timbre matching his, she told the duo, "You just take people in your house and don't know where they came from or nothing about them? They, *whoever they are*, could drop a serial killer off at your house, and you would just let them in." She shook her head, her face showed obvious disgust.

"Yes, dear, we do! We are confident that the people who come here are sufficiently vetted before they are brought to our home," the man's wife chimed in.

Their charge got up from her seat and stood in front of the couple, taking the reins of the conversation from them. "Okay, I get it! I just can't live like this again. This is the second time this has happened to me in my life!" she shrieked at the couple.

"The second time!" the Smarts said at the same time, the cadence in their voices the same. This was the first time they'd heard a client had been placed with a family for a second time. Both thought this odd and questioned inwardly whether this client should be with them. Perhaps she had issues not uncovered during the vetting process, or she had been incorrigible somewhere else and had to be moved to another safe place.

The couple looked at each other and looked back at the girl in front of them, hand on her hips, resolve showing in her eyes and on her face.

"What do you mean by 'the second time'?" his wife asked. Her husband was sipping from a glass of water poured from a pitcher on the table beside him.

~~~~~

"I am Kieta Toures, and I am from Mali in Timbuktu, West Africa. A woman from another land, I came from a large family of nomads, which grew smaller as time passed. Our custom was when you were able to work, you were removed from the home to learn a trade. The youngest child, I saw my father take my brothers and sisters when they were about twelve years old away, one at a time, then return to our camp without them . . . A brother, a sister, and on and on until everyone was gone, except me! I heard my mother cry when he took one and hush upon his return then go on about her business like nothing was wrong. I can remember her weeping and moaning like that several times while growing up. My mother died when I was young, so I took over some of her chores, got the sticks for the fire, made gruel from animal parts and grass for us to eat bread too! I watched two others who predeceased her, and I moaned and wept until the old man came back. Again, he was alone. When I tried to ask him where my brother then my sister went, he told me I better get out of grown folks business!" Her words and thoughts tripped over one another as she attempted self-disclosure. And her voice broke while she spoke.

Her host family gave her the space and let her air her concerns. She, in another place in time past, gave them little attention. The man laid his glass aside, poured water for his wife, and passed it to her, while the Toures girl continued to vent.

"Then one day, out of the blue, he told me it was my time to go into the service. He didn't even give me a chance to think about it or discuss it! He told me to get my stuff, so I bundled my few belongings in a rag and followed on his footsteps until we were beside the main highway." *Hic . . . hic . . . hic.* Hiccups broke her speech.

Mrs. Smart pointed to the water, and seeing her movement, Kieta broke her stride long enough to wave away an offer of water. Instead, she drew in a couple of deep breaths and resumed her reveal. "It was not long before a truck came along. We hitched a ride on the back of a truck. Its driver stopped where Papa told him to stop. He took me to the Soyinkas' compound between Mali and Bamako." A sob came. "I never thought Papa would do that to me, leave me like that, but he did. He left me!"

The thought of her father dropping her off like he had shook her to the core. It was apparent to the Smarts that the girl was revisiting a stressful time in her life and relating it to her current state of affairs. Neither spoke; however, both were empathetic. *How awful is that for a child no more than twelve years old to be dropped off at a stranger's house with no preparation!*

The blubbering girl, who was double the age she had been when her father put her into the service, continued, "When we got to the back door, their head servant, a woman named Wakesa a.k.a. Kesa Ayinde, opened it! She yelled at Papa and called him a fool because he had not used the doorbell but rapped on the door with his knuckles. When she finished chewing him out, she let me in, took my belongings, snatched them out of my hands, and put them in the trash! I was so scared! My papa left me there, and I never saw him again. That was the first time!" The girl punctuated her verbal tirade by tossing the index finger of her preferred hand in the air.

By the time she reached "the first time!" she was crying uncontrollably, her heart clearly breaking. The Smart woman got up, reached across her husband, took a napkin from the table, and went to her. Handing it to the girl, she put her arms around her shoulders and pulled her close to her side to comfort her. "I am sorry! I am so sorry your daddy left you like that. We are more sorry than you can imagine."

Feeling her genuineness, Kieta leaned in and sobbed a bit more before pausing and asking the woman, "You called me Marie. Who told you that my name was Marie?"

"Come now! Wipe your eyes and sit. Harold and I will tell you. We will tell you as much as we know if that will help." The woman led her back to the chair she had abandoned. She looked to her husband for instructions.

The man, obviously as touched as his wife had been by the girl's reveal, pointed to a package on his desk and asked his wife to hand it to him.

When his spouse handed him the envelope, Harold opened it and removed its contents—a couple of sheets of paper and a booklet. He looked at the three objects then handed one to the girl who was seated in a chair between the two armchairs he and his wife occupied. "Perhaps this will help," he proffered when it was in her hand.

The Smarts' guest took the four-by-six navy-blue colored booklet labeled "Temporary VISA, *United States of America*" and observed its gold letters on the front before turning it over and looking at the back, which was blank.

"Open it," the woman urged her to look inside the book.

She did and was shocked at its contents. First, at her (Kieta Toures) picture being atop the page with Marissa's full name under it. Second, at "Marie" as what she liked to be called was on the next line. Third, by the Soyinka girl's birthday as well as her height and weight as her own. Fourth, a new nationality—African American. She could buy that because she was from Africa and in America. Finally, an address, one totally unfamiliar, was given.

"Am I in Florida? Is this your address?" she asked as she looked at one then the other. She looked to both parties for affirmation of their address.

Both of the Smarts nodded. "Yes, that is our address. Is this somewhere that you could be comfortable for a while?" Harold's asking did more in that moment than her father had ever done. He consulted her about her willingness to stay in Florida with them.

Considering she had no choice, Kieta relented. The only thing she gave pause to was having to use a name other than her own. "I can stay here for a while," she told the couple. "The only thing I have a problem with is assuming Marissa's identity. Isn't there another name I can use? And I would rather not use Marissa's information."

The latter she found so offensive because Wakesa had always taunted her for wanting to be more than she was. She remembered what she said. "You just trying to be like Mademoiselle Marissa. You ain't nothing but a servant. No better than me!" The woman's early admonishments were there to haunt her, creating a greater resistance to using her friend's vital statistics.

The Smart man looked to his wife for a response. They were a team and had done this critical work long enough to know when one was better at providing answers that clients could swallow easily.

Louel made a clapping sound with her hands, drawing the girl's attention to her. Kieta turned to the woman who leaned over and took her chin in her hand so they could see eye to eye.

"Let's be clear on this, child! The little that my husband and I can share with you is all the information that we have. You hold your past. We know nothing about it except the little bit you just told us! Where you came from, what your situation was, why you had to leave your homeland, we don't know anything about it." The woman wiped a path in the air with her right hand, Kieta's chin rested in her left one.

"It would probably be best if you let go of the past and look to the future. That is something we can help you with, not whatever was going on before you came here, just the remainder of today, tomorrow, and days to come. And then only if you want our help! Harold and I will do what we can to make your future bright . . . and certain. Nevertheless, the only way we can do that is for you, and for us, to follow directions given by the agency that placed you in our home."

The seriousness of her situation pointed out with clarity, the Toures girl nodded when the woman told her, "Now you are a bright girl. I can tell that! For the present, we are going to call you Marie. 'Marie' is what was given to us when you were delivered to our home a week ago, in the dead of the night, on a gurney. 'Marie' is the name we gave Jan, our friends and neighbors, as well as the congregation at our church."

The woman paused, letting go of the girl's chin, and resumed. "So Marie it is! It may take a moment for you to get used to it, but it will grow on you. It's what I did when I married him."

Louel pointed to her husband, who looked on and listened. He was not sure where his wife was going with this line of thinking but understood more as she continued her attempts to make Kieta comfortable with the name-change situation.

"You see, my maiden name was Grant, but I gave it up when I became Mrs. Smart."

The man smiled, interjecting, "Yes, she did but not without kicking and screaming. My wife was what they call a 'feminist' back in the day. She wanted to marry but wanted to keep her maiden name, wanted to be called Mrs. Grant-Smart!"

"Yes, but that was then! Harold, let me finish the story!" She jockeyed playfully with the man. She wanted to tell the rest of their wedding tale.

He shook his head, waved her away, and proceeded, "We went rounds about that! I found it offensive, her wanting to marry me but keep her daddy's name! Who ever heard of such foolishness?"

Marie looked from one to the other, hearing passion in both voices as they relived an old argument. "Well, how did you resolve the issue?"

"Her father made us go to a premarital counseling session with the officiant, which was a requirement of their church. Every couple had to participate before he would officiate at their wedding. It proved to be a blessing! She let go of her given name and took mine!"

"Yep, I took his name, and I am glad I did." The woman smiled as she looked over at her husband. "Now I never think about being called Ms. Grant. Mrs. Smart suits me to a *T*."

Her husband acknowledged her thoughts. "Yes, it does!" He stuck his chest out, an act that his spouse noticed.

Waving away the man's prideful remarks, the Smart woman brought the conversation back to the present. "So it is with you, child! You have acquired a new name, although it is through a totally different situation! It has been assigned to you! Just like me, you must embrace the change. You must learn to respond to *Marie* until a change comes!"

"I get it!" Humility showing in her voice, the girl told Harold Smart and his wife, Louel, that she would be "Marie" for as long as she needed to be "Marie." She also thanked them for taking her into their home. *Anywhere was better than the jail in Mali, the last place she remembered!*

The woman jumped up from her seat. "Good! Let me show you around the house!" She offered to show the new girl around their home on Sandalwood Drive and their environs.

"May we start with the room I woke up in?"

"Sure!" The woman wished her husband a good day. She gave him a smack on the lips then turned her attention to their charge.

Chapter Twenty-One

After a short period, the young woman was enrolled at the local university where Harold Smart served as a criminal justice professor. She had been a junior when taken from her homeland and brought to South Florida. With little ado, Marie resumed her studies. Ordinarily, one lost credit, but she was amazed to find that every credit she had had at her former school transferred. She was on track for graduation!

Kieta enjoyed good success at the school but did not make many friends. Crippled by fear of being discovered and exposed, Marie resisted efforts made by classmates and others among the thirty thousand students of all nationalities that matriculated at the college.

A consummate learner, she poured hours into her studies. When she was not studying, she spent time exploring the family's library reading classics that Mrs. Smart pointed out to her. She also went to the theater, dinners, and church with the childless couple and wrote daily in her diary about new adventures in the United States.

The student took care of her personal appearance and frequently joined Louel who loved walking around the lake in the middle of the gated community in which they lived. The woman also taught her to golf, and when the weather was not good, they went to the clubhouse to work out together on the machines. Sometimes they utilized the services of a fitness trainer in the gym. The women grew close, establishing a mother-daughter relationship.

Jan, the Smart's helper, and she also forged a great relationship. The former appreciated how not only her boss but also the girl who was living there supported her work. Everybody cleaned, cooked, and took care of the house.

On occasion, when the professor and his wife entertained guests, Marie helped Jan with the menu, the making of the goodies, and the serving of their guests. Frequently, the two women used some of the recipes Kieta learned in Wakesa's kitchen. The Smarts always made sure their guests knew who the ladies were, introducing Marie as "an exchange student."

Before long, Louel and Harold would add "She's just like the daughter we never had" to the introduction.

And she would reply "A girl could never have found better parents than they. Dr. Smart and Mrs. Smart took me in their home and hearts, deeds for which I am so thankful!"

Despite her current situation, Kieta Toures a.k.a. Marie did not forget where she came from or the people in her past. At first, she let herself remember Mahmoudou Ibrahaim, who had been the love of her life, and her best friend, Marissa Soyinka, hoping she would see both of them again. Both visited her in her dreams. Sometimes she woke with her pillow wet from tears she shed unabashedly when she was in the bed at night. She often wondered if they thought of her as much as she did them.

Some nights, the girl told herself that Doe had died the day the insurgents broke into the Baker Street cottage then pushed such thoughts aside because she never saw his eyes rolled back, his breath stilled, or his corpse in a box. She had not seen a hole filled and shovels of dirt thrown in the cavity in the earth. *I won't believe it until I see it!* Kieta Toures refused to believe the man was dead and kept believing he would come for her one day.

Time flew, it took wings. Half the year had passed, and the two or three weeks she had thought she would be at the Smarts had passed and gone. All in all, things were good, and the young woman felt some of the sadness lift. She had to admit to herself that it felt good to be out of the stockade the insurgents had put her in and away from what could have killed her. To consider that, Mahmoudou Ibrahaim might not have even made it out of the cottage on Baker Street. While three of the men had been dragging her, several others were fighting with her beloved. He might have won. With these thoughts, a glimmer of hope always injected itself. *It had to be Doe who got me out of the jail. I recognized his eyes. If not Doe, then who? Somebody saved me, brought me to the Smarts, and left me. For what?*

~~~~~

Before long, it was Marie's senior year, and she was seriously considering what she would do as well as where she would go from here. She could not stay with Harold and Louel the rest of her life. She knew this, and she talked with them about it.

Conversations with the Smarts always yielded "You can do whatever you want to do, go where you please. No one is searching for you, and you have done no wrong here. Your record is impeccable. You have a clean slate. Had it not been, you would not have been placed in our home and our hearts!"

Her confidence raised and optimism her companion, the girl signed up for and managed to get work-study opportunities, ones that helped fill up her time and put some money aside for her future. She was glad to have dollars to contribute to her own well-being. Even when she served the Soyinkas, she had been paid for her work and made purchases for herself when Nouhoum drove her and Marissa to the marketplace and the mall.

Since her coming to America, the Smarts had been quite generous. Louel assisted her with opening a bank account, one which she and Harold added money to monthly, and insisted that she have a debit and credit card to access her funds.

Soon, Marie was taking care of her personal needs and saving what was left. She never had need of new clothes. The closet had been full when she got there. It still was, most items not even worn yet. "How did you know my size?" She initiated conversation about her beginnings in America with Louel one day while they walked the track in the gym.

"That was one of the few things we did learn about you," she told the inquisitive one and chuckled, a fixture that was part of her personality, before adding, "I know I went overboard. When they told me I was going to get a girl, I did what I would have done if I had been blessed with a daughter—went shopping!"

"Did you and Harold have to pay for them?"

"Actually, we didn't. The agency gave a stipend to use for your care and would continue if you had special needs."

Marie commented, "Must be some rich agency!"

"No more talk about that! If we knew more, we would have told you more. You should know that by now!" The woman stopped walking so she could address the elephant in the room. He just wouldn't go anyway.

"I guess I will have to do my own research." Marie spoke about closing the gap between her past and present.

Louel stopped and threw her hands up in surrender, her patience being tested. The girl's stride broken, she turned to face the woman whose gaze was on her.

Her benefactor spoke first. "That's on you, Marie! You and you alone know why you were spirited out of your homeland and brought here. You and you alone know whether you would be in danger if you revisit the place from which you came. Harold does not know, and I don't know. We never asked, for it may not be safe for us to know. So do as you must! You alone know your story!"

"Some of it!" The girl raised her voice.

Cutting an eye as other walkers approached, the woman shushed her with fingers to her lips and voiced, "Don't speak so loudly. I am right here in front of you."

"Sorry," Marie said.

Both ladies backed off the trail onto a grassy knoll. "Good morning." Both spoke at a couple of the subdivision's occupants.

"Nice day!" one offered.

"Sure is! Trying to get ours in before the sun comes way up!" the other said. "It's going to be a steamer!"

Louel acknowledged the other women's passing comments then waited a minute before she got back on the beaten path, Marie by her side.

When she was sure the other women could not hear their conversation, she told her charge, "Marie, everything that happened to get you from Timbuktu to Florida was orchestrated through a discreet chain of contacts. We are certain the government, perhaps both governments, were involved in getting you out of the straits you were in. If that is so, the CIA would have initially been contacted.

However, once you were on American soil, your case was probably handed over to the Federal Bureau. That's all either Harold or I can tell you! We were hoping that you had let go of any thoughts you had about finding out more information. As for me, I am tired of you bringing it up! So I am going to tell you for the last time to do what you want to do. If you can trace your roots from here to there and back, have at it!"

Sensing finality in the woman's voice, the girl told her, "I will!"

"Okay, missy!" Louel gave her a warning her mother had used when she was young and insolent. The elder of the two picked up their pace, resuming the fast walking she had been doing before being slowed and arrested by Marie's actions.

Seeing that the girl was slowing down, she beckoned with her hand, saying "Come on! Pick it up!"

Marie enlarged her gait and caught up, and they pounded the pavement, good fitness their collective goal.

Silence accompanied them the rest of their exercise period. The more mature of the women broke it when they were almost at the house and approaching the four-car garage, which currently held two vehicles: his Porsche and her Range Rover. "Harold and I were talking about getting you a little car so you can get around on your own," she told Marie a bit of a conversation she and Harold had had the previous evening, one she initiated.

"I was talking about how having your own vehicle would afford you freedom that you haven't had since you have been with us this past year. I take you most places, but there's nothing like having your own car!"

The girl told her she did not need a car. "The only place we go is to church, out to eat, or to the theater. It would be such a waste for me to have one. I like riding the bus too!"

~~~~~

The yellow bus stop was convenient, just a few blocks from an upper-scale shopping mall behind their subdivision, so Marie rejected this notion. "I have never driven a car or even thought about driving one. Back home in Timbuktu, Nouhoum took Marissa and me to school and shopping." A way of homesickness overtook her for the second time that day. She longed to be back in Mali, studying alongside her friend, and wondered if she was pursuing her education in Europe.

Sadness showed on her face, a brooding for which Louel had disdain. Noticing that her accomplice's mind had gone somewhere else, the woman let all thoughts of a car for this atypical young woman rest and didn't even say anything to each other as they entered the house and headed to shower and make ready for the remainder of the day.

At her vanity, while removing the band and pins from her hair before entering the shower, the Smart woman's own thoughts carried her back to yesterday.

While preparing for bed the previous evening, seated on the cushioned gold bench at her dressing table brushing her hair, her mind had turned to how she could make Marie happy. The woman hated to see her sad, not adjusting to her new home like she should, and hear her whimper and cry when she was alone in her room late in the evenings or at night. She and Harold were bending over backward to make her feel at home. *What more can we do?* Her heart went out to her. She would have been equally as disturbed if she had been taken from one place to another, just dropped off. *Twice* . . . her daddy had done it, and someone unknown had done the same thing. Louel shook her head.

Harold, seated on their bed, laptop open, noticed she had stopped brushing and was just sitting, arm in the air. The man cleared his throat, causing her to resume her personal care. "What are you thinking about over there?"

"I was just thinking about Marie."

"What about Marie?" His response could easily have been translated to "I should have known!"

"You think we should get her a little car to ride around in?"

"No!"

Hearing firmness in his response, she turned around to face him. "Why no?"

"Did she ask you to help her get one?"

"No"—she shook her head—"I was just thinking she might. Most of the kids on campus have a car!"

The man reminded her of campus's inadequate parking and how students parked at a distance and could be seen running to class, else they would be late. "The police are always giving them parking tickets. It's just not worth the trouble, Louel."

"Okay," emitted the woman, laying her hairbrush aside and heading across the room. "Okay, I will. I know I am going a bit overboard. It's just that I am trying to do what I would do if she was mine."

"I know you are, babe. You are good like that. Come on over here and get some rest. Get that girl out of you mind. She will be gone before you know it!"

Harold took a breath and assisted his wife with getting under the sheets. He spoke as they worked. "Can't say I will be sad when she is gone. She's getting all the attention around here. I am not used to that! I don't know if I would have agreed to take her in if I had known she was going to be here more than a few weeks like our other clients."

"Aw! So sorry, baby." The woman put her arms around her husband's neck, pulling herself to him. She gave him a passionate kiss, wanting him to do as he had asked her to do—forget the girl they had taken in for a little while.

Chapter Twenty-Two

A couple of months passed—uneventful ones.

The Smart man generally had breakfast of oatmeal and coffee before he headed for his office in the sociology department at the university. He got more coffee there and grabbed a couple of newspapers from the break room before going to his desk.

His normal routine adhered to, he plopped in his chair, set his coffee on the glass desktop cover, and perused the index on the cover sheets of each to determine which articles he would read before his first class. He would read the remainder sporadically during the day, cover to cover, and frequently talk at dinner about what was going on in the world.

Nothing in the first paper appealed to him, but his eyes were drawn to an article entitled "CIA Agent Lost to Insurgents." That one intriguing, he flipped to the page in the "B" section.

Winston Royals's picture jumped off the page. He jumped, his hand hitting the coffee and causing the full cup to spill. The man leaped from his chair, pushing papers and books not yet soaking to the floor on the opposite side of the desk simultaneously, soaking the yet unread article when it fell in the mess.

The unnerved man cleared the mess, putting all the papers in the trash can beside his desk, then headed to the secretary's office. "I have to leave!" he told her. "Please cancel my classes for the day!"

"You all right? You look like you saw a ghost!" the woman wondered about the look on his face and why he was leaving so fast. He had just gotten there, had not even met his first class. She looked at the clock above the door.

Professor Smart did not give her probing a response. Instead, he thanked her as he backed away from her desk. His stride quickened as he fled her office and from the building, got in his vehicle, and ignited it.

His mind on stopping by a newsstand to pick up a paper and get home, he nearly hit another professor who was parking his car beside his as he put his in reverse and hit the accelerator. The man blew his horn, an action causing Harold Smart to focus on what he was doing. "Sorry, man!" He spoke in the air.

When he stopped at the newsstand, he got not one but several papers with the same Associated Press article and called his wife on her cellphone. She did not answer, so he sent a message through voicemail. "Where are you? I am trying to find you. If you are at the club, stay there. I am on my way there!"

Louel was on the treadmill at the gym. It was too hot to walk outside. Feeling the vibrations from the instrument in her pocket, she hopped off the exercise equipment. She took it out of her pants' pocket and checked to see who was calling. Seeing Harold's number, she backed up and sat on a waiting bench before returning the call.

The man, phone in left hand while he steered with his right one, saw the screen light up. He swiped his thumb across the cellphone's screen at half ring and was talking before she put hers to her ear. "Hey, where are you?"

"Huh?" Her first words caused him to repeat his first question.

"Where are you? Are you at the gym? I got something I got to show you." His words tripped over one another.

"Whoa! Hold up! I didn't get a thing you said." The woman got his attention.

"I am outside of the club if you are in there!"

"I am."

"Come out. I am in the car, parked in handicapped, so hurry up!"

Hearing his urgency, the woman went to her locker, got the few items she had placed there, and hurried to the car.

Inside, she leaned over to give their usual greeting, and the man began talking in her mouth. "Whoa! Hold up! Winston is dead! What are you talking about?"

The man reached for one of the papers from the floorboard, right under her feet, and pushed it toward her. "Turn to page 3B," he said as he carefully back out of the parking space.

"Shit! Damn! Shit!" was all the woman could get off her tongue and out her mouth.

"What does it say? I didn't read it all. I spilled my coffee all over it and had to go get another.

Louel read the short article indicating that Winston Royals, an American citizen and independent contractor in Timbuktu who did some work for the U.S. government, had been assassinated. "The agency is certain who his killer was and will use all its resources to find the man and hold him accountable," she told her husband.

"Is that all it says?"

"Yep! I bet these other papers say the same thing." The woman reached for the other couple of papers to take inside the house when Harold pulled into their garage.

Inside their house, they took care of their personal needs, grabbed drinks from a small refrigerator housed in their bedroom, and retired to the large screened-in patio off their bedroom. They could have privacy there. Neither of the other ladies, Jan nor Kieta, would come there unless they were invited. He sat on a small couch, and the woman curled up on the outdoor furniture with her husband.

He laid the papers on a table beside the couch, opened his drink, and seeing her struggle to loosen hers, he reached for Louel's. Both quenched their thirsts, and he turned his attention to the papers. Like his spouse said, everyone had the same AP article, word for word.

In the absence of anything else he could do, Harold did what most who suffered loss did. He commiserated over a man he had met while in service. He told his wife what she already knew. "We got pretty tight when we were in the Middle East and talked about almost everything. He confided in me about his marital woes, and we talked about what we were going to do when we got out. It was Winston who told me he was going to work part-time with the agency when they left the military. He said our experience in security was still needed. As a matter of fact, he got the job first and recruited me."

"I remember." She returned thoughts about the Royals man. "And that turned out to be a good deal for us. Both of us got work to do!" She took her drink, sipped again, and twisted the top on before placing it on the floor. "With good pay! We could never have afforded a place like this if he had not thought of you."

Nodding at the veracity in her comments, he admitted the guy had helped them in a big way. "You are right. He did that!" He finished his drink and threw his plastic bottle twelve feet across the patio into a trash can's open, gaping mouth. In a distance, in the dust, he could see Winston in his mind's eye shooting hoops. The man loved basketball, sun up to sun down when they were not working.

Their seat groaned as his wife raised herself, doing her own version of a free throw. "There!" She gave her effort a hurrah. Noticing that he had given no response, she turned to her husband. His countenance showed sadness rarely seen.

Sorrow showed in his voice as he spoke about the deceased man. "He had a big heart and was easy to get to know. His love for people made him do the things he did. That's why I helped him out with this one." He turned his thoughts to their houseguest.

Sensing his change in thought and mood, Louel asked, "What are we going to do about the girl?"

"There is nothing to do until we receive further instructions from the agency or the Feds." A look of resignation replaced the sense of sorrow she had just seen.

"Are we going to say anything about this to her? You know we told her she would be here a few weeks. Those turned into a couple of months. Now this . . ." She thought about how she had assuaged the savage beast that arose in the girl whenever she started looking back and trying to figure out where she was going.

"No, there is nothing to be said! We will just let it play out. She will be gone whenever she leaves."

Hearing his compassion, the woman leaned over and kissed her husband on the lips. "You are a sweetheart," she told him. "I think she will be all right as soon as she makes some friends and has some transportation of her own."

The man nodded, his mind on whether the man had gotten a chance to get a proper visa in the girl's name before his passing, one in her own name, not Marie Soyinka's.

~~~~~

On campus, the foreigner accessed the language and math labs the university made available for students in need of assistance but found that in many instances, she was more advanced in both subjects than her American counterparts.

It was there that she met Charlotte Gaines, a white girl who served as a tutor. The first day she came, the tutor showed her how to sign up for a password. The program asked for a mixture of letters and numbers. She toyed with several beginning with Marie and a combination of numbers—*Marie3729, 1Marie6, Marie plus Marissa's birthday*, et cetera. Each password she input was rejected. "This password already in use" showed up on the instruments screen. "Darn it!" she spoke aloud.

Hearing her exclamation and seeing puzzlement on her face, the Gaines woman left the side of another student and returned to Marie's cubicle. "Can I help you?" she asked the obviously baffled student using her best customer service voice.

"All I am trying to do is secure a password. I read the directions and am just trying to create one using my name and number," Marie told the woman.

"Let me see what you've got there." The tutor looked at the screen, and seeing the last password attempted, she said, "Oh I see! Your name, Marie, is quite common. There must be millions of Maries in the United States, so try an uncommon name and just any number!"

Before the woman could try to input another piece of data, the boy Charlotte had abandoned to come to her rescue was beckoning her return. "Hey, miss, come here! You didn't finish with me!"

The girl tapped Marie on her shoulder as she was leaving. "I'll be back when I finish with this fool over there! All right?"

"All right!" Marie pondered but a minute then snapped her fingers. A light bulb went on in her head. She knew what she would use—*M-a-h-m-o-u-d-o-u-1*. She typed the letters and single digit one character at a time then nodded her head when the computer accepted it. She told herself, "Nobody will ever take my password. There are many Does around."

She grinned as she completed the last step in the computer's instructions. "Select a hint to help you remember your password."

The girl clicked on the box and found an entry. "What is your husband's last name?"

I-b-r-a-h-a-i-m flew from her fingers on the keyboard and fell on the computer screen. A message, "Your password is accepted," made her wiggle with joy and throw up happy hands.

Charlotte looked over at her, and seeing her exuberance show, she gave her success a "yes" and a fist pump.

The college student dropped by the lab most days for the fellowship. The computer-assisted programs were boring to say the least. She always made a perfect score on the lessons and assumed they would become more difficult as time passed. Marie would do five or six lessons then do homework so she could enjoy her leisure time at home.

When the tutor saw how quickly she was completing the lessons and that she was scoring high, she pointed out how advanced the girl really was. She took the chair from the cubicle behind them and placed it by the girl's side. "How are things going today?" she asked.

"Fine. I am just trying to get to the more challenging lessons in this module. That is why I am doing more than one a day."

"You might not need to do these lessons," the tutor proffered. "I noticed how fast you are completing each lesson and how many you are doing each day. That's part of my responsibility, to track students' progress and performance as well as provide assistance where needed."

Anticipating that she was making an error, the girl said she would slow down and complete one lesson each day.

The tutor clarified, "You have a propensity for languages, and your knowledge of tongues from your own country, England and ours, shows," she told the girl one day when she stopped by her desk. "Your needs pale in comparison to other students who access this lab. Most of them failed English and math when they were in high school or took remedial courses, so those are the ones who benefit from this service and the computer-assisted learning we provide."

"Oh!" Marie showed that she had not understood the efficacy of the lab for others and how it would not serve her purposes. Disappointment showed on her countenance. "But I enjoy coming here!"

Seeing her disappointment, Charlotte argued, "You can still come! If you do, we get a chance to talk to each other!"

A wide grin showed on Marie's face.

Both mature young women, they became fast friends like she and Marissa had been. Soon, they were doing all the things that young women in their twenties did. They shopped, went to movies, got pampered, and did a bit of boy watching. On occasion, they got hit on by fellows on and off campus. And while Charlotte dated a few, her friend, Marie, did not. Her heart belonged to another.

What the Toures woman liked about her newfound friend was she was not nosy or overly inquisitive. She let her tell her story in her own way and in her own time. Before long, Kieta found herself sharing with the Gaines woman how she had found herself on foreign soil.

"I am not sure how I got out of the country," she told her on one occasion while they traipsed across the campus from the academic building to the dining hall. "All I know is when I woke up, I was in the capital city, Bamako, and was on a private plane, leaving my homeland. And then I was here. A couple of men in black suits whisked me away from the airport and took me to the house where I now reside. I can't recall anything that happened between these two events!"

Charlotte stopped in her tracks, causing a break in their collective strides. "Wow! You must be somebody important! A princess or something?" flew from her lips.

Shaking her head in the negative, the speaker offered up a brief explanation, her stride shortening and enough time being given for the hearer to digest some of what she was talking about. "No," Kieta admitted that her heritage had been humble. A child of nomads turned servant, she had been accosted for failing to follow the DOORs rules and separated from the man she loved. "I don't know much about Mahmoudou," she said near the end of their exchange. "We never spent much time talking about ourselves but spent most of our stolen moments in each other's arms and resorted to just trying to be together!"

The Florida sun beamed down on the duo, and sweat beamed on both their visages. They both swiped at their brows and longed for some sunscreen.

"Let's hurry up and get out of all this heat. It must be a hundred degrees in the shade. A person could actually fry an egg on the sidewalk if they took a notion. You can tell me more about that when we get inside," the Florida native said as she quickened her steps, propelling them to the comforts of the air-conditioned dining hall.

Inside, the girls looked around for somewhere to put their backpacks before getting trays for their lunches. Kieta spotted one in a corner that would provide them some space for sharing. Now that she was talking, she wanted to disclose fully to her friend. She pointed at an empty table, and Charlotte followed her lead. The girls put their bags in two chairs and headed for the chow line where both got sandwiches, salads, and beverages.

As soon as the two were seated, the girl from Mali took up where she had left off. "I was just thinking about Doe and whether he had means that would allow me to get out of the country Or if Marissa's dad did it."

"What do you think?" the listener asked before tearing the paper off a straw, putting it in the lemonade she'd ordered. Taking a swig, she gave the coolness a groan of satisfaction.

Kieta took another sip from her drink before saying, "I kind of think it was him. I think my master might have been a bit too perturbed with me to render aid." Sadness showed on her brow at the mention of the Soyinka man. She felt awful about breaking his trust. He and his family had been better to her than her own father had been.

"Did Doe have means to assist you?"

"Not as much as Monsieur Soyinka, but he did have means." Taking a minute to wipe remnants of her lunch from her lips, she added, "He was a businessman, and while I am not sure about his personal holdings, he might have been able to arrange for me to get out of the country." The speaker mused before taking a bite from her turkey club sandwich.

"What did he do? What kind of business did he have?"

"Petroleum. His family had been in the petroleum business for as long as he remembered."

"Uhm! That's good money! Petroleum is of premium value here, there, and everywhere. A gallon of gas costs almost five dollars right now!" Charlotte exclaimed, giving Kieta a real sense of the man's personal worth, something she had never thought about. *He could very well have had the resources to get me out of Timbuktu!* The woman pushed her chest out, pride in him forthcoming.

She shifted in her seat and straightened her corps as her mind fled to the night a couple of years ago when she had been taken from the jail, put in the jeep and taken away from the stockade near Baker Street. She had seen the man's eyes when he had squatted in front of her and shushed her so the others would not hear her. He had also rubbed her cheek with the back of his hand before another man had picked her up and rushed out of the cell.

Click! Click! Click! Pictures of the jail, the jeep, three men, and the man, various scenes punctuated by painful sensations flashed in her mind.

The young woman was certain now that she thought about it that it could not have been Marissa's father who helped her escape certain death. It was him, Mahmoudou Ibrahaim.

Doe! It had been Doe who helped her get out of the country. She would know those eyes anywhere. He used to make her open them when they made love, said he wanted to see her all the way through. No way could that have been the Soyinka man. It had to have been him. The Ibrahaim man had not been overtaken by the DOOR. He had come to her rescue. She moaned.

Her moan drew her friend's attention. Charlotte let her fork drop, and she looked up at Kieta, catching a glimpse of newly revealed thought. "What is it? What are you thinking?"

Kieta wiped the remnants of the meal from her lips and put the paper napkin on the table. "I just had a flashback," she told the inquirer. "I think I mentioned earlier that the insurgents caught me and Doe together, and we were separated, and I have not seen or heard from him since."

Charlotte acknowledged that the woman had indeed shared that particular occurrence. "Yes, you said you were dragged away and put in jail and that you have not seen the man since that day."

Forlorn on her visage, the girl told her friend she did not realize it until the present moment, but the Ibrahaim man had been definitely been involved in her removal from the country. "I just saw his eyes and felt his touch!"

The woman shivered and pulled her arms around herself to capture the moment as she continued to talk. "He was there. I am certain now that Doe was there the night I got put on the plane in Bamako. He was so frail though. He couldn't even pick me, so one of the men with him wrapped me up in a cloth and took me to an awaiting vehicle driven by yet another man."

"Hmmm," Charlotte emitted, "if he was instrumental in getting you out of Timbuktu, perhaps he knows where you are."

Kieta's heart leaped with joy, her hope renewed. Perhaps the man did know where she was. Perhaps she would see him again one day. She could barely contain herself. The woman clutched her chest in excitement and caught her breath. The thought that Mahmoudou might know where she was causing her to swoon, an act that her friend noticed immediately.

"Are you all right?" Charlotte asked as she reached across the table and touched the Toures woman on the left hand that rested precariously on the furniture separating them.

The young woman stammered a reply, "Yes, yes, I am okay. I must go now!"

Both girls let go of their seats and got up to return to their day's schedule. Shaking away thoughts of Doe, Kieta's attention returned to the content of their initial conversation.

"All I know, Charlotte, is I am so glad Professor Smart and his wife took me in and helped me heal. They played along with whoever got me out of the country and placed me in their care, and as time passed, they restored my identity and helped me replace those temporary papers allowed for students and workers with a permanent passport. They've treated me like their own. I will repay their kindness when I complete law school and get a job."

"They are good people, but I know you miss your family. I would," the Gaines woman spoke sympathetically.

~~~~~

After that day, Kieta continued to talk with Charlotte about the goings on in her native land.

On one occasion, the girls went to a large shopping mall near the college. A new store drew her attention, one that sold African attire. The girl from Timbuktu, drawn to the store, just stopped in her tracks and watched workers preparing for what a sign showed "Grand Opening!" A family—a man, a woman, and a girl—were working alongside one another, dressing mannequins posted in front of freshly cleaned windows, their colors sharp and crisp.

Both women stood there a minute, watching as they worked, their rhythms matching one another. In a minute, the girl looked up and smiled at the young women. Kieta waved at her, and she returned the salutation. This time it was she who turned to leave the storefront first.

When they were face-to-face, her friend witnessed a longing in her friend's eye, one that came every time her mind took leave and headed back to Mali. Tears shone in the corners of her eyes, ones she removed with her right hand.

Charlotte asked, "Are you all right? Do you want to go inside? Talk with them?"

"No." The one who had stopped resumed their mall-walking. "No, the little girl working alongside her mother made me think about my family."

Charlotte told her, "I know you must think about them."

Her assertion yielded. "While I do worry about my family, especially my father, I am just glad I am not there right now."

"Me too," her friend insisted. "I am glad you are out of there too. I can't imagine living under those conditions."

As they approached the food court, the woman displaced by unrest in her homeland pointed to a table. "Let's sit there."

The women placed their book bags in two chairs and seated themselves across from each other.

Their conversation resumed momentarily. "Now what were you getting ready to say about your family and missing them?" Charlotte asked.

"Actually, I was just thinking how things got better when I went into the service with the Soyinka family. Monsieur worked, and Madame kept the house and homeschooled the children. It was she who recognized my gift for learning and allowed me to take classes with their older daughter after I completed my housekeeping duties"

Kieta continued to talk about her life before she came to live with the Smarts, and her friend listened.

When she told the girl about the family she had lived with and served in Timbuktu, Charlotte queried further. "Do you think your employer assisted Doe with getting you out of the country? It's apparent they thought a lot of you too."

"Je n'ai pas d'une idée." She lapsed into broken French at the mention of the family she served and loved. "I have not seen or heard from Marissa since the day Doe and I were caught and captured. I really can't say. As I told you before, I really don't know who my benefactor was. All I can do is guess."

"What do you think could have happened to him?" the girl inquired about Kieta's thoughts about her lover after her removal from their homeland. "I know you think he might have been there the night you left Bamako, but what do you think happened to him after you were spirited away from Mali?"

The woman shrugged and shook her head. Her response was insincere. "Him. I really can't say. He probably went back to one of his four wives." In her heart, she knew it was him but did not admit it until recent times. She had not because she would never do or say anything to anyone that could ever cause the Ibrahaim man discomfort or exposure.

Shock showed on her friend's face and in her voice. "Girl, four wives, he had four wives! You were going with a man who had four wives!" her American counterpart spoke, disbelief apparent.

Kieta shrugged her classmate's concerns about the polygamous relation the man enjoyed. "That is okay. In my country, it is not unusual for men of faith to have more than one wife and family."

"I don't know how I could handle that," her American confidante readily admitted.

The foreign woman laughed, a rare emotion. She explained, "It is not like I was part of a harem. I never knew his family . . . and doubt they knew I existed. As I told you before, we always met in private. We never engaged in an orgy! Neither did Doe for that matter. He told me on one of the rare occasions that we talked about his family that he had only consummated one marriage. His other wives were too young. They were betrothed to him by their families, and when they were of age, he would claim the promise."

"Still too much for me!" her friend exclaimed before turning her attention to other experiences in Kieta's life in Mali. "I bet you wish you had been able to complete your education there alongside Marissa."

The Toures girl thought for a moment before responding then acknowledged a desire to have continued her study at the university. "C'etait impossible." She lapsed into the French that occasionally flew from her lips. "I don't know whether it is true, but I read an article in the *Sun Crest Times* recently that told how the terrorists had rushed the university, going classroom to classroom, telling women that they would no longer tolerate miseducation by Western influence and that they were to leave school immediately, get married, and serve their husbands. If that is true, as much as I would have wanted to continue to go to school with her, it would have been impossible." She paused for breath and asked her friend, "Didn't you see the article? It was in the paper a couple of Sundays ago."

Charlotte shrugged and admitted her ignorance. "No, I didn't see it. I don't read the paper much. I occasionally glance at it for local news and wedding announcements, obituaries, social events, and the like, but I never read the international news."

The speaker drew the moment out and used it for a teachable moment. It was apparent that her friend was not merely nosy as some were but rested uniformed because she had enjoyed the freedoms that came with democracy, ones she herself was just now, at the age of twenty-five, embracing. Their worlds, opposite, could become the same if the Gaines woman did not attend to her surroundings and participate by keeping knowledgeable, watchful, and participating in all the rights her country afforded women: to be educated, make choices, work outside of the home, receive pay comparable to that of men, vote, govern, and serve, not be subservient.

Reaching for the Gaines woman's hand, to make her attend, Kieta looked her friend squarely in the eyes so she could see sincerity in her face. "You must pay more attention to the world around you, friend, lest you risk the same *maladie* my country faced. We, Timbuktuians, were united and prosperous at one point, but we grew fragmented and warred among ourselves as the terrorists came in, destroying a way of life that we were accustomed to and enjoyed. If you and your fellow Americans do not pay attention, you may also fall victim to outsiders.

What I am trying to tell you is the same thing that happened in my homeland can happen right here in America." She let her gaze drop when she had finished speaking.

Charlotte acknowledged her own ignorance. "I know. You are right. I must do better!"

The moment passed, and in a minute, their attention returned to the reasons they had come to the mall—just to hang out and do a little people watching. Neither were shoppers. Kieta had enough to share with the other college student. She would never wear all her clothing. Louel Smart, a consummate shopper, had filled her closet and continued to bring her items of clothing she like when her host shopped for herself.

"Come on. Let's get something to eat. I am ravenous!" Kieta jumped up first and headed toward the restaurants encircling the mall's dining area.

Her friend, on her heels, called after her over in the din that had increased in the food court since their arrival about fifteen or twenty minutes ago. "What do you want?"

Kieta turned toward a restaurant with Indian cuisine. "All that talk about home makes me want something flavorful. I think I will get some beef curry."

"I will go over to Chick-fil-A and get a grilled chicken sandwich and an order of waffle fries." Charlotte pointed toward the restaurant across the dining area.

"Okay, get me some *limonharri!*"

"Will do! I will get your favorite beverage." The woman translated "lemonade."

Chapter Twenty-Three

Little did the Toures woman know, Doe no longer had a family. His immediate ones had gotten out of the country when he was hospitalized after the motorcycle-truck collision he was involved in while trying to rescue her from the insurgents. He no longer resided in their homeland either. The man had been reduced to being a runaway. The man had been lost to the insurgents who exacted a vendetta on him because he refused to become one of them. He would have been an asset to DOOR or any other of the numerous groups that formed in and around Timbuktu.

Fuel was necessary for their vehicles, and the businessman had contacts they did not have. Since he failed to cooperate, they started blowing up his tanks, cut off access from his providers, and caused him to be separated from her, his *cherie*. Mahmoudou Ibrahaim grew blind with rage then exacted revenge on the man who had been involved in this final act.

She also could not tell her new confidante, Charlotte Gaines, for she did not know that Doe, in a weakened state, was recruited by foreign fighters while recuperating from the accident that nearly took his life. He fought against DOOR and other insurgents before feigning cooperation with Winston Royals and his group with hopes of finding her. A budding extremist, he also found himself involved in some burnings. The town hall, the governor's office, and an MP's residence were incinerated under his command.

Most notably, he had shot dead the man responsible for their separation. The Ibrahaim man shot him point-blank because he took her from him in an attempt to make him a loyalist then ran for his life, his mind on finding and saving her.

When the insurgents could not find him after Winston's death, the maddened men had used petroleum from his few remaining storage tanks to light up his immediate family members' emptied cottages, those of other known acquaintances, and killed innocent men, women, boys, girls, and children who could not give them any information about the man they sought.

Mahmoudou Ibrahaim had satisfied a vow he made to himself when the men had taken the love of his life from him on Baker Street almost three years ago. He had had to take the CIA operative out before he left their homeland on his own accord; otherwise, Dubuya might have gotten away scot-free. Because the man he killed was an American citizen, one of their "elite," his name was placed on the list of international terrorists.

Likewise, Kieta could not express to her friend how the homeless man soon grew weary of the lifestyle or how he longed for a bed with a firm mattress and some pillows, one which could hold both of them. The floors of vacated buildings the man slept in grew increasingly harder when he was hanging out with the homeless and other runaways.

Nor could she tell of the night she, Kieta Toures, visited him in a dream, transporting him to another more peaceful estate. Of how, in the morning, the man left his trusted weapon in its spot beside his bundle and walked away from the life imposed on him by the loss of first, his *cherie*, and then his family.

Or how, with his mind on where in the devil Winston Royals sent her, he made his way to the airport. He stole his way on a plane, in cargo storage, and made his way to the United States in search of his beloved Kieta. The woman had stayed in his head and his heart and occupied his dreams. How, he purposed when he found her, he would take her to the city they had discussed, New York City, and make her his wife then live happily ever after.

Kieta's conversations with Charlotte had so many empty blanks she could not fill in. The one thing she could do was provide a description of him to her friend. She knew him from head to toe. After all, he was her man, and she was his woman. At least, that was the way it had been.

"He sounds handsome!" her friend remarked then asked the woman a.k.a. Marie about his hue, the color of his hair, whether he was hirsute or clean-shaven, and the color of his eyes.

The woman described her man to a *T.* "Tall, dark, and handsome. His skin a shade darker than mine like toast, just turning from brown to burned, deep brown hair. His piercing eyes so deep they almost cut into my soul. He was clean-shaven most of time, his skin as smooth as a baby's butt. However, I am convinced the last time I laid eyes on him he had a beard." She grew warm all over and nearly dampened her underpants as she remembered his feel, his touch, Doe's manly odor. The woman crossed her legs.

Her passion articulated, it brought a thunderous reply from her friend.

"Damn!" The woman let a rare expletive explode from her lips. "Some fine man!" she told Marie. "No wonder you can't get your mind off him!"

Marie clasped her hands, prayer style, and bobbled up and down where she stood, her legs weakened by desire. "I just wish I had a picture of him. I am so afraid I won't know him when I see him again. So much time has passed, and if he is anything like me, he has changed some."

Charlotte assured her, "You will know him! Your heart will let you know when you see him again. Such love as you have described can never be forgotten."

After a pause, she continued, "How long will you wait for him?"

Kieta hunched her shoulders, admitting, "As long as it takes. That's how long I will wait—as long as it takes."

"I just can't relate yet. But I hope I will find and know the love that you have described," the Gaines woman spoke, her voice low and tone longing.

The other woman saw how sad she was growing, reached over, and drew her friend to her side and assured her, "You will find love! You will find it right there in the city! New York is full of men, professional men, all kinds of men. There is one for you, and you will know him when you find him, and he will know you. That's the way love does you. It puts itself in your life when you least expect it."

Her mind flashed back to how she had been doing her work at the Soyinkas' compound, love the last thing on her mine. Obviously, Cupid held her number in his hand. She spoke more. "A phone call did it for me. Doe was trying to call someone else. However, he dialed the wrong number, liked the sound of my voice, so he called every day. That man wouldn't give up and relented until we met and fell in love. That's how that nymph, Cupid, inserted love in my life. He will have his way with you too!"

Once Kieta Toures opened up with the woman, she not only dreamed of Mahmoudou Ibrahaim but also started searching for the man. The woman looked for Doe in every face she saw. She pledged to herself that she would find him.

~~~~~

In the meantime, everywhere Mahmoudou went, he looked for her face in the crowd. In Seattle, Washington, USA, he initially found himself working odd jobs. The man, rescued from the hold on the plane by fellow countryman, found a safe haven. He was sponsored by an antiterrorism organization. Through this organization, he met more of his countrymen who had escaped the goings on in Timbuktu and got assistance with the temporary visa, which allowed him to remain there while he decided what he should do, whether he should continue to work for the small amount of cash given to day laborers, undocumented individuals from many countries as well as those who had visas, or go to the college and complete the degree in business management he had started in Timbuktu so long ago.

He found himself brainstorming with a mere acquaintance one day, and soon, he talked himself into fulfilling a dream to go to New York to live, work, and get that elusive degree. He decided once his schooling was completed he would secure employment in the petroleum field in the United States. He had experience with that.

But how would he get there? The Ibrahaim man labored and saved, saved and labored, did overtime whenever that was available, and begged any worker who could not go for his shift. He noticed how much more he could earn and put back.

Not working, he utilized the public library Downtown Seattle to search and research colleges in New York. Ms. Folsom, a librarian, noted his obvious intensity and soon gained his confidence. She helped him make application to college and study for entrance tests, which he passed with flying colors. He also received a scholarship for minority students.

The woman secured lodging for him with a friend who had a flat near Central Park. In his mid-thirties by then, he soon found himself in the city at the university in New York pursuing a degree in business administration and working at a nearby Waffle House restaurant as a short-order cook, a job that did not require a great deal of training. It was open twenty-four hours, seven days a week. Tips and a flexible hours, his perks.

Regardless of where he was, what he was doing, day in and day out, Doe's mind rested on starting up again in this country and finding love lost when his homeland had been invaded and ravished by the insurgents.

Kieta Toures rested the wind beneath his wings, his raison d'être. He told himself frequently, willing her to hear with mind and heart, what he spoke aloud, "Don't give up! *Cherie*, don't give up on me. I will find you. No mountain is too high, no valley too low, no river too wide." His mind channeled a song he heard playing on the jukebox at the restaurant. Admittedly, the United States was a big country, but he vowed he would find her.

At the university, he also took full loads and participated in work-study on campus. His obvious experience created a climate where he served the business administration department as a student aide. When he didn't have his head in the books or was not working, he took to the gym on campus to work out. It helped keep his mind off the woman, a hard job for a man who enjoyed pleasuring women. He had had a wife and his *cherie* to attend to his needs when in Timbuktu. His hand became his best friend when distressed. The man did not know how long he could remain loyal.

One day he took a walk in the park with his landlord and enjoyed the walk. After that morning, he rebutted the sterility of the gym and exchanged it for a busy climate, walking first then jogging on the trails in Central Park early in the mornings and late evenings, his preference those nearest to the Hudson. The trees were denser and gave off more shade. The water was calming. It was nothing like the desert land he had escaped years earlier.

Chapter Twenty-Four

When the girls were close to graduation, their attention turned to what they should do after graduating from the Florida college: go to work or get advanced degrees. The foreign girl wrestled with her decision more than her accomplice did. She was an orphan, on foreign soil, with a host family providing safe haven for an unspecified length of time. Charlotte, from a family that could provide her with necessary support, did not have such concerns.

The latter girl's finances certain, she convinced her friend to confide in the Smarts. "I think they will do everything they can to help you transition from undergraduate school to work. Both have educations, good work ethics, and value what advanced degrees can help you achieve. They can help you get financial aid. He has contacts that my parents don't have."

"I will talk to them, see what they say!" Kieta relented and talked to her benefactors. She brought it up when they were having supper that evening.

When they had finished the main course and were enjoying coconut cake, her favorite, and coffee, she began, "I was thinking—"

Before she could finish her sentence, the Smarts playfully engaged her by parroting "I was thinking," a phrase the girl used almost every time she initiated a conversation. This phrase, something that had been discussed before, brought the three to laughter.

"Stop playing with me." She toyed with them. Her face grew serious, so the adults gave her their full attention.

"I was . . ." She raised her hand to cease the phrase she had admonished them about. "Okay, Charlotte and I have been talking about what we plan to do when we graduate in the spring, and she told me I should talk to you all."

The man took the lead. "What are you thinking, child?"

"I don't know whether I want to go to work or I should get an advanced degree first."

Louel inserted her opinion. "I think you should do whatever makes you happy. If going to work on a job just to have a check is what you want to do, is what will make you happy, then do that. If the advanced degree will provide an opportunity to do work that you enjoy and get better income later that will sufficiently meet your needs, then you should do that."

"Uhmmm . . . money now or more money later? A job I don't like now or doing a work that I value and enjoy later?" the girl voiced what she had gleaned from the Smart woman's views.

The professor eyed the two as they conversed. In a minute, he cleared his throat and set his cup on a saucer beside his plate. Both looked to him for his thoughts.

"You know we have been talking a lot, but I don't recall you ever saying what it was you want to do with your life. Do you know? Can you share your interests with us?"

"I am not exactly sure, but I am thinking about law . . . international law. I keep thinking how I might advocate for young people like myself who are between lands, allegiances . . . I don't know whether that would do it or whether it is missionary work that I should do," she stammered as she tried to sift her thoughts and clarify for herself what she should do.

"Is this the same thing that Charlotte plans to do?" The man was interested in knowing whether peer pressure was influencing her decision.

"No, not really! She wants to do law and be a public defender."

Seeing his brow raise, Kieta kept talking. She gave a full reveal. "I guess you could say we kind of want to do the same thing but serve different populations. We have been talking about going to New York City, going to law school there. I was the one who actually brought it up. I was telling her one day how I always wanted to do that, and she found it ironic that we were wanting to go to the same place. I also told her I didn't think I could go now. My future is up in the air. I am not sure whether I need to get out of you all's life and fend for myself now. If I do, I will have to work. When I gave her my reluctances, she asked if I had talked with the two of you. I confessed that I had not but would soon."

Louel smiled and gave Charlotte props. "I am so glad the two of you are friends, and you have someone who gives good advice. That is not always the case."

"I know," Kieta acknowledged the woman's comments. "She is really a neat person. I am going to miss her when she goes to New York. Her parents and she are making applications already."

"Hold up!" Harold stopped her from talking. "Did I hear you say your dream is to go to law school in New York to study international law with hopes of supporting others like yourself in transitioning and embettering their lives?"

"Yes, sir," she answered, humility in her voice.

"Well, young lady, if that is what you want to do, what is stopping you?" He raised his eyebrows as he raised his voice.

Stammering again, she confessed how inadequate she felt when comparing her life and life's chances to those of her friend.

Louel grabbed the conversation like a matador might grab a small bull in training. "Oh, no, missy. Don't go there! You do have a home. Ours is yours! I don't know how many times we have told you that! Harold and I pledged to *you* that we would be there for you as long as you need us. Both of us are college graduates, so we know how to do school if we don't know how to do anything else. We know how to apply for colleges and get grants and loans. Professor over here"—she pointed a finger at her husband—"has contacts. He can help you more than you know. And I can too. So you can stop that feeling sorry for yourself and let us help you get busy. No child coming out of this house is going to be left behind!"

"Damn! You told her!" Harold brought levity for what seemed to be a bit harsh. The man patted Kieta on her hand and told her, "You can be whatever you want to be and do whatever you want to do. Instead of going by the lab, come by my office tomorrow, and I will help you get started."

The Toures girl jumped from her seat, hugged the man, and ran around to the other side of the table so she could embrace the woman. "I got to go! I got to go to my room and call Charlotte!"

At the door, she remembered her manners. She turned around, telling them, "Thank you, thank you, thank you!" She blew kisses to match her appreciations.

Louel and Harold, their hearts warmed by the girl's enthusiasm, took each other's hand. Their thoughts on how things were going to work out for their charge.

"We are going to have to get that identity thing taken care of soon," the man told his wife.

"It will work out," she offered her assurances. "It always does." They leaned over and kissed each other on the lips.

~~~~~

Shortly after Winston Royals's body was returned to Seattle, a funeral was held in his hometown. Harold Smart went to his services as did others who were in the war with the man, several who also started working for the agency before he and Harold signed on. The operatives enjoyed fraternal relationship much like the one the Florida native had been a part of when in college. They fought together, played together, and held each other's affairs confident.

These, the pallbearers, ported their friend's remains with the care they knew he would have given theirs. After greeting the Royals family, pairs or groups of the men found trees to shelter them from the sun while they spoke either about the deceased or other things.

Seeing another agent who served with them, Harold Smart caught up with him when he was making his way to his vehicle. "Hey, man!"

The man returned his greeting, slapping him on the back and hugging him. "I thought that was you I saw over there in the church, but I wasn't sure. You don't look the same when you clean up! Looks like being a professor is agreeing with you."

"You look pretty good yourself!" Smart countered. "I need to talk with you about something important!"

Hearing urgency in his voice, the other man told him, "Hop in! Let's ride out. I will get you back to your vehicle."

"Okay, it's a little way down that way." He pointed away from the cemetery.

As soon as they were buckled up, he spoke to the other operative about the girl he and his wife were keeping. "I don't know where this goes from here. Louel and I decided we would keep her until she was ready to leave our care. The only problem is we need documents with her real name on it *if* she is in no danger."

"No problem," the agent told him when he was getting out of his car. "I will see to it! Get your ass out my car!"

Both laughed. Harold was giddy with relief. "Thanks, man. I owe you one!"

~~~~~

A week or two passed before her corrected documents were in the mail. Her name, *Kieta Marie S. Toures*. What she liked to be called, *Marie*. The Smarts decided to keep them under wraps for a while and, when they were certain she could handle what they needed to tell her, give them to her.

As her relationship with Charlotte grew, she grew to love her host family as much as they loved her. She even brought the girl by the professor's office. Soon, Charlotte started dropping by their house to pick her up and take her to the mall, a movie, or concerts on campus.

Everything calmed down; all adjusted their lifestyles accordingly. When Christmas came, the Smarts decided to give the Toures girl the gift they had maintained for her. Now that she was finishing school and headed where destiny was leading her, the question about who she could identify herself as needed to be resolved. Along with purchases for the holiday, Jan decided she would wrap this one in a number of boxes, small to large. She got a small box and wrapped it first, and as she found another a bit larger, she inserted the smaller one into that.

Thanksgiving came and went. Christmas on its heels, Louel exhibited the spirit she always had. Her joy was intensified this time because she and Harold had another in the house this Christmas. The following Monday, she was up before Harold at Jan's side and jabbering endlessly about how to make the holiday one Kieta would remember.

"I know one thing she can do! She can help with all the decorating we do around here. If that don't help her feel special, I don't know what will" was the helper's cool response.

When the woman was off her heels and out of the earshot, Jan told herself what else the girl could do. "She can help take all that mess down. Ain't no sense in what Ms. Louel does, not this year but every year! She puts trees everywhere, even in the toilets. Lawd, that woman know she is crazy about some Christmas."

She put breakfast fixings on the tray and pushed it the short distance from the kitchen to the dining room. As she entered the room, she had another thought about what the visiting girl could do. Her mouth spoke aloud what was in her heart. "You ask me what that girl can do! I tell you what else she can do! She can get her lazy butt up on that ladder and string some of those thousands of lights too!"

"What? Did I hear you say something?" Harold looked up from notes he was making until he heard her voice.

The woman shrieked, her yells causing him to jump.

Harold asked her, "Are you all right? Is something wrong?"

She put her hand over her heart, which was racing. "Naw, Mr. Harold. You just about scared me to death! I didn't know nobody was in here. I just finished talking to Mrs. Smart in the kitchen, and I thought she went back into the bedroom to get you to come on and get your breakfast!"

Jan took a cloth napkin from the cart, wiped her brow, and uttered a final "Lawd, have mercy!" before pushing the breakfast cart all the way to the table.

So together, Louel, Jan, and Kieta decorated the house for the holidays. This proved to be one among the most exciting times the girl had ever had. The three of them got the decorations out of storage. When they were laid out in the garage, they sorted them according to their color. Every color in the rainbow as well as those in the basic Crayola box was represented—traditional reds and greens, silver, gold, white, blue, yellow, orange, and purple. Hordes of it!

Astonished at the volume of bulbs, bobbles, bangles, beaded chains, stars, and boxes of garland, the Toures girl asked, "Where are we going to put all this stuff?"

Jan provided the answer. "Child, this woman is a Christmas tree-loving woman! We are going to put a tree in every room, every nook and cranny there is in this house! And we are going to decorate the outside too. Our house is going to be the best one in this whole subdivision!"

Hearing the woman chuckle at Jan's alluding to their subdivision's annual decorations contest, the girl looked to her to tell her more about the contest, but before she could respond, a white truck loaded with trees passed their driveway. The logo on the truck's door, The Nursery Surrounded With Trees, claimed their full attention. Louel left their sides to help the driver back into their yard.

Her assistance was not warranted. A man jumped out of the passenger side of the truck and trotted over to where she stood, hand raised and ready to guide the driver. "I got it, ma'am," he told her as he waved the backing driver straightaway until he was close to the garage. She stepped over, and he claimed the spot she relinquished.

The driver halted when he heard the man's "Whoa! That's good enough!" He hopped from the Nursery's truck, work order in hand, and came over to the familiar woman. "How are you doing today, Mrs. Smart?"

"Fine now that you are here with my trees!" Delight showed in her voice and on her face.

"All fifteen of them," he told her as he pointed to the work order. "The sizes you ordered. Do you want to have a look at them before we bring them into the house and set them up?"

"No need for that! Your work speaks for itself! We will get out of your way while you do your work."

"Okay, let's do it!" He headed to the truck bed, his accomplice on his heels. The two men started taking the trees off the truck.

As soon as Louel was back on the side of the garage that held the decorations, the obvious first-timer, surprise showing on her face, asked, "Are we going to put up *all* those trees?"

"That's what I was trying to tell you, child," Jan answered.

For lack of anything else to do or say, the Toures girl just stood there gawking. The size of some of the trees was shocking. She shook her head.

Momentarily, Louel snapped a finger to bring her back to the present. "Okay, there is lots to do, but we won't get it done standing in one spot. First, let's decide which colors we want in what room. We know for sure we are going to use the gold and silver in the living room and dining room. The larger trees will be placed there. These are the ones for which we have the most decorations. You first, missy. What color do you want, and where do you want to put it?"

A task she found overwhelming, Kieta bowed out, asking, "Can't I just help this time? Once I see where they are placed today, I will be more capable of choosing the next time."

Louel let her slide but gave her something she could do, something that would not take much thought. "I tell you what . . . Take everything gold and put it in the living room!" Seeing the men taking a huge tree in the front door, she cautioned her, "Don't get in their way!"

Everyone involved in the tree placement and trimming put their noses to the ground and did not come up for air until the truck bed was empty, the trees were in stands, and boxes and bags of decorations were placed around the walls of each room, their colors coordinated to match furnishings, curtains, spreads, and floral pieces.

The trees in their places first, the men used their dollies to help the ladies complete their work. When their work was completed, Jan offered refreshments, which the men refused.

"Go get my purse out of my bedroom," Louel said, pointing at Kieta. The girl turned and started to go but stalled. She had only seen the Smarts' bedroom once and that was on the day she got the official tour. No one had made the place off-limits. She just respected their privacy. Her feet failed her; she stopped walking.

Seeing her confusion, the woman shooed her onward. "Go on, child. Get my bag out of our room. It's on a chair beside the dresser. You will see it from the door!"

Kieta rushed into the bedroom and was out before there was time for her to be missed. She handed the Michael Kors handbag to the woman who withdrew her matching purse and gave the men a hefty tip. Its value noted, both thanked her profusely and pledged to come by and help more if she needed assistance.

"When we are outside and can't reach as high as we want, I may just do that," she said as they were leaving the house.

Needless to say, the girl was winded by bedtime. She had not worked that hard since she left the Soyinkas' house to go to school on her last day there. But she could not sleep because thoughts about home refused to let her rest. She remembered how Madame Ruby had celebrated the holiday, but nothing she did matched what was happening here. The Soyinka's' library was always decorated in greens and reds with a bit of white for the annual Christmas party. Another was in the living room where presents for opening on Christmas morning were placed. Both held a variety of ornaments, store-bought and ones the children made in their art classes. *Who would have ever thought a person would have more than two Christmas trees in a house? I wish Marissa, Taurence, and Ife could see them!* The girl's final thoughts about Louel's infinity to overdo everything, even decorating for the holiday, was voiced aloud in the darkness before sleep finally came replacing them.

The Smarts and their charge participated in a round of holiday parties, every one equally as magnanimous as the other. All met with increasing fondness for a livelihood the girl was enjoying. No point in the period, however, would be as memorable as Christmas morning when the family met around the huge tree in the living room to open their presents, Jan not there because she was spending the yuletide season with her own family.

"Come! Let's open our presents!" Louel led the way into the living room where they exchanged gifts: perfumes and colognes, gift cards, books (paperbacks and audiobooks—contemporary fiction from their favorite authors as well as some classics to place on the shelves in the Smarts' library), pajamas and robes, house shoes, and new toothbrushes because the woman changed everyone's out every three months.

One huge box remained, it having been secreted near the back of the tree bathed in gold ornaments, feathers, chains, and trinkets. The woman clapped her hands and rubbed them together. Excitement showing all over her countenance, she pointed to it as she asked her husband to give it to Marie.

He laid the last of his presents atop the stack he'd made beside the armchair he had taken when they came into the room. Out of his chair in a minute, he kicked wrapping paper aside as he shuffled over to the box. A bit heavy, he pushed it over to the girl, letting it rest right in front of her.

Kieta's mouth fell open. "Is this for me?" she asked.

"Yes, it is." The two pranksters chorused. "Open it! Open it!" the man said as he pushed it a bit closer.

"Do you want to guess what it is?" Louel asked when she was removing the wrapping paper, exercising care not to tear it up. Finding it too pretty, she took the time to fold it, the same care that had been taken when unwrapping all her gifts; however, her ritual was brought to an end by the Smarts encouraging her to hurry and open the box.

Seeing there was a box inside the box, this one equally as ornate as the larger box, the girl comprehended why Louel had been seeking boxes of various sizes while they shopped. "Aw, so you are playing games," she told the woman standing over her. "How many boxes am I going to unwrap before I find the tiny one with the car keys in it?" Her thoughts were on the woman's continuous badgering her to let them get her a car and for Harold to be able to teach her to drive before she left their home.

Louel laughed, and her husband joined her.

"Okay, which one of you is going to tell me what kind of car it is?" the girl asked when she had made her way through four boxes, retrieving one the size of a paperback book.

"Hurry up!" The woman was jumping up and down, unable to contain herself.

Kieta leaned back in her chair and opened the present, its gold wrapping paper more splendid than the covering on any of the other presents. She pushed the white paper inside the box aside, expecting a gold car key to leap out at her.

It was not a key. Seeing the box's contents, she grew quiet. The blue of the visa with emblem pressed in gold on its cover almost took her breath. She looked up, looking first to the man then to his wife. Tears of joy welled up in her eyes.

Both Smarts had not anticipated her obvious overwhelm but rushed to her to comfort her. He, at the side of her chair before the floodgates open, rubbed her back soothingly. The woman left her side, nudged the discarded paper and boxes aside, and knelt in front of her. She used her thumbs to wipe away the droplets from Kieta's leaking eyes before they could become a storm. The couple looked at each other, their eyes met, their thoughts on how they should have given the gift without upsetting her.

"We are so sorry, Marie," Harold told her. "We didn't mean to upset you. We just—"

"No, no, it is all right! I am just surprised. I didn't have any idea . . .," she stammered, words to express the joy she was feeling refusing to come.

Her knees aching, Louel got up. "Look inside it, see what it says," the woman told the Toures girl. Her words the same as when they showed her the temporary visa that came with her the night she was delivered to them for safekeeping.

Kieta took her new visa from the tissue Louel had encased it in and read aloud what they wanted her to see: her new name, her own followed by Marie, the label she had been given, an *S* instead of Marissa's last name, and her given name, Toures. She traced her fingers over *Kieta Marie S. Toures*, and a smile crossed her face.

Sighs of relief escaped her benefactors.

"I am Kieta Toures. I can use my real name." She tapped her chest with a finger, her pride showing through.

The professor told her she was who she was and should place her name as it was in the visa on applications for colleges, entrance exams, and the LSAT used for admission into law school, any legal documents. "However, Louel and I would appreciate it if you would continue to use Marie while you are here."

Confusion showed on her face but was erased by Louel. "Since we introduced you as Marie to Jan, our neighbors, and friends, we just thought it would be better to keep it up. There is no reason to explain a change. At least, that's what we said."

"We will do what you need for us to do, child," the man assured her that everything was all right.

Her bladder full, she almost wet her pant when she got the surprise. Kieta got up from the seat. "Marie it is! I will be Marie as long as you want me to be. I got to go!"

"Go ahead!" The woman shooed her out the room.

Harold and she flopped back down in their chairs by the time she was out of earshot. "Glad that is done!" The man spoke first.

His wife agreed with him. "Me too! For a minute there, I was not sure whether we had done the right thing."

~~~~~

Her identity certain, and with apprehensions about support for her continued schooling removed, Kieta Toures and Charlotte Gaines threw themselves into preparations for the next phase of their lives. They took the LSAT, and both passed with flying colors; made applications to law schools all over the United States like the professor suggested; and got accepted to all programs for which they applied but flew to the preferred city, New York, and had interviews and were accepted.

Both initially found housing on the campus, opting not to room together or share space. Kieta kept her assigned one, an efficiency apartment. The Gaines woman's parents, however, helped her acquire a larger apartment near the campus. Each did what her financial aid would allow.

Louel Smart did for Kieta what *real* mothers did. She accompanied the young woman to school, luggage filled so much that they had to pay the excess baggage fee at the airport, the four bags they checked over fifty pounds each. Each of them also took a carry-on and a backpack on the plane. The exhausted women had to wait nearly an hour before taking their bags from the turnstile and rolling them on a cart to the exit. A waiting cab transported them through the busy streets from the airport to campus housing.

Other students and their families were unloading when they got there. Students helped each other take boxes, bags, and luggage to their new lodging, assistance they truly appreciated.

At Kieta's new home, they passed the first night resting, the girl in her bed in the one-room apartment and Louel on the couch. The girl had offered it, but the woman refused the comforts of the full bed after they had dressed it together. "It's not like I haven't ever slept on a couch," she told the girl, a statement that gave her pause.

The girl had been so into herself and what was happening with her that she knew very little about her benefactors. he Smarts had told her they had been middle class, a system she barely understood. In Timbuktu, there were two kinds of people she was familiar with—the haves and the have-nots. But the Smarts enjoyed an affluent existence because of their military retirements, his employment as a college professor and their work with the agency. This was as much as she found out about them in the many, many months she had been at their home on Sandalwood Drive. In bed that night, the girl told herself she would learn more about them during the week Louel was spending in the city with her.

The next day, the two women shopped at nearby stores for accessories to personalize the fully furnished campus apartment. Against the girl's wishes, her benefactor filled the pantry with foods—canned goods and lots of Ramen noodles because that's what sustained her when she had been a college student. The woman overfilled the refrigerator with waters and juices to keep her hydrated.

In addition, she assured her bank account at the bursary on the campus was opened, checks ordered, and a debit card gotten, its password placed in the contact information on her own cellphone just in case the Toures girl got caught up in all the excitement and forgot it.

It took only a couple of days to do errands, so they spent the remainder of the week exploring New York. They had researched shows and gotten tickets on the Internet for one on Broadway they had never heard of before they left home, so they saw a matinee that day too. Both women enjoyed the production immensely and pledged to see the Rockettes later. Another day they took a taxi to Ellis Island to see the Statue of Liberty and went to Ground Zero to see the progress being made on the place where the Twin Towers had been before the planes flew into them.

There, Kieta did not know about the terror that had taken over New York City in September 2001, so she listened attentively as Louel and the taxi driver reflected on that day's events.

"Where were you that day?" the woman asked him.

"I was here in New York and witnessed the whole thing!" The man placed extra emphasis on *whole*. "I had picked up a fare and was headed this way. A woman from Georgia was up here to see her cousin who lived over in Jamaica. I was picking her up in front of her hotel and was fixing to take her there. I just happened to look up while she was closing the door." His voice grew louder as he recounted the terrifying event.

"The tower that was right there went down first." The man pointed from skyline to the street and back. "A plane flew into it! I saw it with my own eyes." He paused a moment to catch his breath and continued, "I froze, couldn't move a muscle! I was sitting there just like I am sitting here now, trying to get myself together. All of a sudden, the woman in the backseat started yelling!"

The driver shook his head. "What was she screeching about?" the man asked, anticipating they were wondering too. Neither had time to answer his question. He continued to share what he had seen that eventful day. "She saw another plane before I saw it. My mind was transfixed on the spot where Tower I had been, so she called my attention to the second plane . . . I realized she was screaming because a second plane came out of nowhere, and before we could do anything, it flew right into the other tower! It started crumpling too right before our eyes." The man stopped short, he needed a cleansing breath, a short one.

He resumed, "Before long, they were saying on the radio that we were under a terrorist attack! I was so scared. I just wanted to get off the street and get home. I just wanted that woman to get out of my car so I could get out of the city before something else happened."

At the mention of the word terror, Kieta Toures's mind returned to her own homeland. The girl thought about how beautiful Timbuktu had been before the insurgents came. It was a beautiful city, a cultural center. What happened to it? Once the terrorists came, factions were established, and the warring groups tore up the city, looting first then trashing businesses that had been there for a long time. They broke into the museum, took artwork, and pillaged the library, taking classics that were on its shelves for booty.

The man kept reliving that awful day. "Anyhow, that woman must have heard me thinking. She jumped out my car, ran back into the hotel, and I drove around trying to find somewhere safe. I wasn't the only one! Seemed like the whole of the city was trying to get somewhere. Anyway, I was trapped in the city and couldn't get back to the office or to my home. It was one big mess up in here that day! Whew!" He wiped beads of sweat raised by memories of September 11.

At least, you all didn't just let it stay there! The Malian's mind was on how the people in America had cleaned up quickly and built the area up again. *Not in my homeland! Rubble stays where it is forever!* She wondered if the cottage on Baker Street was wrecked and torn up after she and Doe were discovered or bombed and burned. She recounted how insurgents used explosives and incendiary devices with reckless abandon even on private property. The girl told herself how fortunate she was to be in the new land.

Time flew while the two women learned the city. Another day dawned, and with its dawning, more items on the Floridian's bucket list were checked off.

"I know you are going to Central Park," her husband had told her when she was making an itinerary for the week.

"You know I am!" was her answer as he encouraged her to enjoy the trip to the fullest and expressed regrets that he could not go with them.

A consummate walker, Louel had always dreamed of hiking a few of the six miles of walking trails in Central Park; however, she was not certain how they would do it, on their own or take a guided tour or entertain other options found online. They did their research before leaving Florida.

Kieta told her, "Let's just go there and decide when we are at the park."

"My, my, you are the practical one. I am so glad you are here with me." She paused. "Or should I say that I am here with you." The woman chuckled.

"Either way, it's six of one or half a dozen of the other" flew from Kieta's mouth, her expression so much like that of Harold Smart until it gave Louel pause. Like she, her husband passed many hours with the girl, talking, and soon, she held on to his every word. The woman shook her head. Her mind turned to her husband. He had taken them to the airport a couple of days ago. She thought about how he looked when saying good-bye to them at the departure gate. He had given the girl a fatherly hug, and she moved away when he was bidding his wife farewell. Louel had seen how his eyes had gone watery and knew he was thinking how much the two of them were going to miss the girl. The woman chuckled.

"What's on your mind?" the girl asked.

"I was thinking how much you sounded like Harold when you said 'six of one or half a dozen.'"

"Oh, how I was using one of his *professorisms*!" Kieta made up a word to describe the bon mots the man frequently used. "Charlotte started teasing me about that a while back. She would say I should have been the professor's daughter, that I had started talking just like him."

"Really!" Louel exclaimed, surprise showing in her voice. "I will have to tell him what an awesome influence he had on you. I think he would like that!"

"Not just him! But you too," Kieta told the woman, her mind on how much like parents they had become so much so that she didn't know what to call them. They answered to her meek Harold and Louel, courteous Professor and Mrs. Smart, and facetious Mom and Pop when they were being nosy about her and Charlotte's business. "You guys have been so good to me just like a mum and dad. Sometimes I have been tempting to call you mum, but I didn't know how you would take it!"

Louel held out her hand to the girl on the couch beside her and took hers in her own, and grinning, she flushed with pride. She replied, "You can call me mum anytime you want." They squeezed each other's fingers in agreement.

"I bet Harold won't get mad if you call him dad either!" Hearing the news come on, she told the girl, "We better go to bed. It's going to be a long day tomorrow." Her thoughts were on telling the grieving man about their conversation: how the girl felt about him, her, and them.

Kieta went to the bedroom to shower so the facility would be ready for Louel's use when her *mum* finished talking with the man they both loved. She smiled at the thought of having the woman as a surrogate; she was perfect.

Early the next morning, the women took the subway to the park. Outside of it, they found a booth where tickets for tours could be purchased. The women did not get in line right away, for they were not sure which one they would take—a walking tour, a pedicab ride, a horseback buggy one, or wait for the Red Bus tours. The women had talked about riding the double-decker bus when they had seen it earlier in the week or just take off on their own, walk leisurely and stop whenever they wanted.

Both took brochures from a rack beside the hut and sat on one of the open benches nearby to map out their day. There was so much to see: Strawberry Fields, Bethesda Fountain, Poets Walk, Bow Bridge,

Dakota Building, and The Ramble. The list of sites to be seen went on and on.

"How about we take a guided walking tour first?" Wisdom showed in Louel's words. "It's going to get warmer as the day goes, which it would be better time to catch the Red Bus later." The woman pointed to the brochure to show a spot at the end of a walk tour where they would find a ticket booth for the bus that would take them around the remainder of the park.

"Sounds like a winner!" Kieta said as she was getting to her feet and smiling to herself about the words she had just uttered. Harold Smart often said this when supporting the women's many contentions and ideas. She was amazed that she was thinking and acting like these people she had known just two years.

Seeing her smile, Louel asked her what she was thinking about. "Nothing," she told the woman. "Look. The line is growing. You wait here if you want. I will get in line and purchase our tickets."

"Okay."

"How much is the walking tour?" the girl asked.

"Just thirty-six dollars each," the Smart woman told the girl who was reaching for her wallet.

Her maternal instinct kicking in, Louel told her surrogate, "Use your debit card. It's not a good idea to pull out cash here. There are too many people around." Her mind was on some of the things that had happened in the park in previous years: a couple of females accosted and raped in the park, a gang claiming it as its territory, and several incidents involving the homeless who were taking up there.

Attention drawn to their surroundings, Kieta looked up and around, seeing the number of people in the park increase as she headed to the end of the line to secure their tickets. She heard the din of the park: people talking, loudly and in whispers; the pitter and patter of feet on the ground and trails; neighs of horses anxiously waiting riders to mount carriages for rides through the park's many acres; the river running; and in a distance, music from a carousel.

In ten minutes, the two women, tickets in their hands, went to a spot in the park where a woman held a sign "Two-Hour Park Tour." They joined a group already gathering in an area under a large tree. When they were in place, their guide counted the people in the group aloud, one to twenty plus, and pointing to the two women with her pencil, she said, "Twenty-nine . . . and thirty!" She recorded the number on her log, joking with the cadre while she wrote. "If I start with thirty, I have to end with thirty. If I lose just one of you, I will lose my job!"

Everyone in the group laughed.

"How many of you have been to Central Park before?" She sought information about the group of men and women. A couple raised a finger.

"Great! You two will serve as my assistants and make sure everyone leaves the park more informed than when they got here this morning."

"We won't be much help," the female tourist commented. "We took a Red Bus ride around the city yesterday and decided to come here today when we were back at our hotel last night."

"Okay." The guide looked at her watch, checking to see if the nine o'clock hour had arrived. Seeing she had another minute before the tour started, she pointed to the Toures girl and asked, "Is this your first time in New York?"

"Yes, it is. I am going to law school here. I've read a lot about the city and the park, and am excited about seeing as much as we can see in one day," Kieta Toures readily answered the woman's question.

"Great! I know you will love the city. I came here ten years ago to go to school and ended up getting a job in the park. I have been here ever since." The woman spoke directly to the girl. "Hope you enjoy it!" She raised her arm to check the time.

The minute hand on her watch at twelve, their park guide began her spiel in earnest. "As you probably noticed, we are at Columbia Circle. We will be walking northward and will catch some of the sights here in the lower two-thirds of Central Park." The woman pointed in the direction they would go, their eyes followed her pointing pen. Pausing to check their attention, she told the group, "I walk fast but can adjust my pace to suit you. I will slow down if I need to. Let me know, okay?"

Some nodded to show understanding. Others showed agreement by saying, "Okay."

The guide continued, "We will not be keeping to the trail you see in your brochure so don't be alarmed if we step off the path. Just follow me! We will not get lost. I have worked here for five years.

They can't put everything on the itinerary. So you will not only see spots advertised in the park's brochures but will also see some hidden bridges, secluded parks, and some other surprises that crop up as we proceed. I am going to show you as much as we can in a short time. I will be jabbering most of the way but feel free to ask questions as we proceed. Okay?"

The woman started to walk but stopped short when she noticed something dangerous. She pointed with her pad to a tourist's shoe that was not tied. "Better tie those shoes up before we take off! We don't want anyone to get tripped up."

"Oops," emitted the man and leaned down to tie his walking shoes. While he did that, everyone looked at his or her shoes. When prepared, the group took off, their pace brisk.

~~~~~

At the end of the tour, Louel took a bill from her wallet to tip the guide and thanked her for what she found to be an awesome experience. "This was the best tour I ever took. I wish my husband had come with us."

When the guide was compensated, she left the group and prepared to show Central Park to another group of tourists.

"That was some tour! She about wore me out," Kieta admitted she could barely keep up with their guide as soon as the woman left. "It's a good thing I have been walking with you. She about had my tongue hanging out! Can we go over there and get a drink?" She pointed to a cart where a vendor was selling water and other beverages.

At the cart, the women got water, drank all of it, and placed their emptied bottles in their purses to fill with water from fountains situated close to restrooms in the park. Four dollars for a bottle of water was a bit much.

"Harold and I have to come to the park together the next time!" The woman longed for her husband. They went most places together. "I was thinking, when we were over near Summerstage, how nice it would be to go to a concert, a Bruce Springsteen one there! I am going to try to get tickets for his birthday!"

Kieta smiled to herself, her fear of being abandoned by the couple she had grown fond of diminishing. When they came to New York for his birthday in the spring, they would surely come to see her. "That would be great!" she spoke more to herself than to Louel.

To round out their day in the city, the women enjoyed the ride on the Red Bus, their seats on the top in the open air, causing both to exhilarate. These were better than the ones on the inside. Both enjoyed the sights, sound, and smells of the city before getting off at the place where they entered Central Park that morning. They took the subway back to the stop closest to Kieta's apartment.

There, they showered and dressed, Louel in a smart pants suit she had brought with her and a shawl to throw around her shoulders and the Toures girl in jeans and a light sweater. The chill a certainty because New York in the early fall was nothing like sunny South Florida. "You think you are going to be all right in that?" her mentor questioned whether she was going to be warm enough. "It gets quite cool in some restaurants!"

Kieta returned to her closet to secure a vest to add to her ensemble.

Outside, they hail a cab to the Tavern of the Green near 67th Street, a restaurant recommended by a couple on the walking tour. Louel called the establishment as soon as they were back at the apartment to see if reservations were required, to make theirs if such was the case. Theirs made, both women were excited about what they later called Our New York Experience.

Their culinary experience included selecting from a menu fit for royalty. When the waiter asked for their drinks, Kieta ordered tea; however, Louel got a glass of water and studied the drink menu. "Neat!" she said as she looked at it.

"Neat what?" Kieta asked.

Louel turned the menu upside down and turned it toward her table mate so she could see that cocktails were named after New York's boroughs: Bronx, Brooklyn, Manhattan, Queens . . .

Noticing the waiter returning, the onlooker said, "You better hurry up and decide. He's on the way back."

"A Manhattan!" Louel decided to have that one.

"Okay, I will put this in and return for your order!" The man hastened to a nearby bar to get it.

Curious about why she had selected that one, the girl asked Louel about her choice.

The woman shrugged and told her, "No particular reason. You know I am not much of a drinker but decided to get that one because we are here." She pointed at a map on the menu, a bold star beside its location.

"So if we had been in the Bronx, you would have gotten that one." Kieta touched the stop where that borough was shown.

Louel nodded and pulled the menu back to her side of the table, picked it, and studied it a moment before asking, "Do you know what you are going to eat?"

The girl looked at the menu again, commenting, "I could just use a hamburger from Wendy's. You know that's my favorite."

The Smart woman encouraged the girl to stretch her limits. "You know what they say! When in Rome, do what the Romans do! We are in New York, so let go of the Wendy burger craving and eat what they have on this delightful menu."

"Okay!" The exasperated diner tried to find something different. She let her fingers trail along as she read every item on the menu, coming up for air when she heard the waiter speak to Louel.

"Your drink, madame." The waiter placed a napkin on table and set the cocktail on it.

The woman picked it to take a sip, so he turned to the girl for her selection.

"I will have the Tavern Burger." She spoke of the sandwich made of prime brisket and short rib and American cheese, noting that the twenty-four dollar burger came with a dill pickle and salt and vinegar chips. "Can I still get that?"

"Yes." The man pointed to the menu to show that the sandwich was available all day.

"Okay. Thank you!" she told the man.

"You are welcome." The man did not reach for the menu; the girl had not closed it. His thoughts, *She might change her mind and order something else after her friend orders.*

He turned his attention back to the Smart woman. "And you, ma'am?"

Louel ordered a Truffle Caesar salad, one composed of baby green romaine, basil, and garlic parmesan croutons, and after a pause, she had the man add Prosciutto di Parma.

Her dinner date followed along as her mentor ordered, looking at the items she called out and adding the prices—salad, eighteen dollars, plus nine dollars for a sliver of ham—noting the woman had spent the total of her meal already and not selected an entrée. Together, their tab was already sixty-seven dollars, not including tax and *the 20 percent preferred* tip shown at the bottom of the menu's pages.

"Your entrée."

"Uhmm . . . I'll have the Scottish organic salmon with roasted artichokes, marble potatoes, and citrus aioli!" Louel spoke with finality in her voice. She closed the menu and handed it to the man who reached for the one Kieta still held but not before she noted "*thirty-four dollars*" for Louel's main course.

"Is either of you having dessert?" the man asked. "I can take that as well, or if you prefer to wait until you finish your meal, I will take it then."

Both women waved away the notion of having a dessert.

"Whew," Louel said when he was out of earshot, "that was hard. I almost ordered the prime meal entrée then shrimp. That salmon got me!"

"I got my burger! I hope it's good."

"I'm sure it will be delicious!"

"What's aioli?" the girl asked about the citrusy bit of the woman's menu.

"Aioli. It's sort of like mayonnaise! I'll let you taste it."

While waiting for their food, their attention turned to clothing, how fashions differed according to where one lived. A conversation that ended with Louel telling the girl, "Some of what you have will do but let's do a little comparison shopping tomorrow."

The girl, a simple dresser, argued that she would make do and purchase anything needed for special occasions or when the season changed. "I know I am going to have to get winter wear. We already talked about that. I can do that later."

Louel did not let it rest. There was definitely going to be some shopping when morning came. After one last night on the couch, they got up early, the woman first. She wanted to get as much shopping as she could get in in one day.

After a small breakfast, they took a cab to a mall that had the same department stores as the one in Florida. Kieta got a few things there. She, a frugal being, would only buy the things she needed.

Her duty done, Louel hailed yet another taxi to take them to Macy's, a treat Louel was giving herself. She had made the case for shopping at the "world's biggest" store before they left Florida. When her husband told her she didn't need to go shopping because she already had everything, hairs on her back raised. The woman, hand on hip, argued, "No one comes to New York City and not go to Macy's. No one!"

When the cab stopped on the corner of 34th and Broadway, Louel paid him, while Kieta gathered her few packages together and got out the car. Outside the vehicle, she looked upward and outward. She whistled audibly.

"What?" Louel, who was beside her, asked about her noisemaking.

"This is one big store. It covers the whole block!"

"I know. We better get in there before they sell everything." The woman laughed at her own joke.

Kieta's stomach rumbled, so she asked if they could get something to eat first.

"Sure. Let's see what we can find." Both women looked up and down across the street, finding the perfect place. Louel took the lead, and they went to the corner to cross to the other side.

The women paused before noon to get the Wendy's cheeseburger Kieta had wanted when at the fancy restaurant. After brunch, they took to the New York pavement again to go across the street to the coveted Macy's.

Needless to say, the store did not disappoint Louel. The woman shopped. Full-priced and clearance items from designers, American and foreign, claimed her attention. She bought everything she wanted for herself and got a few items for the following year's birthdays and yuletide season.

While her mentor shopped, Kieta found seating near or inside dressing rooms. There, she occupied her time with games on a Kindle, a gift from the Smarts, and watched a clerk who assisted the shopper by passing items into her in the dressing room, some which Louel gave a thumbs-up and others which the woman passed over or under the door for the helper to return to the rack.

By suppertime, the woman had amassed a fortune in clothes and accessories. "Let's get out of here." She touched the girl on the shoulder to gain her attention.

"You're through?"

"Yes, I think I have done enough damage! Harold is going to kill me when I get home," the woman said as they headed to the register where the clerk had taken the items she was going to purchase.

When they were at the counter, the Smart woman took her credit card from her purse and watched as the woman who had assisted her pass item after item to the clerk who input prices into the cash register. She did not blink when the total showed, just handed her American Express card to the cashier then sighed as she began to consider how she was going to get all of the boxes and bags back to Florida.

The Macy's employee read her mind. "We can ship this to you free of charge, ma'am."

A smile spread across Louel's face. "Thanks, I appreciate that!"

"We will use the same address that's on your credit card if you like," the woman responded.

"That will be great! How long does it take to ship it?" Louel asked.

"We will ship the items right away! They should be there in two to three days."

"Great!" The shopper was glad she would be at home before the boxes arrived.

Having heard Louel and Kieta talking, she knew they shared an address. So the store employee turned to the younger woman and asked, "Would you like me to send your purchases as well? We can just put them in the box with madame's."

The girl shook her head. "No, that will not be necessary. I am not returning to Florida with my *mum*. I am staying in New York to attend law school."

"Neat!" the woman told her. By that time, the cashier handed the receipt to the shopping assistant who, in turn, passed it to the customer.

She gave the first strip to Louel but maintained the other. "This one has rewards points on it." Pointing to Kieta with the receipt, she said, "Since miss is staying here, she can use the points next time she comes in. Or you may use them yourself, next trip. However, it has an expiration date. Right here." The woman picked a yellow marker from beside the register and circled two entries: *$500 in rewards points* and *expires three months from today's date.*

"Wow, that's quite a bit!" the older of the two women said. "Can I use it today? Some stores will let you use them the same day and some won't."

"Sure, you can!

Kieta's heart dropped. She was tired. She had seen as much of New York as she wanted to see with Louel and done more shopping than she ever imagined. All she wanted to do now was get back to her apartment, rest, and get ready for new beginnings. Here they were in the store with rewards points and Louel ready to start shopping anew. A clock on the wall showed 6:00 p.m. If the woman started up again, they would be in there until closing at ten. Her mouth flew open.

The girl touched the Smart woman on the shoulder. "I can use those reward points to get winter clothes later. That way, you don't have to add money to my account so soon." She spoke what was on her mind.

"What a great idea! Give the rewards points to Marie." Louel gave up on the idea of trading the points for more items.

The shopper's assistant gave the rewards points to the girl, who dropped the paper in the side of her handbag that held her tablet.

Seeing the casual manner in which the girl disposed of the slip, the assistant told her, "Don't lose it! But if you do, just go to customer service and give Mrs. Smart's cellphone number to a representative, and he or she will retrieve the points for you."

Winded down and ready to go home, Louel asked how to get out of the huge store.

"Are you going to use a cab or Uber driver?" the assistant asked. "I can call either and have one meet you at the exit. That way, you don't have to wait or flag one down."

"Please call!" Kieta said before Louel had time to act. Exhaustion was slowing the older woman's response time.

The woman pointed them toward a Broadway exit and gave a fan for the girl to hold in her hand.

"This will help your driver recognize you."

Again, Louel gave a bountiful tip before heading to the exit.

Having noticed the woman's generosity more in the city than at home, the Toures girl commented, "I don't know whether I will be able to afford New York!"

"Why?"

"Tips. You had been handing out Ben Franklins for the last five days. I don't have money to give away like that."

Louel laughed. "You, silly goose! You will be fine. Tips are based on the total of one's purchases as well as quality of services. Many businesses place percentages one should give. Many leave it up to the customer. So one acts accordingly. Me, I always tip, and because I give generously, I reap bountifully. Have you noticed how servers everywhere cater to me? That's why! That woman back there, she won't forget me, and when I am here again, she will ensure an even greater shopping experience."

Kieta acknowledged, "I get it!" just as they stepped from the department store's exit.

A cab pulled up, and the driver got out to let them in. "I will take that," he said of the fan the shopping assistant had given them.

"See," Louel told the girl when they were in their seats, and the man closed the door.

"I get it!" Kieta yawned a yawn she could no longer contain. She was exhausted.

~~~~~

When all the shopping was complete, the surrogate, satisfied that the girl knew how to get around in the city, how to access and use the subway, even how to hail a taxi, turned her attention to home. She was certain these crucial things could be completed without a hitch.

However, with difficulty that a mother hen generally possessed, she attempted to release Kieta Toures to whatever the future would behold, an act that caused another watershed moment.

It was Friday night, the last night Louel would spend in New York. They ordered pizza, New York style, and enjoyed that in front of the television. The crust and ingredients claimed their attention for a while, but the conversation turned as the news came on.

"Dang!" flew from Kieta's lips.

"Dang what?"

"I was just thinking about how I wasn't going to have nobody to eat pizza with next Friday night. We have been having pizza parties every Friday night since I came to your house."

"Perhaps you and Charlotte will—"

The girl cut the lady off. "Seriously, this ain't about no pizza party! I was just thinking . . . I don't know what would have happened if you and 'the professor' had not opened your home and hearts to me!" She reached to give the woman a hug, the first one she had initiated since coming to their home, an act that caused the woman to tear up and sniffle.

"No need to cry or be sad. Everything is going to be all right," the girl told her as she did what the woman had done for her on many occasions when things from her past cropped up, causing her to be sad and become depressed. She put her arm around her shoulder, pulling the woman to her side to close the distance between them. Both women leaned in and over, their heads touching. A tight squeeze of appreciation given, Kieta turned the woman loose.

Louel reached for her handbag, which was on the floor beside the couch. She put it in her lap, reached inside, and withdrew a tissue to wipe her eyes when the girl released her. "I didn't know I was going to be such a wimp," she spoke, shaking her head at feelings she had acquired while Kieta had been with them. She blew her nose that was also leaking and took a compact from her purse to check for smudges in her makeup and to fix it where needed.

While the woman busied herself, the Toures girl pulled her cellphone from her purse and snapped a picture of the woman.

"Hey! What are you doing?" she yelled at the girl, trying to grab it from her hands.

Kieta jumped up and out of her reach. She laughed at the woman trying to get off the couch and at her. "Uh-uh! You might as well sit. You are not going to get my phone. The professor said you were going to do this and made me promise to send him a picture of you with red eyes! If you come any closer, I will run in the bathroom and send him a text."

Louel begged her, "No, don't do it! He and I were fussing about who was going to be sad when you left home, and I said I was going to be morose but would not be reduced to tears. He bet me I would! Don't send it to him, please. You will make me lose my money!"

Acknowledging how close they had become in the two years that passed since the night she had been dropped off at their place, Kieta told her, "Okay, okay! I won't do it then. He didn't tell me the whole story. I ain't going to get in the middle. Anyway, Professor is probably back at the house, crying. He ain't nothing but a bucket of water either. That's why he didn't come with us! His nest is going to be empty again too. You all will probably have someone else soon."

The Smart woman waved away her argument.

After Winston passed, they had poured blood, sweat, and tears into this girl, and while they had not intended to do so, they fell in love with her. Neither wanted to have to cut ties like this again. "No, no way! We no longer work with the agency. We haven't worked for them for quite some time."

Shocked at this revelation, Kieta wanted to know more. She retook her seat on the couch and asked, "What? What are you saying? You were not getting paid to keep me the whole time I was at your house?"

"That's right! We did everything we did because we care for you!"

The girl's hand flew to her heart, overwhelm threatening to overtake her. Tears showed in her eyes this time, her thoughts on how lucky she had been. The Soyinkas had taken her in when her father abandoned her and had treated her like their own. And here she was, with the woman some of her clients labeled a modern-day Harriet Tubman, hearing that everything she and her husband had done for her was because of love, not the money she thought they were being paid to keep her.

"You mean to tell me you were doing all that you have done because you cared for me?"

Louel's turn to be the comforter, she told the weeping girl, "Yes, child. Harold and I love you more than you can imagine, have for quite a while. We hope you will keep in touch and come home when you have a break! We will keep your room for you. Come whenever you want to come, stay long as you want. And when you have found love, married, and have a family, bring them with you. Our home will always be your home!"

The women hugged and cried until it was time for Louel to catch a ride to the airport and go back home to her husband.

Chapter Twenty-Five

Now that she was actually in New York, Kieta kept to the campus and her studies. She started making more friends. She and Charlotte took some of the same classes and sometimes studied together before going home, a habit acquired when they were in undergraduate school. They frequently ate out together or joined a group of law students.

But the latter's free time was soon taken up by a boyfriend she found once in the city just like Kieta predicted on a day when they reminisced about her beloved Doe.

~~~~~

The Gaines girl generally had cereal, fruit, and a beverage before heading off to school; however, a lit "Open" sign of a nearby Dunkin Donut shop drew her attention, so she decided to break her routine and grab a pastry and cup of coffee, the second week in the city.

That particular morning, she got dressed early so she could get the treat and eat it before catching the subway. Inside the shop, the line was a little longer than anticipated. She checked her watch and decided she would have it "to go" instead of "dine in."

Her turn came in about fifteen minutes. At the counter, it barely took the server another five minutes to take and fix her order—a lemon-crème-filled donut and a large cup of hazelnut coffee with cream and two sugars. She was getting anxious. She didn't want to miss her train.

So engrossed with thoughts of being late for class, she took her order, and when it was in hand, the girl pivoted to head out the door. Her mind so full, she turned too quickly, spilling her coffee on the man behind her.

The customer behind her saw the melee coming but couldn't prevent the inevitable. His clothes were fixing to get soaked with the large cup of hazelnut-flavored coffee with cream he heard her order. The man jumped backward, his movements too late. He watched the cup fall out of her hand in slow motion, her squeeze tightening its bottom to maintain a hold, which was obviously not going to happen.

Her efforts went awry as the hot liquid splashed on her hand. The woman held on to the bottom of the cup with her fingernail, but when it was clear, she would not be able to break its fall. She threw her corps backward to avoid a soaking, a maneuver that became necessary when the lid popped off, releasing the hot beverage into the air between them.

Just as he anticipated, the liquid fell from the cup's brim, hit him dead on, and cascaded down the front of his clothing, making uneven splotches head to toe. The cup fell and bounced a couple of times, coming to a rest atop one of his newly polished dress shoes.

He took it like a champ though. Its warmth did not reach his skin because he had on a dress suit. He was glad about that. The man brushed the amber liquid off his clothes with his hand but gave up quickly. It was to no avail.

Mouth open, the girl watched everything in slow motion. She blushed with shame, raising her head to apologize.

"So sorry, so sorry," she stammered to his chest. Her eyes had yet to meet his as they followed the bagged lemon-crème-filled donut to the floor. Both gasped loudly and bent simultaneously at their waists to pick the pastry, their actions causing more chaos. She fell backward, her butt hitting the counter's wall, and the two of them bobbled heads, bumping the side of their temples when arising.

He got the donut first and stood, his hand on her left elbow as he drew her up with him, chivalry his companion.

Up, she looked into a chiseled face of the man she had sprinkled with coffee. "Sorry, so sorry," she emitted when her senses returned.

The man took charge before she could do more damage. "Sit over there and get yourself together. I'll reorder yours."

She did as she was told and watched while the man handed the coffee-stained bag over the counter to the server who tossed it into the trash.

Hearing the man reorder hers and say, "I'll have the same thing she is having," Charlotte took money from her bag to pay for her order and his. The hair on the back raised when the server asked, "For here or to go, sir?"

"Here!"

Here! Charlotte looked at the restaurant's clock, her thoughts were, *He said, 'Here.' If I stay here much longer, I am going to be late for class, something I can ill afford to do!* She shook her head at the straits she found herself in and wished she had kept to her routine—had some cereal before she left her apartment. If she had followed her instincts, she wouldn't even be here, getting ready to have breakfast with a stranger.

"Oh well!" she told herself and sighed a sigh of resignation as the server put the coffees and donuts on a tray and pushed it toward the man who stood with wallet open.

"No charge, Detective!" the young woman told one of the establishment's loyal customers. He frequently breakfasted there and, on occasion, took some donuts or breakfast sandwiches to work or got coffee late in the evenings and gave their gift cards to family members and friends.

"How about hers?" He pointed his head in her direction.

The server waved his offer away, so he picked the tray up and took it over to the table where Charlotte sat.

"Sorry, sorry. I am so sorry!" she apologized profusely as he set their breakfast on the table before taking the seat across from her. He scooted the chair to be closer to its edges and placed his donut and coffee to the side before pushing the tray with hers across the table, stopping when it was directly in front of her.

While he was doing that, she pushed the five-dollar bill she had removed from her bag toward the man.

He pushed the money back at her and looked over at her to chastise her. Their eyes met for the first time.

"Sorry—"

The man cut her voice off with a wave of his hand, flick of his wrist, and his thoughts. "You know any more words besides sorry, sorry?"

Admittedly, the Gaines woman had never been at a loss of words. She talked with everyone she saw. Her parents had accosted her on many occasions for being too loquacious. Her mother or her father said when talking about their daughter, "She talks when she ought to be listening, needs to keep her opinions to herself, and can talk the bark off a tree." Things contradictory to what she experienced that fateful day. There she was, tongue-tied. She couldn't articulate what she felt. He, whoever he was, had unnerved her. The entire situation had her in a thither.

The man was not experiencing any difficulty. He was fully in control of his emotions and faculties.

She looked on as he kept talking. "Is it all right if I join you?" he asked. "My mother would be disappointed if I didn't show good manners!"

The Gaines woman nodded.

"What's the matter? The cat got your tongue?"

"So sorry . . ." Her good manners kicked in. "My mother also taught to apologize when I have wronged someone."

He laughed, shaking his head and reaching over to take her small hand in his huge one. "Kudos! You got me! How about we eat our breakfast? I got to get to work and looks like you got somewhere to be too."

"Okay" came out.

"Grace?" he asked, more to impress her than anything else. Jason Pitts was not a religious man.

"Sure," she said for lack of anything else to say.

He murmured a couple of lines of a thanks audibly while she said hers silently and then turned to his coffee. "I need a sip of this before it grows cold." The man removed the top from the coffee cup and poured more sugar from a container on the table.

She did not wait for him to drink. Charlotte put the cup to her waiting lips, pursed them, and blew on the beverage to cool it down a bit before drinking.

"Nice, kissable lips," the observing man spoke under his breath when he had a sip of coffee.

Her hand shook. So she put the cup aside and turned her attention to her donut. She fingered the pastry lightly, turning it to the spot where the lemon filling showed before biting it. It was full of sweetness, the lemon filling oozed out of it, a bit appearing in the corner of her mouth. She licked her lips, moaning inwardly at the goodness of the treat. It was much better than the cereal she had been eating for a couple of weeks.

Seeing remnants of filling on her face, the man across her reached with a finger and removed the cream from her face. To her surprise, he licked it off his finger. The alarming act made her heart merry. She smiled.

"Sweet!" he said throatily.

The woman almost swooned. His voice was sweeter than the morsel of pastry she had just consumed. Full already, she laid the remainder of the pastry aside and wiped the corner of her mouth with her napkin, careful to leave his touch there. Charlotte drank from her cup and watched the man polish off his donuts. He had ordered two for himself.

Her thoughts were on how she could sit there and watch him eat all day. She was smitten, totally taken over by a man whose name she did not know or had not heard. The only thing she knew was he was an officer of some sort. She had heard the server call him detective.

His donuts gone in a few bites, he drank more coffee and cleared his throat before speaking.

"I didn't catch your name," he told her.

She smiled. "I didn't say it!"

He threw his hands up. "Well, are you going to tell me? I think you owe me that. You wasted your first cup of coffee all over the front of my suit and shoes, so you could at least tell me your name."

"So . . ." She started.

"Surely, your name can't be *so sorry!*" he teased her, his laughter booming and filling up the every cavity in the restaurant.

She shook her head. Gathering herself, she told him, "I am Charlotte Gaines, and I am glad to make your acquaintance." She reached an outstretched hand across the table to shake his.

He gave her a firm handshake, pumping just once before releasing the member. "Nice to meet you, Ms. Gaines. My name is Jason Pitts."

He looked at his watch, shook his head, and told her, "And I am late for work."

She opened her mouth to apologize, but he raised his hand to stop her while pushing his seat away from the table. "I have to go around the corner and change so I won't be smelling like coffee. What's on your agenda today? What you got going on?"

They stood simultaneously and headed toward the opening door, wading through the horde of customers entering and leaving the donut shop.

"Not much," she told the man. "I have to study a bit then get ready for class. I just came around the corner to get a cup of coffee."

At the mention of lodging near the establishment, he asked, "Where you stay around the corner?"

"Berkley Apartments," she said as he placed his hand on the small of her back, steering her through the growing crowd and rows of tables.

As the man opened the door, he asked another question, "What number?"

Without pause, she told him, "K-3."

He stopped dead in his tracks. "What?"

"K-3," she repeated.

Jason laughed. "K-3 Berkley!"

The woman, whose steps arrested when his halted, showed assent with a mere nod and grunt.

He looked to her honest eyes then replied, glee in his voice, "Naw, can't be! You can't be my neighbor. I live in K-5 Berkley."

"I do." She led the way. Momentarily, they turned to the right, their strides matching, although her legs were shorter than his. It was she who chuckled this time. "Howdy, neighbor!"

In a minute, they entered the apartment's courtyard, took the elevator to their floor, and each went to his or her own door. They gave each other a smile, put their keys in their respective keyholes, and went inside. On the other side of their door, they paused and let their backs hit the door and stood there a moment, shaking their heads side to side in disbelief.

Jason hurriedly dressed and got a taxi to work. He generally took the subway but had missed today. He had spent more time in the coffee shop than he usually did.

Meanwhile, Charlotte tried to study but to no avail. The woman found herself reading the same sentence twice, thrice, more times than she usually did but not recalling what she had just read. Her mind was on the man she bumped into at the donut shop.

Finally, she laid the book on the desk, got up, and wandered around the apartment doing much of nothing, picking a piece of paper or lint from the brown carpeted floor, plumping pillows on the couch, and meandering over to the refrigerator in the four-hundred-square-foot efficiency apartment her parents had helped her secure to remove leftovers from fast foods she had placed there earlier and disposing of such.

After cleaning that area, she went in the apartment's tiny bathroom to straighten towels on the rack and replace tissue on its holder; it had fallen off when she had used the toilet earlier.

The woman opened the door to the bedroom and looked at the plush headboard's plum coloring, reconsidering the floral printed bedspread and curtains she had recently purchased. Everything looked so girly.

Charlotte just could not imagine Jason Evans lying there . . . *Stop, girl! He probably already has a woman. Ain't no man that handsome walking around free*, she spoke in the air.

Hearing her voice aloud uttering thoughts of the man who was right across the hall, she slapped herself on the face. *You better get back to your books!*

She gave her studies as much attention as she could, her mind wavering periodically. Later that morning, she tried to no avail to reach Kieta but left a voicemail telling her to call her ASAP.

Kieta returned her call between classes.

The Gaines girl told her about the encounter at the restaurant, ending with a breathless "Girl, I was so embarrassed. My thoughts like my words were tripping all over one another. As much as I like to talk, I couldn't get but one out!"

What was that one?

"Sorry! I kept trying to apologize, and there he sat, all smug, taking over my life and telling me what to do! Owww!" The girl told her bestie how insecure and helpless he made her feel. "He had me like a puppet on a string and was ordering me around. That guy pointed to a table and told me to sit, and you know what I did? I sashayed over to the table and sat. Owww!" Charlotte railed at her responses to his commands. She paused for breath.

Unable to get a word in edgewise, her friend explained to the Gaines girl what was happening. "Child, that's him! He's got you panting like a puppy! You won't know no peace until you eat a little of that meat off them bones!" she shrieked gleefully at her friend.

"What you talking about?"

"You know what I am talking about. I told you that you were going to find someone and fall in love. I told you!"

"Who said anything about love?'

"I did! That's something I know a little something about." Kieta grew serious. "You see, love is not something you plan for. It just happens. Love finds you when you are not looking for it. And when it does, it has its own way. It makes you feel some kind of way, so I know how you feel, a bit overwhelmed. That's the way I felt when I met Mahmoudou Ibrahaim. Love took over, and we went with it! I am glad we did. We lost each other along the way, but I am glad we let love have its way before we got separated. I believe it is better to have loved and lost than never to have loved at all. All I can say is don't fight it. Go with it! And see where it takes you! Let Cupid have her way with your heart!"

When her friend stopped giving advice, Charlotte told her, "I hear you! We will see."

"Okay, where are you going for lunch?" Kieta changed the subject.

"I'm not going. I haven't left the house since I went down to Dunkins. Girl, I am still full!"

Looking at her watch, the Toures girl told her, "You are going to miss class if you don't hurry up and get out of there."

"I know. I am just not feeling it."

Her friend decided to let it rest. "Okay, I will catch up with you later. Then we can talk about him some more. By the way, what's his name?"

"Jason, Jason Pitts." Charlotte removed the phone from her ear and turned the instrument off. She powered it down less it ring again. The woman did not want to talk to anyone else.

Off the phone, she decided to get comfortable. The woman removed the pants and shirt she had worn out that morning and put on a housecoat and her house shoes. Feeling the need for total freedom, she also removed her bra then took her ponytail lose, letting her auburn locks fall freely. Charlotte ran her fingers through her hair, opting to braid it and put a rubber band on the end to keep it from coming loose. When she had prepped herself, she took to the books with a vengeance, not coming up for air for half a day.

The Pitts man was equally as enamored, and his married partner, Ward Berger, had to listen to him banter about the girl most of the day—as soon as he was in the car, between cases and conferences about cases, at lunch, and until he let him out of the vehicle.

By the end of their shift, the other detective was declaring that Jason had found his soul mate. "Man, that chick really got to you! You need to stop by the jewelry store on the way home. You ain't even got a little sugar, and here you are, just about to hit the knee and go to begging for her hand," he told him before he dropped him off at the curb in front of his apartment building.

Jason didn't fool around with him, his mind elsewhere. He jumped from the passenger seat and hit the ground, almost trotting.

"Bye," his partner spoke to his back through the rolled-up window. The man hit the entrance almost before he pulled back into traffic.

As soon as he was inside, the Pitts man showered, washing off a day of crime watching and stopping as well as investigating cases assigned by their department head. He draped a towel around his waist, went to his living room, put some music on, and decided to make a sandwich and have a beer or two before watching a little television.

He fixed a turkey sandwich, put a few chips from an open bag on it, and grabbed a jar of Kosher pickles from the refrigerator, putting a couple of spears on the side of his plate. He headed for the couch but returned for a couple of oatmeal raisin cookies for dessert.

Soon, his mind returned to the woman across the hall. Jason wondered what Charlotte was doing, whether she was having supper and what it would be like to share his own meal with her. His manhood stirred beneath the towel. He looked down, admonishing his penis. "Down, boy!"

Across the hall, she looked up at the clock. It was almost six, well past time she generally ate her supper. While it had taken a good deal of her morning, she had managed to let thoughts of the man on the other side of the door across the hall rest. She was able to do it after she and her bestie had cajoled each other about two men—the one she had just met that morning and the one Kieta Toures had loved and lost.

Charlotte pushed the books, her PC, and pieces of paper as well as pens that littered her small table toward the side against the wall, leaving room for her supper. She meandered over to the refrigerator to remove contents for her meal: turkey, white American cheese, lettuce, tomato, relish, and rye bread from a bread box on the counter.

She let her fixings rest a moment while she went to turn the television on. It was on CNN, but she was not in the mood for news. She advanced the channels until she reached the 900s. Music channels were found there: Christian, country, folks, rhythm and blues, popular hits, and so on.

The woman chose a show matching her mood. An old love story was on the Lifetime Channel, a couple with their lips locked, his hand running through her hair, her arms around his neck. Romance on the tube and in the air, she felt a stirring in her private areas. She tried to shake away the feeling and returned to the countertop to complete her meal, adding chips to her plated sandwich before grabbing a couple of cookies from a nearby bag.

Jason Pitts put his paper plate in the trash can beside the refrigerator, making a mental note to take the bag down to the chute at the end of the hall for disposal the next time he went out. *Out!* His mind fled across the hall, so he turned to follow it.

When he threw his door open, a change in the temperature took place, causing him to look down. Seeing and remembering that he was in a state of undress, he shut it as fast as he opened it and returned to his bedroom for a pair of pants and a pullover. He didn't bother about putting on his boxers but thought a little aftershave might be a plus. So he headed for his bathroom to put some on.

In the bathroom, Jason rubbed his hand on his face. Feeling the stubble, he considered whether he should shave. *The heck with that!* He took aftershave from a shelf in the medicine cabinet and sprinkled some of the fragrance in his hand and rubbed it on his face, neck, and shoulders.

Charlotte jumped when she heard a tap on the door, almost knocking her Pepsi over. She wondered who it could be. She had had only one visitor since she moved to the apartment, Kieta. They had spoken earlier, but neither had made mention of coming over or getting together later in the day.

At the door, she peeked through the tiny peephole, squinting then peering. "Shit!" she exclaimed in surprise. It was he, the guy she had met that morning, and he was at the door. What was she going to do? She wrung her hands, threw them up to her face, and twirled around, and her back to it, she slid down the door until she was seated on the floor, all actions that surprised even her.

The man tapped softly again, willing himself not to push it open and just go in there and make her his. He spoke her name three times as he rapped on her apartment's wooden door. "Charlotte! Charlotte! Charlotte! Are you in there, Charlotte?"

His neighbor held her breath to keep quiet. He put his ear to the door, listening for her footsteps, some movement over on the other side of the portal. Hearing nothing, the man was preparing to leave.

A whimper of anticipation escaped her. She really wanted to see him. So the woman started to breathe again, pulled herself up, and opened the door for the man. The Gaines woman took a misstep and fell forward. Jason caught her, pulling her to himself, an act that left both swooning when their clothes touched. Sparks shot from both of their psyches.

Neither said a word, just stood in her doorway, holding each other and rocking like they were on a dance floor, the music having stopped before they could will themselves to separate.

Jason took Charlotte's face in his right hand, tilted her face upward, peered into her eyes, and seeing want in her eyes matching his own, the man kissed her ever so gently. She returned his kiss, pressing her way, pushing her tongue further into his mouth cavity, and they waltzed their way into the apartment with lips locked and eyes closed. He shut the door behind him with his foot. They loved each other's lips until they were on the couch. He was in the seated, and she was on his lap.

When they came up for air, he spoke first. "I have been thinking about that all day!"

"Me too!" She admitted she had studied under duress. Now she was glad she had finished her schoolwork so she could freely enjoy the evening's promise.

She then took the lead and nudged his jawline with her nose, his stubble prickly but quite nice. The man rubbed his face on the side of hers and turned his lips back to hers. They came up for air then the woman sniffed the aftershave on his face, kissed his cheeks, and followed the trail of aftershave he made, ministering to each spot with her hot lips.

"Damn!" The man invoked, picking her up and walking with her in his arms until they were at her bedside. He knew the way. All the apartments in the building were laid out the same. She tightened her arms around his neck and let herself be carried to the bed. Her closed eyelids fluttered but opened when he laid her on the bedspread. Jason's experienced fingers were unbuttoning her top.

"Wait," she said. "Let's pull the covers back." She attempted to get up.

"Uh-uh." The Pitts man shook his head to indicate she did not need to get up. "I got it!" He raised her upper body with left hand and used the other to maneuver the floral bedspread. When he was at her waist, Charlotte raised her hips to help him. Both used their feet to kick the coverlet to the foot of the bed.

Momentarily, they were between the sheets. His unhesitating confidence caused the virgin to follow the experienced man's lead. Their first coupling easy, they made love as if they would never do it again. There were four hours that passed before they were satiated. They fell asleep in each other's arms, she before he. All too soon, morning came, and the two enjoyed what he called a quickie before he escaped to his man cave to make ready for the workday.

While watching the man leave, Charlotte mused about his energy. Jason Pitts was full of it. The man had sprinted out of the doorway, leaving her a bit battered and bruised, almost helpless. Her legs and the rest of her body just wanted to lie there the remainder of the day; however, her mind took the lead, so she got up and went off to school.

Chapter Twenty-Six

Soon, the Pitts man and the Gaines woman were an item. Early on, they spent most nights in her apartment. When his lease was up, the two lovers shared the one apartment as they looked for another larger one in Manhattan, which was no easy feat. The price of housing for middle-class workers and students who came to the city was exorbitant. A two-bedroom apartment like the one the pair was searching for cost as much as $2,700 a month.

It took several months, but an apartment became available near Central Park and close to the college Kieta and Charlotte attended. So the two of them moved there.

Needless to say, Kieta was their very first visitor. Charlotte had spoken of her often, but her friend's beau had not yet seen her. The man was glad to meet her. They hit it off right away, something the Gaines woman was happy about. Her friend's approval important, she also began to think about telling her family about her boyfriend.

After the initial visit to their new apartment, *the woman from another land*, as she referred to herself when her comfort level with new acquaintances increased, relaxed. She frequently dined with them and, on occasion, spent the night with her friend if the man was gone to a conference or for training.

As time passed, and comfort levels were established, she told the Pitts man snippets about her life and how she had come to be in the

USA. A hopeless romantic himself, his partner teased him for being "whipped," the detective pondered about the man she had loved and lost.

"Dang, buddy! I hate that, especially how you and your old man got separated like that," he told the girl one evening when they were hanging out. "I don't know what I would do if I got separated from my baby."

"It's hard!" she said of her separation from her beloved Doe, sadness showing in her face. "Some days are worse than others."

"Do you reckon he could have gotten out of the country too?" he asked. "You said he might have been there the night you were put on the plane."

Her mind returning to the night she was spirited out of Timbuktu, she tried to recall as much as she could. "I don't know. Like I told you, I am not sure, but I think Doe was there. I didn't see much or hear much for that matter. When that man put a rag over my face, I caught a whiff of something. That's all I can remember."

A consummate investigator, Jason probed further each time the two of them talked. One day he asked if there was anywhere in the country he might go *if* he came here. "Did you all ever talk about coming to America?"

She started to tell him they had never discussed coming to America, but did not—at least she didn't respond to his question right away. Puzzlement showed on her brow. A conversation about where she would go if she came to the United States came to her, a conversation she had not thought about until Jason asked the question.

Kieta was not sure whether she could let herself think her beloved might be there and had not found her. So she told Jason, "Not that I came remember. We talked about so much!"

He noticed she had cleared her throat, an action that let the interrogator know he was getting somewhere. Exchanges between the two of them had always flowed freely, no sign of nervousness evident until this conversation.

Kieta left soon. Her thoughts on the day so long ago when Doe and she were dreaming aloud and talking about traveling in Europe and in North America accompanied her the short distance between her friends' apartment and her on-campus one.

It was around the time the insurgents were wreaking havoc in the city, and the two of them were in the cottage on Baker Street commiserating over the future in general. She told him that she wanted to flee, and he asked where she would go if she could go anywhere in the world she wanted to go. "Or was it in one of our daily telephone calls?" The Toures girl found herself speaking in the wind. "It really doesn't matter when we talked about it. It's what we said."

A voice she had not heard a long time spoke in her head, clarifying, "Where would you like to go if you could go anywhere you wanted to go?" She smiled at its authenticity and true concern about what she wanted.

Her gait changed, and she hopped from one foot to the other like she had done in the desert when she was a child.

"New York! I told him New York!" she told herself. "I am sure I said New York City!" The woman laughed aloud, her glee too large to contain.

Her beloved's next question was "And just what would you like to do there?" She felt with her hand where he had touched her on the face with the back on his hand while they daydreamed together.

We were lying on the bed in the cottage on Baker Street! She was certain now that she had not dreamed they had the conversation when she was in bed at the Soyinkas' compound or fantasized about what they would do and where they would go when Doe rescued her from solitary confinement where she had been placed in the jail.

She was certain she had told Mahmoudou Ibrahaim that she would do some research on New York, which she had. And they had spoken about coming to the city, but fate had removed this piece of memory.

By that time, she was home alone in her apartment where she allowed herself to feel. She shuddered at the thought that Doe could have come on the same plane and be in their midst. She wondered what he looked like. It had been over two years since she had seen him. Kieta closed her eyes and tried to see his face; it had escaped her.

Now that she was not sure if she would even be able to identify him if she saw him on the streets, in the park, on campus, anywhere, she started to cry. The girl took to the couch and cried herself to sleep.

~~~~~

Sensing he had touched a nerve, Jason waited a while before he asked about Doe again. His purpose for asking was only because he wanted to see if he could find out whether the man was in the country. He had access to technologies that helped find people, one he would apply when he could *if,* and *only if,* she wanted to run a search to see if the man might be in the country.

Jason did not mention how unnerved the girl had become to Charlotte. Kieta didn't either. He didn't want his girl to be angered and accuse him of being too harsh with her friend. As for the Toures girl, she enjoyed their relationship immensely, so she never mentioned his invasion into her privacy.

The next time the threesome went to dinner, Kieta saw a couple of West African couples. As they passed the table, she greeted them in French, "Bonsoir! Comment ca va?" They returned her salutation with "Bien! Et vous!" Jason and Charlotte kept on their waiter's heels and were seated, their napkins in their laps by the time she joined them. The man pulled a chair out for her, and she sat.

"Do you know those people?" the Gaines woman asked. Their circles enlarging as time passed, they no longer knew the same people.

"No! They are from Timbuktu. I am certain of that," she told her friends. "I just spoke to them." She picked up her menu.

Jason, having decided what he wanted, laid his on the table. He was curious about how she knew those people were from Timbuktu but hesitated to ask. He gave in but exercised care not to offend her. He wanted to know how she could tell one set of brown-skinned foreigners from another. "Does either of those men look like your Mahmoudou?" he spoke gently.

She turned her head aside to look at the couples anew. "Not really," she replied. And she pointed with her head to the one facing him and told Jason, "That one, the man facing you, shares his skin color," before talking about his height, weight, hair, and eye color.

As she described him, the investigator made a mental note of the attributes she gave and decided he would go to the IT department at the New York City Police Department, give a description of

Mahmoudou Ibrahaim, and see what they could come up with. He wanted to see what he could find out if he could have come over too.

~~~~~

Before he could get to that, he and his partner, Warren Berger, were summoned to their boss's office. The man's secretary called each of them on their cellphones. They were out on the field together. Jason, getting the call first, cut it off when the woman gave him the message.

Afterward, she rang the other man. When Berger got off, he asked Jason, "Do you know what that's all about?"

The man hunched his shoulders. "I don't have any idea. She didn't say, and I didn't ask."

"What's with you?" His partner accosted him. "You are always the interrogator, so I thought you would have asked that dame what she wanted."

His mind on how he had offended the Toures girl with his questions, he told Berger, "I am learning. Sometimes you just need to listen and not say anything. That way, you won't offend anybody."

"Damn, man! You are becoming a real pussy. Since when did you start worrying about other people's feelings?"

The man waved away his friend's assertions. "Shut your face and drive! Boss will tell us what he wants when we get there." He leaned back in the seat and rested until they were at the precinct.

Inside, they took the elevator up to the fifth floor and walked right past the secretary and into their boss's open door.

The man looked up from his desk, and seeing the two coming, he said, "Well, if isn't the Pennsylvania boys!" They looked at each other, pissed because they had to put up with the jackass who had given them a name that had nothing to do with anything. One's last name, Pitts, and the other, Berger, the man had decided to call them that when they were paired together, although neither one was from the Keystone State.

"What's up, boss?" The men parroted each other.

The man handed registration information for a technology conference to be held in Las Vegas the next week across the desk. "I know this is short notice, but I need you fellows to go out there and see what it is about. Can you do that?"

"Sure, who wouldn't want to go to Vegas?" Berger expressed delight at being able to get out of the city for a few days.

"How about you? You got something on your agenda to keep you from going?"

His eyes trailing down the paper, he nodded as he told the man he was ready to get out of the city for a minute too. "I have never been there. It should be fun." He looked over at his partner, his thoughts on how he wished he could take Charlotte instead of him.

"I ain't sending you all out there to gamble and play!" He looked at his watch and toward the door. "I got a meeting." The man got up and walked toward a coat rack in the corner of his office. "My secretary will make arrangements. Keep up with your receipts. Finance raises hell when we fail to do that."

The following Monday found them at the Las Vegas Convention Center. They had flown to the city on Sunday evening and caught the shuttle to the hotel. There, they checked in and did what tourists do—explored the strip for a few hours, got some supper, and played a little quarter slots. Neither man was a gambler, so by midnight Pacific time, the men from the East Coast were sound asleep.

Before long, room service called, bringing them out of semicomatose states. Warren vaulted from the queen-sized bed, grabbed the bag with his toiletries in it, and flew past the foot of Jason's. "Order some coffee!"

His partner rolled over, dialed room service, and ordered a full breakfast: steak and eggs over easy with white toast and pastries for himself. He paused, his pause so long until the person taking his order had to ask twice about a beverage. "Coffee, coffee, two pots." Then he shook his head as he responded to her questions about condiments. "Uh-uh! No cream, no sugar!" He let the phone fall on the cradle and rolled over to catnap while waiting.

Out of the shower pretty quickly, Warren slapped the bottom of the covers just below the sleeping man's feet. "Get up, Sleeping Beauty."

The Pitts man rolled over and sat up on the side of the man, stretching and yawning with reckless abandon. He was exhausted, the time change affecting him more than usual. He and Charlotte had passed the night doing what young lovers did when departing: satisfying each other, their lovemaking like the first time every time. Jason had tried to get a little shut-eye on the plane, but his partner talked like a parrot, from east to far west, his mind on what kind of trouble they could get in while there.

"Breakfast almost ready, honey!" The man toyed with his friend who still was not fully awake.

A rap on the door broke their exchange. "You get it while I take a leak," Jason told him as he headed to the bathroom.

By the time the man finished showering and shaving, the other man had polished off his breakfast and was seated at the table in front of the hotel window, eating one of his pastries.

"What the f . . . You are just trying to make me whip your ass!"

Laughter rang loud in their room. Warren, forever the prankster, took the lid off his plate to show him that his was intact. "My baby put this in my bag before I left. You know I hardly eat sweets, but for some reason, I am hungry as a bear." He polished of the remainder of the tart and the rest of his coffee.

His clothes on, Jason walked over to where the man sat and opened the sliding glass door to let some of "Sin City" inside then sat down to eat his breakfast.

"I don't know how you get by on donuts and coffee! Especially now that you got a woman. You gonna have to have more than that to keep your strength up! Women will take it out of you!"

"Check and see what time the shuttle runs. We can't be late for that training!"

~~~~~

At the convention center, they found the site for their meeting. A sign on the outside said, "Identity Solutions." When they entered the room, it was almost full. They found their seats with little difficulty; theirs were up front, marked *Reserved*.

The room buzzed with excitement. New York City detectives and other attendees were looking forward to hearing about a new machine that could generate a likeness that was more accurate than previous technologies and seeing it do what was advertised.

Like most of the workshop participants, the duo had perused a brochure about the new technology and read a bit about what wonders it could perform. Supposedly, the cutting-edge imaging machine the company was selling could translate words and turn those words into images, flat ones and tridimensional ones. It could also use the same data to make a bust of a subject.

So nearly everyone who signed up for the training looked for the marvel as soon as they entered the room. However, nothing out of the ordinary was there, just a laptop and a medium-sized printer on a table at the front of the room. Both instruments looked just like the ones they had in their workplaces.

Jason said to his partner, "They probably won't show their invention until this afternoon. We are going to have to listen to this fast-talking joker all morning!" He pointed with his head in the direction of the man making preparations for the session.

"That's what I was thinking. I wish we could change seats with some of those fellows back there." Like the man beside him, he used his head instead of his fingers for a pointer.

When the hour came, they watched as the facilitator turned the computer on, and while it was booting, he removed a notebook from the conference bag he had rolled in the room. They saw him remove a CD from its sleeve and prepare for the presentation. He clicked his heels, calling attention to himself.

"Good morning! I am Gerald, your facilitator . . ." A middle-aged man, he used a PowerPoint presentation to first talk about the company Identity Solutions and then to show them how the machine was constructed and what it could do and how it could support their investigations, make their detective work easy. Last, he gave some case studies in which law enforcement had used the product and given the research on its efficacy. He trumpeted how much money departments could save if they used the program to help find fugitives, lawbreakers, as well as illegal aliens—people without visas and passports, ones who had let theirs expire.

Jason, a technology geek, was mesmerized by what he saw on the screen—the graphics clear and crisp, movement between frames fluid, and the narrative concise and easily understood. Once its purposes were clear, he was anxious to see if the machine actually worked.

When the group broke for lunch, he hung back so he could talk one-on-one with the facilitator, Gerald Smith, his bio on the inside cover of a folder they had found at their reserved seating, impressive yet elusive. The Pitts man thought he must be "genius." It took one to do what the man said the computer could do. "Go ahead. Save me a place," he told his partner.

Not surprised by the man's actions—Pitts was the "details man" on their team, a master in the interrogation room—his skillful questioning aided their team in cracking cases others did not.

Knowing this, Berger went ahead to save a place for him. He would come along when that "one" question he always had was answered. When he was in the dining area, he quickly found seating. Place cards with their names on them were on round tables. Theirs was with law enforcement officers from neighboring states. Introductions made, the group shot the breeze about first, one thing then another, while the waiter began to serve them.

Back in the meeting room, Pitts engaged the workshop facilitator. "That is the most fascinating thing I have ever seen."

"I know! I've shown it a dozen times now and become more intrigued as I train officers like yourselves all over the country." Smith spoke about the gadget, enthusiasm on his face.

The facilitator let Pitts out of the door. He hit the light switch, and the two men walked the few yards to the dining area side by side.

"So you were not on the ground level. You had no part in developing the product." The New York detective answered one of his own questions.

"How I wish I had been! I wouldn't be here," the man responded. "Actually, I was a middle school teacher for twenty years and got tired of dealing with kids, so I sought out a new career. When this job came along, I jumped at it because I could do what I love to do. I could still teach! I just train people on it."

"Yeah, but you know that program inside and out!"

Smith told him, "I am just as intrigued as you! The inventors trained a cadre of facilitators on it, and every time I present, new questions arise. Sometimes they come from workshop participants like you. Other times, I will be in front of an audience, talking, and one pops in my head. When that happens, we take those questions back to the company for answering. On a couple of occasions, the produce was tweaked because of questions generated when we trainers were in the field showing and selling the product."

Disappointed that the man had not been involved from the blueprint to production but impressed by his obvious intelligence, Jason headed off to find Warren. At the table, everyone expressed enthusiasm about the machine and wondered aloud about its cost. The participants wolfed down a full meal, appetizer to dessert, in no time. They were looking forward to the afternoon session.

His prowess recognized by the trainer, the man called on Jason to help demonstrate how the machine actually worked. "How about helping me with the demonstration, Mr. Pitts?" The man gestured for him to come up front.

"I bet you have a favorite girl," he said as he pointed to the chair on the side of the table facing the audience where the man could sit.

Jason's partner provided an answer. "Yep, he sure does!" His response caused some in the class to laugh. "You just need to ask me about it. I ride with him every day!"

"Ahhhh, it's like that." The facilitator, an eyebrow turned up, added levity to the situation.

The Pitts man, seated behind Smith, looked through the man's arms and mouthed at his partner. "Shut your face, asshole."

Warren Berger, always the class clown, was in stitches, his tomfoolery noticed by the facilitator.

"All right. Let's get down to business!" The former teacher regained the man's attention and turned back to the man Berger was taunting.

"Okay, Mr. . . ."

"Jason!"

"Okay, Jason." The man's voice changed. It was as if he was going to put the man in a trance and have him come out of it when he "snapped his finger."

Smith droned on, "I am going to ask you a series of questions about your girl. Nothing personal, mostly physical attributes. You should answer each question to the best of your ability. Please do not try to trick the machine. If you do, we won't get a chance to know your girl's full beauty."

Seeing how serious the man had become, the detective sat upright in his seat and planted his feet flat on the floor. His oath, "Okay, I will answer to the best of my ability."

The facilitator took a seat in front of him, his back to the others, and asked, "What is your girl's full name?"

"Charlotte Gaines."

He repeated Jason's girlfriend's name, recording it on a chart, "Charlotte Gaines. No middle name?"

No middle name. Jason paused. He could not remember a middle name. So he shook his head.

"Please speak loudly and clearly when you give a response. The machine cannot comprehend nods and gestures, Mr. Pitts."

"Oh! Okay!" Jason was beginning to regret being a guinea pig.

The facilitator turned toward the remainder of the trainees. "If this is to work as it should, everyone else must keep quiet. Do you understand?" Coming to a quiet, the others showed they comprehended that the results of the experiment could be affected by peripheral sounds.

"This works best when the subject is in a soundproof booth, and the interrogator is outside, asking the question via microphone."

He turned his head to Jason, who by now was sweating. *This can't be that serious* were his thoughts.

The facilitator cut the machine that looked like an ordinary printer on and began the questioning in earnest. It took an hour. A lot of useful information was attained in those minutes. Jason Pitts gave the Smith man a description of his girlfriend: her weight, height, bone structure, skin tone, eye color, the shape of her face whether round or oval, the length of her neck, etc.

When he had finished what seemed like a thousand questions, the facilitator punched a button on its side. He turned in his seat to watch it do its job, his mind on how much it reminded him of a soft drink machine in the break room at work. You push one button, you get Sprite, another strawberry Sprite, cherry Sprite . . .

Before he could recall all the flavors of the beverage, the machine sent the image described to its printing function, and it made magic. Identity Solutions's product spat out a perfect image of Charlotte. It did that instantaneously, a feat not unexpected—that was its job;

however, a little surprise, a pleasant one showed on the man's face when Smith handed the photograph to him for scrutiny. He smiled.

It didn't stop there. The new technology whirred, whined, and soon spat out a bust much like ones found in a museum but much more lifelike, as it was in color, not plaster, a result that shocked the New York City detective to the core. He nearly jumped out of his skin.

"Damn!" spewed involuntarily from his lips when he saw his girl's likeness. The picture fell from his hand, floated in the air, and hit the floor.

Seeing his reactions to both, the presenter took that to mean the machine had once again proved its authenticity and efficacy. He asked the man, "Do you happen to have a picture of her in your wallet?"

"Sure do!" Jason said, his eyes on the 8 ½ x 11 color portrait the facilitator retrieved from the convention center's floor.

He took his cellphone out, went to an album he had labeled "Just CG," and scrolled until he found a clear headshot he had taken in the last couple of weeks. He handed it to the instructor, watching the man's face to see his response.

Smith picked up the photo the printer had generated, held it side by side with the one on the phone, and compared the likenesses, finding them "uncanny."

Looking at the volunteer, he asked, "Can we share the pictures with the group for comparison purposes?" He could see how anxious the others in this premiere session with the new product had become. They were stirring in their seats and mumbling, some voicing their desire to actively participate.

The facilitator raised his hand and voice to calm the crowd who was becoming boisterous with excitement, similar to that of the middle schoolers he had taught. "I wish I could let everyone have a chance," he told them. "But this thing costs a mint to operate. This one will have to suffice!"

He asked the detective if he would take both from table to table and show both likenesses. "How am I going to hold all this in two hands?" he asked.

"Not the bust," the instructor said. "They can see it from here. These two pictures should suffice." He pointed to the hard copy and the one on the iPhone.

Needless to say, all of the workshop participants were impressed. Conversation turned to implications for solving criminal cases.

"It helps if the information given is accurate," the man told them. "There is no feature to determine if a person is being honest. It is not a lie detector. The machine only yields a likeness based on descriptions you give. If you say a subject has blue eyes, you get that color . . . No specific hue is there, just blue. So you still have to exercise caution when using this technology. Specificity is the key."

One questioned, "So Pitts was so good because he knows his woman like that?"

Laughter from the group turned the session from serious to more folly. *Could you do a full body bust? What if she had one tit bigger than the other one? Or was cross-eyed?*

"You must be talking about that woman you got." Jason pointed to one of his joking friends before the presenter returned their attention to the utility of the image-producing machine.

While admitting the machine definitely had its uses, the Identity Solutions employee acknowledged that it could not detect a liar. "As I was saying, it only works if a witness's description is accurate. If false information is given, it will not give a true picture of a perpetrator, only the one that the person gives." He paused as Jason was near the end of the last row then resumed his lecture when every viewer had seen the pictures, the printed one and the one on his cellphone, side by side.

For a moment, the room refilled with lilt and blabber of the men talking about probable uses of the machine or just making jokes. The instructor cleared his throat, calling them back to attention. "Yes, you are right. Accuracy may also be impacted by the length of time an individual has known the individual, how many times they had seen a person, or by one's relationship with an individual, whether that person is a mere acquaintance or whether it's a loved one."

By then, Jason was almost back at the front of the room. "How long have you known your girl? I would say it's been at least a year." The presenter attempted to validate his assertion.

"A year!" Jason's partner called out from his seat on the front row beside his friend's empty chair. He laughingly added, "I can tell you that! It's been one whole year. He has been bending my ear about her day in and day out."

Everyone in the room cracked up. Many could identify; for some reason, single detectives were always paired with married partners. Jason blushed but asked when he was up front, "Can I have this?"

"Don't mind at all." The facilitator assured him it was all right to take the picture and the bust home. "There is nothing we can do with it! I have a box and some bubble wrap in my bag. You can use that to make for easy shipping."

Chapter Twenty-Seven

Needless to say, the Gaines woman was pleased with the likeness when he brought it home the following day. "And you did this just by describing me!" Charlotte turned the bust around and around, tilting her head from side to side, trying to see just how accurate it was. She went to a mirror on the living room wall and put it up beside her face, checking its ears against her own to see if he got the shape right.

"I guess you do know me!" she told the man standing beside her.

He winked salaciously at her and offered up, "Every inch of your body. I know what's mine and what's not." The man slapped her butt lightly, and she cocked an eye at him.

"Stop," she said. Her interest had been piqued, so she wanted to know more about the imaging solution.

"Yes, this is cutting-edge software and hardware. I know everybody will be down in the IT department playing with the new computer and image printer!"

"No, they won't!" he told her as he took his shoes off and headed to the bedroom to shower. "It costs too much money to play like that."

Charlotte thoroughly examined the picture, paying attention to each feature. "You sure he didn't copy the one you had in your wallet? That thing might have been a copying machine."

The man stopped, turned to her, and told her that he was equally as amazed at how the one she held had been generated. "No, like I told you, the man had a list of about fifty questions about physical features, et cetera. He had me to sit up front and speak into a microphone. The machine collected the data and interpreted it then spewed that picture out just like that!" He snapped his fingers.

"The bust too?" she asked.

He shook his head. "No, it took a bit longer, maybe five minutes or so. I was so enthralled with the photo that I was not paying attention to the machine. As a matter of fact, I didn't even recall him saying anything about the bust being created."

"So you weren't paying attention?" She shook her head.

"No, it wasn't that. He talked about flat and raised images as well as multidimensional images, but I just didn't have this in mind," he told her. "As a matter of fact, I don't think anyone did. A collective gasp came out when that machine spat out this likeness of you. Everybody in the room was surprised. But I guess that was the way it was supposed to be."

Curiosity kept the conversation alive. She suggested, "It was just like using Siri on the cellphone. You just say, "Okay, Siri," then ask your question, and the computer seeks your answer."

"Yes, something like that," he agreed. "Let me get my shower. I am ready to get a bite to eat. Th chicken salad, chips, Coke, and chocolate chip cookie I bought for lunch on the plane is gone."

Charlotte laid the picture on the table with her schoolwork. She decided she would get a frame to put it in later and set the bust atop a bookshelf.

Her bestie came over the next night. Needless to say, Charlotte was more than anxious to show the picture and the bust to her friend. She took her hand when she was at the door and practically dragged the woman over to the spot where the bust rested.

"What a marvelous likeness of you!" the Toures woman exclaimed. "How long did you have to sit for it? Did you find someone in the village to do it? What street? New York City has some real talented street artists." The woman's thoughts tripped over one another before her friend could tell her the source of her gift.

"No, it wasn't like that. I didn't have to sit at all. You remember that meeting I told you Jason and Berger had to go to, the one in Las Vegas?"

"Yes, you spoke about that, but I didn't realize it was happening so soon," the woman replied.

"Neither did I! He came home and told me about it, and before I had time to get back to you, the secretary had e-mailed their hotel reservations and plane tickets. There wasn't anything to do except get in the car, get to the airport, and get on the plane. It happened just like that!" Charlotte snapped her fingers to show the turnaround time between the Pennsylvania boys' conference with their boss and going to the conference.

The woman continued talking as she moved toward the kitchen area. "Anyway, they attended a workshop in the city, and when the trainer finished showing the company's new product, he used Jason for a guinea pig. He will have to explain how he ended up with that thing."

"I look forward to hearing the story. He always has interesting stories."

"Yes, he does! They both do, him and Berger. You wouldn't believe some of the stuff they tell me." The woman opened the refrigerator door, peered inside, and found the meat she was going to cook.

"Come on. Help me make dinner and let's catch up on what you have been doing while we are waiting for him to get home."

"I need to wash my hands," her friend said as she headed to the bathroom.

By the time Kieta joined her at the counter, she had also taken the salad fixings out of the refrigerator. Charlotte handed the items to her. "Here, you make the salad and dress it. You make the best salads!" she spoke nostalgically. "I haven't had any of your cooking lately. I was longing for some of your fresh yeast rolls the other day. You are going to have to make them for us sometimes."

"I love salad," the woman said as she prepared the requested dish. "Wakesa taught me to make it. She would make vinaigrettes with oil, vinegar, fruit juices, and spices to die for and let it marinate in the fridge overnight. The next day, she would take whatever greens she had and chop them, then pour some of the potion over them, then add raisins, currants, dried fruit peels, nuts, and generous chunks of fresh fruit before serving it to the family."

"She is the one who taught you to make bread too?" Charlotte asked.

"Yes, that and about everything else I learned about housekeeping." Kieta thought about the woman who had taken her in her charge the day her daddy had left her at the Soyinkas' kitchen door, and her visage showed a bit of sadness, which did not go unnoticed by her friend who was seasoning the chicken to put in the oven.

"Was she nice to you?" she asked the woman who by now had completed the salad and was covering the dish before placing it in the refrigerator.

Up and out of the appliance, her hand still on the handle, Kieta retorted, "Actually, she was a bitch!"

Her tone drew her friend's full attention. "Sorry, you want to talk about it?"

Kieta slid in a chair and spoke candidly about her life in the Soyinka household. "My dad dropped me off there one day when I was about ten. That woman worked the fat off my bones! She treated me like I was her personal servant. Kieta, do this! Kieta, do that! Girl, you better not drop that!" She mocked the woman as she shared her early years in the service of that family.

The two young women talked about the woman's early years in Timbuktu until the chicken was done, the oven's timer the only thing that kept it from being crisp as bacon. While Kieta had previously given Charlotte an abbreviated version of her story, she had not gone into details about these early days. She barely ended their conversation with "I don't know what I would have done if it had not been for Marissa and Madame Soyinka, of course" when the apartment door opened.

It was Charlotte's beau. Jason entered, two bouquets of multicolored freshly cut flowers in the crook of one arm. He hurried to Charlotte and gave her a peck on the lips as he handed her the top bunch. And turning to the woman resting in her seat, he offered up, "Here's another for the chef's assistant! I hope she let you make the salad." He pointed his head toward his girlfriend.

"Merci beaucoup!" Kieta pronounced gratitude in a language rarely used. All that talk about the Soyinka household had taken her there.

"You are welcome!" he told her as he kept moving toward the bathroom. He told the women, "I am going to freshen up. I'll be back in a minute."

Kieta looked at the bounty in her arm; let her eyes feast on the beauty of the pinks, yellows, reds, and green; and grew even more nostalgic. She raised them to her nose and sniffed, their fragrance was as sweet as any bouquet Madame Soyinka had ever had at the house in Timbuktu.

"Hand them to me. I will put yours in here." Charlotte reached for the flowers to put them in the place in the refrigerator away from the salad bowl. "They will keep fresh until you are ready to go home."

The woman pushed the bunch of flowers toward her friend, her mind wandering and her thoughts turning toward kindnesses not experienced since she had last been with Doe. Her friend saw her eyes well up. A tear also escaped the corner of one eye, an action that did not go unnoticed. It was clear that the Toures girl was all in her feelings that day, and everything from food to flora took her to secret places.

Charlotte took a couple of Kleenex from a box on the counter near the stove and passed them to her friend as she asked, "Are you all right?"

Kieta took the tissues, blew her nose, and disposed of them before rinsing her hands in the sink and drying them with a nearby dish towel. "I'm okay," she admitted to being in her feelings. "It's just that Doe has been on my mind so much lately! I've even been dreaming about him. Just seeing you two lovebirds just brought memories back. That's what it has to be!"

When she got up to put the tissue in the trash, the young woman took a few extra from the box to hold in her hand. These she laid on the counter and rinsed germy hands in the sink. "I hope you don't mind. Some people don't like for you to wash your hands in the kitchen sink."

"Some people, not me!"

"I know you are not like that, child!" She turned the conversation to her friend's relationship. "What I was going to say to you before I got teary-eyed is I am so glad you found love, Charlotte and that it found you! No greater thing can happen to a friend as wonderful as you have been to me since I came to this country. I used to think that way about Marissa. Now it is you that I think that way about. I want the best for you always!"

The girls hugged each other. "There is no one I would rather have had than you for a friend! God bless you too! I hope you will find love again."

By then, Jason was in the room. "What's going on in here? You all being so friendly without me. Come on over here! Let's have a three-way hug." He beckoned the women with his hand.

In a minute, the trio had enjoyed a group hug and were seated at the dinner table. The man prayed over the garlic roasted potatoes, salad, and oven-baked chicken. They enjoyed a wonderful fellowship with one another.

That night when they lay in their bed, Charlotte's mind returned to her friend and the man she had lost, Mahmoudou Ibrahaim. She told Jason the entire story the woman had told her. It was a compilation of the many snippets the Toures girl had told him. He shook his head with disbelief. "So she really has not heard anything about him or seen the man since they spirited her away from that prison in Mali and put her on the plane to the United States."

"That's what she says."

"Do you believe her story?" the man asked.

Charlotte expressed support for her friend with "Jason, I would stake my life on anything that she says. That's how much confidence I have in her and anything she says or does. As for trust, I have relatives who I wouldn't trust with her dime. Her, anything and everything!"

The detective in him took over. "Now she said she has been dreaming about him. Do you think she is trying to hint at having actually seen him or having heard from him but not wanting to come out and confess for fear of reprisal?"

Noting the change in his voice, she sat up. "To answer all that, sir, if she said she was dreaming, then she was. If she had seen him, she would have told me. She wouldn't play around with me like that or mince words. That is one woman who says what she means and means what she says."

The man, sufficiently accosted by his girlfriend, raised his hands. "I don't mean no harm. I was just asking."

Charlotte laughed, and he joined her. When they got themselves together and were back in character, friends talking about another friend's concerns, he told her, "She might be having those dreams for a reason. He might be trying to get to her to find her! Love is like that! I know if I lost you or had you sent somewhere to keep you safe, I would eventually look you up even if it was only in my dreams."

She looked at him and saw the traces of love in his eyes, heard them in his voice, and mewed, "Awwww, babe. That is such a sweet thought. I would do the same for you!"

They kissed, a romantic overture that took them back to their own care and concern for each other. He loved her to life, and she loved him more.

Morning came soon, and when he was on the way to work, Jason told Warren Berger about Kieta and Doe. At least, he told him as much as he knew. "I was kind of thinking about seeing if I can find out anything."

"That will probably be like trying to find a needle in a haystack!" the veteran officer told his younger partner.

"I know, but maybe he is in the States, on a visa or something. We could check with immigration."

The driver told him, "You know we have to have a reason. We just can't be checking on folks just because we can. Confidentiality requires proper protocol for searches."

"It ain't like I don't know that. I am just trying to figure how to help a friend out!"

"Man, love has took over your mind! You better leave that alone! We got enough legitimate business to take care of, so I'd let that be if I was you." Berger gave his fifty cents' worth of advice.

The Pitts man did let it go that day but resolved to utilize resources he had to conduct a search. However, he did not tell Charlotte what he was up to. He went his own way. He did not want to disappoint her or Kieta for that matter. Besides, he knew if he told his girlfriend, she would aggravate him to no end, her never-ending questions turning from simple asking to nagging in a heartbeat.

Time kept doing what time did. It rolled along, days came and passed as did weeks and months. Almost a year passed before the Gaines woman decided to play Cupid and help her friend. get back into the dating game. She brought it up while they dined on the balcony late one evening.

"Uhm!" she uttered after sipping from a glass of chardonnay she had poured from the bottle on a table the two shared.

"That good?" he asked her. His question brought her from reverie to reality.

"What?"

He pointed to the glass she still held in her hand.

"The wine! You make a little noise, and I took it to mean that you were enjoying your drink."

She put the wine glass on the table and told him what was on her mind. "I was thinking it's time for Kieta to get out and find someone to date. She just can't keep hoping that man is going to jump out of her dreams and back in her life. Her birthday is coming up soon, and I was thinking we could have a little get-together for her and invite a few people over here for her to meet."

Jason didn't have a problem with that. They had ample room for a small party. While neither were partygoers nor entertained bunches of people, he was comfortable with Charlotte's idea. "What do you need me to do?" he asked. "How can I help?"

"One way you can help is with the guest list," she replied. "Perhaps you can invite a couple of single guys from work or from the gym."

He paused then told her, "I know a few guys, but I am not sure of their status. We don't talk much about that, but I will see what I can find out."

Excitement garnered by his willingness to help with the party caused her to clap her hands in glee. "Yeah!" she cheered. She jumped up and performed a bit of a routine she had done when she had been a high school cheerleader, ending it with a leap on one foot then went inside to get some paper to write on.

Jason laughed heartily as she jogged into the living room and came back with a pad and pencil in hand so she could begin her party planning in earnest. "You got a calendar on your phone?"

"Sure," he told her as he picked his iPhone 6 from the table and flipped to the application. "What you want to know?"

"Friday or Saturday? What date do you think we should have the party?" He told her it did not matter but gave dates for the four Fridays and Saturdays in August, three months away from the current day. She chose the last Saturday in the month.

"Are you sure you are off that day?"

"Sure." He leaned over and showed her the calendar on his phone. "See, I don't work any fifth weekends."

Her understanding of scheduling appointments on the application not good, she asked how she could tell if he was off or not. Pointing to the date and showing her a small almost invisible dot under the dates on the calendar, he verified that he could be at the party and would help her make Kieta's birthday special and memorable.

Just about every waking moment Charlotte had for the next several weeks was used for planning, organizing, or securing something for the party. Since it was not a surprise party, she involved Kieta in every aspect of it, especially the guest list. When they finally finished, the guest list comprised twenty-four people: a few couples, some singles from their school, Jason's employ, and a couple who lived in their apartment complex.

The hostess also considered what they might give Kieta for a gift.

"She is quite simple," she told Jason while moving around in the apartment, cleaning. "And she doesn't like lots of fragrances or jewelry . . ."

Charlotte stopped dead in her tracks and snapped her fingers.

His eyes, which had been following her, arrested when she halted.

"I got it! I know what we can do! I don't know why I didn't think of it earlier."

"What?" he asked as he noticed that she was standing right in front of the picture he had brought from the workshop.

She reached out, took the framed picture off the wall, and turned to him, showing him what had claimed her attention. "I know what we can do, Jason. We can get a portrait of Doe made for her."

"Hold up!" he said as he rose from his seat. "I hear you thinking out loud, but that won't work. The reason you wanted to have this party was so she could meet somebody. You said you want to help her move on, get her mind off the past."

She spoke flippantly. "I know what I said. But that is not what I told her. I told her we wanted to give her a birthday party. She has never had one, so we wanted to be the first ones to give her one. I didn't say we were trying to set her up with anyone, silly!"

Jason knew he was fighting a losing battle, so he asked, "How we are we going get a picture of someone we have never seen?"

Charlotte took him back to the night he had come home from Las Vegas with the framed picture and boxed bust, gifting her with memories she would otherwise not have had. "You told me how both of them were made. And you said if a person knew specific details like shape of the face, color of the eyes, and texture and length of the hair, he could just speak that into that Identity Solutions machine, and it would generate the picture."

"You didn't hear everything I said," the man argued profusely. "You stopped listening as soon as you unwrapped the picture! I also said it was quite expensive."

His argument was falling on deaf ears. "How much does it cost to get it done? I have a little money in savings and will be getting my excess from financial aid soon."

"It's not about the money! It's the principle of the thing. This is not what you had in mind that night on the patio."

She did not relent. "Come on! A lady has a right to change her mind," she told him.

Jason Pitts shook his head. "Come here. Let me see if I can talk some sense into your head."

The woman flopped down on the couch beside her lover, and he pulled her close to him.

"Look here, babe." He took her chin in his hand and kissed her on her lips. "There is nothing in the world I wouldn't do for you. Right now, I am thinking that's not possible to get a picture like that done. You know what we have to do if we want to use that thing. No, you don't! Let me tell you. We have to fill out a requisition to use anything in the IT department, and it has to be approved by the captain who checks with finance to see if it's in the budget. What the hell am I supposed to do? Stroll my ass in there and tell him my girlfriend is having a surprise party for her bestie, and she wants me to have a picture of her boyfriend generated and put in a gold-plated frame so she can remember what her long-lost boyfriend looks like?"

The look on his face and his gestures drew first a smile then a chuckle from the annoyed girl. This time she took his chin in her much smaller hand, looked into his eyes, and told him, "Yep, you can do it like that if you want to! Or you can make friends with the guy who runs that lab and get him to cut you a deal." Then she kissed him, pecking his chin, cheek, forehead, and lips until she had his full attention again.

He reciprocated and pulled her onto his lap. The two lovers let go of all that which was dividing them and turned toward that which was important—her, him, the love they shared. Jason and Charlotte engaged in a bit of foreplay, drawn to a close by the timer on the oven letting her know the casserole she had placed in the oven earlier was ready.

She got up off his lap and turned around to extend a hand to him. "Come on. Get up and make drinks. I will plate our food and bring it to the table."

Charlotte took the Mexican corn casserole from the oven. As the recipe suggested, she set it on the stovetop to rest a minute. She put salad from the fridge in bowls, which she placed on the table while their entrée was resting. Shortly thereafter, she heaped spoons of the casserole on their plates, set his in front of him first, and put hers on her placemat.

"New recipe?" her mate asked about the mixture of corn, hamburger, chips, and spices he tasted as soon as she put it in front of him.

"Yes, one of those somebody put on Facebook," she explained. "It kept being reposted, so I thought I would give it a try."

She tasted of the dish and gave it a nod of approval too. "I will make that again."

Toying with his salad while the casserole cooled, the man turned their attention back to Kieta. "This salad is nothing like sister girl makes." He used one of the terms of endearment he heard some of the brown women down at the precinct use when talking about their friends and acquaintances.

"I know," the woman beside him admitted. "This salad is kind of bland. I don't know what she does to make hers so good." She shrugged. "I am going to keep trying though."

Between bites, they continued to talk about the party. "I am looking forward to it," he admitted. "Berger is a little pissed though. He wants to come and bring his old lady. I told him it was for singletons only."

"All I know is we are going to have a good time and some good food!" Charlotte assured him. "Kieta and I are having lunch tomorrow. We are going to complete the menu. You know I was going to cater, but she wants us to prepare all the food ourselves so that's probably what we will do . . . cook it ourselves."

"That works for me!" he said, scraping the remains of his salad on his fork with a finger. "As long as you let her make the salad."

She agreed with him. "That and some fresh bread! She used to make it on special occasions when we lived in Florida. It was so good, hot, straight out the oven, slathered with butter! I could actually make a meal out of that!"

~~~~~

Just as they had planned, the girlfriends met at a restaurant near the park. Both had bowls of soup, salad, and a beverage before making out the menu for the party. Kieta recounted the fixings she and her mentor had done for the Soyinka family. Laughingly, Charlotte told her, "All I know is you got to make the salad and the bread. Jason and I don't care if that's all we have."

"I can do that! It's nothing to making yeast bread. If you want, I can teach you how."

Charlotte waved off her friend's desire to teach her to make bread. "No, not me. I can't stand the feel of dough on my hands. If you just make me some every now and then, I'll be satisfied."

"Okay," Kieta agreed. "I will make extras so you can put them in the freezer, take out a few at a time, and bake them for the two of you."

That same day, the Gaines woman had an epiphany. If Warren Berger and his wife could come to the party, he would help Jason get "the gift" made for the honoree. She told her lover so that very evening and secured his partner's address for mailing of the formal invitation.

The invitation went out immediately, and the RSVP was returned pronto. Jason also saw a change in his friend's attitude. He stopped being so playful and did not taunt and tease his partner about being "whipped" like he had done a lot lately.

Consequently, he confided in him about the straits the woman from Timbuktu was in when they stopped for lunch, ending the reveal with "The insurgents came, found them together, jailed her, beat the hell out of her, and locked her back up. Somebody, she thinks her fellow, spirited her away from the country in the dead of night. Next thing she knew she was in Florida!"

"Damn! What a story! She deserves a party, all she been through, and a ton of presents!" Warren Berger showed empathy toward their friend.

Jason retorted, "That's what we were saying! That's why we want to do something special for her!"

"If there is anything me and the wife can do to help, just let us know!" Berger took the bait just as Charlotte had anticipated. "I ain't never met her, but it sounds like she is some special kind of woman, all she been through, and in law school, making good grades." The man shook his head in disbelief.

A few days later, the Pitts man confided that the Gaines woman wanted her friend to have a framed picture of Doe as a birthday present. He told his partner, "My girl has been worrying the heck out of me about getting a picture of that dude done for her!" He cut to the chase. "So I went down to IT and checked out the place. I am trying to figure out who has access to that Identity Solutions machine and to see if I can cut a deal with him. Do you know anybody down there?"

"Sure, I know somebody. I'll check it out and get back to you Monday!"

Jason gave a sigh of relief. He was glad he had had an inroad into the technology department. Nevertheless, he didn't feel right about what he was doing. His conscience was whipping him for a couple of reasons: he was breaking the department's policies and was involving other people in an act that could lead to suspension from their jobs all the way to termination of their employ. The nagging feeling stayed with him all day, and when it was time to go home, he almost told Warren Berger to forget about it. His partner had a family, wife and children to take care of.

A seed of doubt planted, it took hold. "Maybe I just need to forget about the picture!" popped up constantly during the weekend, thoughts the man tried to exercise away. He went to the gym, jogged in Central Park, rode his bicycle, did everything physical because that generally helped chase away the blues.

His actions were not lost on the Gaines woman. "What's eating at you? Is it time for you to take your annual physical?" she asked him.

"Neither," he answered her questions. Instead, he lied to her. "Late summer does that to me! The weather is just right, so I am just trying to get it all in before fall. It gets cool here early."

A native of Florida, she found his response plausible. "It's hot down south all year round, so I get that."

The weekend dragged, and when Monday finally came, Jason was up and out a couple of minutes before Charlotte made breakfast. His bed, literally growing harder as he lay there waiting for time to go to work, he went to the Dunkin Donut shop where he met the love of his life. There, he called Warren, an early riser himself. "Pick me up at the donut shop," he told the man.

"What's the matter? Did she kick you out of her bed? Is she tired of your ass already?" the man teased and taunted Jason.

"Neither, just pick me up here!"

"Okay, I am on my way!"

"Not now," Jason told him there was no need to hurry.

"It's all right. My old lady ain't fixed any grub yet. How about I pick you up, and we swing by IHOP or somewhere. That way, I can get my breakfast, and you can get some pancakes or something."

"That will work!" Jason pushed the donut in front of him aside. Peaches and raspberry sauce on a stack of three pancakes, much more appealing than the cake donut he had just ordered. He sipped from the cup of coffee a few minutes before heading to the exit to wait on the sidewalk for his ride.

He didn't have to wait long for his ride and the other matter that had claimed his attention the whole weekend.

As soon as he had one leg in the car, his partner started talking. "I took care of that little business for you. My wife's cousin works there, so I just asked him. He gave me this questionnaire. He says all you have to do is to have her complete this, and he will see what he can do with it."

"What? I didn't know you had family on the force," Jason told him, his mind on how he had worried about finding somebody in the department to help with Kieta's gift.

"You still don't know I have family in there. That's nepotism!" The giver of the coveted gift made it clear for his partner that he should forget what he had just revealed.

"Okay! I get it!" Jason showed his partner that he understood.

The brief but important exchange having taken place, Warren told Jason, "Buckle up!" Then he craned his neck to see if he could pull out into traffic safely. "This traffic ain't no joke!" he said when his front end was on the busy avenue, the rear trailing as fast as it could.

Hearing the click, he told Jason the survey was in a large, brown envelope in between the seat. "He told me to get this back to him ASAP, and he will get the picture done and to make you promise never to let on where you got the picture from if anyone asks!"

"Cross my heart and hope to die!" Jason gladly swore secrecy. He couldn't wait to get home that evening. He knew his girl was going to love him to death that night. She was going to get the coveted gift. The man started whistling where he sat.

Chapter Twenty-Eight

At first, Charlotte and Jason thought they could use information gleaned from conversations with the girl to complete the questionnaire but soon realized it required more details than they could produce. They remembered the Toures woman's story but soon admitted they could not cast characters like Mahmoudou Ibrahaim if they were doing a movie or a play either.

So the woman broke down and told Kieta what they wanted to give her for her birthday. "I was thinking about how you were saying that while you see Doe in your dreams, you are not certain that you would recognize him if he walked up to you on the streets and tapped you on your shoulder. I asked Jason to see if he could get a picture like that one done for you." She pointed to the one on her wall, the one he got at the Identity Solutions training in Las Vegas. The other girl's eyes traced the path her pointing finger made.

Surprise showed on Kieta's face, and her heart skipped a beat while the Gaines woman continued to talk. "Anyway, Jason got his hands on the survey, and we tried to complete it. That to no avail because we found ourselves fussing about whether the man had black eyes or brown eyes, how tall he was, what his stature was like, and so on. Neither one of us could remember much about Doe's appearance!"

Charlotte headed to the bedroom, beckoning her friend to follow her. "Come on. I got it in here."

The Toures woman, still processing what it was that her friend was getting at, trailed behind her, stopping at the bedroom door where she watched her friend pick some paper from her nightstand and stuff them back into the nine-by-twelve envelope.

When she had retrieved the survey and was directly in front of her friend, she told her, "Here, take this thing home and fill it out! I will drop by your place tomorrow on my way home to pick it up."

"Okay" emitted the visitor, deciding to cut her stay short and to head home.

Urgency in her friend's voice propelled her out their apartment and back to her own to complete the questionnaire, a task that proved to be daunting even to her. It had been years since the Toures woman had seen Mahmoudou Ibrahaim. However, since he invaded her dreams on occasion, she felt that the image would be accurate.

Once she took the papers out of the envelope and reordered them, the woman set about reconstructing Mahmoudou Ibrahaim's image, reading the whole document first and responding to those items that came easy—height, weight, bone structure, eye color. Others like the shape of the eyes, more oval than round, as well as approximate distance between each took more time.

True to her word, Charlotte stopped by her brownstone the following day. The women plopped down on the couch and chatted about their day before Kieta offered her friend a cool beverage.

"I thought you would never ask," the visiting friend said. "I know you have some lemonade. You always do!"

Kieta chuckled and acknowledged how well her friend knew her. "You have kept my story on your heart. You remember how I fell in love with the beverage the first glass Wakesa gave me the day I came to the compound in Mali," she said as she removed a pitcher with a small amount of drink in it from the refrigerator. She pushed it toward the Gaines woman and said, "This is all that I have. However; I can make what you Americans call an Arnold Palmer because I have a full jug of sweet tea."

"Oh! That sounds good! Give me a large glass, please."

"Okay." Kieta reached in the cabinet and shoved glassware around until she found a couple of large mugs.

Drinks made for the two of them, Kieta set both on coasters on her coffee table. "I've got chips and nuts," she said.

"Chips, please. That will hold me until suppertime." The Gaines girl expressed appreciation for the snack.

Her hostess function taken care of, the Toures woman plopped down on the couch and leaned over to retrieve the envelope the woman had given her. "You won't believe how long it took me to complete these fifty questions!"

Charlotte told her, "I bet I do too. Like I told you, it was more than a notion for the two of us together. Tell me anyway though!"

"Five hours. It took me five hours to complete this." She gestured with the envelope. "Five freaking hours!"

"That's longer than it took for us to take and pass the LSAT! What were you doing? You didn't have to think about much. Girl, you knew that man. Anyway, that's the impression I got!"

Charlotte's speech brought fond memories of Doe, especially when she implied that she knew his sexual proclivities, so she should have found it easy to answer the questions. Kieta smiled, her thoughts on his lovemaking. What he had done for her sustained her even now. In her dreams, she still felt his touch. So it was not this that she forgot; it was other things that were vague.

Silence permeated the air, lasting too long for the other girl. "Yoohoo, you still with me? Or somewhere else?" Charlotte tapped the sofa, causing the daydreamer to return to the present.

Kieta shook away memories and handed the envelope to Charlotte. "Here. I can't wait to see what it looks like." She smiled more to herself than at her friend.

~~~~~

When the photo was ready, Jason went to the IT department to pick it up and brought it home. "Dang, that's a good-looking fellow," the Gaines woman evoked when she took it from its wrapping. "I am going to take it downtown to the frame shop and get it matted and framed. That girl is going to love it!"

"I just hope it looks like him," Jason argued.

Holding the picture out, looking at it anew, his girlfriend told him, "I don't think it will matter much. This is a good-looking picture."

Feigning jealousy, her beau told her, "Hey, you better stop gazing on that man and come over here and give me a little attention. After all I went through to get that thing done, I need a little appreciation."

She laid the image aside and turned her attention to him. "How was your day, honey?"

~~~~~

Back at the IT lab, the uncanny happened. Once Mahmoudou Ibrahaim's picture was generated, it was matched with others in a facial recognition databank maintained by the agency. An alert identifying him as a suspected terrorist showed up. When it did, the technician contacted Jason's partner to let him know that the man was on the list, and he had informed the Central Intelligence Agency.

One thing led to another, a chain of events that was unanticipated, unforeseen, as well as unfortunate followed the "red alert." When it was received, the agency instantly recognized Winston Royals's killer and assigned the case to two agents to seek the man out, capture him, and make him pay for the loss of one of their own.

Meantime, Warren Berger kept this bit of information close to his chest. Jason's partner had overstepped his authority when he had utilized the police department for personal gain. The senior member of their team, he could be demoted, lose his job, or be terminated, so he swore his in-law to secrecy as well. "Man, don't ever tell nobody about this shit! No damn body. I ain't even going to let this on to my partner! You better keep your face shut too!"

The IT clerk assured him, "You ain't got to worry about me. I don't even know why I let you talk me into this. I got a wife and a family. She's pregnant and about to drop one soon. I need this job, so your secret is my secret!"

Chapter Twenty-Nine

Kieta, still refusing to date, spent time in Central Park, running a little and exercising. The woman was trying to move the longing for Doe from her head, heart, and deep in her loins. She was not a regular sprinter though. It was just when lust wanted to overtake her that she went there to beat it down.

One night she dreamed that Doe returned. He slipped his hard, naked frame in her bed and was under the sheets with her. The man pulled her to him, and she let her body mesh with his . . . his lips were on her neck. He nuzzled and nicked at her skin with his teeth. A feverish warmth cascaded down her corps, reaching her womanhood.

She groaned in her sleep and woke up with sighs of ecstasy escaping her parted lips and her bed wet where she urinated on herself. The woman got up, went into the bathroom, removed her wet lingerie, and decided to shower before returning to change the bedding. A cold shower would have to do. She could not put on her jogging shoes and run.

Needless to say, she could not go back to sleep after such a dream. So the Toures woman found herself at the kitchen table nursing a cup of Joe laced with a fair amount of hazelnut syrup and considering whether it was time for her to move on, to seek new love. That was what Charlotte and Jason told her she needed to do. One of the reasons for the birthday party was so she could meet someone and move on.

~~~~~

Several miles of New York City blocks away, Mahmoudou Ibrahaim woke with a start. He had dreamed of his *cherie*, Kieta Toures. They were in the cottage on Baker Street, the one he had rented from his friend, Kunto Boro, for their privacy. He and she were there. They were joined by their love and lust for each other. He was on the bottom and she on top, riding him as if her life depended on it. He felt himself being swallowed up as she pulled his manhood with muscles trained to please him and only him. The pulsating of his member brought him from reverie to reality.

He woke up, pain deep in his groin! "Ahhhh!" the man growled at the dream. Doe got up to go to the bathroom to relieve himself. Unable to return to sleep when he was back in bed, he used his hand on himself as he consciously planned the tryst he would have with her when he found her.

~~~~~

Mahmoudou Ibrahaim had indeed been lucky when he arrived in the States. A stowaway found by his own countrymen who helped him get on track, he kept his head down and experienced good success.

After completing a bachelor's program in business in three years, the man was recommended for and took a position with a firm in New York City, excelling. His work ethic was impeccable and noted by everyone he came in contact with. Soon, he was at the table when discussions were held about fuel consumption, distributions, and markets worldwide.

The more successful he became, the more the women in the office chased him for themselves or to make introductions for a blind date. Soon, his boss's wife was in on it. Everyone was trying to find him a wife, and conversations about him moving up when he was married became more frequent.

Needless to say, he was a hit at office parties as well as company dinners. All were interested in how this dark brown-skinned hunk of a man managed to come to the United States, establish himself in record time, and be in the fast lane. He was up for a promotion soon. Frequently, the women would switch place cards at the dinner table to sit beside him, to bend his ear, and to find out more about him.

Despite their best efforts, Mahmoudou Ibrahaim never let his story escape his lips so it could be told and regurgitated at will but would turn any question about himself or his past on a dime, causing the listener and inquirer to reveal more of herself than he did. Doe had thoughts only of his Kieta.

The more he thought of her, the more he ran. He kept up the running in the park, sometimes before work, sometimes after work. One day he caught a glimpse of a girl who looked like his *cherie*. His pace halted, and he turned around, but she was around the curve by then. The man considered turning around and following the woman. He shook such a thought from his head for fear of being accused of stalking. However, he continued to come more after work to see if he would see the girl again.

Months passed before he caught a glimpse of the same woman. She was not running this time but stretching and preparing for a run. He had come up on her so fast that he did not have time to cut his speed or brake. A safe distance away, he pulled up to wait for her to pass, but she did not. The girl ran in the opposite direction. "Damn!" escaped his lips before he decided to continue his run. That could not have been her though. She did not wear braids like the girl he had seen on two occasions. She permed and relaxed her hair just like the Soyinka women did, and she wore it short.

He shook thoughts of the woman away for a moment, fully considering asking one of the girls at the office out the next day. His idea, *This shit is going to run me crazy! I need to stop chasing ghosts and get a life!* He changed his mind almost as soon as he decided to move on.

It took almost a half year of playing "a cat and mouse" game before he finally saw that it was indeed the woman he had known in Timbuktu. Once he was certain that he had found his *cherie*, he ran past her on a couple of occasions, checking to see if she had an idea who he was, but she did not seem to notice him. Soon, it became apparent that she was listening to music while she ran. Mahmoudou saw the earbuds in her left ear and that her eyes were on the trail. This was smart since the path was not as smooth in some places as it was in others.

After careful deliberation, the businessman changed his strategy. Instead of running, he bought a book with him and perched on a park bench and pretended to read. He dressed casually instead of in running gear and wore shades to protect his eyes from the sun's glare. The man found a shaded spot about twelve feet from the trail where he could see runners and other park dwellers clearly and those lurking there could also see him too.

The man took watch and found his beloved Kieta Toures, and when courage made itself felt, he inconspicuously followed her to the campus. From a distance, he watched her go into the building where she resided. When he was sure she would not come out, he moved closer to the building, observing its three floors and stairs on the ends and in the middle of each set of apartments.

It looked like a hotel had been converted into a dormitory, a practice quite common in college towns with growing enrollments. He wondered which one of these could be hers and if she lived alone. Or had a man? He shook thoughts of another man away. He could not bear the idea of his beloved sharing space, especially her bed, with anyone else. She was his!

At home that evening, Doe paced the floor like a madman. He couldn't eat or sleep. His mind was consumed with thoughts of how he would approach her or if he should approach her. Perhaps she had forgotten about him, had someone else.

He went to work the next day, and finding that he could not concentrate, he decided to take a few days of vacation. The Ibrahaim man's request was granted without questions. By ten o'clock, he had taken the Metro, gotten off, and was at her living quarters. His mind was on just walking up to the door and knocking on it until she opened up and let him in. At the newfound place, he stopped. He did not know which door was hers. So he turned on his heels and went home to rethink his approach.

Mahmoudou Ibrahaim stalked Kieta Toures, shadowed her for a whole week, anticipating how he would approach her and what he would say when he had her full attention. He took a seat on a bench and watched her leave early on Saturday morning. He was dressed in his running outfit and shoes, waiting for her to come out for a run.

The woman came out but was dressed in street clothes, not the running outfit she had worn the last four Saturdays. He look down at himself and almost laughed. His best laid plan was going awry. A taxi came to a stop between the few yards that separated the two of them, and she got inside. "Damn!" His expletive of choice escaped his lips. He got up, stomping the ground where he stood in frustration while she mounted the vehicle.

~~~~~

The two agents assigned the Ibrahaim case went over to the precinct close to Manhattan to speak with the chief about the wanted man.

One asked, "How did you all manage to find him?"

"I have my sources," Jason and Warren's boss spoke tentatively, not wanting to reveal that an employee in his IT department had breached an IT usage policy he had enacted. "All I can say is when the data from that questionnaire was inputted, a likeness of Ibrahaim's picture was generated. As soon as it was done, a pop-up appeared on the computer screen, bringing him to the attention of the bureau and the agency. That new facial recognition machine we bought last year caught his ass!"

"Must be linked to someone in the upper echelon," the other agent replied, his eyes on the man on the other side of the desk.

"Can't say!" was the reluctant response given the former's assertion. The man shook his head. As much as he wished he could reveal his source, the chief could not. He did not know which "jackass" down there had caused the alert. He had told himself he would choke the living shit out of whoever did it when he found out.

He did not want to appear weak, so he took one for his team. "We don't have any additional information we can give you, boys." The man dismissed the inquirers.

The agents just decided to let it be. *What it was was what it was!* Nothing more could be achieved by sitting in the office over at the precinct talking with a man who obviously did not know as much as they did. The senior one looked at his watch then back to the man he shared office space with and said, "I am ready to go when you are ready."

His partner jumped up from his seat, saying as he rose, "All right! Let's go do this!" They took the elevator to the garage where their vehicles were parked, and within the next few minutes, they were headed to stake out the place where they felt sure the man would appear: his job. He had taken a few days off but was back and following the regular schedule. When he was not working, he was checking the girl out, observing her movements, and determining when he would make his move. All the agents had to do was wait and watch.

~~~~~~

Their full investigation done, and certain that they had their man, the two men in black stood in the building's shadows, observing Mahmoudou Ibrahaim's movements. "Oh well!" one said to the other. "This just ain't his day! How about we just pick his ass up now and take him down to the station?"

"No!" the other interjected as he placed his hand on his partner's arm. "We been chasing this joker for almost five years. What's five more days?"

"You are a hopeless romantic! That's what you are," Agent One argued with the other.

"Naw, it ain't that! We gotta make sure one plus one equals two!"

"Yes, you right! Let's go get a coffee." The men watched as Mahmoudou Ibrahaim turned and headed for home before they removed themselves from their perch and headed off to enjoy the remainder of their Saturday.

"What are you going to do?" one asked the other.

"I am going to hit some balls! You wanna come?" The agent swung his imaginary club.

"I ain't into that golfing!"

The speaker stopped. "Next week though! Right?" His friend nodded in agreement.

Doe stood watching the woman. He had not seen her for nearly five years, and he was struck by how little she had changed. She had put on a few pounds, but they looked good on her, so did the permed short cut she wore. It suited her to a tee. To read the books on the table in front of her, she wore glasses, narrow square ones with glossy black frames that fit her face. The spectacles made her look both scholarly and sexy. Kieta Toures was every bit as beautiful as she had been the first day he had seen her on the streets of Timbuktu.

The man walked over to the table where she sat. "Hello, beautiful!" he spoke, his voice full of admiration.

Chapter Thirty

In the law library, Kieta heard a familiar voice and turned her head to meet its sound. "Doe, Mahmoudou!" she exclaimed, teary-eyed. "You are here. I can't believe you are here."

"*Cherie*, I didn't think you would want to see me again after what happened," the man confessed, his eyes meeting hers.

The Toures woman opened her mouth to speak. She had rehearsed in her mind a thousand times what she would say when she saw him again, not if but when. Kieta never doubted the love of her life would return to her someday, somehow, so she practiced what she would say when he made his appearance. The woman even did it in front of the mirror, just as she did when she was learning lines for a play or making an argument in front of the courts.

But that had not helped. The man present, she was more nervous than she had even been on a stage or in mock trials held in front of her professors and the class. Plays were make-believe, but this was real life, and no sound was coming from her lips. She knew her lines, but she couldn't get them out.

Likewise, Doe was certain of his own lines but could not believe what a wretched job he was doing with his own delivery. A confident man, he had never balked when speaking. But now when it really counted, words escaped him. There was so much he wanted to tell her about what had happened since she had been torn from his arms by the insurgents.

She still in her seat and he standing, they moved simultaneously, turning to meet each other. He reached for her hand and helped her to her feet. Up, he drew her close to himself. The woman lifted her head to see his face. Their eyes met, and the two held each other's gaze. Their fingertips touched, and finally, their hands grappled with each other's until their fingers were intertwined. They drew nearer, each feeling the heat emanating from one to the other. Fluidity escaped them; the movements were not well orchestrated. Their awkwardness created a gulf that had not been there when they had last seen each other.

Both were unaware that they were joined in their reunion by men in the shadows.

"Let's get out of here!" the Ibrahaim croaked, the frog in his throat distorting his normal timbre.

The student gathered her belongings and led the way through the stacks, in the elevator, past the librarian's desk, and outside into the open air. Neither spoke as they began the promenade toward her environs, their footsteps matching as they headed to her lodging.

Normally, she let her bag of books drop before taking her key from her purse to unlock the door. That day, she handed the backpack to him. She stepped inside her small apartment, holding the door open for the visitor.

The man paused in the entrance way and studied her living quarters and the decor. He saw an artist's drawing of him, bearded with a prayer cap on his head, hanging on the wall in the living room. "Who is that? Malcolm X?" he asked about the American he had learned about since coming to the States. Several people at work had told him he resembled the man.

She playfully punched him in the side as she shut the door. "No, that's you, silly. That's my Doe!"

Still standing and looking at the picture over the dining table, he asked, "Where did you get it?"

"My friend Charlotte's boyfriend works for the NYPD. They have some kind of imaging machine down there that generates pictures if a person can give specific details about a person's features—eyes, ears, nose, etc. They input data, and from what I understand, it spits out a likeness. Anyway, he had a picture of her done, and I liked it, so they had one of you done for me. The two of them gave me a birthday party and voila!" She pointed a wagging finger toward the photo in walnut frame. "That was my gift, a likeness of you. I think he and I did pretty good." She looked at the man back at the picture, all the while smiling, satisfaction showing on her face.

Kieta turned to him, asking as she gazed into his eyes, "Qu'en penses-tu? What do you think about it?"

Still standing and giving the photo his full scrutiny, Doe rubbed his chin and turned his head from side to side, admitting, "That's not bad! I think it accurately reflects the young Mahmoudou. I've got a little gray since then." He brushed at his temple and sides of his head with open palm.

"You look the same to me," she complimented him. "Just like I remembered."

He took her face in his hand; tilted her chin upward, giving his eyes full access to her features; and then spoke throatily. "And you, you are still the most beautiful woman I have ever known." His words made her blush.

Their eyes caught, and they beheld each other's beauty, the moment held and not broken until she changed the subject. "Come on!" she took his arm, inviting him to continue to walk with her as she went from room to room, sharing her sparsely but elegant six-hundred-square-feet apartment. The kitchen with laundry room on the side, she paused to show the bathroom on left just inside her fairly nice sized bedroom. A neatly dressed, full bed in the center of the floor, and a desk beside a window replete with books, notebooks, and pens caught his eye.

The tour completed, he told her, "My apartment is much like this, just large enough for me."

A sigh of relief came from her. She was certain that if Doe was sharing space with anyone, he would have told her. He was always forthright with her. She could not think of a time when he ever kept a secret from her. "At least, that was the way he had been when we were back home in Mali," she told herself.

"Asseyez-vous!" she told the man, pointing to the couch facing the New York Skyline. He sat, and she offered him a beverage as she proceeded toward the refrigerator. "Tea or water?" she asked.

"A bottle of water if you have it."

She took two bottles of spring water from the cooler's shelves and returned to the couch where she took a seat beside the man. He took a swig of his before taking the one from her hand to open it. She was struggling with the plastic cap. When he handed hers back, their hands touched, and coolness from the water was replaced by a warmth that shocked the woman. Their eyes met. She turned from him, else she would be enveloped in warmth and consumed by lust in his eyes.

"Okay now." She probed while scooting toward the couch's arm to give a bit of distance between him and her. "Tell me where you went after that night."

Mahmoudou Ibrahaim took up their story where her memory had left off, his words exploding, their speed as rapid as the guns he still heard in nightmares. "*Cherie*, when we put you on that plane, I went crazy! All I wanted was to get my hands on those bastards . . . I wanted to kill every one of them . . . I didn't care whether I lived or died . . . I just wanted vengeance for what he had done to you because I wouldn't cooperate with them. I swore on my grandmother's grave that I would hunt them down, kill the shit out of every last bastard that conspired with the American, Winston Royals, to make me do his biddings. I was going to mow the whole motherfucking lot of them down."

His reveal left the man exhausted and emotionally bereft. There were tears streaming down the man's face as he told the Toures woman about the assassination of the American operative, Kunto's reaction, and the inevitable separation from his childhood friend.

"He was drinking like a fish, and he tried to get us equally as inebriated, just kept offering beer and liquor from a cooler he kept beside the couch. I watched until I couldn't take it anymore. Disgust just overtook me, and I put a bullet right between his eyes!"

A loud gasp escaped from the woman's lips, and she threw her hand over her mouth to quiet herself.

Doe kept talking, rambling about the loss of his livelihood, his family, having been homeless then a stowaway—one who rode the plane with the deceased on a jet to Seattle where he had been found by some brothers from Mali, ones who had been instrumental in helping his acclimate to the new world; how he never forgot about her; how he recalled the conversation about where she would like to go in the United States; how he got to New York; and how he found her, his *cherie*.

She held herself as she watched the man unravel. Shivers threatened to overtake her, and she did not know what to she should do next, whether she should stop him or just let him talk, get it all out of his system.

Her mind turned toward what assistance she could get from the outside. She thought, *Maybe I can call Charlotte and Jason, and they can come over.* His sobs greater still, she pondered about calling 911. He appeared to be coming apart, right there in her apartment. What to do?

Mahmoudou felt her fear. He took a tissue from a box on the coffee table and wiped tears from his leaking eyes and blew his nose. He was feeling stuffed up, and his head was hurting, stabbing pains hitting him between the eyes. Yet his chest was deflating. The more he told her, the better he felt. It had been a while since he had been able to speak freely.

She relaxed but waited for him to make the next move.

His mind back in Dubuya's ornate tent in the desert, he told her, "And then it was over. I saw what I had done. The enemy lay dead at my feet. I had really done it, and I had to act cool. I did not want Kunto to know how scared I was. He was already freaking out. As for me, I was ready to shit my breeches but could not let on what I was feeling. I had to lead my buddy out of that tent, go out by the fire, eat a morsel and take a drink with his men, and act like nothing had happened."

He swallowed and drew a breath. She closed the gap between her and the man, reached for him, and pulled him into her arms. Doe hung his head and sobbed, this time with total relief. And Kieta just sat there stroking his hair, letting him get much-needed relief. How long they sat there she couldn't tell. The sky lost its blue and turned gray.

Her stomach growled, bringing her attention to the present. "Do you want a bit to eat?" she asked. "I have meat for sandwiches."

"That would be great," he told her before getting up to go to the bathroom. The urge to relieve himself set him quickly in motion.

~~~~~

337

Reunited by fate, the immigrants spent a full week together, being watched by roving eyes. Ironically, she was on holiday. He called human resources at his employ for a few more days of vacation. They holed up in the apartment, talking and making love, trying to make up for time lost.

One agent grew restless and wanted to arrest the Ibrahaim man while they had him in their sights. The other, a hopeless romantic, wanted to give them a bit of time before separating the lovers.

The former reminded his partner, "Winston was one of us! We don't want to lose this bastard!"

"I know." His senior waved away his impatience. "Don't be quick! Let's dot our *Is* and cross our *Ts* and make sure he is the right man. We don't need a fuckup."

The underling threw up his hands.

Noticing his gesture, the former added another thought. "He ain't going nowhere anyway not as long as she is putting out like she is."

His partner laughed. "Man, you know you are about as lame as they get! Nobody I know says 'putting out'!"

"What they say?"

"Hitting that azz, man! That's what everybody say now."

"Whatever! All I know is if he is busy, his mind ain't on us!"

"You reckon it ever was?"

"You betcha! Ain't no way in hell he kill one of our men, come over here, and think he is just going to assimilate. He has probably been looking over his shoulder in his sleep."

"A killer with a conscience, huh!" the driver said when they were in the parking lot.

The other man shook his head. "I didn't say he had a conscience. I just know he has more smart than some would give him credit for. I can't wait to hear his story, find out how in the hell he got out the country and here in the Big Apple. And how he found the girl!"

By the end of the week, the agents were ready to pick the man up and take him in. They went to the law library and waited there. The men knew her routine. His too. Kieta Toures would go there immediately after class to study before heading home. Now that Mahmoudou Ibrahaim had found her, he would without a doubt come to the building, walk her home, have dinner, and then copulate. Lovers were predictable like that.

The Friday of his takedown, before he or she could enjoy greetings, the two lovers were joined by a gun-wielding man who stepped out of the library's stacks and poked the man in his side as he uttered, "Long time no see, Mahmoudou!" His accomplice, by his side, reached for and pulled the man's resigned arms from his sides to the base of his back and cuffed him, speaking as he placed the manacles on the man's wrists, "You are under arrest for the murder of one Winston Royals, an operative for the Central Intelligence Agency."

The other agent gave the man the Miranda rights. "You have the right to remain silent. Anything you say can and will be held against you in a court of law. You have right to an attorney . . ."

Mahmoudou Ibrahaim lifted his head, his pride showing. The man had no regrets about what he had done to avenge the love of his life. He gave her a small nod, the edges of his mouth showed satisfaction as did his eyes. Doe did not resist arrest. He could live in a hole peaceably now that he was sure that his *cherie*, Kieta Toures, was fine.

A shocked Kieta witnessed the arrest of the man who had loved her from afar but given his freedom away just to see her one more time. She pushed one agent aside, and as close to her man as she could be, she slid down his frame and held on to the man who was cuffed in silence. Tears ambushed her, and she started to wail. Everyone on the fifth floor in the library turned to the sound and saw attempts to lead the man one way and the student the other direction toward her seat. Her neatly manicured nails clawed at his khakied leg, almost renting it in anguish.

Momentarily, the agent removed her hands from Doe's corps and assisted her to her seat where he identified himself. "CIA, ma'am. Sorry to interrupt your reunion, but Mr. Ibrahaim is under investigation for terrorism and has entered the United States unlawfully. We have been in pursuit of him since he arrived and were watching to see where he was going. Perhaps you have information that would be useful to us in our war on terrorism." He sat in a seat across from the woman then removed a clean handkerchief from the inside pocket on his jacket. He handed it to her to wipe tears that cascaded from her eyes in sheets.

"How did you find him?" she stammered, almost choking on her words, thoughts, and saliva. The man confessed that an officer at the NYPD had generated a photo of Doe, and having been sure it matched one of Doe seen in a notebook of terrorists, he had notified their field office in New York, and they had observed him for a while.

"What's going to happen to him?"

"I don't know." The man feigned ignorance as he got up from his seat to leave and join his partner and the accused outside. "Here is my card. I will call you soon. However, if you can think of anything that might be of help before then, give me a call."

The woman closed her eyes, her only mental image being that of a statue of three monkeys with hands over their eyes, their lips gripping each other in silence. Kieta Toures spoke truthfully. "I haven't seen anything! I haven't heard anything . . . I know nothing!"

Made in the USA
Lexington, KY
14 June 2016